GREEN AND PLEASANT LAND

Steve Shahbazian

KELVERN BOOKS

Copyright © 2019 Steve Shahbazian

ISBN-13: 978-1-9161460-0-6

Paperback edition

Written by Steve Shahbazian

Cover Design by Caroly Nisu

Published by Kelvern Books

This is a work of fiction. The story and characters are fictional. The politics and history are fictional. The groups and events are fictional. Apart from the named references to specific historical figures, the England depicted is fictional. These do not represent any actual people, groups or events. Any resemblance to real life is purely a sad indictment of the times.

www.steveshahbazian.com

For Caroline, Karina, Rae, Nichole, Karine
and everyone who helped me write my novel

Acknowledgements

With thanks to Richard Waters, Jan Singh and Dylan McKay for reading my novel, The Literary Consultancy for manuscript assessment of the early drafts and for Maya Berger for editing the final version. Thank you also to Caroline Natzler, Karina Vidler, Rae Stoltenkamp, Nichole Beauchamp, Karine Crabbe and everyone in Caroline's writing group, who helped me with the writing. Finally, thank you to Caroly Nisu for designing the cover and for Greg Claeys for kindly writing a foreword.

Works quoted or parodied within the novel:

'Meditation XVII' from *Devotions upon Emergent Occasions* by John Donne (1624); 'This Sceptred Isle' speech from Act 2, Scene 1 of *Richard II* by William Shakespeare (1597); extract from 'Ængla Tocyme' from the Old English version of *Historia ecclesiastica gentis Anglorum* (*Ecclesiastical History of the English People*) by the Venerable Bede (c.731); with apologies to William Blake for parody of *Jerusalem* (1804) and George Orwell for parody of "old maids biking to Holy Communion through the mists of the autumn mornings" from *The Lion and the Unicorn* (1941), Secker and Warburg, p.11 (see also former Prime Minister John Major's speech to the Conservative Group for Europe on 22 April 1993, which misquotes Orwell).

Winston Churchill's 'Finest Hour' speech in the House of Commons on 18 June 1940: House of Commons Debates 18 June 1940, Vol 362 cc51-61; http://bit.ly/2duhtf6
[Contains Parliamentary information licensed under the Open Parliament Licence v3.0; https://www.parliament.uk/site-information/copyright-parliament/open-parliament-licence/]

I would also heartily recommend anyone interested in chindogu to read Kawakami, Kenji (1995) *101 Unuseless Japanese Inventions*, Translated from Japanese by Papia, Dan, London, Harper Collins, particularly pp.140-1

FOREWORD

Amidst the gloomy anticipations of a post-Brexit vision of a Little England bereft of world influence, in a world burning as a result of its consumerist excesses, Steve Shahbazian has conjured up a different vision of our future. England is again an industrial giant, if under the influence of Japanese culture. But the masses fare no better than in the early days of capitalism, their vast estates defined by violence and poverty. And there is resistance to this new, soft totalitarianism. In the great tradition defined by Orwell, we accompany one man's quest to penetrate the sordid corruption of the new regime, avoid an apparently inevitably collapse into tribalism and anarchy, and establish a better society.

Shahbazian keeps up the pace in this compelling and atmospheric novel. He portrays a bleak, apocalyptic scenario populated with parallels close enough to feel realistic today, and realistic enough for us to feel the contemporary satire on civilisation unravelling to the point of threatened collapse. Too close for comfort, we feel time and time again, as we wonder whether this is the price of survival, and one we would readily pay ourselves. This novel will keep you wondering about the future, and fearing it – and wondering whether we are all fiddling while England burns. And that is all to the good....

Gregory Claeys
June 2019, London

PART I

1

The view through the window was set to slow motion. Roger Tyson stood in his office with a morose expression, watching the procession of late-night shoppers to the sound of a funeral march. On his desk, sat the notes of the speech he was writing. It had got no further than the title, "The Death of England."

At his command, the window reverted to transparent and the wall retracted. With a deep sigh, he stepped onto the observation deck and surveyed the scene. A big red sun hung over the English Channel, casting the Chrysanthemum Bridge in a warm glow, while a never-ending stream of bullet trains rushed across, taking their passengers to and from London. He turned to the skyscrapers of New Folkestone Business District and the elevated expressways that threaded their way through like flickering streams of red and yellow, before casting his gaze up to the shimmering holographic company logos. His mood briefly lightened at the sight of the famous Greenwood Oak, but as the information service announced the business news, he grew anxious. The Eikkei index of 100 leading shares had hit another all-time high.

He bit his lip and stared out in gloomy contemplation, only to be interrupted by an election drone, which had hovered into view. He looked up with annoyance as it projected a broadcast for the ruling English Liberal Democratic Party. "Don't let the other lot in," it shrilled, depicting rival politicians as cabbages. "Vote for the natural party of government – for a nation at ease with itself." A rival drone zoomed in, playing a cartoon of the

Government as turnips. "Kick them out," it trilled. "Vote for change. Vote for the Democratic Party of England." The two drones battled in the sky, trying to drown each other out before buzzing away.

"Tomodaore," Roger muttered. "All fall down together."

With a sigh, he rested his hands on the railings and looked out to sea, his eyes fixed on the horizon. Tall and strongly built with a face that seldom smiled, he still cut a commanding figure, even if at over sixty he lacked his former physical strength. While many found him intimidating, those close to him said his intense pale blue eyes reflected a deeper, sensitive nature. It was a side few saw. Always difficult, he had grown unclubbable with age, preferring to retreat into the past than spend time with others.

The sun dipped below the horizon and he drifted back into melancholy, remembering the time after the Great Incident when levelled cities and food queues were common. He thought of the reconstruction efforts and the study missions to Japan. He recalled how he had given up a promising career in the Self Defence Forces to found a small kaisha called Greenwood and how, under his leadership, it had grown to become England's largest keiretsu; a worldwide constellation of affiliated businesses. Yes, he thought, it had truly been an economic miracle. England had become the world's most dynamic economy and he, Roger Tyson, its pre-eminent businessman; not just a public figure, but to many a hero.

As he stood in the fading light, those days seemed long gone. He looked inside at the Samurai Sword of Honour he had won at Sakura Military Academy as leading Officer Cadet, feeling like the product of a bygone era. When he had first warned that boom was turning to bubble, he had been listened to with respect, but when, instead of crashing, the economy had grown faster than ever before,

4

he had found his judgement called into question. It had been a rude shock. He was out of touch, old fashioned, stuck in the past; even within Greenwood, the criticism had become voluble. Publicly, he remained defiant, but privately he grew embittered. The whispering was one thing, but the rumours of a boardroom coup were another matter. He knew the politicians were stirring it up, he knew they wanted him out, but no-one would listen. He gritted his teeth as the fruity voice of a Ministry of Economic Policy, Trade and Industry spokesman (or MEPTI, as it was known for short) emanated from the media screen.

"We live in a New Era," it announced. "In the long run, the economy can only grow."

Roger turned around as a fresh wind picked up, blowing his thick grey hair everywhere and spattering him with salty sea air.

"It won't last forever," he growled. "We're no different from those ruined civilisations in the sand."

He ordered the screen off and returned inside, briefly looking back as a large banner was unfurled from the Chrysanthemum Bridge. BE HAPPY, a smiley face said as fireworks marked the start of another Government Sponsored Celebration, LIFE IS GETTING BETTER. With a disconsolate pout, he left for home.

The evening turned cold and Roger boarded his private aircraft, ordering a sake from the robot valet as he flopped into his favourite armchair. Damn them! Damn them all! Damn everything but the sake! As the aircraft lifted off, he activated the internal wraparound screen and watched as New Folkestone and the Chrysanthemum Bridge receded into the distance. Within minutes, he was flying over the London Dormitory Suburb of Kent, one of the many resi-dential complexes that surrounded the cities, commonly known as "the barracks." He watched the endless sequence of gigantic blocks that seemed to march across the landscape, then zoomed in on the gangs as they fought amidst the garbage mountains and burnt-out vehicles, torching cars and tossing burning mattresses out of windows. The sight filled him with sorrow. Once model homes, the barracks had become no-go areas that even the police wouldn't enter without an armed escort. They were an alien world, dominated by warring ganglords and beyond government control. Law and order counted for nothing. Behind the perimeter walls, furigans ruled.

The aircraft continued over the eighty storeys of Lansdowne Tower, centrepiece of the notorious Deer Park Estate, and Roger turned to the news.

RIOTS ERUPT AGAIN IN MIDLANDS PREFECTURE

TEENAGER SHOT DEAD

SHOPKEEPER FIGHTS FOR HIS LIFE

He selected the last story, watching the CCTV footage of the attack. A portly man in a tank top stood behind the counter of a well-kept electronics store, attending to the multitude of screens on the rear wall. Seconds later, a gang wearing balaclavas and fluorescent long johns burst in, screaming and waving metal bars. The shopkeeper hit the floor as they leapt over the counter and curled into a ball as they set about him. After about thirty seconds, they ran out of the shop, screeching and laughing, except for one who squatted over the counter to leave the gang's calling card. None had attempted to take any money. Roger's hands tightened as if ready to wring their necks. If there was anything noteworthy about the attack, it was that the man had survived.

He retrieved his speech and began writing. *If there's hope, it's with the Government – if only it would wake up.* He quickly crossed the last part out, feeling his anger return. Only the Government had the power to solve the problem, yet it did nothing, responding to furigan violence by withdrawing police patrols, making sentences more lenient and increasing their financial aid – everything he considered wrong. As he entered Central London airspace, he recalled his last speech.

"This is appeasement," he had thundered. "Give them what they want in return for a quiet life. If we don't get tough now, we'll have to send the Army in."

Ministers had reacted angrily, accusing him of "alarmism" and "exaggeration," but others had been more forthright, calling for him to be banned from the media. He had avoided censure, but only just. Criticising the Government might be acceptable, even something of a national sport, but criticising furigans was not. There was a Political Consensus and everyone adhered to it. Beneath the official line there was no good or bad, only different, lay a deeper unstated message – society was bad and furigans its victims – and to say otherwise meant being marginalised or worse. As the saying went, the peg that stood out would be hammered back in.

He gulped his sake down and stared woozily at the shiny new buildings in Nagata-Cho. While furigans slipped out of state control, the rest of society found itself enmeshed ever further. An extensive state apparatus had sprung up to regulate life, overseen by four new Commissions – executive bodies with plenipotentiary powers that reported directly to the Sori Daijin (who in previous times was known as "Prime Minister"). The Commission for Fairness rooted out abuses of power; the Commission for Wellbeing controlled social relations; the Commission for Lifestyle regulated culture and the Commission for

7

Identity managed media representation. Indignation bubbled up from the pit of Roger's stomach. Furigans might be left alone, but if *he* failed to comply with their "administrative guidance," he would face a heavy fine or prosecution – and it would only get worse. He looked down at the incomplete Sori Daijin's Department, whose skeletal frame dominated the district. Once that was finished, his impotence would be complete.

What could he do? He put the empty glass down and let out a belch. If the Government was weak, the opposition parties were no better. Though they traded insults and attacked each other vociferously, there was little to differentiate them – and all supported the Political Consensus. The same was true of the media. Despite the hundreds of stations, none ever questioned it and none would have anything to do with him after his speech. Roger, however, retained hope. The evidence might be impressionistic – boozy chats in the pub, snippets of conversation on the train – but he knew the people would support him.

"Democracy has become a rigged choice," he once said. "But if the politicians won't listen, the people will. They can see what's happening. They hate it. They want an end to it. And if they had a voice, they would be unstoppable."

He looked at the image of the shopkeeper frozen onscreen, anger welling up within him. He could contain himself no longer, the anger was too strong. He picked up his speech and shouted the words out. Furigans were the enemy.

He breathed out, unable to write the words down. Not only was this controversial, it was subversive. No, he couldn't. He couldn't. He had to. His body seized up. A message had arrived: a reminder from the Commission for Fairness. Compassion Day was approaching.

It had been nearly a year since the last event – the world's largest celebration of Niceness, as its organisers, the Compassion Foundation, had billed it. Roger had arrived at Tokugawa Square in the early evening, taking his seat onstage as a grey politician droned on, ignored by the crowd, who, divided into groups, taunted each other like rival football fans. A commotion broke out backstage, breaking his concentration. He turned around as a large entourage proceeded through the cordoned-off path and Sori Daijin Bill Harris arrived, taking the large throne-like seat centre stage. Roger looked at him, dressed in a fashionably sharp suit and a new pair of designer glasses, and nodded an acknowledgement. Bill responded with his trademark matey grin, then for a fraction of a second it vanished, replaced by a steely glare. Roger felt a searing contempt, but before he could respond the grin returned and Bill was laughing with his Naikaku colleagues, full of camera-friendly bonhomie.

In contrast to his run-ins with others in the Naikaku, relations with Bill had been cordial, if cool. It was as if their careers had crossed, like escalators travelling in opposite directions – Bill the media darling and Roger the dinosaur. Although they had never been in conflict, it was under Bill's administration that the Political Consensus had hardened into dogma: soundbites had replaced argument and name-calling masqueraded as debate. Worst was the vitriol reserved for anyone deemed out of line.

"True, no-one's ever liquidated," Roger had grumbled, "but there are plenty of character assassinations."

Roger watched Bill with suspicion. He might have been more political thespian than ideologue, but the Political Consensus made him bulletproof. Criticism never stuck and somehow it was always the critics who found themselves attacked. So slippery, Roger thought, so underhand....

Firecrackers broke the hubbub, fizzing and crackling through the air as the compere opened the event. Immediately, the crowd turned to the front as Niceness Mentors worked their way through them, smiles fixed to their faces as they clapped and chanted "Ha-ha-ha, he-he-he, ho-ho-ho." Roger watched the crowd repeat the chant, then looked to the edge of the square. There, serious looking Compassion Stewards stood in fancy dress holding aloft electronic placards that alternated between LOVE NICENESS and LOATHE NASTINESS.

The event began with a brief montage of warm sunsets, gambolling lambs and children clutching teddy bears on the screen accompanied by gently lilting music. There were "oohs" and "aahs" from the crowd before a short film with a group of furigans in bobble hats and freshly pressed long johns began. As usual, they looked into the camera with big round eyes and frightened expressions while a voiceover admonished people to be Nice, its tone at once patronising and hectoring. The furigans skipped through a meadow of buttercups in slow motion as the sun's rays beat down on them until they came to a hill. At its crest stood a smartly dressed family with their backs turned to them. The furigans stopped and looked up to the summit. The camera zoomed in on a young furigan girl, one big tear rolling down a rosy cheek. The image faded out, leaving the legend, "Let's try to be nice for once, eh?"

The next film was a furigan screaming and snarling into the camera, the sound muted. His face filled the screen as he lunged forward, coating the camera lens with flecks of spittle. He backed away and made a slashing gesture then lunged forward again. The film played in a loop then stopped. "Shocked? Angry?" a voice admonished. "Have you thought about how he feels?"

"How can we do this to them?" a voice behind Roger trembled.

"What kind of a society treats its vulnerable like this?" said another.

Roger looked around and bit his tongue. Everyone except him was nodding.

Throughout the square, the mood grew subdued as the crowd was pummelled with images of helpless furigans being bullied, the voiceover repeatedly chiding viewers for being heartless. A young man near the front held his head in his hands before putting his arm around the girl next to him as he began to sob.

"Synthetic emotions," Roger gagged.

He looked away, catching the gaze of a woman in her mid-thirties with glossy brown hair and chestnut eyes. She looked at Bill and rolled her eyes with a smile. Amanda Cooper had been a rising star within the Liberal Democratic Party, tipped as a future Minister of Finance, but her career had stalled when Bill had become Sori Daijin and she had suddenly been sacked. Roger had met her at a business conference after she had become a Member of the National Diet and they had instantly established a rapport.

"You're the only person who sees through this madness," he had said. "I feel as though I live in an alien world."

"You have to speak out," she had replied. "The Government fears you."

She had leant in, their faces almost touching, her voice barely a whisper.

"Bill's propaganda is slick, but it hides a lot of dirt. If people knew the truth, there'd be an uprising."

Roger had known exactly what she meant. Officials acquiring assets they could never have earned, funds unaccounted for, misappropriation, embezzlement, cronyism; the rumours were abundant, but nothing had ever been proven. It was tantalising, frustrating, elusive. If only it could be made public. If....

The square darkened and the gentle piped music was replaced by a low hissing noise. Amanda slipped away as Roger faced the front. NASTINESS, the screen flashed against footage of ordinary people walking down a street, IS ON THE RISE. The Stewards thudded their placards on the ground as the film cut to footage of Bill addressing his last party conference.

"Nastiness is the menace we must always guard against," he said as films of people screaming, war and corpses appeared onscreen. "There are those who don't want a Nice society. They poison minds: picking on the weak and vulnerable, blaming them for our failings. Nastiness is a conspiracy for power and its forces are growing. It must be stopped."

The crowd began to get agitated; anger and hatred flashing across their faces.

"Nastiness is evil," a stentorian voice boomed, the words appearing onscreen to reinforce the message. "Stamp it out!"

The crowd began stamping and shouting, crying out for the Forces of Nastiness to be punished. Roger reeled, feeling the relentless pressure to conform. This was the insidious thing about the Political Consensus. There was no law forcing anyone to conform, nor any forbidding dissent. Language had been loaded so as to make support obligatory and opposition impossible. To celebrate furigans and condemn society was to be Nice, the supreme political virtue, whereas to criticise furigans and praise society was to be Nasty, the ultimate vice. It was a simple choice: to be branded Nasty meant an end to one's career. Free speech hadn't been abolished, only distorted so the Political Consensus dominated by default.

The compere returned to the stage, accompanied by the Shacho of the Compassion Foundation and a pop singer. The hissing noise stopped and the light brightened as anticipation replaced anxiety.

"And now for the moment you have all been waiting for," the compere announced, "the naming of this year's Figure of Hate!"

The crowed hushed as the singer stepped forward to the podium and opened an envelope. Roger winced.

"This year's Figure of Hate is," she beamed, "Phil Tucker!"

The crowd cheered as the name flashed onscreen in huge letters. A wheeled trolley bearing an effigy emerged from a hatch then trundled slowly down the trackway as the crowd pelted it with rotten eggs. A group of youths leapt over the barrier and bashed the effigy with baseball bats before being escorted out by security.

The trolley reached the front, where two stagehands removed the effigy and the compere handed the microphone to the Shacho of the Compassion Foundation.

"We're all aware of this man's vile malopinions," he said, "Stirring up hatred, using Nastywords and calling the Helpless 'furigans.' We thought this sort of Nastiness had been eradicated, but it shows how far we have to go."

Roger watched as the screen played a short film of Phil spliced together from old interviews, interpolated with clips of people being beaten. It was like the furigan violence, except actors playing furigans were attacked by actors dressed in suits. The effect was instant. Whenever Phil appeared, the crowd became a snarling pack, baying for his blood. The couple who had been in tears earlier were now screaming at the screen and waving their fists.

"Furiganism," Phil said in his plummy accent, "is an attack on civilisation."

At the sound of the word "furigan," the crowd threw itself into a frenzy, egged on by the Compassion Stewards, who banged their placards ever harder, shouting "Death to the hater!"

"Phil's a decent bloke," Roger protested, but no-one could hear him above the din.

The lights dimmed and the crowd went quiet as a soft drum roll began. The singer collected a torch from the corner of the stage and approached the pyre, her smile now gone. She stopped and held the torch aloft, then with one dramatic movement set it alight. Fireworks lit up the square while music boomed from loudspeakers and the crowd went wild, yelling and jeering. Onstage, Bill chuckled while his fellow ministers gloated.

"We're making fools of ourselves," Roger cried. "A society that hates itself and loves its enemies is finished."

The spotlight returned to the stage for the closing message. Roger scanned the square as those onstage stood up to sing "Let's build a nicer society." Apart from a few individuals, the crowd was paying no attention, whooping and cheering as they looked for things to smash. In one corner, a group of Compassion Stewards had broken away and were charging down the streets chanting "Phil oroshi, Nastiness oroshi." Roger watched as the screen switched to the news, where a reporter was running after them.

"A group of revellers," the reporter puffed, "Have left the square to protest outside novelist Phil Tucker's home."

He stopped as they reached the writer's home and smeared his windows with filth, one man running up to the front door and urinating in his letterbox before coverage ended abruptly.

Roger watched in horror, trying to imagine what Phil must have been going through. *You can stand up for yourself in a fair fight, but not at Compassion Day. It's a ritual, a human sacrifice, victims thrown to their foes – and*

I'm next. He looked at the remaining Stewards watching him through narrowed eyes, and his horror turned to hatred. *I know you bastards hate me. I know you want to do that to me. Well, screw you!* As Phil's image disappeared from the screen, his defiance evaporated. Phil Tucker was nothing. It was him they wanted, and how badly they wanted him. To them, he was Nastiness incarnate: his speeches and attacks on furiganism nothing more than a campaign to seize power and make himself Shogun. Worse, the image of him as a power-hungry nationalist was not confined to the political classes. Murky dealings, secret links to the military, allegations of a criminal past; nothing had ever been substantiated, but nothing had gone away either. He could blame the media all he liked, but if ordinary people saw him as a would-be tyrant....

He looked up, alone with his enemies in the emptying square, unable to bear it any longer. If being accused of Nastiness was irritating, the prospect of being slandered filled him with dread. What could he do? He had little personal appeal and the media were hostile. With a shudder, he turned to leave, only to find Bill blocking his path.

"I want a little chat," Bill smiled.

Roger gave him a surly look and the grin faded.

"Some of your recent comments have caused us concern," Bill said. "There's a feeling you're not fully behind us."

He paused as the Compassion Stewards marched off.

"But I know you better. I know I can count on your enthusiastic support. Next Compassion Day, we will finally eliminate Nastiness."

He grinned and left, leaving Roger to stare at the effigy's charred remains.

The aircraft began its descent, snapping Roger from his thoughts. Nervously, he reached into his coat pocket and pulled out a brown envelope. Inside was a sheet of paper, a military intelligence report.

Assessment on the Threat of Insurgency

Enemy: the Movement for Supreme Love (known colloquially as "the Muhonin") – a chiliastic religious cult with its own underground army. Highly motivated, disciplined and exceptionally violent, its aim the total destruction of society.

Muhonin Strategy typically follows a three-staged insurgency:

Stage One: aggressively recruit new members, build up arms, form alliances with anti-social elements such as furigan gangs.

Stage Two: mount hit-and-run attacks against the state, typically beginning with assassination of low-level officials.

Stage Three: full-scale attack: pin down civil forces with furigan allies in coordinated nationwide rioting while Muhonin attack and destroy state targets.

Assessment: Muhonin weaponry at least as sophisticated as those of the Self Defence Forces, possibly including chemical and biological weapons. Stage One should be considered complete and Stage Two ready.

Threat Level: IMMINENT

Roger stared at the page, thinking of the Muhonin holy book *The Divine Prophecies*, which prophesied that humanity would be cleansed through violence in a "Supreme Rebeginning." They had launched numerous insurgencies to bring it about, none of which had succeeded, but all of which had caused massive bloodshed. On their own, neither furigan violence nor Muhonin insurgency could bring down a state, but together, with the Government weak and society fragmented, an uprising could well succeed. As the aircraft touched down, he began writing furiously:

OUTLOOK BLEAK: barracks at crisis point – Muhonin ready to strike – government blind – state failure – social collapse – consequences unimaginable

The limo took him the remaining distance home, stopping in the security bay outside the gates of Suzuki Hall. The Head of Security strode from the guardhouse and saluted as a tracked bomb detector scanned beneath the vehicle. Roger smiled back, trying to hide his disquiet. A Muhonin Insurgency would sound so far-fetched as to be ludicrous, yet the threat was real. He had to speak out, but it wasn't just the media he had to worry about. He thought of his wife Jane's growing friendliness with Bill. If he were made Figure of Hate, would she stand by him? The gates swung open and the limo glided down the oak-lined driveway, halting by the statue of a girl playing a violin. As he stepped out, he could already feel isolation enveloping him.

Jane was in the front room, hunkered down with a glass of red wine, watching an old black and white film and wearing a collarless tweed trouser suit. Petite with short red-grey hair, she was and everything he was not: cheerful and gentle with a warm smile and infectious laughter, a person who was the focus of every social occasion. However, while friends said she was the person they liked to be around, those who had fallen out with her told another story: of warm smiles replaced by icy glares and friendships abandoned at a stroke. She was not was a member of the Robinsons for nothing, they said. Hers was the wealthy industrial family from Derbyshire of whom it was said that "steel ran in the blood."

Roger tiptoed past the ikebana display and bust of Winston Churchill and sat down beside her.

"Good day?" she said without looking up.

"Fine. You?"

She nodded an "uh-huh," still absorbed in her film.

There was a long silence as he watched the small tracked robot rake the gravel in the karesansui garden. She turned the film off and looked at him, her arms folded.

"Have you reached agreement with the board yet?"

He grunted.

"You're turning a minor spat into a keiretsu-wide problem, Roger. Find a compromise; those directors only want to expand the business." Her expression softened slightly. "Come on, let's enjoy a glass of wine together."

She poured a glass, but he would not be moved.

"This is no spat," he said. "Bill's behind it."

"Bill?" she laughed. "I think you're suffering an incipient megalomania. Nobody's trying to force you out and nobody's trying to take over Greenwood."

His expression turned dark.

"While we're blathering on about Compassion Day, our enemies are arming. A failed state, Jane – it could happen here. The Government is supposed to be our sword and shield, but Bill's stuffed it up. Look beneath the surface; we're heading for disaster."

"Roger, stop this nonsense," she cut in. "The state is not going to fail and society won't collapse. It's make-believe, the talk of the lunatic fringe – and if you continue to talk like this, you'll end up making yourself Figure of Hate."

She smiled sympathetically and put her hand on his knee.

"You're a brilliant businessman, but also a political novice. You're too thin-skinned to succeed in politics. I see how much their lies hurt you, but you will insist. Stop listening to cranks and focus on Greenwood, where you can still be a hero. Why sacrifice everything?"

Why sacrifice everything? He scowled as memories of past disappointments bubbled up and a deep voice boomed inside him: *You've never achieved what you were capable of and you never will. You lack what it takes for greatness. Retire. Keep quiet. Give in.* He sank back as he remembered the intelligence report. He was all that stood between the people and the Supreme Rebeginning, but what could he do? He was alone, devoid of political power, he had to get to his enemies before they got him, but his enemies held all the advantage, except one. Bill. He was hiding something – something bad, something worse than corruption…. His insides froze. No, he could never give in. He had to go on, impelled towards the one thing that truly terrified him.

Jane smiled and put an arm around him.

"I'm sorry," she said, giving him a kiss. "I'm only trying to help. We're a team – you the visionary and me the realist. Kudasai, Roger, don't get drawn into a reckless political adventure."

He looked at her, his eyes melancholy.

"Let them make me Figure of Hate. I will be Sori Daijin. I have to defeat the Muhonin."

Fear shot across her face. She took his hand, her face etched with concern.

"Roger itoshii, listen to me. There are some things you just can't say." She squeezed his hand. "I don't want you to get killed."

A loud explosion ripped through the air, scattering gravel against the window. They sat alert for a minute then went outside. Apart from some wrecked streetlights, there was little damage. They cuddled up close as people groaned and a woman cried for help. He looked at her with a grave expression as police sirens wailed in the distance.

"It's happening," he said.

2

The police had arrived and sealed off the area, quickly identifying a faulty gas main as the cause of the blast. An accident, Roger pondered as he inspected the site, but what if it had been a bomb? He scoured the news reports. Not one had considered the possibility.

He wandered down the avenue of elm trees, his spirits sagging. Even in this quiet residential district, he was surrounded by the Political Consensus. The road was lined by information screens praising the authenticity of furigan culture, while the walls were covered with posters saying DEATH TO NASTINESS and NATION-ZOKU OUT. He stopped as two groups of children hurled stones at each other, one dressed as Goth-zoku, the other as Punk-zoku, two popular Lifestyle Groups. A small boy, his hair spiked up in a Mohican, was caught by the rival gang and punched repeatedly. Roger was about to step in when the parents appeared, ushering the children away and casting him wary glances.

"They're just playing, you old fool," a mum yelled.

"Nastiness," jeered the small boy, throwing a stone at Roger, which bounced gently off his shoulder.

He walked on in disgust, ignoring the parents clapping. *Blowhard, fuddy-duddy, reactionary, Nastiness and now this! I might be the outcast today, but it'll be you tomorrow. You too will find out what it's like to be Figure of Hate.* He looked back as they shepherded the children indoors, thinking of the cities with their walls, gatehouses, razor wire, shutters, barriers, alarms, security cameras and bulletproof screens; it was the architecture of siege, not harmony. Division was engraved in the landscape and fear expressed in physical form. *This is Bill's England, no bond or belonging; everyone alienated from everyone else. It's madness, we're destroying ourselves. We need to rediscover our unity. We need to be a nation again.*

He trudged on, realising how out of touch he was. While people still talked of society, "nation" had become a Nastyword that only people like him used. He might as well be speaking another language. Was it possible to have a nation if people no longer believed in it? His despondency grew as he remembered a student debate.

"The nation is dead," the speaker had said. "It's a defunct concept, an outmoded construct, a repugnant relic we have liberated ourselves from.

"It's who we are," Roger had replied to whistles and catcalls, "It's our soul – the sum total of our history and heritage. We've just forgotten it."

The audience shouted him down with cries of "Nationalist" and "Nastiness" while an academic took the microphone.

"This is exactly the sort of blinkered, old-fashioned notion that belongs in the dustbin of history. Society has moved on, Tyson San. You're living in the past."

There was loud applause and the academic stepped down from the podium to shouts of "You tell him" and "Nastiness Oroshi." Roger sat fuming, the words of one of England's long forgotten writers circling around his mind.

No man is an island, entire of itself; every man is a piece of the continent, a part of the main. If a clod be washed away by the sea, Europe is the less. Any man's death diminishes me, because I am involved in mankind, and therefore never send to know for whom the bells tolls; it tolls for thee.

The sight of the academic sitting down looking so pleased with himself had stirred a rage within him. Roger stood up, waving his fist as the words shot from his mouth.

"You can't build a society on division. Belonging is human nature. When we're part of a nation, we're part of a community: we feel a bond to each other. Shared identity is the keystone in the bridge. Take it away and society collapses: alienation replaces belonging, hostility replaces civility, savagery replaces humanity. We end up with tribalism – a permanent state of war."

This time there was no booing or hissing; the audience just laughed.

Roger arrived outside the Professor of Human Zoology's office in a state of anger, replaying the debate again and again in his mind, unable to find the winning argument. *Bloody intellectuals, arguing that good is bad and bad is good. How do I win? I need to understand what's going on.* He paused. Professor Helen Rowe might have been regarded as a controversial ideologue, even an extremist, but she was the foremost expert on furigan culture, and if anyone could provide answers it was her.

She opened the door and beckoned him in whilst on the phone. Slim with an angular face, short fair hair and square glasses, her neat appearance and precise movements stood in contrast with her office, which was cluttered with pictures of residential complexes and furigans. Shaved heads, scarred faces and heavily tattooed bodies, faces clad with metal so that no skin was visible, old men coated in war paint, girls with necklaces of bones; he looked at them with revulsion and sat down. She finished her call and took a sip of coffee.

"What do you want this time?"

"I've decided. I'm going to do it."

"There's no point," she said, putting her coffee down. "You won't achieve anything—"

"You said," he interrupted, "we need to take on our opponents. What happened? Last time, you complained I was complacent."

"Give up." Helen slunk behind her desk. "We're a society in hatred with ourselves and it'll take an intellectual revolution to change that. The Political Consensus is too deeply entrenched."

"Only because we never challenge it," he said, "Think of the furigans—"

She held up her hands.

"We've been through this before," she said with exasperation. "There's no such thing as *the* furigans. 'Furigan' – or to use the correct Niceword 'the Helpless' – is a label given to disparate subcultures hostile to civil society, a bit like the terms 'yob,' 'thug,' 'vandal' or 'hooligan,' from which it's derived. They have no common identity and they don't constitute a class, race, or group; they're simply the parts of society that have rejected their own culture. How can you expect to win if you can't get the basics right?"

"In other words," Roger said, ignoring her question, "they're like the warlike tribes on the frontiers of the ancient empires. They were disparate groups too, but they united and overran their neighbouring civilisations."

She shook her head and pressed a button. A persistent boom-boom-boom thudded from the speakers.

"The furigan vid," she announced. "The old-fashioned music video reduced to its most basic elements. This is Bubo-dog, one of the biggest artists – a hero to millions."

Roger snorted derisively as a snarling figure waddled into view, his hair clumped together in two horns and his two remaining teeth ground down into fangs.

"Look at that moron," Roger said. "He's got his trousers around his ankles."

"It's a sign of status," Helen said. "He's saying: I have so much power, I have no need to run away."

Bubo-dog jumped up and down on the spot and yelled a stream of gibberish. His voice grew ever louder as he gesticulated in demented fashion. Soon, he was throwing himself around in a frenzy, bashing his chest and screaming so loudly his speech was unintelligible. After several minutes, he urinated on the floor.

"Why are we watching this drivel?" Roger said as it finished. "He's like a wild animal."

"Not wild," Helen corrected, "feral. Wild animals have to survive in nature; they cannot afford to waste energy on recreational violence."

"So what? It's nothing more than a mindless celebration of stupidity."

"No," she said. "You're thinking in instrumental terms. Furigan violence is not a means to an end, it is the end itself, a form of hedonism. Furigans indulge in violence because they enjoy it. They despise us and take pleasure in making us suffer. When they attack us or vandalise our property, they feel dominant. Bubo-Dog is urinating on all that you stand for. He's urinating on you."

Roger folded his arms as she selected a new vid. A fast, shallow drumbeat began as a group of clowns strode into a heavily vandalised basement.

"The Fun Deth Staff," she said.

The clowns stood in a ring as an indistinct figure was pushed into the middle, falling to the floor before staggering to its feet. The largest clown strutted forward and clubbed it down, stamping on its head in time with the beat. The figure tried to stand up, but the clowns closed in, launching themselves, punching and kicking it to rhythmic squawks of laughter. After a minute, the figure got on all fours, breathing heavily and dripping with blood. The beat stopped. The leader grabbed the figure and slit its throat. The staff whooped with delight and touched fists as the body fell in a heap. Roger turned the vid off, an unpleasant feeling shooting up his spine.

"Helen, what's the point of this?"

"To show you why you're wrong." She pointed to the pictures on the wall. "Clothing is a uniform: an expression of who we are and what we stand for. They are making a statement: we don't look like you, we don't speak like you, we don't act like you – we're not like you. Furiganism is love of the barbaric and hatred of the civilised: to speak in grunts, unable to read or write, is to be strong and virile; to be educated and employed is to be weak and impotent. Rudeness, aggression and violence equal glamour, while manners, politeness and intelligence are beyond contempt. Who'd want to be a nurse or an engineer when they could be Bubo Dog or the Fun Deth Staff? This isn't some minority interest; this is mainstream culture and politics can't change that. The warlike tribes you mentioned may have fought their neighbouring civilisations, but they aspired to their cultures. Today, it is us aping them. This is a culture war and we are losing."

As he looked again at the pictures, Roger thought of the Lifestyle Groups in Tokugawa Square. Aristo-zoku, impeccably dressed in tweed, with their horses and stately homes; Rugian-zoku in shabby clothes and unkempt hair; Bling-zoku with crowns, maces and heavy jewellery;

Gepid-zoku with puffy clothing and makeup; Geek-zoku casually dressed and hunched over electronic kit. It wasn't just furigans and Muhonin – society according to the Political Consensus was a loose confederation of Lifestyle Groups, each officially recognised by the Commission for Wellbeing and each with its own media channel. The challenge seemed insurmountable.

"So how do we win?" Roger sighed.

"We don't," Helen said. "Politicians may occasionally condemn the extremes of furigan behaviour, but to attack furigans themselves...."

Her voice faded away as the energy drained from her face.

"We have a duty," he whispered, "to save our country. Remember?"

She drew back, her face lined with worry.

"You can't question the Political Consensus. They'll accuse you of extremism. Bill invented the Forces of Nastiness so he could lump his critics together and get rid of us. He'll cook up some imaginary conspiracy and...."

She backed away as if gripped by an unpleasant thought.

"Helen," he said, stepping towards her, "why were you blacklisted?"

He caught a glimpse of her face. Was she trembling? Could he detect a tear? After several minutes, she turned around.

"Now, if you would excuse me, I'm late for my next appointment."

Roger left for London Shinjuku, feeling utterly frustrated. *You encouraged me to do this and now you've gone cold. Stupid vids. Why don't you tell me something useful?* His dismay increased as he arrived at the station, noticing all the adverts for Compassion Day. He made his way through the barriers onto the escalator, where a giant animated reminder enveloped him on the wraparound screen. Doe-eyed Manga-style furigans with little snub-noses implored the passengers not to bully them while angry commuters in suits grabbed them by the scruff of the neck, their fists clenched, ready to strike.

"Kudasai, don't hurt me," squealed a little furigan girl, following him down the stairway, "kudasaaaaaaiiiii!"

The screen went blank and Roger felt himself back in Tokugawa Square with the synthetic emotions and the baying. He looked at the expressionless sea of pressed suits and polished shoes, seemingly oblivious to the message. *It's a case of goodies and baddies, only we're the baddies. Why can't people see the subtext?* His stomach lurched. Lurking behind the furigans was a menacing figure bearing an uncanny resemblance to him.

The passenger flow stopped abruptly as he reached the bottom. The escalators had stopped and the passengers were crushing up together in the airless space, fidgeting and cursing as the dingy strip lighting and low ceiling exaggerated the sense of confinement. Roger loosened his collar and tried to see what the holdup was.

"Does anyone know what's happening?" a woman behind him asked as the plaintive sound of piped saxophone music filled the space.

"Probably a jinshin jiko," he said, straining to look around, "We'll be moving soon."

"Jinshin jiko?" a gruff voice muttered. "They needn't bother jumpin'. I'll bleedin' well push 'em under."

Roger ignored the remark, catching sight of two men in grey suits behind a grill in the distance. A uniformed member of staff caught up with them, pointed at something and all three disappeared from view. A bomb scare? It was standard procedure in such an event to announce something innocuous, like a power failure or jinshin jiko, to avoid alarm, and the Subway would almost certainly be the Muhonin's first target, probably combining nerve gas and explosives for maximum panic.

The minutes passed and the grousing became more persistent. Roger stood calmly in the stuffy atmosphere as elbows and knees jabbed into him.

"Come on," he whispered, "make an announcement."

"Let's get a bloody move on," the gruff voice yelled. "They're not letting anyone onto the platform."

"I can't breathe," complained the woman behind.

Roger looked at his watch; they had been trapped for half an hour and nerves were fraying. *Stay calm, Tyson, take charge; it won't take much now to spark a panic*. The lights flickered, then went out, enveloping them in darkness. Before he could act, they were back on. The passengers started moving and the tension evaporated as if nothing had happened.

Was it a bomb? Roger mulled it over then put the thought to one side as the train glided over the magnetic guideway and the suicide screen doors opened. Immediately, passengers jostled to get onboard, while the robot packers in peaked caps and white gloves crammed them in. As he boarded, a group of businessmen tried to force their way in, only to be held back by the packers. The doors slammed shut and he watched the mass of seething faces as the train pulled out of the station. If people were pushing and shoving now, how would they cope in a real emergency? Still troubled by intelligence report, he turned to the faces in the carriage, which had settled into a sheep-like neutral. Mindless furigans and obscurantist Muhonin might make strange bedfellows, but their alliance made perfect sense. They had a common enemy – a stupid enemy that was joining them in attacking itself. Roger felt his anger grow as the desire to say the forbidden surged within him. *They're parasites, bloody parasites. What do they make? What do they produce? Nothing. They're dependent on us, and if they destroy us they destroy themselves – they destroy everything.* As the train rushed through the tunnel, riots, terrorism, panics and stampedes mounted into one apocalyptic vision.

"Chikan! Chikan!"

The sound of a woman's voice pierced the carriage. Everyone looked around. The woman turned around to a man behind her, who grinned sheepishly, his hands hovering over her buttocks. Roger barged his way through and grabbed him by the scruff of the neck.

"Domo arigatou gozaimasu," the woman said as the train halted. "It's nice to know there's some civility left."

Roger escorted the chikan off, only to be pushed back as a group of mature students dressed in furiganista fashion barged past, white noise blaring from their noise generators. He stood on the platform, watching angrily as they wiped their feet on the seats and threw food waste at each other, oblivious to the elderly couple forced into the only free space at the far end. They gave him a despairing look as the train left before disappearing from sight.

The sun went behind a cloud as Roger slunk down the Hirohito Boulevard. *This country has gone down the toilet and into the shit. We're not the nation that survived the Great Incident. We couldn't survive, we don't deserve to.* Overcome with pessimism, he called Amanda.

"I'm bringing my speech forward," he said. "Could you find me a venue next week?"

She looked taken aback.

"Next week? Have you forgotten about Compassion Day?"

"Forget that. This has become urgent."

"This is a terrible idea, Roger," she said. "The mainstream media won't broadcast your speech – *Eikoku!* and

Igirisu no Koe won't even return my calls. You'll bring a whole load of odium down on yourself and for what? A tiny venue in the suburbs? It's not worth it."

"Kudasai, Amanda." He smiled. "Next week."

She nodded and he ended the call, a tear forming in his eye as his mood grew maudlin: green fields, clean streets, smiling faces, he could see his country. *Dear England, please remember me. I believed in you when everyone thought of you as Nastiness. I was Figure of Hate for you. I sought power for you.* No, it wasn't the name-calling or the slurs; he'd suffer them gladly. It was.... He thought of the furigan vid and hurried on. He had to win. The prospect of defeat was simply too dreadful to contemplate.

When he got home, there was a message waiting from his old army friend, Dr Mark Alexander. There was no text, only an article from *The Utopian*, a media station commonly known as "the Subversive Service" and reputed to have close links with the Muhonin.

"Not like Mark," he said as the headline *POLICEMAN EXECUTED* appeared onscreen. Beneath it was a coarse, grainy picture of an underground car park. Two figures in police uniform hung from an air duct suspended by its arms, their heads slumped forwards. Their wrists had been cuffed together and their jackets and shirts ripped apart. Clearly visible in the centre, the stomachs had been sliced open with the entrails spilling onto the floor. Roger turned the screen off and looked away, but the image would not leave him. Although no group had claimed responsibility, only the Muhonin disembowelled their victims.

3

The audience crammed inside the squat brick community centre. The news that Roger would be speaking had exploded through the social media, creating an excitement that threatened to overshadow Compassion Day. Would this be it, the time he finally attacked the Political Consensus? The Live Commentary was predicting a fight and nobody expected him to hold back. Roger took his seat, enjoying the mounting controversy as he watched the audience fidgeting in the airless space.

"Aren't you concerned about the reaction?" the host whispered, glancing to a group of men with scarred faces on the fringes.

"The people must be heard," Roger replied.

The host straightened his tie and looked at him askance.

"Remember, when you go home to your mansion, we'll still be here. We don't need a populist troublemaker."

Before Roger could respond, he stepped forward.

"Ladies and Gentlemen, we're very fortunate today to have not merely a great businessman, but a man of great moral courage. Despite repeated attempts to silence him, he has made it his mission to speak up for ordinary people like us, so would you please give a warm welcome to Roger Tyson."

Roger stood up to loud applause.

"Today," he announced, "we face the gravest crisis in our country's history. We face war – a war between civilisation and barbarism. Do not think of the Great Incident. Then, friend and foe alike believed in civilised values: even amidst the bitterest fighting, there were rules and honour. This war will be unlike any other, a war without uniforms, armies or battles, a war of casual aggression, random violence and savagery – pitiless furigan savagery."

There was a ripple throughout the audience.

"They'll crucify him, absolutely crucify him," a woman whispered.

"And what do our leaders say?" Roger's voice grew louder. "They tell us *we* are picking on *them* and we must apologise. What sort of government does that? One without morals – or backbone. We, the law-abiding citizens, are being abandoned to furigans in the name of the Political Consensus. They call it Niceness. I call it betrayal."

"Hear! Hear!" shouted a voice in the audience.

"This is not merely wrong," Roger bellowed, "it's obscene. Furiganism is not culture, it's the negation of culture – an anti-culture inimical to everything good. Worthless, barbaric, stupid; it has no place in society. I shall say it and I shall say it loudly: furigans are our enemy."

"Too right," someone shouted.

"They make our lives a misery," shouted another.

Roger waited as they were hushed up, but the agitation was now audible.

"We used to have a strong state and a harmonious society. Now, we're nothing but a patchwork of warring tribes held together by an economic bubble. Society is disintegrating. Only strong leadership can save us."

There were loud cheers and raucous applause as people stamped their feet and yelled, "You tell 'em."

"We're being sold out. Furigans are worthless scum and the people who love them are fools. The Government should speak for us, not our enemies. If it won't stand for us, it should stand aside."

The words burst forth, Roger punching his fist repeatedly into the air, as if battering an invisible foe. The audience stood up in a pandemonium of noise, shouting and banging chairs as the angry faces merged into one in the stifling heat.

"I'm afraid we don't have time for questions," the host said, looking around anxiously as Roger sat down triumphantly.

"Who cares?" said a stooped old lady as Roger rushed off for his next appointment. "He's only interested in himself."

The host tried to speak, but it was too late. The men with scarred faces were smashing up chairs and hurling them at the windows.

Roger raced into Central London in his limo, energy coursing through body. Pleasure quickly turned to anger as he read the Live Commentary. *Rabid rabble rousing, crude demagoguery* and *stirring up base emotions*, the reaction was uniformly negative. Worse still, a small group of protestors was blockading the entrance to his London office.

"Bloody Action Groups," he cursed, "First they fill up the Live Commentary with their lies and now this. Damn them."

"Security," he shouted into the intercom as a man with spiky green hair ran around filming. "How long have they been there?"

"About half an hour," the Head of Security replied.

"Half an hour? How did they get here so quickly? Get them removed at once."

"They're only looking for publicity, sir."

"Don't talk such garbage, man. Someone knew in advance about my speech. Get a team by the rear entrance now."

As he spoke, a man with a purple-painted face pointed him out and began shouting "Roger Tyson, Robber Baron" with the others following in unison, waving their fists defiantly.

The car reversed away, giving Roger a chance to see the assortment of brightly coloured clothes and furigana-style long unkempt hair. *What a bunch of scruffs. I'll bet they spent hours in front of the mirror trying to look like that.*

The security guards formed a cordon by the car park entrance, behind which the protestors had regrouped, shouting and waving their fists. Roger looked at them with contempt. *Self-righteous little shits; how dare you try to silence me on my own property. If I had my way, I'd set the dogs on you.* The limo glided to a halt and he stepped out as a security guard opened the door. There was a loud yell as a protestor broke through the cordon and charged towards him.

"Quick. This way, sir." A security guard put his arms around Roger.

Roger pushed him away and stood up straight.

"Yeah, big man, scared of me," screamed a teenage girl with bright blue and gold hair. "You can't ignore what the people think. Warmongers like you need to be taught a lesson."

She jabbed a finger in his face as the others barged through, the security guards in pursuit.

"Would you kindly allow me into my building," Roger said.

"We know what you're up to, you old dinosaur," shouted a tall man with a bright red ear-to-ear Mohican. "Stirring up trouble so you can seize power. Well, it won't work. We don't want your nationalism or military dictatorship."

"I don't want those either," Roger said over the jeers. "Now, let me through."

"No way," he shouted, waving his fist. "Roger Oroshi. Nastiness Oroshi."

Roger gritted his teeth as the others joined in the chanting.

The security team was joined by reinforcements, who hauled the protestors away. Roger watched as two security guards grabbed the arms of the man with the bright red Mohican.

"Get your filthy hands off me," he yelled, wresting himself free before two more came and grabbed his legs. "You won't stop us. You don't speak for anyone, fat cat."

"And who asked for you to speak on their behalf?"

Roger glowered at him as he was hauled through the barrier, still struggling to break free.

"We know your secrets," he shouted, eyes bulging and teeth bared. "You won't keep them hidden forever."

The barrier lifted and he was ejected.

"Do you need anything, sir?" The Head of Security opened the door.

"Military dictatorship?" Roger muttered. "Where do they get this stuff from? They could at least think up something original."

He gathered himself and entered, but as he walked through the corridors his anger returned. Every wall was festooned with posters for Compassion Day, put up on the orders of the Commission for Fairness. "Say No to Nastiness" and "Nastiness is Narrow Mindedness" were followed by "Malopinions and Malemotions – Don't be afraid to seek help." He stood outside the boardroom, incandescent with rage. *I can't escape it, even in my own keiretsu. Not only are critical opinions wrong, they're pathological too.*

The doors slid open and he strode in, the directors standing to attention as large wall screens displayed the keiretsu's activities worldwide. On one, robots assembled parts for a prototype Fifth-Generation Supercomputer. On another, designers pored over the keiretsu's product range. On a third, the workforce from an automotive plant lined up to sing the company song.

"Let's get straight to business," Roger said, sitting down. "It won't have escaped anyone's attention that our performance has fallen below that of our competitors, nor that we are the only Big Six keiretsu not to have embarked on a major expansion programme. There has been pressure for us to follow suit and Emma Bland has submitted a proposal for our consideration. If this meeting of the Rijikai cannot resolve the matter, it will have to be escalated to the Shachokai. Bland San, would you talk us through."

Everyone looked at Emma as she stood up, her blonde hair bathed in the afternoon sun. Young, determined and conscientious, Roger had noted with approval how she would not be pushed around.

"Domo arigatou gozaimasu, Tyson San. I joined Greenwood because we were number one. Cars, trains, computers: our products were the best, the epitome of monozukuri, but now we lag behind in every sector. Sales are flat, market share falling and share price low. In fact, if it fell any lower, we would be at risk of takeover. It's time for us to rediscover the spirit that made us number one. We are living in a New Era and technology is revolutionising life. The other keiretsu recognise this and have expanded, while we have remained stuck in low-yielding sectors. We must do likewise before it is too late."

Three young executives, Pete Northmore, Jeff Scott and Michael Dean, nodded and tapped the table as she sat down.

"Bland San," Roger said, "we're still the most profitable of the Big Six and have the smallest debt burden. Our competitors' margins are perilously thin. If we pursued a sales maximisation strategy like them, our profits would vanish overnight."

Colin Hayden, Greenwood's second in command from Delhi and Roger's oldest friend in the keiretsu, nodded in agreement.

"Kudasai, tell me," Roger said, "what financial return have these New Era projects generated to date?"

"We have to think long-term," Emma said. "Short-term loss is inevitable, but if we fail to invest now, we'll leave the field free for our competitors."

"These projects are highly speculative," Roger said. "There's no guarantee they will ever generate a return. Take the Fifth-Generation Supercomputer: nobody has managed to build a working prototype, let alone receive any orders."

"The market begs to differ," Pete interjected. "Look at our competitors' share prices."

"I've been around long enough to recognise a fad," Roger said. "Are we really living in a New Era in which gravity can be defied or the old one where what goes up must come down?"

"Shacho San," Michael interrupted, "We know you think the economy is about to crash, you've said so on many occasions, but the fact is you've been wrong every time."

"I don't claim to be a fortune teller," Roger snapped. "Look at debt levels and property prices; do you think these are sustainable?"

"This pessimism is misplaced," Emma said. "These old valuations are misleading indicators."

"History disagrees," Roger said.

Discussion came to an abrupt halt as the executives shook their heads and huffed. Jeff stood up and faced Roger.

"They may be intimidated by you, but I'm not," he said. "I'll say it: you're the one holding this keiretsu back. While you've been playing your political games, you've neglected business. The economy will crash, society will unravel, furigans this, Muhonin that... you've lost touch with reality."

Christine Barratt, the keiretsu's statutory Commission for Fairness representative, turned to Roger.

"I think what he's trying to say," she said with a toothy smile, "is that, while we hold you in the greatest esteem, we are greatly disturbed by your speech. If anyone else uttered such malopinions, they'd have to retake their mandatory edutainment. Inciting Nastiness is a very serious offence. The other shachos understand this."

Roger scowled, nauseated by the very sight of her. *Everything about you is repugnant: your unctuous smile, your false chumminess, your mockney accent, your affected use of furigan slang, your empty claims to follow football, your contempt for business. You pretend to be an ordinary person, but you're as superior as any aristocrat: you wouldn't dream of using the subway or setting foot in the barracks – unless it was a photo-opportunity. Yes, a typical member of Bill's new elite: smarmy and fake right through.* He gritted his teeth as she put the news on, knowing she carried the authority of the Sori Daijin.

"The Government," said a reporter, "has condemned a speech made today by Shacho of Greenwood Keiretsu, Roger Tyson, in which he called on the country to prepare for war. Minister of the Interior, Antonia Richardson, described his comments as 'utterly despicable' and accused him of 'trying to give Nastiness a respectable veneer'."

The report cut to the protests before Roger angrily turned it off.

"Barratt San, this has nothing to do with the matter at hand."

"On the contrary," Jeff butted in. "When you speak, we suffer a backlash. How long will it be before our products are boycotted? There's a consensus in favour of expansion and we won't let you block it any longer."

"Let's put it to the vote then," Roger said. "All those in favour of expansion."

Five electronic displays lit up green.

"And for consolidation."

Four displays lit up red. Colin looked at Roger with a sigh and pressed his button, followed by Roger.

"Six votes," Roger said. "Consolidation it is."

There were cries of disbelief.

"Unacceptable. Bloody unacceptable," Jeff shouted. "Consolidation? This is a ruse to sling us out."

He walked out with the other executives close behind, while Emma approached Roger.

"I'm serious about my proposal, Tyson San. If it's rejected at the Shachokai, I shall be forced to reconsider my position."

"Shachos may have dabbled in extreme kouha politics in the past," Christine smiled, "orchestrating bond market strikes and using front groups to sabotage official policy, but those days are gone. I'll see you at Compassion Day."

She smiled again and left with Emma.

Roger stormed out, his face red with fury.

"I know their game. Trying to move me to a desk by the window. I'll show them."

Colin chased after him, struggling to keep up.

"Wait, kudasai," he panted.

Roger turned around as Colin stopped to catch his breath.

"Don't do anything rash. They're using Christine to provoke you. They want to mount a rebellion at the Shachokai."

"Bill's put those stuffed shirts up to it," Roger said. "He wants to bankrupt us, so he can take control. Political games, indeed."

"Roger, listen," Colin said with a weary expression. "We're part of England Inc and we can't keep defying the

39

Government. As Greenwood's Fukushacho and your friend, I must tell you: your hard line is making it hard for us to support you."

Roger smiled and patted him on the shoulder.

"Domo, Colin, I appreciate your candour. Tell me, you don't really believe this New Era nonsense?"

"What I think doesn't matter," he said. "You're going out on a limb over this."

Roger winced and left.

The light was fading by the time he reached Okinawa Wharf, giving the unoccupied buildings a desolate appearance. Roger walked down the street as a gust of wind clattered the detritus from the nearby building sites against the high wooden fences and forced him to bow his head. It subsided long enough for him to notice a screen half-concealing a block of derelict offices earmarked for demolition. Alongside a picture of him was the headline *THE COMING WAR?*

"Where is this collapse of civilisation?" said commentator James Ashley. "It's nothing but a kouha fantasy concocted by Roger Tyson."

Roger listened, filled with loathing, as the angelic face continued his critique.

"His horribilistic hate-filled Nastyspeech, talking of 'furigans' and 'enemies,' inferiorising resi-urban culture, shows how evil is becoming mainstream. It must stop. If we allow him to Nastify politics, we are as good as allowing him to turn society into a prison camp. He must be made to atone for himself at Compassion Day."

"Stupid little puke," Roger shouted. "What do you know?"

The wind picked up again and he pressed on, unable to suppress his fury.

He reached Kenzo Tower, where he had arranged to meet Dr Mark Alexander. An ebullient character nicknamed "the schoolboy" at Sakura Military Academy on account of his chubby face, floppy hair and fondness for pranks, he had stayed in the Self Defence Forces and become a successful medic. The two had been in regular contact before he suddenly disappeared from view four years ago. Roger walked into a deserted lobby area and took the lift to *The Rupert*, a small pub on the tenth floor. The doors slid open, revealing a dingy room with drab grey walls covered with pictures of armoured fighting vehicles. A solitary figure was sitting in the far corner staring at a pint glass. Roger approached him, studying the drawn face and sunken eyes.

"Mark?"

The man looked up.

"I urge caution," he said.

"Caution?"

"Your speech was ill-advised."

Roger sat down, shocked.

"Ill-advised? This is a national emergency; we agreed someone had to speak out. What of it anyway? Bill's a playground bully pushing around the little kids. What can he do? He's never been in a real fight."

Mark shook his head.

"This country's rotten, Roger. No morals, nothing; not even basic respect for human life...." His voice faded away then picked up again. "They say they never see it coming. One minute you're safe then *puff*, you've gone."

"Mark." Roger looked at him sternly. "I know the risks. We agreed, our country comes before personal safety."

"They're watching you – the workmen outside your house, the random passers-by – you've made more enemies than you realise."

Roger leaned forward.

"Mark, what's going on? I must know."

Mark's voice faltered as he got up to leave.

"This is the end," he said.

4

A vista of sprawling retail cities and entertainment complexes spread out ahead as the expressway entered the ribbon development of the Outer London edgelands. Animated billboards with jaunty superheroes and exotic aliens advertised the latest holographic cinemas and upmarket virtual reality suites. *Virtua, Immersion, Astral Traveller*; Roger watched the names flash past, trying to ignore the media criticism without success.

"What society does Tyson think the Helpless are part of?" said one commentator. "This is their government, too. Does he really think they should be disenfranchised?"

"Imaginary culture wars, hatred of resi-urban culture, blaming the Helpless for their plight," added another, "scarcely a malopinion was left out. Tyson's speech was a frightening vision of hatred and vitriol to further his lust for power. Let's not forget his entire career has been built on hiding his Nastiness behind cod Churchillian rhetoric."

"You fools," Roger punched the screen. "It doesn't matter if an opinion is Nasty, only whether it's true or false. If it's true, then Nastiness is right. If it's false, Nastiness is irrelevant."

He looked skywards with a pugnacious expression and remembered the cheers, but as the Compassion Day blimp asked people to nominate their personal Figure of Hate, his doubt returned. Were the people listening? Would they rise up?

"You might be prepared to brave the obloquy," Helen had said, "but that doesn't mean others will be. Don't underestimate the Political Consensus."

He looked at the blimp, vexed. What exactly was the Political Consensus? There was no written doctrine and nothing was formally stated, yet it was everywhere, a set of attitudes and assumptions accepted without demur. Its proponents might claim no such thing existed, but hatoha values such as caring and compassion were sanctified, while kouha values such as drive and determination were denigrated. As far as his opponents were concerned, he was speaking another language; one as incomprehensible as it was wrong. He gnashed his teeth in frustration. It was a barrier he couldn't get past.

Helen was waiting in the station cafe with a fed-up look. Sitting by herself as heavy rain was forecast on a giant news screen, Roger looked at her half-pityingly. *Poor Helen, you think you can hide in your ivory tower. There's no escape.*

"How are you?" he smiled.

She looked at the empty tables and gave him a bored look.

"Cheer up." He patted her on the arm. "You're my foul-weather friend. We need to stick together."

"Forget it, Roger. You can't win."

He pulled up a chair beside her. "Come on, explain the Political Consensus. You understand, I don't. Help me."

She breathed out, trying to muster some enthusiasm.

"In the old days, rulers thought they could stamp out opposition by banning dissent, but it didn't work. People could see they were being controlled and rebelled against it. Today, they don't make that mistake. Instead of banning dissent, they label it Nastiness. Genuine free speech means accepting viewpoints we disagree with, but the Political

Consensus means either you parrot hatoha slogans like a mantra or you're denounced. It isn't a consensus at all, it's an unstated orthodoxy designed to shut down debate. By maintaining the illusion of free speech, we believe ourselves to be free when we're not."

"It's how the elite thinks," he said. "Go down the pub, ordinary people don't think like that. Why can't we tap into that? How can it be so difficult to shift when the vast majority of people hate it?"

"People are stupid and lazy," she said. "So they whinge. Big deal. They complain from time to time, but they want the Government to do their thinking for them. They happily regurgitate their catchphrases and slogans, thinking they've come up with the ideas themselves. It's a well-known phenomenon: it's called passive cognition."

She slunk back and stared into space as if she would rather be anywhere else. Roger watched as a new govermercial appeared onscreen.

"Life is getting Nicer," it chirped as smiling furigans and Muhonin helped old people across the street. "But more needs to be done."

Helen looked at him, her face taut as if ready to deliver a lecture.

"You know your problem?" she said, her voice a crisp staccato. "You're so focused on action, you can't see the power of ideas. Ideology is more than thought control, it's a means of rule. Take Nicewords and Nastywords. If you load oppositional words with negative connotations, then critical thought is stifled. If you load supportive words with positive connotations, then people can't avoid thinking in the prescribed way. Who wouldn't want to be Nice or support the Helpless? Who'd want to be Nasty or use Nastywords like furigan? The result: words have been divorced from meaning, so thought no longer represents reality. Now, ideas can be manipulated at will. Furigans are the Helpless – except when they express kouha opinions: then they become hooligans – and we are the Oppressors, whatever we do. Hatoha equals caring and compassion, so anything bad they do becomes good, while kouha equals hatred and aggression, so anything good we do becomes bad. Nothing needs to be banned. By thinking in the prescribed language, we conform without realising."

Her face broke into a knowing smile.

"What is Nastiness, anyway, but the doctrine of original sin in political form? In the past, people believed humanity was inherently sinful and only the grace of god could save them. Nowadays, we believe we are guilty of the sins of hatred and aggression and only the grace of government can save us. The Muhonin and furigans have become our inverse: the noble savages whose innate goodness – a kind of original virtue, if you will – must be protected. We're the sinners, so we accept the sacrifices we're forced to make, and they're the godly elect, so we accept the privileges they're granted. And most importantly, we accept a government that works against our interests. Grovelling to furigans isn't merely a policy choice, it's the only moral course of action."

She sat back triumphantly with a sour smile.

"So now do you see? People submit to Bill because he is the Force of Niceness leading them to salvation and hate us because we are the Forces of Nastiness leading them to damnation. Ideology is the very basis of his authority. People might not like his Government, but as long as they accept the Political Consensus, they support it by default."

Roger shook his head.

"Have faith, Helen," he said. "Once Bill has been dislodged, the Political Consensus will go with him. It can be defeated, but I can't do it alone."

"I know how much you want to be Sori Daijin and I wish you well, I really do... I just don't see it."

"Kudasai, Helen," he said. "I'm asking as a friend: what is it they're so afraid of?"

She hesitated and got up to leave.

"Roger, my job is all I've got and I don't want to lose that. I'm sorry."

The rain beat down as the limo turned off Upper Tamada Street into Katayama Yard. A few smokers huddled under a small awning outside *The Princess Kirsten*, while the pub sign – a beautiful young lady with long blonde hair and a wistful gaze – rocked in the breeze. Roger smiled as it rekindled memories of old times, drinking with army friends, business meetings in Greenwood's early days, going out with Jane, before dashing across the cobbles. He stopped in front of the window and read the notice, "Join us for a traditional karaoke knees-up!" He pushed the door open and walked in, engulfed by warm air and laughter.

The pub was full, making it difficult to see anything, except a screen high above the bar showing the football results and highlights of the national Sumo champion-ships. He eased past a fat man standing by the entrance and pushed his way through to the lounge. Amanda was sitting by the coal fire and black and white photographs of Victorian London, engrossed in a book. He sneaked up behind.

"Roger!" She hugged him and kissed him on both cheeks. "How are you?"

"All the better for seeing you," he smiled. "*Dr Kishi-moto*? I didn't know you were into literature."

"I thought it was about time I started," she smiled back.

He looked at her face, flushed with happiness. There was a warmth about her that made his problems seem to float away. Helen might listen, but Amanda enjoyed his company. The thought lifted him and he ordered a tokkuri of sake.

"I told you, Roger," she said, "nothing inflammatory – calm and rational always wins the day. We can't afford to sound so alarmist."

"It's the only way we'll get heard," he said. "Otherwise, the media will ignore us."

He looked at her as the bar droid wheeled over two sakazukis and motioned for her to come close.

"Have you watched the Subversive Service recently?"

"No." Her expression changed. "Why?"

"Ladies and Gentlemen," bellowed the landlord, "it's time for a traditional Princess Kirsten karaoke knees-up. Gather round! Gather round!"

A wave of people heaved forward towards the karaoke machine. Roger put his chair close to Amanda as the noise rose.

"Earlier this week, two policemen were disembowelled in the barracks, but there's nothing on the mainstream media. This isn't them treating the barracks as a foreign country; this has been embargoed."

"Embargoed? What for? It's not like we've never had terrorism before."

She looked at Roger, her manner no longer relaxed.

"And for the first song," the landlord bellowed, "'Woman from Tokyo'!"

A loud cheer erupted from a group of large red-faced men in rugby shirts bunched up next to the machine and the pub filled with the sound of the opening chords played on an old piano. Roger looked at Amanda as the red-faced men began singing.

"This isn't just a terrorist attack," he said. "The Muhonin understand the power of fear. They know the more frightened their victim, the more they will give to have peace, so their tactic is to ratchet up the fear to extract maximum concessions. A Muhonin peace is holding a gun to your head and not pulling the trigger, so they alternate between threat of violence and promise of peace until the victim has nothing to give that they can't take for themselves. That's when they rise up. We've reached that point."

The red-faced men belted out the chorus, spilling their Morning Sun Bitters over the karaoke machine.

"But the Muhonin couldn't topple a state?"

He paused, his expression serious.

"Amanda, what's the mood in Nagata-Cho? Has the Government mentioned the Muhonin?"

"No. Never. They've vaguely mentioned trouble with hooligans and organised crime, but nothing more. They're confident – complacent even. More than that, I don't know; I'm not privy to security discussions."

"They must know," Roger said. "They can't be in denial."

The song finished and the red-faced men took a rest, panting heavily. The karaoke started up again with "My Old Man Said Follow the Van" and they leapt back into action.

"Don't bet against it," she said. "Bill doesn't know anything about real emergencies. He's a career politician who's never had a real job. All he knows is how to lie, cheat and stab people in the back. He'll probably announce some security measures for public show while trying to buy them off behind the scenes. He's got away with it for so long he thinks he's fireproof."

"Amanda, we need to use this to our advantage."

"No, absolutely no." She looked at him with alarm. "Bill might not be able to stop the Muhonin, but he can certainly stop people talking about them. If you speak out, he'll have the Public Prosecutor throw the book at you. The laws are so subjectively worded – hate, anger, fear – you'd be pro-secuted for inciting Nastiness, no problem."

He flopped back, suddenly drained of energy.

"Then we're in deep trouble."

Roger's mood dropped lower as the entire pub joined in the chorus in a convivial fug of beer and song. *We're back where we began. I'm caught in a pincer: Bill on one side and his boardroom stooges on the other. They won't oust me. No, they'll move me to some meaningless position, where I'd be forced to toe their line: under keiretsu arrest, ready to be made Figure of Hate.* He sank back further, his shoulders slumped and his eyes moist.

"It's gone too far," he sighed. "Even if we got into office, we'd still have to fight the Muhonin and, by then, it'd be too late. It's not like the old days. We lack the fight. Maybe my critics are right, maybe I am an old fool, out of touch with the modern world."

"No." She rubbed his arm and smiled sympathetically. "Don't let them get to you. It's what they did to me. I could see the dangers of an economic bubble and I wasn't going to keep quiet, so they started casting aspersions: I was ambitious, a schemer, a political hack – all the things they are. It really hurt. For ages, I was too upset to speak about it, and then I decided: I wouldn't let it get to me. I know Bill wants me out of the Diet, but I'm not giving in. That's why I wanted to speak to you. The boardroom dispute is a diversion. While you're fighting your executives, Bill will get the Action Groups and his tame journalists to smear you – and that's not the worst of it. He's dangling the prospect of seats in the House of Councillors in front of Jane—"

"I knew it," Roger cut in. "No wonder she hates me criticising him. And she says I'm being disloyal."

"Roger," she said tartly, "all she cares about is her own standing. Bill would never do it, but her family's so blinded by ambition they can't see it."

She leaned in close and held his hand.

"In politics, you'll be free. That's what she's afraid of. She only wants you in that keiretsu, because her family's the largest shareholder. The moment she thought you were a barrier to her family's ambitions, she'd ditch you. Hell, she'd denounce you for Nastiness if she thought it'd curry favour with Bill, only she knows she can't run Greenwood without you."

He drew back, biting his lip.

"I can't, Amanda," he said. "She's my wife. I can't ignore her."

"I understand," she said, "but don't be fooled into thinking Bill is anything but your enemy. If you think you can force him into changing course, forget it. He won't. Ever. You need to win over the public."

Roger sank back in his chair.

"People think I'm a hardliner, Amanda. Nobody listens."

"They do." Her voice was soft. "They see you as the one person to stand up for them. You inspire them, you give them hope. Don't forget, Churchill was considered a Victorian throwback until his nation needed him."

She retook his hand and smiled.

"Now, I don't want to hear any more gloomy thoughts. I have a plan."

The song came to an end and the red-faced men patted each other on the back. Roger looked at her as they returned to their seats, feeling his spirits rise.

"Okay," he said, "we're agreed: I make another speech. What do you suggest?"

"I've heard rumours of a sex scandal within Bill's inner circle," she smiled. "It'd be awfully inconvenient if the media found out."

"After all," he grinned, "the public has a right to know."

He refilled the sakazukis, handing one to Amanda and holding the other aloft.

"To our political partnership: you on the inside and me on the outside. Kampai!"

Amanda's face lit up.

"I always said you were wasted in business. To us. Kampai!"

He gulped down his sake and looked at his watch.

"Is that the time? I've got to go. Jane and I are off to the theatre."

"What are you going to see?"

He pulled his overcoat on in one swift movement.

"*Dr Kishimoto*. The stage version."

He gave her a wink and left.

The media screen burbled in the background as Roger travelled home, Elgar's Pomp and Circumstance March No. 4 ringing out from the speakers. *Dear Amanda, when everything else is misery, you are joy. You will be a success in everything you do.* He closed his eyes and smiled. She had a *joie de vivre* that was irresistible, yet he couldn't help noticing there was something restless about her. She seemed to flit from one interest to another, her only constant her love of politics. It was as though there was something missing in her life. As he lost himself in thought, news of the policemen's deaths broke. He turned the sound up as gushing eulogies and armchair punditry alternated with images of sobbing crowds and high-rise towers.

"Where are the facts?" he cursed as a reporter appeared in front of a perimeter wall, with the caption *River Meadow Complex* onscreen. "This is nothing but emotion."

"The Ministry of the Interior," she said, standing amidst a sea of flowers, cards and teddy bears, "has released a statement calling for calm. It has not named any suspects, but says the attack was most likely the work of a criminal gang or hooligans."

"What lies!" Roger cursed. "No criminal gang is strong enough to attack an armed police patrol. As for hooligans...."

He stopped and searched the news for more details. Nowhere was disembowelment mentioned.

The news stopped and the screen went blank. Roger sat up with alarm as a deep voice announced, "There now follows a public broadcast by the Sori Daijin."

A sombre Bill Harris appeared from the Kantei, sitting behind the famous oak desk. Dressed in a black suit, his hair undyed, Roger could barely recognise him. At a stroke, the dashing young reformer had become the elder statesman.

"Today," Bill said, "we are peoples united in mourning. The tragic deaths of these brave policemen are a brutal reminder of the cruelty disfiguring our country. While we must not forget what has happened, we must also understand what drove the perpetrators to this appalling act, for it is all too easy for us to condemn. The Forces of Nastiness have sown discord, fear and hatred and now they are mobilising to exploit this tragedy. I urge you kudasai to remain calm. Your Government will implement tough new security measures to combat Nastiness, which from tomorrow will become a criminal offence. This year, Compassion Day will become a Day of Mourning to commemorate the dead policemen and all victims of Nastiness. Together, we will overcome this fear."

He looked into the camera and the broadcast ended.

The sight of Bill's long face sent Roger into a rage. *Nastiness killed those policemen? How can you say that and keep a straight face? How can you come out with all these stupid clichés and platitudes? Oh, it's hopeless. If I speak out, I'll be arrested and jailed. If I do nothing, I'll be sidelined and sacked. I'm stuffed.* As his car slowed to a halt, he picked up a handwritten letter from the seat beside him.

Dear Tyson San

> *Life in the barracks is unbearable. Every day we are*
> *threatened and attacked when we go to the shops or*
> *take our kids to school. When we're at home, we have*
> *bricks chucked through our windows. I can't go on*
> *any longer. Help us.*

He clutched it tight, weighed down with doubt. There was
no escape. As he used to tell himself in the Army, it was
better to go down fighting than to surrender.

5

The temporary traffic lights turned red. Cars tailed back
into the distance as the Metropolitan Expressway became
one gigantic military checkpoint. Armed police and
security guards swarmed everywhere as tracked robots
searched beneath the stationary vehicles. Roger waited
listlessly, his mind elsewhere. The Action Groups had
stepped up their campaign against Nastiness and hostility
to him was increasing – even within Greenwood, where
staff openly predicted he would be made Figure of Hate.
His own keiretsu. His own staff. Figure of Hate. He listened
to the sound of the helicopters circling overhead, feeling
hunted.

"Stay in lane," boomed the public address system. "Wait
for the scanners to pass."

A gantry swept overhead making a loud beeping noise
while a security official in a navy-blue jacket and crash
helmet marched over from a temporary cabin. Roger sat
up, feeling his pulse quicken. The man was heading
towards him. *This is a pre-meditated stunt. This....* Roger

relaxed: the man had stopped at the car beside him and was waving the driver over.

"Really, do I look like a terrorist?" An exasperated voice came from inside the car. "I'm already late for my meeting."

A middle-aged businesswoman stepped out and was escorted away, leaving Roger relieved yet angry. *This is pure political theatre! Fixed check points won't stop a mobile enemy. It's us that get caught – and that's the whole point: we're being inconvenienced to fool us into thinking something's being done.* He looked again at the police cars and helicopters. *No, it's worse: we're being treated like criminals, because we must be made to fear ourselves. Loathing Nastiness is not enough, we must loathe ourselves, we must feel guilty, we must internalise the propaganda.* He checked his inbox, but Emma hadn't replied to his proposal. In frustration, he turned to the media screen. Three furigans were being interviewed in the middle of a rain-soaked pedestrian square with fortress-like buildings towering all around.

"How do you feel about the negative stereotypes used to portray the Helpless on the media?"

They looked confused. The interviewer tried again.

"How do you feel about being called 'furigan'?"

"I don' keh," said the first, the others laughing.

"Do you think the Government does enough for you?"

"Naw," cut in the second, "They don' give us nahfin'. They should give us mo."

The documentary cut to the interviewer speaking to camera as he walked down a desolate arcade of boarded-up shops and half-demolished walkways.

"We've let down the Helpless. Deprived of the recognition we take for granted, it's no wonder they seek support from their own structures, which we deride as gangs."

Roger cursed, wanting to punch him, then switched over to another station, where three Muhonin in cult uniform, a jacket worn back to front over a night gown, faces hidden by ski-masks, were being interviewed.

"People often say they have difficulty understanding your ideology," the interviewer said. "What are your core beliefs?"

"We take issue with your question," said the first Muhonin. "We have no ideology. We believe in peace and love."

The interviewer smiled.

"Don't take what they say at face value," Roger shouted. "Question them. Challenge them. Don't give them free airtime."

He switched channel again: a govermercial.

"He called me a Rodney," said a sad-looking man.

"She called me a berk," said a dismal-looking woman.

"Have you been called a name?" the voiceover said. "If you have, report it to the Anti-Taunting Watchdog. Your Government is making tackling name-calling its number-one priority. Because name-calling hurts feelings."

Roger searched the channels, but it was the same everywhere: friendly chats with furigans, celebrations of resi-urban culture, govermercials berating people for not being sufficiently Nice. He clenched his fists. *Spinelessness elevated to a point of principle; no wonder we're in a mess....* He looked outside again, feeling once more unsettled. What if it was more than political theatre? What if the state's weakness was more apparent than real? Could he have misread the situation? He thought back to his military training, remembering how dragnets were set up and suspects handed over to the Security Services for processing. Why was the Government keeping the disembowelment secret? Why was it stopping people from mentioning the Muhonin? He thought of Bill's broadcast with increasing apprehension. The feeling of being hunted grew ever stronger.

The businesswoman hurried back with a scowl, slamming her door as the lights turned green and the public address system boomed "You are clear to pass." Roger prepared to move, his mind focused on the pincer. Behind the rebels stood Christine and behind Christine stood Bill, but was he really behind the opposition to him? When Bill had first been appointed to the Naikaku, he had been friendly to Greenwood and the two had worked together harmoniously, as Jane had been at pains to remind him.

"He's an honourable man doing a difficult job," she had said. "He's your best friend in the Government, if only you'd realise it."

He had scoffed at the idea, but as a light rain spattered the windscreen, the thought began to trouble him. There was no way she could be right. Bill? He was too crafty, too cunning, too... what was it? As the car picked up speed, Roger reflected on his sudden rise from obscure junior minister to England's longest-serving Sori Daijin. He could still see him grinning outside the Kantei that first historic day. It had been a landslide. Young and urbane, he had wooed voters, promising to sweep away decades of rule by crusty old grey men and clean up politics. He had been as good as his word, appointing four new commissioners and removing anyone who opposed his "modernisation." Within a year, the Political Consensus had gained quasi-official status.

"This is a coup," Roger had complained. "Opponents are accused of Nastiness and sacked, while supporters are praised for Niceness and promoted."

But it hadn't stopped. Power became ever more concentrated in the hands of a few associates, leaving the mighty Liberal Democratic Party little more than a personal cheerleader. Where previous Sori Daijins had come and gone, Bill had become a permanent fixture, his stranglehold on Nagata-Cho almost complete. No, Roger thought, he was neither honourable nor a friend. He was untrustworthy and ambitious, just as Amanda had warned.

"Democracy's a fiction," she had said. "People might talk about England Inc, but there's nothing behind the façade: the Naikaku never meets, the Diet is packed with placemen and the ministries are controlled by the Commissions.... It's like the royal favourites of the *Ancien Régime* with everyone dependent on the king's patronage. Opposition is impossible."

"It's completely unconstitutional," Roger had fumed. "People ought to be concerned. We need to warn them...."

"They're not interested in constitutionality," she had said. "They want a comfortable life. As long as they feel affluent, they don't care what the Government does. Bill knows that and is expert at playing on their anxieties. While the economy booms, it's easy for him to accuse us of scaremongering and frighten people into thinking any opposition to him will bring the party to an end. We've got to be careful. He's used the bubble to gain control of the LDP: he allows his cronies to extract bribes in return for their political support. The hotter the economy, the larger the kickbacks and the greater his power. He's stoking this bubble deliberately. Once he's strong enough, he'll take you on."

Roger shook his head as the limo sailed past the lines of warehouses. No, no, it couldn't be. Bill was too soft, too showy, too superficial, too weak. They had to be bold, not cautious. He returned to the screen as a repeat of the Mike and Julie Show came on, with Bill once again the main guest. The hosts cooed and simpered, welcoming him onto the sofa alongside a pantomime horse and a celebrity sumo wrestler.

"I remember when I were a lad," Bill said. "I used to go fishing with me mates when we were supposed to be at school."

Roger let out a hollow laugh, remembering how a newspaper had interviewed his school friends afterwards, revealing that no such escapade had ever occurred. Bill's media spokesman had brushed the matter aside with a curt "recollections of past events always differ" and the matter was soon forgotten, but for Roger it still rankled. How many times had Bill dodged serious interviews? Was this really the man he should be so afraid of?

"We need to be more robust," he had told Amanda. "This fear of Bill is overdone. He might be king of the dungheap now, but if society collapses, he will collapse with it. The Muhonin and furigans are his enemies too. Sooner or later, he's going to have to confront the fact."

"No," she had said. "To him, we're the enemy: we're the ones barring his ambition, not them. Once he has his Sori Daijin's Department, he'll concoct some conspiracy and accuse us of plotting against him. We'll be purged and the way will be clear for him to abolish the Imperial Crown. Then, he will declare himself president."

Roger had roared with laughter.

"Declare himself president? The fool must be even more deluded than we thought. He's building sandcastles while the tide is coming in. It would be laughable if it weren't so tragic. Come on, Amanda, really!"

"You should take him more seriously," she had said. "Forget his softline rhetoric – in public, he'd never say anything unpopular. It's what he does in private you should worry about. In person, he's very convincing, charming, modest and self-effacing to the point of shyness, and he'll always give you his undivided attention. That's how he takes people in: he pretends to be your friend while getting his allies to attack you. The false modesty masks huge vanity: look how he can't go anywhere without a huge motorcade or how he commandeers the Emperor's official aircraft to go on holiday. He sees himself as saviour, leading his people to the hatoha promised land, like a religious leader of old. He's completely convinced of his own rectitude: if he does something, it must be good, no matter how crooked or immoral. It makes for a nauseating mixture of high moralism and low politics."

"But he doesn't believe," Roger said. "This constant profession of passion; he's trying too hard to convince."

"Oh, he does believe," she had smiled. "He believes what he says with the utmost sincerity – when he says it. The next day he will believe the exact opposite with equal passion. He can convince himself of anything. That's what makes him so persuasive. If you aren't careful, he will catch you out."

Roger gritted his teeth. Bill Harris, skilful and controlling politician, yet weak and cowardly leader; it was a paradox. He had ruthlessly defeated his opponents, yet the merest hint of trouble from the Muhonin or furigans led to cringing displays of servility. Was the softness an act or was his political mastery an illusion? Was he just a petty crook who'd sell his country for personal gain or a political mastermind with carefully concealed authoritarian ambitions? Who was the real Bill Harris? The more he thought about it, the more elusive he became.

The car parked itself in the upper storey of an Outer Suburban car park, where Colin was shuffling about in a corner in an attempt to keep warm. Roger greeted him with a quick bow.

"Have you got it?" Roger said.

Colin nodded and handed him the files.

"Watch yourself. Christine's orchestrating an attack. She's been accusing you of using Greenwood as a springboard for your political ambitions and spreading rumours you're planning to fire the board."

Roger puckered up his face, the thought of her filling him with disgust.

"Don't do anything rash," Colin said.

"I won't," Roger smiled. "Let's separate Christine from her lackeys."

Roger slapped Colin on the shoulder and climbed inside his limo.

Within minutes, Roger was back on the expressway, flicking through the files spread out on the seat. *Christine might be protected, but her little boys aren't. What are their weaknesses? Ah yes....* He smiled, only to be interrupted by the communications screen. He sat up, startled. It was Bill Harris.

"Konnichiwa," Roger said gruffly.

"Konnichiwa," Bill smiled. "I trust I am not intruding."

Roger looked at him, dressed in a smart pinstripe suit, his manner assured, as though ready to deliver a good-natured homily. There was something almost boyish about him, a fresh-faced innocence that seemed to say, "I might get up to the occasional prank, but I'd never do anything bad – honest."

Bill cleared his throat.

"I wanted to speak to you about Compassion Day. I need your help."

"My help?" Roger spluttered. "What happened to Phil Tucker was a disgrace."

"I don't like what it's become any more than you do," Bill smiled. "But I'm limited in what I can do: the party's been hijacked by hatoha extremists and the Office of the Sori Daijin carries less authority than you think. The public may not always like the Action Groups, but they support their general principles and I have no choice but to accept what they do. You know, I've stuck my neck out a long way to defend you, but there are some in the Naikaku who wonder whose side you are on. If it hadn't been for me, you, not Phil, would have been Figure of Hate."

"If opposing appeasement means being made Figure of Hate," Roger said, "so be it. I stand up for my principles."

"Why now?" Bill's smiled broadened. "You've attended every Compassion Day for the last ten years and, now our popularity is faltering, you discover you have a principled objection?"

"I've not changed my views one bit, Harris San," Roger said through gritted teeth. "I have always been proud to be English, and that, I'm afraid, is something your generation doesn't understand."

"I sympathise with your nostalgia," Bill said, his smile narrowing. "But this isn't the England of forty years ago. People don't think in terms of public duty or national service – and they most certainly won't put collective obligations ahead of their own desires. We have to balance many different groups with their competing demands and it's not as easy as you think. If we were to appeal to one group at the expense of the others, the whole country would come crashing down. Do you really think that imposing your vision of society will bring harmony?"

Roger's face puffed up with indignation.

"No, Bill, it's this wretched hatoha mush is turning us against each other. In the past, we survived because we were tough. Look at us now, a snivelling bunch of wet blankets blubbing at the tiniest triviality. Our lives are so comfortable we drown ourselves in pity, desperate to convince ourselves we suffer hardship. It's pathetic."

"Churchill was a great sentimentalist," Bill said. "He wasn't afraid to be seen crying. You know, you've honed the role of the tough leader so well, people don't realise you have your vulnerabilities, too."

"Don't patronise me, Bill," Roger snarled. "What about you? All this empathy and emotion, is that real?"

Bill ignored the question.

"I know you're a good patriot," he said, still smiling. "But there are many who think differently. They don't understand old-fashioned values and see your stoicism as coldness – they confuse you with people like Helen Rowe. Do you really think I want to keep you out of politics? Do you really think I want to abolish England and make myself president? I'm no more the hatoha bogeyman than you are the kouha villain. There are a lot of false rumours being spread by people with agendas and it suits them to set us against each other. I'm no fan of the Political Consensus, but your association with known kouha extremists makes it very difficult for me to contain the hatoha extremists within my own party. They want you to stay away from the Day of Mourning and give them the excuse they are looking for. Their mistrust of you runs much deeper than you realise."

Roger folded his arms.

"Okay, what's the reason for this call?"

"I want peace." Bill's expression turned serious. "We worked together when I was Seimujikan for Health and we can do so again. I don't ask you to agree with me on everything, but I do ask that you support the Government line. I promise you this: there will be no Figure of Hate at the Day of Mourning. I can help you, Roger, but I need something from you if I am to restrain the extremists."

Roger sat quietly, deep in thought.

"Domo arigatou. I appreciate your offer, but I must remain true to myself."

"I understand." Bill's smile returned. "But I fear this will end in tragedy. Sayonara."

Bill hung up, but Roger was far away. Peace? Opposed to the Political Consensus? It went against everything he knew, yet he couldn't discount it. If Bill was merely a figurehead, maybe he did need his help to face down the hatoha extremists and, if the country could be saved without a costly political confrontation, then he could hardly ignore his offer. But what if it were a ruse? If Bill was in charge, then his soft appearance was a sham and, if the hatoha extremists were his pawns, then his offer was a trap. Roger sat pensively as another govermercial came on. It was Bill, sitting in a cosy armchair, wearing a woolly pullover.

"We in government," he said, putting down a book, "aren't a bunch of bureaucrats sitting behind desks. We're real human beings with real hearts – which is why I'm introducing our new mascot, Granny Government."

A life-size mascot, a granny with hair in a bun and knitting needles, walked onscreen with children dancing around her singing, "Granny Government, we love you."

"We're here to look after you." Bill grinned with a fatherly wink. "Because we care."

Roger bashed the screen, more frustrated than ever. *Bill opposed to the Political Consensus? He* is *the Political Consensus. His entire persona is constructed from the same hatoha values: celebrate one and you celebrate the other.* The car slowed down and he looked at the temporary checkpoint ahead, feeling his anxiety return. The threat was mounting. If Bill were preparing to attack him through the media, he didn't have time to be cautious, but if his offer were a trap, he wasn't able to take action either.

There was a tap at the window. Roger turned around and the feeling of being hunted returned: a police officer stood outside, his baton pressed against the window. *The boardroom rebellion must be a feint. Someone knew about my speech, someone is concealing the disembowelment, someone....* The officer tapped louder. Roger looked out nervously. Never mind Figure of Hate, there were other ways to keep people quiet.

6

Roger watched the pleasure boats on Cherry Blossom Pier, remembering his first Compassion Day. Fearful of being the only keiretsu not present, his Shachokai had begged him to go. The feeling of duress had been bad enough but having to join in the emotional display and glib catchphrases... the mere memory made him sick. Then, the moment he had dreaded. He was standing at the podium, awkward smile fixed to his face, waiting to present the award for best new artist. He could feel the retching inside, every sinew in him desperate to get out. Four louts in food-stained dungarees strutted onstage, baring their backsides to a cheering audience. Before he had even finished intro-ducing them, they had snatched the award and hurled it away, yet it was he, the fuddy-duddy from industry, who was mocked afterwards. Anger boiled within him. Never again would he abase himself. Never.

The memory brought him out in a sweat. He closed his eyes and breathed out, trying to let go. In his mind, elevated expressways soared over landscaped parks as bullet trains raced past high-rise towers.

"You know when you are home," he had once said. "The orderly queues outside the virtual reality suites, the unmistakable smell of automated pubs serving frothing pints of bitter, old maids stuck in traffic jams on their way to the sales in the autumn mists. This is my England."

He opened his eyes and surveyed the London skyline, remembering how nobody at Sakura Military Academy had considered him officer material, let alone a potential

Sword of Honour winner. How he had been ridiculed! He had been dismissed as an English Napoleon and laughed at for his talk of duty, yet he'd been the one holding the prized samurai sword at the passing out parade. He smiled, remembering his triumph with pride. *I didn't give in then and I won't give in now. Our country is worth fighting for and it isn't lost yet.*

His equanimity returned as Jane arrived and she took his arm, walking with him down the Koizumi Embankment.

"We've received a new grant," she said. "Isn't that great? We won't have to close our youth leadership programme."

"That's wonderful news," he said. "I would most certainly like to be part of that."

They reached the Hokusai Chashitsu, a small wooden tea house overlooking the adjacent Takemitsu Gardens, and walked through the sliding doors.

"I've been thinking," she said, taking a seat beside a photo of a bullet train rushing past Mount Fuji, "I've been overhasty. On reflection, I think going into politics would be an excellent idea. You could be my man in government."

He looked away, studying the fake shoji windows and the alcove, which had been mocked up to look like a tokonoma, before returning to her.

"Jane, you said I was a political novice."

"Yes... I did." She folded her arms. "I mean... no more talk of a furigan apocalypse. Look what happened after your speech."

"A made-for-media protest," he snorted. "A handful of professional agitators trying to manufacture an impression of widespread hostility, nothing more."

"Roger, think about our positions," she said. "If you go on like that, you'll just make us social pariahs."

"Social pariahs?" he spluttered. "Jane, social position means nothing in a collapsing society. It's like having the best room in a sinking ship."

"Oh, what rot," she said.

He leant in, his eyes intense, "Surely, you don't believe those policemen were killed by Nastiness."

Her smile disappeared as she scrutinised him with narrowed eyes.

"Where does this rubbish come from? Helen? It's not Amanda, is it?"

There was a long silence as he looked at the print of Hokusai's *The Great Wave off Kanagawa* on the far wall.

"Yes, I might have guessed," she said. "You'd believe anything that manipulative woman tells you. All she cares about is becoming Minister for Finance. She thought she could pressure Bill into appointing her as Minister for Finance, but she got caught inciting backbenchers to revolt over the proposed tax rises. Now, she's trying again using you. Once she's got what she wants, she'll drop you. She'll rejoin the Naikaku and you'll be Figure of Hate."

"I'd expect better of you," he said, unable to hide his irritation any longer. "Repeating the lies they put out to justify getting rid of her. I've known her for many years and she has always kept her word. She's a loyal friend and right now she's the only ally I have."

"Listen to me, Roger. She's very bright and very attractive, full of hugs and kisses, but it's all false. Perhaps you can't see it, but I can. She's trying to draw you into an affair, so she can blackmail you. You'd be ensnared, like all her previous 'allies'."

Jane sipped the remains of her tea and gave him an accusatory look.

They walked into Takemitsu Gardens and strolled along its meandering path as the noise of the city disappeared behind the screen of trees. Roger looked at

Jane, trying to work out what she was thinking. The anger had gone, replaced by a tight-lipped concentration.

"I will support you," she said, breaking the silence. "But not to destroy yourself – and certainly not to attack the Government. It's disloyal and, dare I say it, unpatriotic. Every time you attack them, you make it harder for them to defeat our enemies."

"This charade has nothing to do with defeating our enemies," he said. "The security services know who they are, so why aren't they targeting their bases?"

"You don't know they aren't," she said. "We don't know what they're doing behind the scenes."

"That," he said, "is what worries me."

They continued in silence over a wooden bridge past an ornamental pond. She stopped by a pavilion and her expression softened.

"I've spoken to a friend in the party and they'd be happy for you to join. I want you to take up the offer. My family has worked damned hard and what have we got for it? Nothing. We've been shut out of politics because, unlike you, we're not from the elite. Bill recognises what we've accomplished, he can see the contribution we could make in the House of Councillors and has offered to help. My family has done a lot for you and the least you could do is show some gratitude. Stop treating Bill as your enemy. Make your peace."

"He only wants control of Greenwood."

"Oh, you are stubborn. He recognises your achievements. There's an amakudari job in Government, if only you'd realise it."

"Jane, I won't be fobbed off with some pointless sinecure. When I left the Army, you said I could be anything I wanted. I will be Sori Daijin and your family will receive their honours. Have faith in me. Don't you want to be First Lady?"

She rested against a stone lantern and looked at him sceptically.

"Roger, at long last my family is getting the recognition it deserves and I won't let you jeopardise it. Stop this confrontation."

She kissed him on the cheek and they parted company.

Roger climbed into his limo and ordered it to the Geisha Club, fuming. *How could you fall for such a trick, Jane? Do you really think your family can cut a deal with Bill? So he offers you an honour or a seat in the House of Councillors – what then? With me out and your shareholding reduced, Greenwood would be his. As for the idea he'd offer his most prominent opponent an amakudari post... even the mildest sinecure would be anathema to his Action Groups allies. You've lost your judgement. No, it's that wretched foundation. You want me out the way, so you can build up your alliance with Bill. I'll bet you're assisting the board-room rebels. I'll be fired and left for the Action Groups.* He cracked his knuckles. *Just you try, Jane No-one else can run Greenwood. Side with Bill and you'll sink with him.*

The limo pulled up in a discreet West End side street where two doormen in black suits greeted him, their necks and arms covered in irezumi tattoos of dragons and warriors. Roger smiled and walked into the foyer, where the executives were waiting: Jeff the blunt Yorkshireman, Pete the upper-class city boy and Michael the coarse Londoner; all in their thirties, all highly ambitious. Roger smiled at them contemptuously. *I made it the hard way. It wasn't about flash status symbols back then. Seniority was respected: superiors were spoken to in reverential language and shachos commuted to work with their staff. With you, it's all instant results and easy money. You think you can get to the top without putting in the hard work first. I've seen your files. You know-nothings won't be so cocky.*

Before he could speak, they were greeted by a hostess dressed as a geisha.

"Konbanwa," she smiled. "Welcome to the Geisha Club, my name is Kiko. Come this way, kudasai."

She led them through a long crimson tunnel with thin extruded light tubes that cast a warm light on the shunga art on the walls. They walked past the pictures by Kyosai and Shigenobu of copulating couples with oversized sexual organs before the tunnel opened out onto a curvaceous pink room. They stopped briefly on the platform and watched the scene. Drunkards in expensive suits laughed boisterously and geishas served drinks, while bouncers watching a discreet distance away. Kiko smiled, leading them down the steps and past a man pouring his heart out to a geisha who smiled sympathetically.

"Nobody loves me," he sobbed. "Nobody cares. I live in an empty world."

She put her arm around him as he blubbed into a silk handkerchief. Next to him a man with a pencil moustache was whispering into the ear of a voluptuous geisha, who burst out in fits of coarse laughter. He grinned rakishly then launched himself, slipping his hand down her kimono. Kiko took them up a flight of stairs to a white pod-like structure floating above the main lounge.

"Aki will be with you shortly," she smiled. "Enjoy your stay."

The room contained two curvilinear leather sofas either side of an oval table with a plate glass window overlooking the main lounge. Michael watched as the doormen pulled the man with the moustache off the sofa and escorted him out of view while Pete and Jeff watched Roger suspiciously.

"It seems we've reached an impasse," Roger said, as Kiko returned with some beer and a bottle of champagne in a bucket of ice. "I've no desire to repeat the arguments;

the main thing is to reach an agreement before the Shachokai."

"Tyson San," Jeff said, looking him in the eye, "this is about more than expansion. Authoritarian leadership has no place in keiretsu: you're a shacho, not an absolute monarch. Change your autocratic ways or the Shachokai will change them for you."

Pete and Michael nodded.

"You have a nerve," Roger said, his voice cold. "I'm chief executive, not chairman, and I won't be bounced into anything by threat of rebellion."

"Rebellion?" Pete said in clipped tones. "You may have founded Greenwood, but that doesn't make it yours. England Inc means party, state and keiretsu working together in harmony. You can no more defy government policy than the City of London can pass a law against an Act of the National Diet. Greenwood has fallen behind because you keep defying MEPTI's guidance. The consensus of the board is the consensus of England Inc. If there's a rebel here, it is you."

Roger laughed then leaned forward aggressively.

"In the past, staff showed respect. Never did they question their superior's judgement and you'd do well to remember that."

"Respect, my arse," Michael sneered. "We're sick of your dewy-eyed reminiscences. Was it hard work and entrepreneurial flair that made Greenwood or was it MEPTI channelling state orders your way? If it hadn't been for them, Greenwood would have failed like thousands of other small kaishas." He opened another beer as Jeff stared Roger hard in the eye. "Face it, Tyson San. The state made you."

The lights dimmed and a light show of jagged shapes projected onto the ceiling, bouncing in time with the music. Pete and Michael loosened their collars and knocked back their beers, while Jeff and Roger eyeballed each other. The music grew louder as a spotlight illuminated the entrance, where a girl appeared, her lithe figure instantly capturing the executives' attention. She tossed her long brown hair and sashayed towards them as they banged their fists on the table. Roger watched the lustful faces following the thrusts and gyrations in front of them, readying himself for the fight as the lights came on.

"You must take me for a fool," he roared as she left. "MEPTI's Industrial Plans were for public consumption. Sure, they drew up plans and issued guidance, but nobody took any notice. Keiretsu working together under MEPTI's guidance for the national good? A myth. As for their joint ventures, well... you try getting competitors to give up their commercial secrets. The only way they could get anything done was to throw drink at the problem. The fact is the Defence Agency was struggling to find a supplier who could provide quality military equipment at an affordable price and I was the only person able to do it. Without me, there would have been no England Inc."

"That still doesn't address the shacho issue," Pete said.

"There is no issue." Roger raised his voice. "This Government wants tame keiretsu and that means getting rid of shachos that stand up to it. Once you've done their dirty work, they'll put their yes-men in and you'll be ditched like last year's lover. So tell me, who's the rebel?"

The music returned with a thudding boom. Roger smiled as the executives forgot the row and focused on the shapely silhouette in the doorway. They cheered as she walked towards them. The next moment she was writhing up and down on Michael's lap, her flesh millimetres from his face. She loosened his tie and unbuttoned his shirt, sliding her hands up and down his chest as sweat dripped down his face. Pete and Jeff were on their feet, calling for her to come to them. Then, with a wink, she jumped off,

71

fixing her attentions on Jeff, while Pete and Michael knocked back another drink. Roger watched them leering and closed his eyes, remembering a talk he had given to shachos of Greenwood's affiliated businesses at a Friday luncheon club.

"As we know," he had said, "hierarchies used to be command structures: individuals above commanding individuals below."

A holographic display showed a pyramidal organisational chart with arrows from the top box flowing downwards to boxes below.

"Today, the individual has been subordinated to the group, so that hierarchy consists of groups nested one inside another."

The pyramid image was replaced by an origami box, which opened up revealing a series of progressively smaller boxes inside, like a set of Russian dolls.

"But leadership is still critical – the leader is the source of vision and initiative; the person who binds individuals into teams."

The shachos shook their heads as the boxes returned inside each other.

"Our culture is built on consensus," said one. "Superiors act on behalf of the group: listening, coordinating, harmonising. Leadership is a relic."

"You're wrong," Roger said. "The leader is the innermost box. Without it, everything else implodes."

He crushed the boxes with his fist, ending the presentation. What applied to the keiretsu also applied to the country as a whole. If the innermost box was unsound the entire structure would collapse, but what was going on in the centre of power? Infighting within Bill's inner circle? A power vacuum? He might be the innermost box at Greenwood, but as far as the state was concerned, he was on the outside. He needed to get inside. He needed....

He opened his eyes with a start. Aki was on his lap, stretching herself up and down the length of his body while his executives whistled and clapped. She smiled at him with gentle chestnut eyes, put her arms around him and pressed her body close. He gulped, unable to look away. She was so beautiful, so sweet, so innocent looking, so... Amanda. Panic swept over him. He felt helpless, like a child. Then, she was in the doorway blowing a kiss. The lights came on and he came to: his shirt was covered in sweat. He quickly buttoned up his jacket and looked at the executives, who were too drunk to notice.

"Okay," Roger said, gathering himself. "I propose a compromise: a limited expansion, no questions over leadership; no-one gets moved and no-one gets fired. Do I have your agreement?"

Three drunken faces looked back sullenly. Jeff nodded.

"It'll do," he said. "But there's still no consensus."

"On the contrary," Roger smiled. "This is exactly how consensus is formed. Here's to throwing drink at problems."

He held up his glass for a toast.

"To the Geisha Club," Michael said lolling forward. "Much better than any no-pan kissa."

Pete laughed at nothing in particular and they all held up their glasses.

"To Greenwood," Jeff said, holding a bottle aloft. He took a large swig with more going down his shirt than his throat.

"I think our business is done." Roger stood to leave. "Sayonara, gentlemen."

Pete and Jeff bid Roger farewell, but Michael had fallen asleep. Jeff gave him a prod and tried to wake him. Michael grunted, but would not be roused.

"Put him in the taxi when it comes," Roger said.

Softer music was playing in the main lounge as the evening wound down. A few hardcore drinkers remained, some slumped, others rambling incomprehensibly.

"Roger, old chap, how the devil are you?"

Roger looked up to see Dr Frank Carter, a senior figure in MEPTI with a reputation as a hard drinker, sitting on a sofa, with Chairman of the Liberal Democratic Party, Jim Minto, beside him, swaying around attempting to stay upright.

"Haven't seen you at the rugger for a while," Frank said. hunting for something to drink on the table in front of him. "Where have you been?"

A hostess removed the empty bottles and produced a new one with a flourish.

"Domo, itoshii," he beamed. "What would I do without you? Don't you love this place? The hangover's frightful, but always worth it."

He winked at the geisha, who smiled back, but Roger was staring wistfully into space.

"Frank, it was never a selfish ambition to be shacho. England Inc meant something. Keiretsu, party, MEPTI: we were building a New Japan. It wasn't always perfect, but look at it now. Respect for seniority, group orientation, long-term focus, consensus; they're empty concepts – and it's down to Bill. The previous administration understood business. Never did they treat us as the enemy."

"Well, you've certainly caused consternation with your speech," Frank chuckled. "They think it's jolly unsporting."

"Jolly unsporting? Frank, what's going on?"

Frank's face fell as his mood grew maudlin.

"You're so right, Tyson old boy. We've been sidelined at MEPTI. The Commissions tell us what to do... and you too, if that bloody Sori Daijin of ours has his way."

Frank took a large slug of whisky and straightened himself.

"He's planning to create a Commission for the Economy and put the keiretsu under his control. Ostensibly, it'll be to 'coordinate economic planning' or some such piffle, but we all know its real purpose will be to seize keiretsu assets. The state won't take you over directly – far too obvious. No, he'll use its powers to put his cronies in charge – reverse takeovers, forced mergers with shell kaishas, that sort of thing. Keizai ichiryu, seiji sanryu! The economy is the one first-rate thing we have left; if our third-rate politicians take control of that, too... we'll be a proper third-world country. All the things that made us great – MEPTI, the keiretsu, England Inc – gone. Oh, how I long for the old days."

Roger contemplated the comment as Jim propped himself up and looked at him, trying hard to keep still.

"Watch yourself. He'll e-engineer an ici... incident to discredit you."

For a moment, the mood was serious, then Frank began laughing.

"You know what the engineer's motto is?"

"No, Frank, I don't."

"Spanner, screwer, lever, bolt."

He chuckled to himself and began singing.

Roger settled the bill and returned to his limousine. It was past midnight and he could feel the tiredness catching up with him. He threw himself inside, wondering what Jim had meant. He was the one senior figure in the Liberal Democratic Party he could trust and not one to invent things, but it was too late. The lights from the pachinko parlours merged into one red blur as he drifted off to sleep.

He awoke with a jolt as his limo came to a sudden halt. He checked the forward display: a small family car was blocking the road, a furigan gang in balaclavas and pyjamas attacking it with hammers. The leader jumped up and down on the bonnet, taunting the occupants, while his gangmates smashed in the windows and tore off whatever they could. Roger climbed out and strode towards them.

"Get away," he shouted. "Leave them alone."

The gang ran off, leaving detritus strewn across the street. He peered inside, where a young family was cowering.

"They've gone. Are you okay?"

They staggered out, shocked but unharmed.

"Yes, thanks," said the mother as Roger helped the children out.

"Were you there long?"

"An hour or two," said the father. "It felt like bloody ages."

"Do you need a lift?"

"No, but that's very kind of you," she replied. "The breakdown service should be here soon."

"We came from Tyburn Park Complex," the father added as it arrived. "We can thank our lucky stars we didn't break down there or we'd have really been done for."

Roger helped them back in the car and watched them leave. His neighbourhood was an odd place for people from the Tyburn Park Complex to come, never mind a furigan gang.

The sky had turned dark by the time he had reached home. As the gates opened, he noticed figures lurking in the shadows. They made no noise and didn't move. It was the gang he had encountered earlier. He turned into his drive, casting the car's rear lights on them, then watched them merge back into the murk as the gates slammed shut.

7

Roger paced around his office frenetically. The Day of Mourning was only a day away and there was no guarantee that his agreement would hold. Would Christine push the executives into voting against him? He couldn't discount it. Would she organise a media attack? That was almost guaranteed. He peered outside nervously and watched the government-sponsored party in Ishiguro Park. A small crowd had formed, lounging around on bean bags and picnicking under parasols as they waited for the free film. He scowled, recognising what was playing. Fast cuts of murder scenes, grieving victims and soldiers marching underscored by music that buzzed and scream-ed like hornets. It was the latest govermercial.

"Sinister forces are at work," boomed the voiceover as people fled in terror and rows of body bags filled the street. "Nastiness is threatening our way of life."

Roger put his hands over his head trying to shut it out, then gave up. *It's useless. You can't fight against it. Wher-ever you are, the Political Consensus is always there to wear you down.* He looked at the crowd. Though no-one seemed to pay govermercials much attention, they seemed to assimilate their message as if by osmosis. It wasn't so much persuasion as normalisation; passive cognition, as Helen called it.

Yet something had changed. Gone was the breezy reassurance of earlier broadcasts; in its place a sense of imminent doom as if Bill had recognised the public's fears and redirected them at him. Roger watched as made-up newspaper headlines flashed across the screen – *NASTI-NESS ON THE RISE; CRIME WAVE HITS CENTRAL LONDON; MURDER RATE AT ALL-TIME HIGH* – remembering the poster on the subway. *Now the Muhonin have struck, hat-ing me is not enough. People must be made to feel afraid.*

They must think I'm the threat. His feelings of dread returned. Bill's allies controlled the media, and the moment they chose to vilify him he was on his own. He looked at the crowd, much bigger now the film, an ultra-violent Manga cartoon, had started. Surely, people so apathetic to politics they barely bothered to vote didn't believe the propaganda. Surely, they would see through the smears. Surely....

He sat down, recalling the snippets of conversation he'd heard. *They're a complete shower... a bunch of crooks... they've buggered everything up... we got no free speech... more effin' Political Consensus....* Rumblings, complaints, outrage; discontent was never far away, but always muttered sotto voce where the Commissions couldn't hear. Then every so often, a change would come over the people and protests would erupt as if from nowhere. He could see the angry faces and the journalists doggedly pursuing ministers. How powerless the Commissions had been! An increase to Diet Members' allowances, a proposed internal passport; the people had risen up and the Government backed down. If they could do so once, they could do so again.

Roger banged his fist on the desk. *Bill knows he's vulnerable. He knows the public could topple him; that's why he treats them as the enemy, frightening them with Nastiness and Figures of Hate. Keep 'em weak and keep 'em scared – this isn't apathy, it's disempowerment. The people might be strong, but they need a leader. No. Bill's profiting from appeasement, but the people don't know, they don't realise how much danger he's putting them in. Leadership isn't enough, I need proof.* He stood by the window and looked out over Ishiguro Park, hands on hips. *We will have a strong state and a harmonious society. Bill's clique will be swept aside and England Inc revived. It will be a democratic revolution, a restoration of proper government. Pain is no barrier, I will prevail.*

Amanda was outside, ready for their appointment at Kurosawa Studios. She gave him a hug and they walked to his car bay. He opened the door for her with a smile.

"Ooh, how civilised," she laughed in mock surprise.

He closed the door, feeling a glow inside. Figure of Hate, Action Groups, boardroom rebels, furigans, Muhonin; where everything else in his life was drudgery, she was joy. Where others kept their distance, she remained loyal; where others saw a gruff exterior, she saw warmth. His enemies could do what they liked – with her, he was not alone. Yet as they drove along, he noticed something else. As she gazed out of the window, there seemed to be a sadness about her. Was she, too, unhappy? He thought of the rumours Bill's Naikaku had put out, accusing her of being duplicitous, deceitful, scheming and unprincipled and felt a pain within him. *What they did was horrible. Jealousy's a terrible thing and Bill's Naikaku full of it. They've hurt you, Amanda, and I won't let it happen again.* She turned around and the sight her large brown eyes made his heart beat faster. He wanted to put his arms around her and hold her, but he didn't move. With a gentle smile, she rested her head against his shoulder and the Political Consensus faded into insignificance.

The reception robot escorted them to Holo-Studio 5. After a short Safety and Wellbeing briefing on the dangers of malemotions, the doors slid open to reveal a familiar scene. The garages, underpasses and walkways could have been anywhere in the barracks, but this complex existed nowhere. Roger looked disdainfully at the furigans milling around with cups of coffee, their accents resolutely middle England, and took a seat. The Studio Manager, Hilary

Wilton-Spence, bumbled in and adjusted his bright blue bow tie before sitting beside Amanda.

"We're doing a drama about life in the complexes," he said, peering over his half-moon glasses. "Challenging perceptions of the Helpless as senseless brutes."

"I see," Roger said. "And what if those perceptions are correct?"

"I don't know," he replied, "I just get paid to do this."

The director called "action" and the actors took their positions in the underpass. A furigan girl approached the gang leader and uttered some gobbledygook Roger couldn't understand, before the scriptwriter rushed onto the set and filming stopped. Hilary got up from his seat, throwing his papers on the floor.

"What now?"

"This scene is flat," the scriptwriter shouted. "I keep telling you: we need an antagonist."

"Such as what?" the director shouted back.

"I dunno, anything: a social worker, cop, politician, last year's Figure of Hate."

"Yeah, that might work," the director mused. "We could have him take a pop at the kids, calling them names and pushing them around like."

"And what if he sues you for slander?" Roger said.

"He's got a point," Hilary said, taking his glasses off and giving them a polish.

"Who cares?" the director said. "It would make good drama. Let's give it a whirl."

Filming resumed with an actor standing in as Phil Tucker. Roger stormed out, his fists clenched in fury, Amanda following close behind.

"Now you get it?" she said. "This is how they deceive us. While the real barracks are pushed out of sight, a sham is being broadcast into every home and people believe what they see."

"But why don't they question it?"

She looked at him sympathetically.

"The media's so central to our lives that we believe what we see onscreen is real. In fact, it's more real than reality: emotions are heightened, drama sharpened, issues simplified. Someone tells you Fred Bloggs got mugged, it's an anecdote. You see Phil Tucker bashing the hell out of some cuddly furigan kid, then it's real. We live in a computer-generated hyperreality and Bill is in charge. The Political Consensus tells us how to think, the govermercials tell us what to think and the Commission for Identity ensures that every media station conforms. Any programme maker must depict furigans or Muhonin as helpless or they will be fined for being Hurtful or Upsetting – or prosecuted for Nastiness. Real life counts for nothing. They've decided that we are the Forces of Nastiness; and if people believe it, then we are the Forces of Nastiness."

"But it's not true."

"It doesn't matter whether it's true, only that it's believable. As the saying goes, an unquestioned assertion is as good as a truth."

Roger was about to speak, but Amanda was interrupted by a phone call. He stood back and thought again of the sham furigan world. *Phil never attacked anyone, but once you're seen as a monster, you're wrong whatever you do. Fiction is now the common currency of debate and Phil is a furigan kiddie-killer. If you're powerful, lies are a weapon. If you're powerless, the truth offers no protection.* He looked at Amanda, who was talking excitedly, troubled by the implications. If the Government insisted the Forces of Nastiness had killed the two policemen, then the Forces of Nastiness must have killed the two policemen, but would people believe it? He looked to Amanda as she finished her call.

"What was that about?" he said.

"Watch the news this evening."

She gave him a wink and hurried off.

Roger felt a wave of optimism as he left the studio. *No, the truth matters. People accept the Political Consensus because they have no alternative, but once its monopoly is broken it will lose its force. People will see they're being lied to. Granny Government, Bill's offer, Nastiness... the Government's ready to crumble and all I have to do is push. I listen to people, meet them, speak to them. Apart from publicity stunts, when has Bill or anyone in his clique done that? They don't meet real people, they don't know what they think. They live in the same districts, eat at the same restaurants, send their children to the same schools and hold the same views. They're delusional, living in their own closed world, believing their own propaganda.* He stopped, doubt gnawing away. *No, someone knows about the disembowelment. Someone is hiding it. Who?*

Roger checked his inbox as he sped towards Greenwood's London HQ. There was still no reply from Emma. He tried calling, but she was out. *Damn her! Where is she? I can't have her reigniting this dispute and have those three saps going back on their agreement.* He was about to call again when a news headline caught his attention. With trepidation, he opened *GREENWOOD: THE UNTOLD STORY*.

With Roger Tyson at the helm, Greenwood has been characterised by an unwillingness to play by the rules. But the indulgent atmosphere of yesteryear is gone. No more can he use the keiretsu as a platform to influence politics. No more can he airbrush out his links to kouha elements within the military. It is no wonder he appears so fearful. With his grasp of Greenwood weakening, he can see his past catching up with him.

Defence orders, MEPTI preference, Robinson family funding, the Roger it depicted alternated between bully ruthlessly crushing rivals and puppet pushed to prominence by others. He stared at the screen, his fingers pressed against his lips, waiting to see who had made it. *The Morning News – I might have known. If the Action Groups are the footsoldiers of the Political Consensus, Kobiyashi Media Group are its cheerleaders. They pretend to conduct investigative journalism when they're acting as Bill's mouthpiece. Digging up facts? Repeating whatever rubbish his Comms Team spoon-feeds them, more like. I know who's behind this pathetic rehash of old canards and unfounded allegations.* He thought of Bill's combative Press Officer and ex-Kobiyashi employee, Andy Hunt, with unalloyed disgust. *I know you. First, you soften up the victim by accusing them of Nastiness, then you smear them with malicious rumours, then you accuse them of something so heinous no-one will speak up for them. It won't just be a fight you get. Oh no, I'm going to enjoy hurting you.* He picked up his briefcase and punched the screen closed.

The board stood to attention. Roger strode inside.

"Right," he said, taking his seat, "let's get through this."

The board members nodded their assent and he rushed through the items, his manner getting more emphatic as they approached the main item.

"There's been a lot of talk about consensus," Roger said. "Consensus means finding common ground and accepting the majority verdict. It does not mean forming cabals and threatening rebellion. There's no place in this keiretsu for insurrections. Anyone that thinks otherwise can find new employment."

He looked at Jeff, Pete and Michael, their dismissal notices ready in his briefcase, but they said nothing.

"Since the Rijikai, I and a number of senior colleagues have worked hard to find a compromise, the main points of which have been circulated. Does anyone have any comments?"

Emma spoke up.

"This is just your initial position with a few token new projects thrown in. It will do nothing to stop us shedding market share to our competitors."

"Do you reject it?"

"If the Shachokai approves this proposal, I will accept," she said. "However, I would like my reservations noted."

"Then we have consensus," Roger said as the Shachokai approved the proposal. He declared the meeting closed and got up to leave. Emma was looking at him, her disappointment mixed with anger.

"I'm serious about expansion," she said as the board members left. "I can't speak for the others, but I believe in my proposal. You'll have my resignation tomorrow morning."

"I take it you didn't see my message." Roger gave her a gentle smile. "These new projects need someone committed to run them and I would very much like that to be you."

She scanned through her inbox and found his message. She nodded, but there was no smile.

Colin was waiting outside, his expression livid.

"What are you playing at?" he said.

"If you're going to give me a lecture about England Inc and MEPTI, don't."

"I'm talking about you picking a fight with the Government. We can't afford to make an enemy of them. What if they cut their orders?"

"It would be nothing we couldn't handle."

"Stop being obtuse," Colin said. "It's a fight we can't win. They can levy taxes, print money, enact legislation, conscript soldiers, declare wars; we can't. We both know the economy is going to hell, but you must see we need to have them onside."

Roger sighed and patted him on the shoulder.

"Colin, old friend, you and I agree on so much. Your faith in the Government is touching, but naive."

"He's right," a voice echoed from further down the corridor. Christine emerged from the lobby area. "Accusing me of stirring up rebellion's a clever ploy. You might have deflected attention from your failings as shacho, but you're not fooling anyone about your politics. Stick to business, Roger mate. We don't need a Shogun."

He turned to her, hands on hips.

"You have some nerve, Soukan Barratt. I warn you to keep out of keiretsu affairs. You can't push me out."

She laughed, then her expression turned sharp.

"You can browbeat your subordinates, but don't think you can browbeat the state. If I were you, I'd stop right now; before you're too far in."

The lift arrived before Roger could reply. She smiled and the doors slid shut.

Roger returned home feeling a vague disappointment. Had he resolved the dispute or won a minor tactical victory? He slumped in his armchair, unsure. The mood detector found some rugby for him to watch, but after a few minutes of muddy non-action he got up. *Christine and Bill chose not to fight that battle. They're attacking me where I'm weakest. Damn!* As he fretted, the mood detector alerted him to the breaking news, *BILL HARRIS AIDE IN SHAREHOLDING CONTROVERSY*. He looked up and opened the report, rapidly forgetting his disappointment.

> *Documents revealing that top Bill Harris aide, Jonathan Green, had not disclosed shares in English Landholdings have been received by the Eikoku Keizai Shimbun today. Green San purchased the shares with a loan from its financial affiliate prior to flotation after giving English*

Landholdings the green light to participate in the Government's Urban Regeneration Programme two weeks earlier. Opposition figures called this a clear violation of the Ministerial Code and called for him to be investigated by the Committee for Public Standards. Green San has denied any wrongdoing and has issued a statement saying that the transactions were perfectly legal.

Roger beamed as the press harried Jonathan Green as he left the Kantei.

"I've nothing further to say," Jonathan said, getting into his car and driving off, journalists chasing after him, still asking questions.

Go on Christine, spread your lies. You can't stop it now. This isn't idle chit-chat or gossip; your scandals are out. He clapped his hands in delight, replaying the report again and again, laughing until his ribs hurt. Jane entered the room and with a gruff laugh he replayed the report.

"There'll always be the odd bad egg," she said, putting her bags down.

He grinned, unable to contain his glee.

"They're all bad, the whole damn lot of them."

8

Roger had been dreaming of Greenwood. It was the early days and he had mounted a hostile bid for Satori Holographics, a long-established but struggling family firm. Hostile takeovers were unheard of and the Satori Shachokai had mounted a lengthy press campaign against it. "Our kaisha has a proud history," they said. "Greenwood only cares about the bottom line." The commentators had taken their side, accusing Roger of being a spiv.

"I have nothing to apologise for," Roger had said. "Satori is a publicly traded kaisha and if its owners accept my bid, then that is their right."

He had prevailed. After the takeover, the Satori Shachokai had been fired and the kaisha restructured into Greenwood Holographics. Productivity had improved and Greenwood taken its first steps to becoming a keiretsu.

Roger raised his head groggily, remembering the sourness he had then felt. *Nobody remembers that we too had been targeted for takeover. They expected us to fail and I proved them wrong. I reinvigorated England Inc. But who cares about that now? Hostile takeovers are back out of fashion. They want softies. They want "collaboration." They want Bill Harrises.* However, it hadn't only been the hostile takeover that had proved controversial. Rumours of state involvement and a policy of building Greenwood into a national champion had swirled around and though nothing had been proved, suspicions remained. Roger got up and stomped around the office with a grumpy expression. Jonathan Green was on the news, walking briskly past journalists, refusing to answer questions.

"The Sori Daijin," said the reporter, "last night expressed his full confidence in Green San after a parliamentary investigation found he had broken no rules."

Roger looked at the information service with consternation. Not only had the Government's ratings recovered, they had improved. Filled with renewed urgency, he fired Amanda another message:

This isn't good enough. The inquiry's ignored his questionable business dealings. Even if Bill sacks him, he'll pretend it's a one-off. We need evidence of systematic corruption.

He switched the screen off and sank back into his seat. *Bill's fireproof. All people see is a goody-goody school prefect. Even if they find him slimy, they can't imagine he could be bad – and now he's turned this into an attack on me. So bloody what if he's spared me Figure of Hate? He's got the media on his side, twisting the facts and quoting me out of context like they always do. That's what's so damaging. That's why people....*

A loud alarm rang out, marking the start of the Day of Mourning. Roger buried his head in his hands, wanting it to go away. However, even barricaded in his office there was no avoiding it. He watched on his private viewcam as his workforce, all wearing black Anti-Nastiness ribbons, lined up in front of the "Be Nice" posters and began sobbing. *Victory at the Shachokai? I'm as distant from my own colleagues as the crowds in Tokugawa Square.*

There was a buzz at the door. Roger sat up, his muscles tense. Christine? Had she come to make sure he attended? Could Compassion Stewards have gained entry? He looked at the monitor and relaxed. Ben Chatsworth, a young colleague whom he mentored, was standing outside.

"Sorry to disturb you, Shacho San," Ben said with a bow, "Would you like to join us for the Day of Mourning?"

Roger looked at him in his dark suit and black ribbon. He was sporting a black eye.

"Are you okay?"

"This?" Ben said. "Oh, a mugging, nothing serious."

"Nothing serious?"

"You are coming – to the Day of Mourning?"

Roger hesitated, feeling a pang of guilt. Always polite and ready to listen, Ben was how he would like his executives to be, yet he could never hide his disappointment with how his boss rejected the Political Consensus.

"Shacho San, why won't you come?"

Roger looked away as Ben's eyes betrayed his disappointment, then put the screen on. Crowds of people wearing black ribbons paraded down Murakami Street in floods of tears, some carrying candles, others pictures of the dead policemen. Behind them, electronic displays projected happy images of Lifestyle Groups, furigans and Muhonin interpolated with previous Figures of Hate. Roger pointed as a group began chanting outside the National Diet Buildings, the flats of their hands pressed against their foreheads and their eyes screwed up in concentration. Beside them, a sign read "meditating for peace."

"Look at that ridiculous charade. It should never be allowed to intrude on private grief."

"Shacho San," Ben said, "they're expressing their grief in their own way."

"That's not grief, Ben, it's hysteria. Those loonies don't know the first thing about the dead men. Tomorrow, they'll be "meditating" for the next fashionable cause. Why won't I come? This nonsense has nothing to do with the policemen; the Government couldn't care less about their deaths. All it wants is emotion – thought-stopping emotion."

"That's so cynical," Ben said. "Ministers are human, too."

"Only just," Roger frowned.

"Come on," Ben smiled. "I think it's good we're trying to have more Compassionage and Inclusionality. Isn't it better to include people within the system than shut them out? We can speak to them, educate, persuade."

"You can't include things that are fundamentally opposed," Roger said. "Eventually, one or the other must give way. We're the ones being educated and persuaded. We're being roped into their system."

Ben went quiet as the policemen's families floated paper lanterns down a river. Roger felt tears well up. Amidst the overblown emoting, it was a moment of genuine emotion. Did the families know their loved ones had been disembowelled? Were they aware what agony their final moments would have been? He grimaced as the image of the dead policeman barged its way into his mind.

"Kudasai, Shacho San," Ben said. "We can't keep living in a state of siege. I know you're a good man, but when you talk in terms of 'us and them' you sound like an extremist. I appreciate all that you've done for me and our keiretsu. Kudasai, do it for the deceased."

Ben waited, desperately wanting him to come. Roger could see the disappointment building in his eyes. He looked down, not wanting to see that look again.

Roger breathed out, feeling deflated. *It's just one day. It will soon be over. Be tough.* He tried to steel himself, but, as he got up to lock and bolt the door, a forlorn Helen appeared.

"Is it okay if I join you?" she said. "The atmosphere's poisonous at the university. I thought I'd be safer here."

He nodded and pulled up a seat.

"Is it like this over there?"

"No, worse," she said. "They're like a lynch mob. I'm afraid they'll ransack my office."

They sat in silence as the procession finished in Tokugawa Square for the final solemnities, Roger watching sullenly as Mourning Stewards bearing "WE HATE ROGER TYSON" signs shepherded their flock into their allotted place.

"You hate me," he bellowed, "but I'm the hater. What happened to compassion?"

Helen said nothing, her eyes fixed on the Sorrow Mentors working their way through the square, encouraging people to express their feelings as they assembled in the front of the giant screen.

"We should apologise to the Helpless," intoned the speaker. "We are the guilty ones. Their plight is our fault."

The screen played live footage of representatives from every Lifestyle Group placing flowers outside the complex where the policemen died to the accompaniment of a sombre drumbeat. As the last flower was laid, the crowd held hands and apologised in unison, a drone swooping low projecting 195 LIFESTYLE GROUPS SPEAK AS ONE onto the night's sky. After a short pause, the speaker led them in chanting the ritual denunciation of Nastiness.

NASTINESS IS BAD

NASTINESS IS WRONG

NASTINESS IS DEATH

"Do you really think you can beat this?" Helen scowled. "People have had it drummed into them for so long they believe it."

The question hit Roger with unexpected force. It was indeed a culture war and there was no guarantee he could avoid defeat, let alone win. He thought back to what she had said and studied the profusion of hairstyles, clothes and argots. Despite the assertion of difference, there was an odd uniformity, as if each group was using its own language to say the same thing. Like the political parties and the media, the Lifestyle Groups might bicker among themselves, but all conformed to the Political Consensus. He looked closer as the camera lingered on the furigans and Muhonin prominently placed at the front of the crowd, struck by the display. *Maybe I was wrong. Maybe it is possible to build a society on division. If we're all different, then we're all the same – and the Muhonin and furigans are simply two more groups. But it can't work. They despise the Political Consensus as much as they hate civilised society. The superficial differences between the Lifestyle Groups are nothing compared to the deep divide separating them from the Muhonin and furigans. Bill may dream he is the unifying factor, but he isn't. By fragmenting the nation, he's opened up much deeper divisions.*

"Helen," Roger said, "is it possible to build a society on division?"

"I don't understand. What do you mean?"

"Is Bill dividing society up or uniting it against us?"

"Both," she said. "A united nation would be a powerful force outside his control and thus a threat, so he's cut us off from our traditional identity and carved us up into tribal groups, where identity can be controlled by his allies. By keeping us divided, the state – or, more precisely, the Commission for Lifestyle – maintains its control. It's basic divide and rule."

"So, if society is divided up into different groups, how is it also united against us? How do you go from lots of little groups with their own identities to one big 'us and them'?"

"There is always an 'us and them'." Helen was emphatic. "However you define society as 'us,' those opposed must be 'them.' The Political Consensus is no different. For all its talk of difference, it's a binary system of good versus evil just the same. Behind the official claim that society is a collection of different groups, neither good nor bad, lies an unstated 'us and them': the powerful versus the power-less, the strong versus the weak, the oppressors versus the victims. *They* are always good and *we* are always bad. The nation is not a shared community, but an oppressive force to be liberated from: who'd want to be part of it when you could be given privileged status like the Muhonin and furigans? With the Lifestyle Groups, we too can play at being victims, we too can opt out of our nation, we too can pretend we are what we're not and we're not what we are. Subversion is patriotic and patriotism subversive."

"But real people don't think like that," he said. "Deep down, people still care about their country. Take football or rugby – they support the national team."

"People are idiots," Helen said. "A useless bunch of big babies who want to be mollycoddled and feel their silly lives are special. Reality frightens them. They'll wet their pants when they realise there's no-one there to protect them. Don't think they'll speak up for you when the accusations start flying. I can tell you from experience, they won't."

They looked up as the screen prepared for its final message, but instead of the booming voice came a soft, insistent voice.

"Nastiness can be stopped. Malemotions can be stopped. We may not mean to be Nasty, but we hate the Helpless even when we're not conscious of it. So, come on, let's mend our ways and feel some empathy. No more Nastiness. Let's all be Nice."

The square was bathed in light and the crowd hugged each other and cheered.

"Forget the people," Helen said. "Our country has become something to be ashamed of. Firm government and strong leadership: it's the only answer now."

She pulled a face as the event closed with a candlelit vigil. Bill hugged a sobbing Chief of Police and stood in sombre reflection for the ten-minute silence, all cameras focused on him. With seconds to go, he bowed his head and a tear rolled down his cheek. There was loud applause and coverage returned to the studio, where black-suited pundits sat around a table, Bill's picture dominating the wall behind them.

"Bill showcased real leadership," said one. "Bringing people together in empathy."

"By being in touch with his emotions," added another, "he's been in touch with the people."

"Our Sori Daijin has expressed our resolve," agreed the first.

"Resolve?" Roger snorted. "If this pathetic display is the worst he'll do, the Muhonin are hardly likely to be deterred."

"They're not the intended audience," Helen said. "The pundits have it the wrong way around: the people are in touch with the Government's emotions. Bill has prepared the script and they have followed. Now they can pat themselves for their emotional correctness and the police-men can be buried with yesterday's news."

She picked up a cigarette and started smoking, her fingers twitching.

"You know, there was talk of creating a Nation-zoku Lifestyle Group once, but it could never happen. Without a common enemy, Bill's society falls apart. We have to be the villains."

She stubbed it out, half-smoked, and turned to Roger with a bitter expression.

"Like I said: there is always an 'us and them'."

They were interrupted by another bang on the door. Roger opened it and a breathless Office Manager, Ann Thomas, rushed in.

"There are thahsands of 'em ahtside," she said. "All screamin' for yer to be 'anged."

He turned on his viewcam. A large crowd of Mourning Stewards had assembled outside the main entrance, banging their placards and calling for him to be arrested.

"We're surrounded," he said, "they've barricaded us in."

Myriad thoughts flashed through his mind. Would they let him out? Storm the building? Provoke him, so he could be arrested? As he looked at the angry faces, he could see them beating him to a pulp and parading his severed head down Murakami Street. *It's not enough to defeat me, I must be destroyed. There can be neither forgiveness nor compromise: for Niceness to prevail, Nastiness must be vanquished. I'll be paraded in public then forced to repudiate everything I stand for and embrace everything I detest. It'll be a lynch mob, kangaroo court and show trial rolled into one.*

"They'll never stop," Helen scowled. "Once they deem you Nasty, you're no longer human."

He ignored her, consumed with hatred as James Ashley stepped up onto a temporary platform.

"People need to understand the true nature of Roger Tyson. Listen to the prophetic warnings, the appeals to the mythic nation; this is the rhetoric of the extremist fringe. Like the militarists of old, he seeks uniformity, regimentation, obedience to the Great Leader. His business empire has been built on fraud and now he wants to topple the Government so he can become Shogun. We say NO."

There were loud cheers. Roger looked outside, feeling sickness rise within him. *Nastiness, militarist, extremism; the narrative has been constructed and there's damn-all I can do. The Muhonin have been airbrushed out and I am the villain. No wonder Christine's so confident.*

He turned to Helen.

"We have to go."

They drove out of the building into the channel that had been kept clear. Either side, angry faces pushed forward against the metal barriers to shout and spit at him. Roger closed his eyes. He could see the protestors' crucified bodies lining the Appian Way; he could hear the screams as he plunged a sword deep into James Ashley's body. He opened his eyes and sat up straight. Helen was staring at the floor in resignation.

"As I thought," he said as they sailed through. "Lots of thunder, but no fire."

"Great. What next?" Helen said. "More speeches? Score a few debating points off Bill? The problem's worse than you think. Furigans aren't merely unsocialised, they're anti-socialised. It's not just they haven't learned to live like civilised human beings. They've learned to live like animals. They've learned their anti-social behaviour will be rewarded. They've learned they can't be touched. And, as for the Muhonin, they could attack sooner than you could get into government."

She turned to the furigan channel and gave him a cold look as hordes of furigans poured onto a street, jeering and hurling projectiles at a film crew as it drove through. As news of scuffles between Lifestyle Groups filtered through on the Live Commentary, he felt his pessimism return. *Bill's kept it from the cameras, but how long will it be before scuffles become riots? If I fail, this will end in inter-communal violence, furigan rioting and Muhonin insurgency, but I can't fail....* Roger could see Bill holed up in a bunker pushing imaginary armies around a map while the Muhonin massed outside, ready to strike. Furigans rampaged and Lifestyle Groups fought each other as the Muhonin slaughtered anyone they could. There would be decades of anarchy: gang against gang, zoku versus zoku, militia against militia; no order, no society, nothing. Helen looked at him with piercing eyes.

"You're nowhere near high office; you're not even in the Diet, so what happens if your politicking fails? Do you really care about our country? Are you prepared to do what it takes to save it?"

She gave him an accusatory look.

"You do know what our last line of defence is?"

He sat back and said nothing.

Roger dropped Helen off and watched the scenery roll past, secretly pleased to be relieved of her company. As he returned home, his calmness returned. The day had been an ordeal, but it was over and he could plan ahead for contesting the Diet seat Amanda had said would be coming free. He sat back as popular quiz show, *Know Your Limits*, appeared on the entertainment screen.

"What country," the presenter asked, "was ruled by Adolf Hitler from 1933 to 1945?"

The contestant, a middle-aged man in a checked shirt, screwed his face up.

"Err, was that Portugal?"

He changed the channel, landing on the talent show, *Point at the Freaks*.

"And remember," winked the host, "to point at the freak!"

A singer ran on stage shrieking completely out of tune as the orchestra struck up. Within seconds, the audience was pointing at her while sirens and hooters blared. The host ran onstage and pushed a custard pie in her face, before booting her off to howls of laughter. Roger changed channels again. Contestants in red crash helmets were bashing their heads against a brick wall. Could Helen be right? One moment bowing their heads in Tokugawa Square, the next banging them against a brick wall, was he wrong to put his faith in the people? He could hear Helen urging him to give up. *Perhaps the nation is dead. Societies can survive corrupt government, but when society itself is corrupt, they die. The house built of rotten wood might look impressive, but it is the first to fall.*

He turned the screen off and took another beer. A message had appeared in his private inbox. Should he answer? He was tempted to leave it but couldn't stop himself. With a sinking feeling, he pressed his thumb against the screen to decrypt.

Furigans and Muhonin preparing for attack. Further executions expected.

He closed his eyes, not wanting to read any more. Decades of anarchy, furigan vids and disembowelments flashed through his mind. Was there time? Could it be stopped? Before he could think any further, he noticed an anonymous call on his private line. He looked up, unnerved. Only a few confidants knew of the number.

"Roger Tyson," he said.

There was no response, the only noise a quiet hiss.

"We know your game," a low voice said. "Make that move and it will be your last."

There was a click and the call ended, leaving a long deep hum.

Roger stood still, gathering his breath and trying not to let the incident faze him. He called for a beer, then stopped. Bob Blackmore, Head of the Eikoku Keizai-dantai Rengō-kai, was on the communications screen. He looked away with annoyance and toyed with not answering, before grunting hello.

"Now then," Bob grinned. "Well done with the Shacho-kai. I'd heard it might prove troublesome."

"What do you want?" Roger interrupted.

"I was wondering...." An uneasy tone entered his voice, "If you'd like speak at our annual conference. I know it's short notice."

"Why should I help you?"

"Listen, Roger. Bill's become very hostile to business. We've heard he's planning to push the keiretsu into bankruptcy by delaying payments on state contracts so he can engineer a takeover."

"Frank and I have been telling you that for ages, but you were too busy sucking up to listen."

"I'm sorry. You were right, okay. Kudasai, pretty kudasai, will you do it? You're the only shacho with the clout to sock it to him. You choose the topic, anything – except furigans, mind."

Roger screwed up his face. *It's a risk: the Eikkei's high and the economy strong. Helen's right: I have no political power base and Bill's waiting to use his new laws against me.* He grinned at Bob and gave him a wink.

Roger rang off and clapped his hands. It was the opportunity he had been waiting for, almost too good to be true. The Eikoku Keidanren annual conference: the media, business leaders, officials and politicians would all be there and he would be the keynote speaker. He laid back in his chair and pressed "massage," relishing the prospect of a fight. *We saw the masses at Tokugawa Square, but how many more stayed at home? Many might have blubbed, but how many more kept their disdain to themselves? Now we will see where public opinion lies.* A smile crept across his face: on the screen, a reporter was standing outside a large suburban home, which he recognised at once.

"Embattled aide Jonathan Green," the reporter said, "Faced calls to resign in what is now being dubbed the 'Hentai Scandal,' following revelations that he had thrown parties paid for by companies involved in the Government's Urban Regeneration Programme. Former call girl Jasmine Smith claimed he would get withdrawal symptoms if he could not get his fix of cocaine and prostitutes. Green San was not available for comment."

Roger punched the air. The Eikkei had closed down and the Government's ratings fallen. He had ridden out the crisis and was on the verge of victory. One more push and it would be over. Compassion Day, the Forces of Nastiness and Figure of Hate marched through his head then disappeared. *You thought you could intimidate me. You thought I'd fall for your false bonhomie. You thought I'd smile as your minions stabbed me in the back. You thought you could brand me an extremist and turn the public against me, but you couldn't break my resolve. Our patriots sacrificed their lives during the Great Incident to defend our country and I'm prepared do the same. The residents in the barracks have nobody and I will never desert them. Never.* He closed his eyes and smiled. Victory was his.

9

Roger drove down Satoru Street, feeling a long-forgotten excitement as the smell of freshly mown lawns wafted in from the on-street air fresheners. People bustled down the cramped pavements into the narrow side streets where the reds, golds and greens of the shop banners reflected in the puddles. He had never paid such everyday scenes much attention, but today was special. Once again, he could feel his pride at building the first driverless expressway; once more, hear the praise as his bullet trains broke the world speed record. A tear formed as he recalled standing next to the Emperor at the opening of the Chrysanthemum Bridge and thought of how it had become a symbol both of Greenwood's success and England's resurgence. Yes, it would be like the old days when he was admired by politicians and feted by the media. As he thought of the Political Consensus, anger surged within him. *To hell with them! I'll speak my mind and be damned. For so long, I've had to keep quiet, nod obsequiously and do as I'm told. No more. Today, they will listen, whether they like it or not.*

He entered the car port and ascended the dark grey lift shaft, listening to the soft whirr of the electric motors. Momentarily, he felt afraid. His courage wasn't unbounded and – why deny it? – he feared being smeared. So far, he had stayed inside the bounds of acceptability, if only just, but in a few hours he would cross into outright rebellion. There would be no backing out. If he failed, he'd be denounced: Roger Tyson the ultimate evil, reviled by all and blamed for everything that went wrong. The thought filled him with terror. He thought of Jane and how distant she had become. Theirs might never have been a romantic match, but there had never been any coldness. Now she seemed to spend more time at her foundation and they exchanged only the tersest of comments. Would she stand by him? Would anyone? As the lift opened onto the private parking suite, he could see his future. His friends had abandoned him, while his enemies attacked without mercy. He was cut off from society, like a limb severed from its body; but unlike a severed limb, he could feel pain.

Roger left his car and hurried onto the upper-level gallery that overlooked the flashing signs and advertisements of Takenake Circus. He looked below as the lights changed and a wave of people swarmed across the expanse – left to right, right to left, diagonally in both directions – then made his way to the private lounge where Amanda had asked to meet him.

"Hi Roger," she said, "What's wrong?"

"I don't know," he said, staring at the faceless glass building opposite. "I understood the world I grew up in. Everything followed rules: two and two made four. Now, it could be five, six, seven, a million. Nothing makes sense and, however much you or Helen explain, I still don't get it."

She took his arm and they walked to the sushi bar, where a high translucent window cast a shaft of light on the cool grey floor. The doors closed, shutting out the noise of the circus, and they entered a tall room with bare concrete walls, wooden tables and bench seats.

"Don't doubt yourself," Amanda said. "You see what's happening. You're the only person with the strength to change it. Look what you've achieved already. You've forced them to pay attention."

He went quiet. Was it her warm smile or her glistening eyes? She had a naturalness he found disarming, yet somehow he felt uncomfortable.

"Stop worrying." She smiled as the service droid collected their food from the conveyor belt. "The fundamentals are on our side: the Government and keiretsu are keeping their bad investments off their accounts and Bill is keeping interest rates artificially low to keep the boom going. You will succeed. You will be a great Sori Daijin."

"And you an excellent Minister of Finance."

She looked at him again. He gulped.

"Amanda." He hesitated. "I really appreciate your help... I couldn't do it without you."

"Domo arigatou, I'm sure you could." She looked down at the table. He looked closer. She was blushing.

"You've done so much for me," she said. "Your confidence in me has never wavered. I appreciate it, Roger. I mean it. Jim approached me the other day – about rejoining the Naikaku."

"And you accepted?"

She put her hand on his.

"If there's anything I can do, you only have to ask."

The midday sun glinted on the smooth glass skin of the Eikoku Keidanren Kaikan Building. Roger entered the main hall and studied the rows of inscrutable faces. Would they listen this time? Would boom turn to bust? The host introduced him and there was an uneasy quiet as he ascended the podium.

"For many years," he boomed, "I warned of the dangers of a bubble. 'How ridiculous,' the critics said, 'We live in a

New Era, life can only get better.' I ask you: can it really be true that London Imperial Palace is worth more as real estate than the whole of California or that England is worth more than the rest of the world put together, as one economist has calculated? No. Combined keiretsu, government and household debt stand at their highest-ever level. This is a bubble."

He paused. He could feel the disquiet ready to break through. He could see the tension behind the inscrutable faces. Should he stop? His voice grew louder.

"Bubbles, however, do not expand of their own accord. This is a deliberate policy to conceal a deeper bubble – an ideological bubble. Niceness, Nastiness, Malopinions, Malemotions; we are living in a daydream world, shielded from reality and forbidden from discussing the truth. There are no Forces of Nastiness. They are an imaginary enemy to distract us from the real one. We all know who they are, but we mustn't say, for the law is on their side. We must end this ridiculous fantasy that our enemies are our friends and our friends our enemies."

The agitation was now palpable. His breathing grew shallow and a thin film of sweat appeared on his brow.

"I have often been accused of alarmism, so I would like to make three points:

One: a stable economy is essential for a stable society. When societies can no longer afford to maintain order, they collapse. By allowing a bubble to develop, we have put our stability in jeopardy.

Two: fifty years ago, we had a sense of common endeavour. Today, we have tribalism. Once the bubble has burst, there will be nothing to hold us together. A harmonious society can survive hardship, but a fragmented one cannot.

Three: it is not possible to buy peace, only to rent it. Civilisation and barbarism are fundamental opposites. If civility gives way, barbarism prevails."

He stopped dramatically, stretching the silence out for almost a minute. The audience began fidgeting and looking around.

"Are we content to be the last generation, the closing chapter on two thousand years of history? We must stop fooling ourselves. While we are fragmenting, our enemies are uniting. Be under no illusion: they will attack – mercilessly, pitilessly, savagely. I call for everyone who cares about this country to stand against it. If we do nothing, it will end in tragedy: state failure, a complete breakdown of order, decades of anarchy—"

"This is Nastiness," shouted an old man, rising to his feet, "I lived through the Great Incident and this is what they said back then."

"Be quiet," shouted a person nearby. "Nobody came to hear you."

"I won't be silenced." His voice grew louder as the ushers gathered round him, "This man wants a police state. He wants to reduce us to servitude."

The commotion increased as audience members shouted for him to sit down, but he continued remonstrating until he was ushered out. Gradually, the audience calmed down and turned to Roger.

"That, I'm afraid, is an example of the delusions brought on by overexposure to the Political Consensus. Nobody is calling for a police state or for servitude. These are deceptions. However unfashionable it may be, I am proud to call myself a patriot and I don't care how shocking that sounds. The truth is the truth: the Muhonin and furigans are our enemies. They must be defeated."

There was silence. The audience looked on horrified, empty seats dotting the hall where people had walked out.

Roger sat down with a resolute half-smile as the host hurried to the podium and declared the event closed. Comments of "He's gone too far this time" and "They won't let this one drop" could be heard above the murmuring.

"If you're right, Bill's in big trouble." The man next to Roger leant over and whispered in his ear, "But if you're wrong...."

Roger ignored him and got up, only to find Bob Blackmore bustling over.

"I know I said robust," Bob said as the anger grew voluble, "but I also said nothing about bloody furigans."

"You wanted bruising," Roger said. "You got bruising."

He left Bob huffing and walked towards the exit, stopping in front of the door. Someone was behind him, someone whose voice filled him with rage.

"Roger, Roger, Roger. So much bravado, but do you really mean it?"

Roger turned around. This time, there was no smile.

"I'd like a word," Bill said.

They went to an empty room and Bill stood by the wall, his arms folded. Was it anger he could detect or another emotion, fear maybe? Roger stood facing him, his hands on his hips.

"I'm very disappointed," Bill said. "I know you only want the best for our country, but with this speech, you've set us back decades."

"I stand by what I said," Roger said. "Furigans don't like you any more than they do me, but they fear me."

"Maybe," Bill said. "But I can assure you the Forces of Nastiness are quite real. By offering them succour like this, you're making it politically impossible for me to defend you. The extremists are using you, Roger." He unfolded his arms and his expression became emollient. "We don't have to be at loggerheads, I wish I could convince you of that. I'm not looking to fight you – I want you in the Naikaku."

Roger watched as he paused dramatically. *A Naikaku post? Don't toy with me, Bill. What do you really want?*

"They see you as a stalking horse," Bill said. "Former military officer, bold, prepared to speak his mind, prepared to take risks; they wouldn't think twice about sacrificing you. I urge you to reconsider before it's too late."

With a polite "sayonara," Bill returned to the party.

Outside, the street was lined with protestors, the scene now familiar. Roger waved to the cameras as he drove past and watched James Ashley address the crowd on the news.

"This is an outrageous attack on the peoples of England. Roger Tyson is appealing to the worst aspects of human nature, encouraging hatred and turning minor discord into social warfare. This is pure, unadulterated Nastiness. He isn't a moderate who can be accommodated, but an extremist who must be stopped. Look at the hooliganism that followed his previous speech. It's time the Government stopped treating him so gently."

Blah, blah, Roger Tyson Shogun, Roger Tyson Nastiness. Stupid prick. He yawned as James Ashley was followed by vox pops.

"Roger Tyson coming to power?" A teenage girl looked aghast, "It's the one thing that frightens me."

"Nah, don't trust 'im at all," laughed a heftily-built man as he walked by.

"And who are you?" Roger shouted. "Friends of Bill?"

He turned to the Live Commentary, feeling the blood pumping through his body. His supporters might have been silent before, but now they were cheering him on.

We've gone mad. It's a mass hysteria. He's being punished because he speaks the truth.

I'm glad I'm not the only person repelled by this emotional incontinence.

He's our greatest businessman and he can be our greatest Sori Daijin

Roger glowered then let out a laugh. Carry on with your childish insults, Ashley; your placards and protests aren't fooling anyone. You can blather on about Nastiness all you like; people know the Muhonin are their enemies. He sat back proudly then let out a loud laugh.

HENTAI SCANDAL – JONATHAN GREEN RESIGNS

Could it be true, a senior Bill Harris ally had resigned? He reread the words, feeling a frisson of excitement. *For the first time in ten years – ten years! Oh, this is good. Although he's sure to bring him back once the outrage has died down, his credibility is wrecked. Yes! He knows he can't avoid a downturn... he's getting desperate. Me a Naikaku post? No way. The Sori Daijin has little power? Rubbish, it's the highest office in the land. The fool's so vain he can't see it's his own weakness. Perhaps he's more rattled by these revelations than his manner suggests. Is there more to this little affair than money-grubbing and prostitutes?*

He read on with growing interest. English Land-holdings had been distributing shares to senior figures in all the major parties and Bill's chief fundraiser, Brian Penney, had been named, although he had categorically denied the allegations. Roger clapped his hands, delirious. *We're witnessing the last days of a dying regime! While Bill and his cronies luxuriate in their embezzled wealth, the state is crumbling from within. Whatever lies beneath the Hentai Scandal, they're finished.* He drove home in no mood for argument.

Jane was watching the news when he got in. He watched himself thundering through his speech, eyes intense and fists pumping as the camera panned to people leaving their seats before James Ashley was interviewed. She turned the screen off and faced him.

"I certainly hope this turns out well," she said.

"And why shouldn't it?"

"Wake up, Roger. People aren't impressed by your bombast. They see a general without an army, a maestro with no orchestra. The only apocalypse is the one facing you."

"Rubbish," he said. "You're so busy toadying to Bill, you can't see what's going on. Whatever your friend might say, Bill won't offer me an amakudari post and the same goes for your father."

Jane breathed in, trying to contain her anger.

"I've spoken to him. His offer is genuine. He's offering you a way out of the dead end you're in and I suggest you take it."

Roger's face went red.

"He's in trouble, Jane, serious trouble – and the Hentai Scandal's only the start. He's scared, Jane. He's never faced an opponent he can't bribe, blackmail or bully, and I won't back down."

"Stop being obtuse," she exploded. She stopped mid-flow and her voice dropped to a whisper. "You have nothing in politics. Leaving the Army was a calculated risk. You had the money and the people behind you to make Greenwood a success. If it hadn't been for my family—"

"Your family nothing," he said. "Your father was losing money until I came along."

"Okay, Roger," she said. "Have it your way, but if it goes wrong, you're on your own. Be ebullient if you must, but don't you dare take me for granted."

The communications screen lit up with a call for him as she left the room. He composed himself and answered, still feeling riled.

"Yes," he said.

"Tyson San," the voice said, "the crash may come sooner than expected. The markets are growing concerned about the true extent of keiretsu bad debt. If the big investors pull out now, we'll have a major panic: liquidity gone, money markets frozen, runs on all the major banks."

"If, may, could," Roger said. "Can you be more definite?"

The voice went quiet.

"Keep watching Country and Suburban. It's been hiding its bad debts for years, but it's running out of cash. If it can't roll over its debt, it will have to approach the Bank of England for emergency funding."

"What timeframe are we talking about?"

"I don't know. There are no details."

"Does anybody else know?"

"No. It's right out this hour."

Roger hung up and poured himself a drink as Dr Mark Alexander's name appeared on the news beneath an old photo of him. He stopped dead, nearly dropping the bottle as a reporter stood in front of a murky copse, cordoned off by police tape.

"The body of missing army officer Dr Mark Alexander was found near his home in South Downs Prefecture early this morning. Dr Alexander, who worked for the Intelligence Service, had been battling with depression for several years. Police have said they are not treating the death as suspicious."

Roger stared at the screen, unable to think or speak. Minutes passed and Jane returned.

"Poor Mark," she said as he replayed the report. "He seemed so unhappy with life."

A tear rolled down Roger's cheek.

"Mark would never do that," he said.

She looked at him sharply and went upstairs. Nothing further was said that evening.

PART II

10

The sun shone brightly but without warmth as Roger crossed the Thames Gateway Bridge. He surveyed the post-commercial landscape of indoor ski-slopes, climbing ranges and preserved office blocks, filled with joy. Country and Suburban had approached the Bank of England for emergency funding and, although spokesmen assured people "the underlying business was sound" and that "the current difficulties would prove temporary," the Eikkei had fallen sharply. The change in mood was perceptible. All talk of a New Era had ceased and, within Greenwood, expansion had been quietly forgotten. Things were better with Jane, too. Though she had been quiet, she was smiling again. Roger, however, remained angry. "I don't care what you regret," he had fumed to himself. "How can you have more confidence in Bill than me? It's wrong... no, it's worse than wrong, it's disloyal."

The thought of her laughing with Bill made him anxious, reminding him how far he was from becoming Sori Daijin. The crisis may have been the turning point he had long predicted, but would history turn? And, more importantly, could he convert crisis into political capital? He pursed his lips, thinking ahead to his meeting with Amanda, and put on the information service.

"Talk of a crash is premature," a commentator said. "Confidence has been shaken, but Country can be saved."

"Boom may be over," another added, "but that doesn't mean we're facing bust."

Roger felt tense. *Country hasn't disclosed how much bad debt it's hiding, confidence remains high and the other keiretsu can still access finance just fine. But what if money markets dried up? Would they find themselves in the same situation? Would they be strong enough to ride out a crisis? A crash, a crash, my country for a crash.* He drifted off into thought as popular game show, *Keep Calm and Carry On* came on.

"The next exercise will test our contestants' courage," shrieked the presenter, jumping in front of the camera dressed as a banana. "Let's see how calm they keep now!"

The contestants sat in an outdoor arena wearing red bandanas, watching as a gate opened and a tiger charged out, savaging a carcass. The presenter continued gabbling as the contestants were blindfolded, while a stuffed tiger was mounted on a tracked robot dolly and wheeled on, accompanied by taped roaring.

"They don't know it's fake!" he screamed.

For minutes, the robot charged up behind the contestants as they tried to escape, the camera zooming in on their terrified faces. Eventually, one fell over and was nipped on the backside with a pair of false teeth. The presenter reappeared and removed the blindfold, revealing the deception, the cue for more canned laughter and gabbling. Roger turned it off in disgust. *Stupid drivel! While people are distracted with rubbish like this, Bill keeps Country's problems hidden. I need to puncture this complacency. I need something big. I need facts.*

As he approached the undulating sail-like arcades of Imperial Docks, his mind focused on Country and Suburban. There had always been something dodgy about it, but what was it? He paused as a news reporter stood outside a pair of palatial gates.

"It has been revealed that several Diet Members, including Brian Penney, have been using the new living allowance created by Sori Daijin Bill Harris to speculate in real estate and property development. The Sori Daijin has ordered an inquiry under Lord Emerson, but declined to comment further, stating it would be wrong to prejudge its findings. Leader of the Democratic Party of England, Margaret Richards, demanded that all concerned should resign...."

Roger turned the sound down. *A whitewash; Lord Emerson's friendly to Bill. As for the opposition demands for resignations, nothing more than parliamentary theatrics. But something's not right. Bill should have sacked Brian and killed the story, but he still openly associates with him – Jonathan, too. Only the other day, he described them both as "good men." What do they have on him? Is it linked to Country and Suburban? And why has Bill gone so quiet? I'm getting warmer, but not warm enough.* He paused in thought as Frank Carter appeared onscreen.

"Roger, old boy," he grinned. "How the devil are you? I trust you heard the news."

"It's not exactly a surprise, Frank."

"No, I can't say it is," he wheezed. "We all knew they'd made some hideous investments. Trying to become England's biggest keiretsu, indeed! This is big, Roger. It's going to affect the Big Six – Greenwood excepted."

"Tell me something I don't know, Frank."

Frank lit up a cigar.

"Look, Roger, this is our opportunity to roll back a few unwelcome innovations. The fact is you're being tipped for a ministerial post. Bill has no choice. He doesn't know his arse from his elbow and his Naikaku has absolutely zero business expertise. Oh, he'd hate it, but a financial crisis would be worse."

"Why not leave him to it?"

"No, old boy," Frank said, choking. "We can't. He's pushing ahead with his plan to create a Commission for the Economy. He thought the bubble had further to run and this little affair caught him by surprise, but he'll be back and, once he's got his damned Sori Daijin's Department, he'll take you on."

"I know that, Frank. What do you expect me to do about it?"

"With you in the Naikaku," Frank said with a grandiose puff, "we could topple him. Right now, there's a lot of hostility in the Civil Service, not to mention in business. The Governor of the Bank of England is opposed to a bailout, and if you blocked a rescue Bill'd be finished. The party's sick of him, they want him out – Jim told me. He's vulnerable, Roger, he just needs to be pushed."

"A Naikaku post, Frank?" Roger said. "Even if I did, they wouldn't let the lame ducks fail."

"Come on, Roger, old chap." Frank took a long draw. "Colin agrees with me and Bob's coming around, too. This is our chance to get our powers back. This is our chance to rebuild England Inc."

Roger paused, his gaze drifting off into the middle distance.

"Tell me, Frank, what do you know about the Hentai Scandal?"

"Me? Nothing. They've been embezzling money through straw kaishas, but everyone knows that."

"What else did Jim tell you?"

"Oh, I don't know; nothing in particular." He puffed his cigar and a wistful look came over him. "We were just saying how it's not like it used to be. Bill's hollowed out party and state, allowing ministers to turn their ministries into private fiefdoms. It's all nepotism now, corruption everywhere...."

He relit the cigar with a sorrowful expression.

"The keiretsu will be next, then the Self Defence Forces. It'll be like everything Bill's touched: idiots put in charge, everything politicised, nothing working. England will be one gigantic slum."

His mood grew ever more lachrymose and Roger let him be. *If Frank knows anything, he won't say or won't remember – all he's interested in is winning his bureaucratic turf war and getting blind drunk. But he's right. Bill's increased his control by breaking up the ministries into small agencies. They're just shells with rival cabals fighting for the spoils, while money disappears into officials' pockets. No, it's not like it was. The state should serve the public, just as kaishas serve their customers. Now, Bill's turned it into an occupying army, seizing anything it can. At least the keiretsu haven't been afflicted – but for how long? If he can ride out this crisis, he'll take over the keiretsu and dismantle the Self Defence Forces. Imagine that! Our army, a collection of warbands indistinguishable from the rabble it's fighting against. It's more than wrong. It's immoral. Bill knows about the Muhonin arms build-up, yet he weakens our armed forces.* He looked at the white masts of Nagano Marina, where Amanda was waiting. *The Hentai Scandal's the key: we need to attack there, but how's it connected to Country? What's the bugger hiding?*

Amanda was sitting in the clubhouse with a far-away expression. They hadn't seen each other since the Keidanren conference, but they had been in touch all the time. Her messages had kept him going, with their smiley faces and warm hugs, always discussing strategy and alluding to promising new developments, but never giving anything away. Her excitement was infectious, yet he felt a nagging doubt, as though she didn't quite realise the urgency of the situation. Okay, so she understood it intellectually, but did she *feel* it? Did she, too, feel the coldness? The thought drifted away as the sight of her lifted his spirits: pink T-shirt, white shorts, sunglasses perched on her head, but no book.

"Well konnichiwa, Amanda. What happened to *Dr Kishimoto*?"

"Roger!" She jumped up and kissed him. "I dunno, it didn't really do it for me."

They entwined arms and strolled through the arcade with its sculpture galleries and indoor gardens to the marina. *Amanda, Amanda*, he smiled, *another passing fancy?* He stopped by his yacht and pressed his hand against the reader.

"We need to move fast," he said as the boarding ramp extended. "We need to turn the financial troubles to our advantage."

"We can't rely on that alone," she said, stepping carefully as she walked up the ramp. "Bill will twist it, like he did the policemen's deaths."

They sailed beneath the East London River Crossing and she stretched out in the sun. Roger looked at her then looked away, feeling the coldness return. Why was Bill so quiet? Why wasn't either Country or the Hentai Scandal hurting him?

"He's been expecting this, hasn't he?" he said, loosening his collar. "He'll let others take the rap, then reappear when the problem's over."

"Possibly," she said, closing her eyes. "He might have anticipated some sort of downturn, but I doubt a full-scale crash. You never know with him."

The river opened up and the panorama changed. Vast power stations and container ports drifted past while the giant blocks of the London Dormitory Suburbs of Kent and Essex sat brooding in the background. Roger watched with foreboding, not wanting Amanda to see his unease. *The façades are monolithic, but behind, everything is fragment-*

ed. I'm not just fighting Bill, I'm fighting disintegration itself.
How do I turn the tide?

"Amanda," he said, trying to sound confident. "The Liberal Democratic Party factions: are they divided over policy?"

"No," she said. "It's a case of whichever party boss raises the most money and throws the coolest parties gets the most media attention and attracts the most followers. The party's more of a brand than an organisation, it's a bit like a franchise operation: each faction runs its own campaign under the party umbrella – there's very little central direction. In fact, there's very little difference between the LDP factions and the opposition parties. That's why there are always so many breakaways and defections."

"If Bill can bypass party and state by forming links with the Lifestyle Groups," Roger said, "what's to stop the factions from doing so or the Lifestyle Groups from setting up their own parties? Bill's not strong enough to hold the party together. Politics will become tribalised."

"Unlikely," she said, turning to one side. "They're a minority phenomenon, like the Muhonin party. People aren't interested."

"Doesn't matter," Roger said. "People are forced into the system whether they like it or not. If they don't pick a side, they lose out to everyone, but if they do, they at least get a small share of the spoils. It's critical. In the past, we could accommodate difference, because we were part of a whole; we could agree to give and take, we could agree to compromise. Now we're fragmented, one side's gain must be everyone else's loss. Eventually, politics will become a cycle of coup and counter-coup. It's our turn to eat, people will say, everyone pushing everyone else aside. Things look stable now, but the Outer Suburbs are only months away from becoming like the barracks."

"Stop fretting about the present," Amanda said. "We're here to create the future. Focus on that."

He stared at the thin metallic towers of the Thames Gateway oil refinery, unable to focus on anything. As news of fighting between Bling-zoku and Grunge-zoku broke, he could hear Helen's voice dinning inside his head.

"Give up," she was saying. "While the politicians are busy milking the system at the top, the masses are busy milking it at the bottom. People don't complain about corruption because they want it to end – they complain because they want to be at the top."

Roger sighed. No, he could no more alter the present than he could order back the tide. As they passed the remains of a jetty, he felt Amanda's hand on his shoulder.

"Don't be miserable," she said. "I've arranged for you to meet Edmund Hope, leader of the England Renewal Faction. He said there could be a wait, but he'd find you a seat in the National Diet. Once you're elected, his faction will leave the LDP and call a vote of no confidence. The opposition parties have agreed to form a coalition with us and together we'd have a majority in the Diet. The smaller parties have always dreamed of uniting into a single party that could challenge the LDP, but there's never been anyone strong enough to unite them. With you in charge, we can unseat Bill. So, kudasai, smile."

She put her arms around him and gave him a kiss. Roger was about to speak when a flustered Ann Thomas appeared onscreen.

"Konnichiwa, Ann," he said, dashing below deck. "What's wrong?"

"The police visited headquarters this mornin'," she said, "investigatin' allegations of malpractice – somethin' about an 'ostile takeover. They said they'd contact you directly. Is it serious?"

Roger paused.

"No. Domo, Ann."

He hung up and hurried back on deck.

"Forget it, Amanda. We don't have time for parliamentary manoeuvring. We need to force the situation. We need to expose Bill's scandals."

Amanda shook her head.

"Be realistic, Roger. Bill's on the defensive, but he isn't beaten. He'll stitch together a deal over Country and, once the economy recovers, he'll be back to his old tricks. Without a political base, we—"

She stopped. The river was filled with police boats, while in the distance a destroyer guarded Thames Estuary Airport making further progress impossible. They stood up as a patrol boat sped towards them.

"The estuary has been sealed off," a policeman shouted down a megaphone. "You'll have to turn back."

"What's happening?" Roger shouted.

"A precaution, sir. The Airport authorities are concerned about spillover fighting from the Outer Suburbs."

"How could it spill over to here?"

The policeman stood impassively, saying nothing. Roger turned the yacht around with a look of disgust. *Spillover violence? That's not even a convincing cover story. Has the insurgency moved to Stage Two? Unlikely. Bill prefers to hush things up. Another show of force? But why? Could this have been ordered by someone other than Bill?* He bit his lip. It was a show of force, but who was showing whom?

The afternoon drifted on quietly, Roger still deep in thought as they passed beneath the Thames Gateway Bridge. Amanda lowered her sunglasses and gave Roger a mischievous smile, her eyes glimmering in the sunlight.

"Roger," she said. "What do you and Jane do together?"

"Go to the theatre, mostly," he said, not looking up.

"That's what she likes," she said. "You don't enjoy it, do you?"

He listened to the water lapping against the side of his yacht, unable to answer.

"You never allow yourself to be happy."

"And you?"

She looked away as a tinge of sadness entered her voice.

"You know, I wanted to be a vet when I was younger. I always wanted to work with animals."

She rested her head against the side of the yacht and the conversation faded away. Roger looked at the buildings as they drifted past, picking out the ones Greenwood had built as he remembered old conversations with Mark.

"Why don't you go into business?" Mark had said after they had left Sakura. "Our country needs businessmen, not soldiers."

"I don't know, Mark. I don't know anything about business."

"Think about it," Mark smiled. "The military needs supplies and there are plenty of reconstruction contracts. Plus, I know a wealthy family who'd back you."

The sun went in as they returned to the marina. Roger looked at the wavelike roof of the arcade, his mind fixed on the police boats.

"Amanda," he said, "what's Bill doing in the barracks?"

"I don't know," she said sleepily. "But I'll tell you who would: Phil Tucker. Andy Hunt made him Figure of Hate after Phil accused him of spreading lies about the barracks, but it wasn't just spite. Phil knows what's going on."

Roger grinned. She shook her head.

"Forget it, Roger. We need that coalition. I'm serious."

"Then the parties must agree to liquidation," he said. "We absolutely cannot let Bill rescue Country and bury all its dirt. Plus, the state finances are in disarray: if it defaults, we're talking state failure. Can you get me the government accounts – the real ones, including the projects Bill kept off the books?"

She nodded.

"I know someone in the Ministry...." She paused and looked at the tower blocks looming in the distance. "Can we go somewhere more glam next time? This place gives me the creeps."

He smiled and she hugged him tight.

Roger climbed into his car pumped up with desire and aggression. Edmund Hope, an opposition coalition; in themselves, they were surely a dead end, but as a lever.... If he could get Phil Tucker to spill what he knew, and if he could block a rescue – the situation would be his! He closed his eyes. He was standing atop the white cliffs of Dover, the Churchill of his times: Bill had been defeated, the Action Groups crushed, the Political Consensus destroyed. As for the Muhonin and furigans... rage welled up within him. He could see the four "artists" in their food-stained dungarees kneeling in a basement, hands cuffed behind their backs and a pistol pressed against the back of their heads. Four shots and the bodies hit the floor. Roger let go of the armrests, leaving two sweaty indentations. He was home.

The car halted and he walked up to the doorway, thinking of Jane, determined to make amends. She had believed in him right from the start and they had worked hard together to create Greenwood, sharing everything – and, yes, he had enjoyed the theatre. He thought of her smile when they first met and the happiness he had felt, but the memory left an uncomfortable feeling. Surely, she couldn't be taken in by Bill?

She was in the hallway boxing up clothes for overseas when he entered and put the parcel down with a look of surprise.

"I'm sorry if I was sharp with you earlier," she said. "Things have been tough at the foundation. We stand to lose our funding."

"No, it's me who should be sorry," he replied. "I appreciate your support, Jane."

She wiped her eye with her cuff and smiled.

"We're just two stubborn characters too proud to give in, but kudasai, kudasai, kudasai don't say anything outrageous. I worry you're going to get yourself killed."

She rubbed his shoulder.

"And try not to think about Mark. He was under a lot of stress."

He smiled and put his arm around her.

They were interrupted by news that Governor of the Bank of England, Robin Shepherd, had refused to provide Country with emergency funding, dashing hopes of a quick rescue. Jane looked on nervously and the mood turned jumpy. Within minutes, pundits were calling for the Government to step in as the Live Commentary filled up with talk of panic and crash. The Ministry of Finance, however, remained silent and the news moved on as armoured personnel carriers surrounded train stations and police boats patrolled the Thames.

"Kudasai, do not be alarmed," Minister of the Interior, Antonia Richardson, announced. "The military mobilisation today was a routine training exercise, Operation Bookcase. I emphasise, you are not in any danger."

Show of force or demonstration of weakness? Whatever it is you're hiding, I'll soon find out. Roger cracked his knuckles as Bex Cook of *Igirisu no Koe* appeared onscreen.

"Hi Roger," she said. "Would you be prepared to give an interview on the Country and Suburban Crisis? We need someone who understands the problem."

He nodded.

"Fab," she said. "By the way, you know you're being tipped for a Naikaku post?"

Roger said nothing and ended the call.

"Itoshii, that's marvellous news," Jane said, cuddling up to him. "Would you join me for some wine? I fancy some red."

They clinked glasses as commentators turned their fire on the Government. Roger swirled a mouthful and savoured the flavour. Whatever history wanted, it would be made to turn.

11

The studio lights flashed as Roger waited to be interviewed. Country and Suburban had suspended operations, causing confidence to vanish and the Eikkei to tumble – an unpleasant surprise to people used only to seeing it rise. As the mood turned nervy, Roger grew ever more confident. The clamouring for a rescue, the calls to ease interest rates; he watched the Eikkei continue its fall, his sense of inevitability mounting. *You can't fight it. Polish the turd all you like; no amount of emergency funding can turn Country into a viable business.* He smiled as the news moved on to a debate in the House of Representatives.

"We were promised growth," said a shadow minister. "But the current shambles is an example of the incompetence of this administration. Does the Minister for Trade and Industry accept his party's policies have failed?"

The Minister for Trade and Industry, Graham Hough, stood up.

"I would like to remind my esteemed colleague that they should not judge this Government on the events of the last few weeks but by the growth we have achieved over the past decade."

He sat back down to jeers from the opposition benches.

"Does the Minister have any idea of the size of Country and Suburban's debts?"

The House fell silent and attention focused on a squirming Graham Hough. Roger smiled as the camera panned to the backbenches where a man in a crumpled brown jacket stood. It was Edmund Hope.

Roger looked at Graham Hough's jowly face as it puffed up with indignation, unable to contain his mirth. *Well played, that man! If we can convince people our diagnosis is right, we can convince them of our remedy, too.* Bex Cook appeared onscreen with interviewer Nick Seldon and gave him the thumbs up. 3-2-1: he was on air.

"Ohayō gozaimasu, Tyson San," Nick said. "The way ahead for Country and Suburban is going to be difficult. What do you foresee happening?"

"Ohayō gozaimasu, Seldon San," Roger said. "We're being misled: Country's problem is not a temporary lack of cash; the business is fundamentally unsound and trying to save it will only squander more money. If it's not wound up immediately, the problem will get worse."

"Does this mean you are opposed to a rescue?"

"Absolutely," Roger said. "A rescue will only postpone the problem – and, let's be clear, this is bigger than one badly run keiretsu. Business, households and government have all expanded too far and borrowed too much, so the Government must stop dithering and bring the failed investments into the open. We need to see the scale of the bad investment and write it off before it can do any more harm."

"Domo arigatou, Tyson San," Nick said, ending the interview.

Roger checked the time and left. As commentators continued to call for a rescue, he knew a solitary interview would not be enough. He needed to be inside the Diet and, most importantly, he needed to know what Edmund Hope knew.

Amanda was waiting in the foyer of Nash's, one of London's most fashionable restaurants, pacing around with a pensive expression.

"Have they agreed to liquidation?" Roger said without waiting.

"They're not happy," she replied.

"Tough," he said. "Push them harder. It's essential we receive a firm political commitment. This coalition can't be more of the same."

She nodded, but he remained worried. *They won't give in without a struggle. They're just as complicit in the corruption as Bill and just as much my enemies. Forced to choose between me and furigans, they'd choose the furigans and, if an insurgency broke out, the Muhonin too. Without a commitment, there's nothing to stop them reneging on their agreement and stabbing me in the back.*

A robot waiter led them to a window overlooking the Thames where a solitary figure with tousled grey hair was doing a crossword. Edmund Hope had been a Diet Member for many years, only briefly holding ministerial portfolio, giving rise to the nickname Mr Spare: "always available but rarely used."

"If Government means compromising principles," he had told journalists, "then I'd rather stay on the back-benches."

Regularly voted the most honest person in politics, he was, in the words of *Igirisu no Koe*, the "moral conscience of English politics". When he spoke, ministers listened. Roger, however, had mixed feelings. He was smart, but too comfortable. His questions hurt the Government, but there was never any follow up. Did he want to change politics or sit back and criticise? As they bowed and sat down, Roger felt unsure.

"Ah, Tyson San," Edmund said in his careworn North of England accent. "At last we meet."

"Likewise, Hope San, it's an honour to meet the leader of the LDP's internal opposition. Your backbench revolts have been the only thing blocking the Bill Harris juggernaut."

"I do what I can," Edmund breathed out as the menu was projected above the table. "Your steadfast defence of constitutional propriety has helped enormously."

"Is there much opposition to Bill in the Diet?"

"Yes," Edmund said, "but it's not united."

"You're talking about the factions?"

"I'm talking about everything. We're not like the keiretsu with a powerful shacho in charge."

"We're not the empires of popular imagination," Roger said as the robot charged their glasses. "Think of us as convoys of independent businesses. Shachos can't order affiliated kaishas around. Our influence depends on persuasion more than any formal authority."

Edmund looked surprise. Roger looked him in the eye.

"We both know the Political Consensus is a smokescreen for Bill to hide behind, but as long as it exists, he can set the terms of debate. We need to defeat it, else he wins by default. The question is how."

Edmund drew in a deep breath.

"It won't be easy. The Political Consensus is the justification for a complex of power that extends from Bill and the Commissions right down to front organisations, like the Action Groups and the Compassion Foundation. It means more regulations and more regulations means more agencies to enforce them – and more power for Bill's allies, so taking it on would mean trying to dislodge some deeply entrenched interests – and they'd vehemently oppose any attempt to reduce their powers."

"It's everywhere," Amanda rued. "Bill has tame journalists, scientists and academics putting out his propaganda while pretending to be independent. The party has no control over them, so it invariably falls into line."

"It's very clever," Edmund said, putting his elbows on the table. "People don't trust the Government, but they trust his 'pets,' because they think they're independent. They don't see the agenda, they don't realise they're funded by the state to promote the state, so they take them at face value. It's a permanent moral crusade with the Action Groups in the vanguard. They're a self-appointed priesthood bullying us into compliance and their power comes from constantly inventing new moral outrages to campaign against. If they actually eradicated Nastiness, they'd be out of a job. So, once one form of Nastiness has disappeared, they invent another – the worse, the better. If you want to defeat them, you've got to mobilise opposition and that means building a political coalition."

"Okay, so we form a coalition." Roger grew impatient. "How do we then win?"

"Win over the people," Edmund said. "Show them we will liberate them from Leviathan."

"Leviathan?" Roger looked incredulous. "The real danger comes from the Muhonin and furigans."

Edmund shook his head.

"Leviathan is always the problem. It's extending its control over us while letting them run riot; our freedom is eroded while theirs is increased. Remember: too much freedom is as dangerous as too little."

Roger looked at Amanda in frustration, but she smiled back as if to say, "bear with him."

"Bill's England is bad," Roger said as the food arrived, "but it's hardly a police state. Look how weak it is."

"On the contrary," Edmund interrupted. "The state's not weak; it's strong – very strong. Ministers might be weak as individuals, but the machinery of government is stronger than ever."

"How is rolling back Bill's petty regulations going to help?" Roger laughed. "If anything, people seem to want more state control over their lives."

"That's because we've assimilated the Political Consensus. If you accept the idea that you're weak and bad, by extension you accept the idea that you can't be trusted with your own life. The state needs us to believe that self-reliance is bad; it needs us to feel vulnerable. That way, we do what we're told. State regulation no longer seems an imposition, but a necessity; not an intrusion, but a means of empowerment. We need it, we want it. We want Granny Government to save us from ourselves."

"And in reverse," Amanda said, "furigans and Muhonin think they're put upon no matter how much freedom they're given. The slightest imposition's too much: whatever they get, they want more. As far as they're concerned, the state is a lazy waiter that never does enough."

"So you see," Edmund said, tucking in, "furigans are strong for the same reason society is weak. Whatever liberties the state gives to one, it must take from the other. If you allow a criminal the right to maim and kill, you necessarily deny their victim the right to life and limb."

"Right," Roger said. "So, we need a strong state to act as our sword and shield."

Edmund put his food down, appalled.

"Emphatically no. You can't solve the problems of Leviathan with more Leviathan."

"How else can we defeat the furigans and Muhonin?" Roger spluttered.

"Gentlemen," Amanda interrupted. "I hate to interrupt this debate, but we're veering off track."

Roger leaned forward, his voice low.

"Edmund, this is our chance to sweep away Bill's clique and restore England Inc. We can't prevaricate. Tell me: what is Bill hiding?"

Edmund shook his head.

"I'm afraid this is a basic philosophical difference and it must be resolved. Else, I foresee grave consequences."

He shut his eyes, as if trying to blot out an unpleasant memory.

"Yes, I remember when Bill first became party leader. I remember seeing that fresh-faced young man who'd stand for honesty and clean out the old backscratching. Yes, I remember thinking: here's someone who truly believes in doing good. We were all so carried away, no-one noticed how he always avoided saying what he stood for and I never thought to ask. New England, New Start. It's been the bitterest disappointment of my life."

"I'm surprised anyone fell for it," Roger said. "I always said he was shifty."

There was a long silence. The robots came and cleared the table.

"We all make mistakes," Edmund said, "but we can also correct them. I know that behind that hard-nosed image lies a good heart. I know that you only want to do what's best for this country."

He bowed.

"Our differences will be resolved."

Roger caught the train, frustrated by the lack of progress. *Idealistic fool, how can he think the state is strong? He knows what Bill's hiding, but this lack of realism will hold us*

back. Yes, we'll meet again. I'll knock some sense into him.
He relaxed and soon the grid squares and skyscrapers of Central London had given way to the semi-industrial panorama of East London, with the twisting avenues and gabled roofs of Outer Suburbia just about visible to the North. The train sped through Hokko Junction with expressways thrusting above and below and slip-roads sweeping round in every direction. He opened his book *Z List England* by Phil Tucker.

> *I visited a delightful pub in Charltonbrook New Town, called the Pit or the Dive, I forget which. I walked in through the vestiges of a doorway to be greeted by four brick walls and a few aged trestle tables. The effect was that of a prison cell with a license to serve. Yet as soon as one got to the bar, all was forgotten: I was greeted by a wide range of regional ales like Old Dom, Cotswolds Glory and Wood End Sour Ale. Best of all, the landlady was eminently knowledgeable and we chatted for many a happy hour, although I confess to nodding off occasionally.*

He detested the Political Consensus, knew Bill's dirt and was sure to be lusting for revenge – who better an ally? Roger grinned. Yes, yes, yes, it was obvious. It would be Bill's effigy burning in Tokugawa Square. It would be…. He put the book down, overhearing three businessmen sitting opposite.

"I have a friend in the Ministry of Finance," said one as they shot into a tunnel. "She said they're stunned – a real rabbit-in-the-headlights job. They never thought it could happen."

"It's been going on for years," added the second. "Sooner or later they were going to get found out."

"But it's not just them," the third replied. "This has got the Big Six sweating; they're all in as deep and running out of cash. People are sitting on their money; if lending ceases, they'll fold. We're talking meltdown."

The train stopped and the lights went dead. Roger stood up, fully alert. Shrieking in the next carriage, loud screams, murky figures steaming through the passageway. A hand grabbed him, an arm was around his throat, another pulling him down. He lashed out and summoned all his strength, wrestling his assailant to the floor.

The lights came on and Roger looked down. His watch was gone and his arm had been slashed. A random attack? A targeted snatch? A biometric mugging? He checked himself as the train crawled out of the tunnel. Nothing else was missing, but biometric information could be used against him: planted as evidence, to frame him. He looked up, feeling deeply uneasy. The three businessmen had gone.

Roger alighted at Thameside Central and left via the footbridge over Yamaha Way, an advertising screen chiming out loudly as he hurried past the luxury apartments of Thameside Towers.

BING-BONG. "Apartment 18A, Burgess Tower to let. See inside the showroom for enquiries." BING-BONG.

He rubbed his ears and crossed the elevated pedestrian square to *The Dog and Lamppost*, where Phil Tucker could usually be found. Inside, it was full of old fruit machines and unused pool tables, but there was nobody around, so he headed to the balcony overlooking Banzai Walk. Phil was standing outside, watching the boats on the artificial lake with a grumpy expression.

"Konbanwa, Tucker San," Roger bowed. "Roger Tyson."

"I know who you are," he replied, not looking round.

"Could I get you a drink?"

133

"Is the Sori Daijin a brainless fool? I'll have a Monkey Puzzle IPA."

"Any good?"

His expression lightened and his voice became the plummy sound recognisable from the media.

"Not bad, it's got the background bitterness an IPA's supposed to have. Bravo, I say."

Roger selected the beer on his communicator, which was promptly delivered by a wheeled service droid.

"People think that I'm posh, because I'm well spoken," Phil said, opening a packet of cigarettes. "I'm not. I come from the barracks, but my mother wouldn't have me speaking like the local lads, so she sent me to an elocution tutor. You can imagine the ribbing." He lit a cigarette up and tucked the packet away. "It taught me a lot."

He rested against the wall as four teenage lads in white boiler suits and black hats walked down the lakeside path.

"I hadn't assumed that," Roger said. "I've read your autobiography. It's very good."

Phil grunted and there was an awkward silence as the lads began fighting, one pushing the others into the water.

"This isn't entirely a social visit." Roger said. "What you said about furigans needs saying, but Bill has been able to pick us off one by one. Together we can hurt him."

Phil laughed, choking on his cigarette. "You want my house covered in filth a second time?" His expression turned serious. "No."

Roger looked him in the eye, but Phil's expression didn't change. He finished his cigarette then stubbed it out on the balcony.

"You have no conception of the barracks," he said. "You live in your big house far away. I'll tell you what it's like. You can't live there, not if you have any scruples. The hard-working people moved out years ago, only the dregs are left... and the ones that couldn't get out, poor buggers."

He looked down his nose at Roger.

"I agree, Tucker San," Roger said, trying to hide his annoyance. "This is why—"

"People think," Phil said, talking over him, "it's what they see on the news: a bit of crime here, a bit of anti-social behaviour there, but they don't know the half of it. The police daren't go there, so you can forget journalists. What we hear about is the mild end of the spectrum. Only yesterday, a young mother was set upon by a gang of teenage girls. They ripped her pram away, doused it in petrol and set it alight; tied her up and made her watch. Where was that on the media?"

"This is exactly what we need to tell the public."

"Forget it. You don't stand a chance."

"Don't I? What's the Government hiding?"

Phil hesitated and gave Roger a sceptical look.

"You really want to know? Look at the Deer Park Complex. One ganglord, Jaxxi, is behind the violence. He runs an extensive criminal empire – narcotics, human trafficking, providing muscle for yakuza protection rackets – and has been absorbing rival gangs through a series of plex wars. Ganglords from nearby complexes have long dreamed of breaking into his empire, but they've never been strong enough – although one, Fuzzz, comes close. The police could arrest any of them any time, but they don't. We all know why, but just you try saying that."

"A furigan power struggle?" Roger said. "What about the Muhonin?"

"Politicians are like furigans," Phil said, ignoring his question. "Individually cowardly, but collectively vicious – and Bill's lot are particularly despicable. What did they hope to achieve with their little stunt? Excrement can be washed off, but they can't unwrite a single word I've written. I'm writing a satire right now, *Reign of Sheep* – I've got some good material from an inside source. Maybe I should add you in. I doubt it will end happily."

"Thank you for your time, Tucker San," Roger said.

Phil grunted and turned back to the lake.

It was late evening when Roger returned home. He looked at Suzuki Hall with its stuccoed walls and large portico surrounded by oak trees, feeling an immense disappointment. Phil and Edmund had been hopeless, his interview had made little impression and now Minister of Finance, Derek Bridges, was due to make an emergency announcement. An announcement. Roger felt a shock. Forgetting everything, he rushed inside and activated the news as Derek stepped out of the Kantei with a dour expression.

"Due to the exceptional circumstances," he said, "the Government, in conjunction with the Bank of England, has agreed to extend Country and Suburban an emergency loan."

"Minister," shouted a reporter, "Country and Suburban today admitted it had made some failed investments. Do you have any idea of the scale of the problem?"

"I've been assured this is a matter of a few unwise investments and that matters are in hand."

"But what contingency plans do you have in place?"

"That is a matter for the keiretsu, not the Government."

Derek got into his car, sullenly ignoring the questions.

Roger checked the information service, trying to make sense of the news. *Bill's done a runner and left Derek to clear up the mess. Or has he? A bailout would postpone the necessary correction and buy him time to put a bid together – then he could use state powers to engineer a takeover. Is he on the defensive or preparing to attack?* He looked away, feeling unsure. The response to the rescue was uniformly positive and, far from crashing, the Eikkei was recovering lost ground, but how long could it be sustained? He looked up as Governor of the Bank of England, Robin Shepherd, defended his earlier decision to refuse funding. *Robin. Of course. Derek tried to screw him, accusing him of running his own economic policy to force him into line. Now, it's Robin's turn to screw Derek.* With a grin, he called.

Robin was sitting disconsolately in front of a cabinet full of porcelain, several reports spread out across the desk. Roger gave a cheery smile, but his expression elicited no response.

"Seems you lost the battle of the bailout," Roger said.

"I had no choice," Robin shot back. "I'm being pressured to stuff the lame ducks with cash and jeopardise the economy. Stability, they say; it's the latest Niceword. What rot! Emergency funding will buy a few months' respite, if that. Once the panic's been forgotten, people will slip back into bad habits and before you know it we'll be back here again."

"You must resist expanding emergency funding or lowering rates," Roger said.

"How?" Robin raised an eyebrow. "Derek appoints the Interest Rate Committee and, without political support, there's nothing I can do. If there were someone in the Naikaku who could argue against this folly, we could act according to our long-term interests – but not unless."

Roger smiled.

"I've drawn up a plan for large-scale liquidation and Bill's in no position to resist. Hold firm and Country won't be the only keiretsu having to face reality."

Robin smiled and bowed.

"Good luck, Tyson San. It is a pleasure to meet someone of sound understanding. Sayonara."

Roger ended the call and checked the news. Country's bad debts had been leaked. Massive investments in retail complexes, office development and golf course construction, all far larger than anyone had imagined; there was no avoiding the fact it was insolvent. He sat back, contemplating the implications. *Emergency aid is no longer enough. If a buyer isn't found, Bill will have to let it fail or take it over himself, bad debts and all. Derek may have granted it a reprieve, but liquidation can't be avoided.* He smiled as the headline *THE SHACHO THAT SAW IT COMING* appeared in the *Eikoku Keizai Shimbun*, then stopped. There, in the small print at the bottom of the accounts, under the heading *Urban Regeneration Programme*, were trillions in Yen Sterling lent to the barracks at artificially low rates. Roger clenched his fists, recalling how the Commission for Social Wellbeing had granted rival keiretsu favourable planning decisions after hiring furigans as "community representatives" and how Greenwood had systematically been shut out. *Of course Derek bailed it out. Even if the state had to take it over, Bill could never let it fail. Only now he has no choice.*

Prepare a bid, he fired off to Colin. *The corruption is coming out.*

12

Ishiguro Park stood deserted as the crisis deepened. Roger watched the leaves billowing in the wind. The news was dominated by boarded-up building sites, half-finished golf courses and empty factories, while images of stock market traders standing by screens full of red with their heads in their hands had become a visual cliché. Despite his bid, Country and Suburban limped on, pleading for more money; however, with no buyer in sight, it was a lost cause. Country, however, was no longer the main worry. As money drained from the markets, the keiretsu too were running out of money, just as he had predicted. Yet, far from working to his advantage, the crisis seemed to be making his life more difficult. The media in particular were unsympathetic to his calls for liquidation and, as fears of a general financial crisis grew, so too did calls to extend emergency funding. Roger gritted his teeth as the Eikkei fell back again and *Keep Calm and Carry On* blared out from the media screen. *Lying bastards! The media knows the worse this gets, the more people want to avoid pain, so they trick them into associating liquidation with closures and job losses, putting out comfort words, like "rescue" and "aid," to fool them into thinking pain can be avoided. Fools! Pain is good. Pain is necessary. Stop worrying, Tyson, there's no alternative: Bill has to accept... Frank's right: I just need to get on the inside.* He smiled as Graham Hough appeared on the news to defend his record.

"It would be madness to let our biggest companies go to the wall," Hough said, jabbing his finger at the interviewer. "We'd bring the economy down."

"As the minister responsible, how would you respond to suggestions that you're trying to sweep the problem aside?"

"No, not at all." Hough smiled. "Keiretsu crises happen from time to time. People shouldn't overstate the scale of this problem. We're in danger of talking ourselves into recession."

"If this is not as severe as everyone believes," the interviewer said, "then surely there can be no harm in liquidating one failing keiretsu?"

Roger laughed as Graham spluttered, unable to find a response. *There's something comic about your bungling, Hough: such little ability, yet no amount of failure can dent your self-regard. Bill's held onto you like a precious gift, no matter how many kaishas you have rescued into oblivion – surely this has to be one blunder too many.* He laughed, imagining a blustering Hough being fired, but his reverie was cut short by a panicky Jim Minto onscreen.

"Short notice," Jim said, out of breath. "Could you get to the National Diet Buildings this afternoon? We have a full-blown emergency: Country's days from going bust: Bill's called a special Naikaku. All options open."

Roger nodded.

"Good man," Jim smiled. "Could you stop by a bit early? I'd like a word."

Roger nodded again, turning to the screen as Jim rang off.

"This is enormous," a pundit said as the Eikkei plunged. "For the first time ever, a Big Six keiretsu has failed. There's only one person with the experience to avert disaster. We've got to accept reality: Roger Tyson has got to be appointed to the Naikaku."

It was good. No, better than good: it was vindication. He reclined his seat as a gust of cool air swirled around the room. *At last. Fear of liquidation has given way to fear of doing nothing. Robin prevented ministers from taking the easy option and they've folded. Bill wanted someone else to be saddled with Country's problems, so it'd drag them down, but no sane buyer would touch it. His saps lack any business expertise and there's nothing they can do. Forget the coalition. If the opposition parties won't agree to liquidation, the Naikaku will.*

He was about to leave when an angry Teddy Smith, Shacho of England's second-largest keiretsu, Eikoku Sangyo, appeared onscreen.

"What's this talk of liquidation, Tyson? Are you trying to destroy us?"

"I don't have time for this, Teddy."

"Find some. We need emergency funding, Tyson: if markets remain gummed up, we'll all go under. Don't you realise the damage a systemic crisis would cause?"

"Don't be a fool," Roger snapped. "This won't stop with Country. Once Bill's got his Commission for the Economy, he'll carve you up, taking the prime cuts for himself and leaving you with the gristle."

"So you keep saying," Teddy said. "We've stuck our necks out for you refusing to touch Country. We're not doing the same over emergency funding."

He gave an uncompromising look and signed off. Roger punched the screen in fury. *And how much bad debt are you hiding, Teddy? Fools like you are doing Bill's work for him.* He stopped as a message arrived from Amanda.

Progress... they're willing to talk. Nothing categorical, but Margaret has said she'd support you in opposing any bailout.

Keep up the pressure, he fired back. *We need to squeeze Bill's balls until his eyes water.*

The white stone of the National Diet Buildings dazzled in the late morning sunshine as Roger stood in front of the heavy stone portico with its squat tower, the House of Representatives to his left and the House of Councillors to his right. He strode up the steps and down the hallway past the busts of every Sori Daijin since the Great Incident – each one from the Liberal Democratic Party. He could feel himself striding into the heart of government, ready to impose his will, ready to join them.

"Glad you could make it," Jim smiled, opening the door. "The Naikaku's in a febrile state. Derek's challenging Bill's leadership again; Graham's blaming everyone else; Fred's trying to nab Graham's post; Antonia's glad it isn't her in the firing line for once and Andy's barking orders like he's Sori Daijin. Forget government policy, it's mayhem."

"Sounds pretty normal to me," Roger said.

Jim smiled. "How does Minister without Portfolio sound?"

"Is Bill offering?"

"He's in no position to refuse. He needs someone the keiretsu trust. Graham will have to go this time."

"Any chance of a permanent post?"

"Can't say," Jim said. "Hough's whining about being made a scapegoat and he's scraped together six back-benchers with links to the Action Groups to block your appointment. The prospect of you in the Naikaku frightens them and they have the Kobiyashi Group's ear – if you know what I mean."

Roger's mind's raced as he left the office, fixated on the six backbenchers. *Hough's too lightweight to be behind them. Bill? Or is it? Could someone be behind him? Maybe he does have less power than I thought. Maybe....* He was barely outside when he was stopped by a woman in her early twenties.

"Excuse me, Tyson San," she smiled. "Would you come this way. The Head of the National Security Committee would like a moment to speak to you. It won't take long."

She led him to the Chief Whip's office and opened the door. The Head of the National Security Committee, Dennis Wilson, was sitting behind a desk.

"Tyson San will see you, Wilson San," she said.

He gave her a lopsided smile and she shut the door. Roger looked at Dennis and entered. Bald and probably in his sixties, wearing a black three-pieced suit, he watched Roger with the air of someone who regarded him as an unpleasant chore while a stone-faced man in a dark suit sat beside him saying nothing.

"Konnichiwa, Tyson San." Dennis stood up and bowed, the man next to him staying put. "Do take a seat, kudasai. Nothing formal; I just wanted a little chat... about a network of kouha extremists within the Self Defence Forces."

He probed Roger with his dull grey eyes as if searching for a reaction then handed him an electronic dossier entitled CHAINSAW. He watched without expression as Roger read the summary with names of serving and retired army officers, including a few old colleagues from Sakura Military Academy.

"Plotting to overthrow the Government," Roger said. "Has this been proven?"

"I can only show you what has been cleared," Dennis replied, his hands clasped. "They plan to stage a series of attacks, which they will blame on terrorists. Their aim is to create an atmosphere of panic to justify military intervention and force the Emperor to dissolve the Government. Then, they will appoint their own figure as an interim leader while a new kouha constitution is drafted."

"What evidence do you have?"

"Tyson San," he said, "we know who's behind it and we're close to rolling it up. The question is: what do you know?"

"I've heard of no such plot," Roger replied.

Dennis stood up and bowed. The man beside him remained seated.

Roger entered the Committee Room and took his seat. Bill sat at the head of the table with Andy Hunt – who, as he was not a Diet Member, should not have been present – to his right, while at the other end a scowling Derek Bridges sat on his own, not speaking to anyone. Roger looked at the burly Finance Minister with his dyed black hair and typically ill-fitting suit, who looked back with the expression of a boxer before a fight. Roger smiled and surveyed the lightweights. Graham Hough was conspicuously absent.

"Welcome," Bill smiled. "Shall we get started?"

The room went quiet as everyone turned towards him.

"I've called this meeting of the Naikaku to resolve the problems afflicting Country and Suburban. Let me assure you, I'm prepared to do whatever it takes. Roger has sent us a copy of his Restructuring Plan for consideration and I urge you all to give it your utmost attention. Roger, would you like to talk us through."

"Domo arigatou gozaimasu, Harris San," Roger said. "Reckless expansion, heavy borrowing from its Main Bank, overinvestment in highly speculative ventures: what we see at Country and Suburban is typical of most keiretsu. As I have said before, injecting more money will not solve the problem: the losses have already been incurred and the longer this situation lasts, the larger they will become. I therefore propose a liquidator of last resort to dispose of the bad investments and salvage the profitable parts – an orderly unwinding now to prevent a disorderly unwinding later."

"Have you considered the psychological dimension?" Derek interrupted. "Inflicting a shock while confidence is so fragile would be catastrophic."

"Let's not forget the political implications," added Antonia. "This Restructuring Plan would lead to an outcry and I don't think it's out of place to point out we've got an election coming up."

"She's right," Employment Minister Fred Abbott said. "People are scared stiff they'll lose their jobs. We can't ignore their fears."

"I appreciate your concerns," Roger said, "however liquidating failed businesses is not a threat, but an opportunity. There may be some closures in the short-term, but in the long-term new kaishas will emerge to acquire their assets and use them more productively."

"Not true," Derek said. "If markets to remain frozen, we'll lose good as well as bad. The Bank of England must provide the liquidity to ensure they start functioning again. Then we can tackle the bad investments. Not before."

"I disagree," Roger said. "We must stop treating the symptoms: markets are frozen because investors are afraid there are more bad investments hidden away. Bring them out into the open and remove them. Confidence will return naturally."

"Who says your analysis is correct anyway?" Andy cut in. "This is a hiccup against a trend of growth. Any fool can see we should be doing all we can to boost the economy."

"The current level of activity is unsustainable," Roger said, growing heated. "We have massive overcapacity in commercial, industrial and residential property; if we don't scale back now, we face a bigger crash later. Your growth is illusory: a product of lax money."

"We can't risk this." Derek brought his fist down on the table. "Your proposal would cause a major economic contraction, possibly a sustained downturn. This problem is manageable if we're prepared to be bold. If we extend emergency funding and dramatically lower interest rates, we can avoid a hard-landing."

"You can't wish away the problem." Roger raised his voice. "You can't unmake a bad investment or un-incur a loss. My plan must be implemented. Now. In full."

The discussion ground to a halt.

"I think we have had a constructive debate." Bill smiled. "Does anyone have any objection to appointing Roger Tyson as Minister without Portfolio with responsibility for resolving the problems at Country and Suburban?"

The Naikaku expressed their assent.

"Liquidation, sackings, restructuring," Bill said. "Whatever you need to do, you'll have my complete support."

"This is an economy-wide problem," Roger said. "Unless I have your support for my Restructuring Plan, I cannot accept."

There was a long pause. The Naikaku members turned to Bill, who looked unusually awkward.

"I'm afraid the remit of this committee is limited to Country and Suburban," he said. "You have argued your case forcefully, but I can't ignore the advice of my Naikaku colleagues. We're agreed that a gradual approach would be less risky."

Roger got up to leave.

"The medicine might taste horrible, but it's the only one that works," he said. "No liquidation, no can do."

"We're giving you a second chance," Andy shouted back. "You guys screwed up. Remember that. We won't let the keiretsu bring the economy down."

He glared at Roger and the meeting broke up without agreement.

"Could I have a word?" Bill said as the room emptied. He waited for a moment and looked Roger in the eye. "It's no secret you're planning to join England Renewal. It's great that you're joining the party, but that road leads nowhere. You could be in the Naikaku tomorrow."

Roger breathed in.

"My plan must be implemented, Bill. We're only delaying the inevitable."

"I'm afraid that's out of the question. Antonia is right: we have an election to consider. After that, your plan will have my wholehearted support."

"Bill, if you don't act now, the economy will crash before there will be an election."

Bill smiled.

"To many that would sound dangerously like a threat. And not just in the Naikaku. There's simply no support for liquidation – anywhere."

Roger hesitated. Could he say no? The economy was in trouble and an opposition coalition, if it ever happened, would be highly unstable. Any ministerial post, even without liquidation, would be better than nothing. Maybe Bill did need his support. Maybe he did want him in the Naikaku. Maybe he was a figurehead. Roger looked at his smiling face, his distrust greater than ever.

"No deal," he said.

He left the room, struggling to contain his anger. *Slippery hatoha politicians! You're only giving way over Country so I'll drop liquidation. You want me complicit in your schemes, so I can't attack you. Don't think you can inveigle me in to oppose a further easing. I won't and neither will the Bank of England.* He stopped as Graham Hough's voice echoed from around the corner.

"I had this under control," he fumed. "We don't need any outsiders, particularly not *him*...."

"It's a definite snub," a muffled voice agreed.

Roger gritted his teeth and turned towards the lifts, only to find Andy Hunt blocking his path.

"Don't think you can play hardball," he said, squaring up to Roger. "You may be someone at Greenwood, but you're nothing here. If the Sori Daijin decides to lower interest rates, then interest rates will be lowered."

"That's for the Governor of the Bank of England to decide," Roger said. "Not Bill and certainly not you."

Andy laughed.

"Doesn't work like that, chum. Robin Shepherd's appointment's up for renewal this year. You know how it works: lean on someone hard enough and they fall over."

He eyeballed Roger and brushed past.

The sky was clear and the Metropolitan Expressway empty as Roger returned home in a state of fury. On the news, six backbench Diet Members were being interviewed outside the National Diet Buildings with a small "Say NO to Tyson" protest behind them.

"Appointing Tyson would be disastrous," said Diet Member Paul Fox, clutching a document. "I have a copy of his Restructuring Plan and it fills me with dread. This plan would devastate industry and ruin livelihoods. And for what? Just so Greenwood can extend its domination. Asking the very people who caused this crisis for solutions is sheer lunacy. The Government must take control. It must create a Commission for the Economy and impose economic planning."

Roger watched with contempt. *Who's funding them? It certainly isn't Hough.... Oh, leave it, Tyson. As long as Robin holds firm, that motley bunch of also-rans, has-beens and never-weres are irrelevant.* He sat back and felt his energy wane as Jane came onscreen.

"So? How did it go?" she beamed.

"A temporary appointment to deal with Country – nothing permanent."

"You accepted?"

He said nothing. Jane looked cross.

"You haven't been swayed by this talk about an opposition coalition, have you?"

"No, I haven't," he snapped.

"It's a pipedream," she continued. "The parties talk and talk, but it never comes to anything. They've no desire to prick the bubble and even if they did, voters always rally around the LDP in times of crisis. They're feeding you false hopes, Roger. Bill wants rid of Hough. He's offering you a chance. Without a Naikaku post, you have nothing. Think about it."

She ended the call with a look of extreme displeasure.

As Roger sat fuming, Derek Bridges announced an expansion of emergency funding, while the Bank of England simultaneously cut interest rates to historically low levels. The opposition politicians had vanished from the screens, except to state they were opposed to liquidation. Roger punched the screen. *Worthless bunch of liars! We need to convince the public liquidation's an opportunity, not a threat and now they do this! I can't trust anyone.* He grabbed his communicator and called Amanda.

"What happened?" he said. "You said the opposition parties would oppose a bailout."

"They assured me," she said. "I insisted...."

"Twist their arms, bully them, make them yelp," he fumed. "I'm not being held up by these jobsworths."

"They're concerned you'd just as soon join Bill's Naikaku."

"They're afraid of holding office, more like," he muttered. "They prefer the safety of opposition."

She looked at him pointedly.

"Bill didn't offer you a ministerial post?"

"Minister without Portfolio."

"You didn't accept, did you?"

"No, of course not."

She said nothing.

"He's testing you, Roger. He needs your business expertise for now. With your support, he could take over your Big Six rivals and if he could make you responsible for the economy, he could fire you when it tanked. Greenwood would be finished and you'd have nowhere to go. Listen, I know you think the party leaders are waiting to sell you out, but with your leadership there'd be no more kow-towing to the Political Consensus. We need that coalition. There is no alternative."

Roger sat stunned into silence. The Eikkei had risen and commentators were praising the Government effusively. He hadn't merely been thwarted, he had been swatted aside. Now he could see why Frank spent his whole time drunk. Whatever Amanda's reassurances, Bill would be on the attack before any coalition could be put together. As he left the expressway, he could see Dennis Wilson's dull grey eyes probing him.

"Don't worry about Compassion Day," they seemed to say, "We have something better lined up for you."

13

The recovery was immediate: confidence came flooding back as firms rehired and households resumed spending, and soon the crisis has faded from memory. It was a blip, commentators said; an irrational panic caused by a single errant keiretsu – and, when Teddy Smith met Bill Harris to agree the acquisition of Country and Suburban, there was widespread agreement the fears had been overdone.

"Contrary to what some might say," Graham Hough had purred, "the economy is fundamentally sound, as this quite painless recovery demonstrates."

Alone in his pessimism, Roger grew increasingly tetchy. He drove across Watanabe Bridge as a brightly coloured pleasure boat sailed below and looked at the newly-built luxury apartments along the river, a procession of pre-fabricated uglitechture. *This is no recovery. It's a return to the bubble... but people don't want to see it.* He shut his eyes, trying to ignore the live coverage of the Diet, where the Minister for Pop Music was calling for every child to have their own television show.

"The junior minister handled the questions adroitly," said a pundit, replaying an earlier debate as coverage returned to the studio. "Watch her body language as she rebuts charges that the Emotion Agency's powers to fine people for getting angry represent an unwarranted intrusion. Look at her posture. See how she uses her gestures to emphasise her passion."

Stupid! Stupid! Stupid! he cursed as another pleasure boat sailed past, lights flashing and music pumping. *Life is returning to abnormal. How long before Figure of Hate is back?* He breathed out, unable to suppress his angst. With the financial crisis over, he was once again Mr Unpopular and, while Graham had lost no opportunity to trumpet the rescue, the Gang of Six had been equally busy attacking him.

"I'll tell you why Tyson's so keen on liquidation," Desmond Grey had told the Eikoku Rōdōkumiai Sōrengōkai Annual Conference. "He wants to strip his rivals of their assets, buy them up cheap, cut jobs and drive down wages. Any attempt to force government into supporting his predatory agenda will be met by our unyielding opposition."

Roger had listened stone-faced as delegates applauded and called for strikes at Greenwood factories, but it wasn't the Rengo he had to worry about. The injection of money would run out eventually, but if Bill could buy enough time, he could attack him before then. Far worse, at some point the Muhonin insurgency would move to Stage Two and all he had was Edmund's offer of a seat. Should he have joined the Naikaku? Could he trust the opposition? As he arrived at Okinawa Wharf, he could see Jane's face after Teddy Smith had emerged from the Kantei.

"You fluffed it," she seemed to say. "Don't let it happen again."

Roger parked in the underground carpark and took the lift to *The Rupert*, where former Joint Chief of Staff, General Sir John Wheeler, was waiting to meet him.

"Konnichiwa Taisho," Roger said as the doors slid open. "How's life in the Self Defence Forces?"

"Morale's low, Tyson," General Wheeler replied, his grey hair and grey face showing no emotion. "We've borne the brunt of Bill's cuts, yet we have to rescue him from every mess he makes – and now he's playing dirty. What do you know about Chainsaw?"

"A classic Strategy of Tranquilisation," Roger said. "Bill's lulling people into a false sense of security while building up his strength. When he's ready, he'll stage an incident and declare a state of emergency. He's fabricated an officers' plot so he can purge the Self Defence Forces. He'll put his own allies in command and turn it into his personal militia ready for when he becomes president."

"That's just the half of it," General Wheeler snorted. "There's been a power struggle within the Action Groups. The moderates have been ousted by the extremists. They see themselves as fighting a common revolutionary liberation struggle with furigans and the Muhonin: Chainsaw is their means to overthrow the state – Bill included. The fool thinks he can keep them in line, but they can see through his sweet talk and have been building up their own militias with the Lifestyle Groups. Not only has the idiot left the country defenceless, he's bloody well tearing it apart. Anarchy and civil war, Tyson; we're that close."

"I understand," Roger said. "But I urge caution."

"Caution?" General Wheeler exploded. "The Muhonin won't wait, Tyson. We can't pussyfoot around."

"We may have to," Roger said. "Bill's ready to purge his opponents. You give him the slightest excuse and he'll have you arrested."

General Wheeler leaned in close, his expression severe.

"Mark Alexander also believed in caution. He knew what was happening – thought he could stay quiet – and look what happened to him. We have a duty, Tyson. We have to save England. Whatever it takes. Are you with me?"

Roger left via the Northern Exit and entered East End District, his mind focused on Edmund's offer of a seat. With his personality, he could turn a minor by-election into a national event. He could.... He paused briefly as an advertising screen played a computer-generated fly-through of a sleek retail and leisure development whose glass and steel towers shimmered in the sunlight.

"Honshu Acres," it declared. "Coming soon."

He looked at the derelict offices behind the hoardings with a sigh of despair. How long would it be before the Muhonin moved to Stage Two? Who would they target? Frank? John? Him? He hurried over the Great Eastern Expressway and cut through a grubby side street, before walking onto the high street. He stopped. Everywhere, there were people dressed in nightshirts and ski masks banging drums and shouting.

"We are the victims," a man shouted down a megaphone. "We are the ones being misrepresented."

Roger looked down as an electronic leaflet arrived unsolicited on his communicator.

"Believe in the Supreme Rebeginning," it said. "Purify your soul and experience Supreme Bliss!"

Roger hit delete, hunting for a way out, but it was too late. A man in a suit, who had been talking to the public, had approached him.

"Come," the man smiled. "See for yourself what Supreme Love means."

Roger stepped forward, aware he was being watched. He looked at the ski masks, feeling nothing but hatred.

"Do not be afraid, my brother. We believe in peace and love."

"But not free will," Roger snarled.

The man's smile remained unbroken.

"You are most mistaken, brother. We *do* believe in free will. We have been given free will so we can come to Supreme Love of our own free choice."

"Free will means the ability to reject," Roger said.

The man shook his head.

"Brother, to reject Supreme Love is the gravest evil. To have seen the light and have chosen darkness is to put one's soul beyond redemption."

"Like those disembowelled policemen?"

The man's expression turned serious.

"You are under a severe misperception, my brother. We do not condone violence, we condemn it wherever we see it, but, in a police state like this, death is inevitable. The media gave those deaths an undue prominence. Why? Because we are the real victims. We are the ones suffering, yet the media says nothing."

Roger clenched his fists and walked on, too angry to know what to say – or care that he was still being watched.

It had gone lunchtime by the time he arrived outside Edmund's house and he was late. Still feeling agitated, he looked at the pitched roof, gables and ramshackle garden, which looked lost amidst the high-rise blocks of Kobe Heights. *What is it with Edmund? He's got the intelligence to achieve, yet he avoids ministerial office. Why? He's an intellectual, that's why. He thinks we live in a police state, like they do. Yes, we'll resolve our differences, all right.* He banged the doorknocker and Edmund opened the door with a yawn, leading Roger down a hallway full of dusty wooden furniture and old ornaments.

"Make yourself at home," Edmund said, entering a sitting room.

Roger looked at the flag of a white dragon on a red background on the wall and sat down by the fire.

"You wanted to meet again. Here I am."

Edmund smiled.

"Tell me," he said, positioning himself in an armchair. "What made you enter politics?"

"Same reason I joined the Army," Roger said. "To serve my country. And you?"

"I studied history and all I could see were the missed opportunities. I didn't want to look back and think I did nothing."

"This is all very nice," Roger said, "but we don't have time to waste talking."

"Don't we?" Edmund leaned forward. "The Great Incident took many years to end, so why should this be any different? Some might say you've made many enemies and have a lot to lose from the current setup. A national emergency would turn the tables quite nicely—"

"Hope San," Roger interrupted, "that's the sort of cheap shot I'd expect from Bill's lot. I didn't need to go into politics any more than I needed to join the Army. I didn't have to have troublemakers camped outside my office calling me Nasty, militarist and whatever else. I could have kept my mouth shut and accepted an amakudari job – goodness knows, I was told that often enough. I might ask why you have avoided ministerial portfolio; do you have some sort of aversion to high office?"

"There's more than one way to serve your country," Edmund said, repositioning himself. "Joining the Naikaku means moral compromise. On the backbenches, I can follow my conscience."

"Conscience?" Roger said, growing irritated. "Oh, how lovely. Anyone can sit and pontificate."

"I'm sorry," Edmund laughed. "I like to play devil's advocate, get people going and find out what really fires them up. I don't doubt your sincerity for a minute. You're not used to being questioned, are you?"

Roger harrumphed.

"The fact is: holding office isn't enough," Edmund said. "We need to know what we are holding office for. You say you want to defend your country, but what is the country you want to defend?"

"I don't follow," Roger said.

Edmund wandered over to the bookshelves, returning with a leather-bound tome. He opened it up and read, his voice transformed into a sonorous baritone.

Ða wæs ymb feower hund wintra and nigon and feowertig fram ures drihtnes menniscnysse þæt Martianus casere rice onfeng and seofen gear hæfde. Se waes siexta eac feowertigum fram Agusto þam casere. Ða Ænglepeod and Seaxna wæs geladode fram þam foresprecenan cyninge, and on Brytene com on þrim miclum scipum, and on eastdæle þisses ealondes eardungstowe onfeng þurh ðæs ilcan cyninges bebod, þe hie hider geladode, ðæt hie sceoldon for heora eðle compian and feohtan.

"What language do you think that was?"

"Don't know," Roger replied, "Some foreign language."

"That," Edmund said, "Was the Venerable Bede's 'Ecclesiastical History of the English People.' That was our ancestral tongue."

Roger shrugged his shoulders, "And?"

"To you, his English sounds foreign, so how do you think our English would sound to him? Think of all those Japanese loanwords you use, not to mention the French and Latin ones. Words like *foreign* and *language*; words so familiar you don't realise they're not English."

Roger took the book from Edmund and looked through it, unable to read the script.

"What relevance does this have?"

"You appeal to England," Edmund said, "but your England dates back no further than the Restoration a hundred years ago. We'd fallen behind and needed to rebuild, so the state sponsored study missions abroad. In Japan, we saw a nation like our own: stoical, polite, resistant to foreign invasion... tea drinkers, even, but most importantly one that had gone from feudalism to modernity through its own efforts. After the Great Incident, the process was complete: we'd absorbed their culture so thoroughly, like those of Greece and Rome before, we didn't even notice it was there. State, business, military; they're all imitations. Your England is an invented tradition; Tyson San, you've gone into politics to restore a sham."

Roger looked at him with incredulity. *Invented traditions? England a sham? What's the fool drivelling about? Don't get drawn in, Tyson. He's an intellectual.*

"Edmund," Roger said, "this is a basic question of patriotism versus anti-patriotism."

"Not so," Edmund said. "Bill can always recast the Political Consensus in patriotic language, redefining England in terms of all those woolly hatoha concepts you detest. A proud history of celebrating softness! The Lifestyle Groups, furigans and the Muhonin the nation, you the anti-patriot. No, this isn't about patriotism. It's a question of Leviathan; everything else is secondary."

Roger clutched his head. *That word Leviathan again. He's not going to insist the state is strong again?* He braced himself for more obscure information.

"You asked me why I avoided high office." Edmund put his leg over an armrest. "I'll tell you. Bill serves Leviathan; he is whoever it needs him to be, but I will never compromise my principles. I'm more than a policy wonk, Tyson San, I have a vision. Amanda is gathering the party leaders to hammer out this coalition and Chilterns South will be coming free: you could stand as the official England Renewal candidate. Tyson San, you are a true patriot and you have the strength of character to be a great leader, but you must ditch your misconceptions."

"Okay, Hope San," Roger said. "You've got a deal: you can do the theoretical stuff... maybe you and Amanda could put together a manifesto. But remember this: I'm in charge."

Edmund smiled.

"You take comfort in being the man of action, don't you?"

"I prefer to trust my instincts," Roger said. "I'm sick of being sneered at by clever-dick intellectuals."

"The main thing is that you stay true to your principles. People respect you for that."

Roger let out a derisory snort.

"No, no," Edmund said. "Principles form the basis of everything we do – it's why this coalition will work. On a personal note, I'd like to say I'm very happy we'll be working together. Amanda's always spoken very highly of you."

"Domo, Hope San," Roger said. "I am so grateful for her. I sometimes think she's my only friend."

"If anybody deserves a reward," Edmund said, "it's her. She's been the victim of innuendo since she started in the Diet. She's young, attractive and intelligent and the others resent it. I can tell you, there's no more loyal person in my faction. She understands what's going on... just like your friend Mark Alexander understood."

Roger looked up, thrown from his thoughts.

"It was said that he had uncovered evidence of criminal activity within the state," Edmund continued. "Alas, he died before he could speak. Tyson San, behind the façade of liberty and democracy, this country's no different from a banana republic."

Roger looked astonished.

"How do you know Mark?"

Edmund stood up and held out his hand, motioning for Roger to do likewise.

"An old custom," he smiled, shaking his hand. "We shall meet again."

"We shall," Roger said. He bowed and turned to leave, stopping as he saw the flag on the wall. "One last thing: whose flag is that?"

"Ours," Edmund smiled. "From before the Norman Conquest."

Roger looked at the shells of buildings waiting to be cleared as he drove back, his certainty shaken. He had never enjoyed debating and Edmund's interminable talk was particularly draining, yet he knew more than he was letting on. Roger thought back to his youthful study missions, but try as he might, he could not dispute what Edmund had said. England had indeed modelled itself on Japan. The Restoration had really been a revolution, ostensibly returning power to the monarchy, in practice replacing the Prime Minister with a Sori Daijin and upgrading the King to Emperor. The Constitutional Revision, too, had been a major change, replacing the pre-Great Incident imperial constitution with a new republican one, again based on Japan. *An invented tradition*, he mused, *a sham*.

The thought remained stuck in his head as he met Jane for the revival of a once-famous play by one of England's forgotten playwrights.

"*Richard II*," she grinned. "The kabuki version. We're in for a treat."

He looked through the programme without enthusiasm and handed it back.

"Well, I'll enjoy it, if you don't," she said.

The first half was met with riotous applause. Jane hurried Roger back for Act Two, sitting down excitedly as the lights dimmed. John of Gaunt and the Duke of York appeared onstage in samurai armour, a gong sounded and John of Gaunt stepped forward to address the audience.

This royal throne of kings, this sceptred isle,
This earth of majesty, this seat of Mars,
This other Eden, demi-paradise,
This fortress built by Nature for herself
Against infection and the hand of war,
This happy breed of men, this little world,
This precious stone set in the silver sea,
Which serves it in the office of a wall
Or as a moat defensive to a house,
Against the envy of less happier lands,
This blessed plot, this earth, this realm, this England.

He stepped back to further loud applause. Jane was on her feet, shouting "Bravo." Roger clapped politely, wondering what Edmund would have made of it.

The play finished with repeated curtain calls. He and Jane had a quick drink and returned to the car. As they sped down the road, he looked out at the elevated expressways soaring above the landscaped parks and the gabled houses nestled in front of the high-rise towers, then inside as a Party Political Broadcast by the Liberal Democratic Party played onscreen. A panoramic shot of the South Downs was followed by Cherry Blossom parties by the Serpentine, a stadium roof opening as a cricket match began and a smiling family collecting their Sunday roast from a restaurant conveyor belt, before closing with the national anthem.

And did those feet in ancient time
Walk upon England's mountains green?
And was the holy Sun Goddess
On England's pleasant pastures seen?

I will not cease from mental fight,
Nor shall my sword sleep in my hand,
Till we have built a New Japan
In England's green and pleasant land.

The words echoed round the car as Bill's face was superimposed over the English flag – a red cross on a white background with a red rising sun in the top left-hand quadrant.

"The Liberal Democratic Party," the voiceover announced. "Our democratically elected Government."

The car halted by a crossroads and Roger sat motionless. Edmund was right. The Political Consensus was patriotism, his England an invented tradition. It was bad enough being a stranger in his own country, but now he had no idea what his country was. *England Inc has no appeal to people today, just as trying to convince people about liquidation was a mistake. Yes, we do need a new vision; something different, something positive, something that will appeal. Maybe getting Edmund to do the manifesto could turn out to be a winner....*

He thought of the by-election and checked the news: sterling was up, the Eikkei buoyant, Bill's ratings back to pre-crisis levels – and there was a new govermercial. He sat up with alarm. The obligatory smiling furigans and Muhonin were still there, but gone were the ordinary citizens. Instead, soldiers in sculpted body armour stormed the National Diet Buildings, gunning down Diet Members and rounding up civilians. A tank rolled forward, its gun pointed straight at the viewer, crushing a furigan

161

holding a flower beneath its tracks. As the hand went limp, the flower fell out and the words SUPPORT NICENESS – STOP THE FORCES OF NASTINESS filled the screen, blood dripping down the letters.

Roger felt as though he'd been punched in the stomach. Chainsaw. Muhonin. How long did he have? As his head dropped, he could feel Jane tapping him on the shoulder.

"A Yen for your thoughts, itoshii," she said. "Come on, you've been funny all evening."

"I've been offered a seat," he said. "Chilterns South."

"Marvellous!" Jane's face lightened. "Father will be pleased. Did I tell you: he's been nominated for a public honour? We'll be a team again: you in the Diet and him in the House of Councillors. So, come on, which faction?"

"England Renewal," he mumbled.

"What, with that old windbag Edmund Hope? Roger, why do you associate with such deadbeats? He's got a dreadful record at getting people into the Naikaku."

She made no attempt to disguise her disappointment and he slipped back into distracted silence, his discomfort growing as police hauled a bedraggled-looking man from his home on the news.

"Retired Colonel Oliver Wells," said the reporter, "was arrested today for membership in a network called Chainsaw, which has been accused of plotting to overthrow the Government. Police have said he is assisting them with their enquiries."

Roger thought of what Dennis Wilson had said. Colonel Wells should be a worried man. He had been deemed a conspirator and would be found guilty. But it was not him they were after. They were looking for a ringleader and Compassion Day would not be enough. The Figure of Hate was for those that could be bullied; for those that couldn't, there was the mysterious car crash, the unexplained accident or Muhonin assassination.

14

Music boomed from every direction as Roger fought his way through the crowds of West End District. All around, people spilled noisily out of the shops and into the medical boutiques, where retail therapists stood ready to help them overcome the recent economic blues. He peered in the chindogu showroom as a girl rolled out a portable zebra crossing across a demonstration road, feeling himself slipping back in time. In the space of a few months, the Eikkei had overtaken its pre-crisis peak and, retail therapists notwithstanding, the crisis had been completely forgotten. Most disconcertingly, the moment he had announced he would be standing for election, the word Nastiness had re-entered the political vocabulary. He thought ahead to the election, knowing party stalwart Tim Hooper would be running against him. A well-connected machine politician, he had widespread support in the media, but did he connect with the people? The sound of a public information screen echoed across the street, bringing Roger to.

"Greenwood's dominance isn't the result of business superiority," bellowed Paul Fox. "No, it uses its generous hospitality budget to cultivate officials and further its corporate interests. This must stop. The Sori Daijin must honour his anti-corruption pledge and cut this overmighty subject down to size."

Roger cursed and headed into a cafe. *Hatred of us is the one thing the Naikaku can agree on and with people like Paul Fox on our competitors' boards, it's no surprise we don't win any state contracts – but this goes beyond muckraking....* He ordered a coffee and peeked outside, his fingers twitching.

"We urgently need an investigation," Desmond Grey thundered. "Not only into his aggressive business practices, but also his influence on politics. He must not be allowed to use Diet privilege to avoid prosecution."

Roger took his coffee and sat down, troubled by the attacks. It was as though the Gang of Six knew the police would be visiting his headquarters, as though they were coordinating their efforts. He thought of Tim and remembered his visit to Kurosawa Studios. Actors didn't exist only on screen; real life itself was a carefully rehearsed drama, with its own cast of stooges, plants and agents. No doubt, the police investigation was a politically motivated subplot, designed to discredit him during his election campaign, but was there a deeper objective? The police had said nothing except to stress its seriousness and their silence made him suspicious. As he contemplated the matter, the word "disinformation" came to mind.

It was simple, Mark had explained: where propaganda was the presentation of opinion as truth, disinformation was the propagation of falsehood as fact; where propaganda aimed to inflame and agitate, disinformation aimed to deceive and mislead. If the Political Consensus was the backdrop, disinformation was the detail. There were four F's, he had said: Falsehoods, Fabrications, Forgeries and Fakes. After the target was subjected to false accusations, they were implicated in a fabricated plot. Next, came the forged documents and doctored photographs to establish their guilt, before the coup de grace: reality itself would be faked. The target would be framed with a staged incident, incriminated and destroyed. Roger sat down nervously. *A characterless dummy like Hooper won't get anywhere. People aren't fooled by his rehearsed gestures and practised phrases... but he's got the media on his side. The Action Groups will manufacture news with their publicity stunts, while Bill's lot churns out its propaganda – including this bloody police investigation. And now every-*

thing gone quiet on Bill's pals.... He sipped the coffee and poured it into the pot plant beside him. It tasted bitter.

A light drizzle filled the air as he left, quickly turning into a pelting rain. He pulled his overcoat tight and dashed into the station, where he noticed a new message: two unnamed financial firms were in trouble. He paused, still breathing hard. *Could it be? English Financial and Albion Investments? They've been concealing dodgy investments for years and they're both connected to the Urban Regeneration Programme through their property affiliates, English Landholdings and Southern Land. It'd be Country multiplied by a million: if Bill tried to rescue them, they'd bring down the state. Too big to save and too important to fail; what answers lie inside?* He reached the platform and stopped. On the news screen opposite, police were raiding a house, dragging out a seemingly respectable man in handcuffs.

"In what is being billed as the biggest case of kleptocracy in English history," the reporter said, "twenty-seven state officials have been arrested for using phoney contracts to divert state assets to straw kaishas. We have this report...."

Roger boarded the train, feeling giddy. *Letting Diet Members take what they like in allowances was bending the rules, but this is theft – not just of money but physical assets too and, if it goes any further, the state will end up an empty shell. Who else knows about these firms? Are officials grabbing what they can before it all goes pop or has Bill given them the nod?*

By the time he had reached East Kensington, the news had sparked a fresh bout of point-scoring in Nagata-Cho: Fred Abbott was attacking Graham Hough's performance at Trade and Industry while Derek Bridges' aides complained about Andy Hunt's influence and Antonia

Richardson's supporters talked her up as a future Sori Daijin. He pursed his lips, thinking about the message. *Ministers openly briefing against each other, factions attacking each other like rival parties.... Could it be? Could it be?*

Amanda opened the door and let him in. A fire roared away in the centre of the room, while a tabby cat was curled up asleep on an L-shaped leather sofa. He paced about as she walked over to the drinks cabinet.

"We've got problems," she said, pouring out two glasses. "These rumours of a police investigation have spooked the party leaders. As long as we've got this hanging over us, I can't get them to agree to anything. What's it about?"

She pushed the cat away and handed him a glass.

"Bill's dredging up old allegations," he said, still standing up. "It's like his claim you were trying to incite a backbench rebellion – there's nothing in it. Have you got any agreement on liquidation?"

"They won't budge."

"Bully them until they do."

"It won't work," she said. "They're afraid of being blamed for any recession and accused of Nastiness."

"Idiots!" he cursed. "If these stupid career politicians don't agree, victory wins us nothing."

"They're what we've got to work with," she said, "I know how much liquidation means to you, but unless we're in office, it's just a talking point. We can't let this hold us up any longer. Without a coalition, Bill wins."

The cat leapt back onto the sofa and Roger sat pensively. *I don't have a choice. Perhaps I could use them to prise the system open. Then they could be dumped in the rubbish where they belong.*

"Amanda," he said, "has Bill put Tim up or are the factions pitching in with their own candidates?"

"A bit of both, I'd imagine," she said. "Bill certainly wants someone to split the vote, but it's not unusual for the factions to field their own candidates. Don't forget, they run their own campaigns under the party ticket, so they often end up splitting the vote several ways and – tomodaore – everyone loses."

Roger's expression grew solemn.

"The system is fracturing, Amanda. I must know what the Naikaku's up to."

She sighed.

"The Naikaku's a charade, Roger. Bill only calls meetings when he wants to give the impression of doing something. Derek's the only minister with his own power base, which is why Bill and Andy are so desperate to get rid of him. He liked to portray himself as Sori Daijin to Bill's Shacho until he was ordered to stop. The others are only bit-part players."

Roger's eyes narrowed.

"So, who's in his inner circle? Are you saying there are outer and inner tiers?"

"If you count the Naikaku as a tier at all," she said. "The inner tier's not government in any meaningful sense: there are no meetings, set agendas, official positions or ministerial briefs. It's whoever happens to be on Bill's sofa at any one time – a band of courtiers, if you like. There's self-styled Minister of the Media, Andy Hunt, a foul-mouthed lout who acts as Bill's enforcer and fancies himself as a ladies' man – he's the one that came up with the idea of using Nastiness to bully opponents; former police chief, Adam Robshaw; Norman Hogg, proprietor of the Kobiyashi Group – he rarely meets Bill in person and usually sends an envoy; Jonathan Green, his fixer and Brian Penney, his cashpoint; then there are the commissioners: Gavin, Suzy, Olly and Babs; Jo White, his aromatherapist, guru and lifestyle coach; and you've got to include his ghastly wife, Lizzie; she's always hovering around. And then there's Sir Gerald Harwood."

"Head of the Security Services?"

"Yes. He's an official, not a true crony, but he likes to be close to decision making and has allowed his role to become politicised. He provides Bill with political intelligence in return for access."

"Is he responsible for appeasing furigans?"

Amanda shrugged her shoulders.

"I've no idea, Roger. Forget them, they're yesterday's men."

The news continued as Margaret Richards launched into leader of the Pioneer Party Brian Collingwood for using Nastywords while Diet Members from the New England and New Frontier parties called each other names. Roger sighed. These were three parties who were to form the coalition.

"I wish I could share your optimism," he said. "If Chainsaw goes any further, there won't be any country to govern."

She rested her head against his shoulder, her hair caressing his face.

"You worry too much," she said. "You need to loosen up."

She touched his hand.

"Roger, what's troubling you? You're very tense."

There was a long pause.

"I'm sorry...." He hesitated. "I'm just no good with emotions."

"There's a lack of love in your life," she smiled.

He sat awkwardly, gazing at the pictures of her: standing outside the Kantei, playing with a dog as a child, standing next to him at a conference.

"You never talk about your husband," he said.

She stared into the distance, her head still resting on his shoulder.

"It was a mistake. I thought he loved me, but he didn't…." Her voice drifted off, then she turned to face him. "Roger, why don't you ever speak about yourself?"

He hesitated, stranded in unfamiliar territory. The prospect of talking about himself made him feel so uncomfortable he wanted to leave, yet as her hair brushed against his face, he found himself unable to move.

"Don't listen to what they say," she said. "I know how much you care, even if others don't. Look at me. You will succeed."

He sat tight looking more awkward than ever as she kissed him.

"She only sees you as a means to an end, Roger. I believe in you. You will win that election."

He closed his eyes and breathed out, feeling her against him, a fellow human being with hopes and fears. *Dear Amanda, not once have you doubted me. When I was Nastiness to everyone else, you alone saw me as your friend; when others wrote me off as a has-been, you alone believed in me. Dammit, we will achieve our dreams.* He looked at her, a young army officer again, ready to do battle, ready to become Sori Daijin. He was a national hero and she the perfect English rose. His ribcage felt so tight he could barely breathe. *National hero. English rose.* He spun round, desperately trying to control the tumult inside him.

"This coalition will work," he blurted, wiping his eye. "Let's do it."

She grinned and hugged him tight. Her eyes were moist, too.

Roger arrived at his office, flinging himself onto his seat as reports of clashes between Emo-zoku and Metal-zoku appeared onscreen. A masked gang daubed a house with "Emo-zoku out" and hurled bricks through its windows.

"We're the victims," shouted one resident. "We never get nuffink, cos the cansel's full of them lot."

"They're always getting preferential treatment," a spokesman for Bling-zoku Action said. "We're being—"

He turned the sound down and let the plaintive sound of Takemitsu's Requiem for Strings wash over him as he searched for news about the two failing kaishas. Nothing, only Graham Hough attacking Fred Abbott for not doing enough to promote Granny Government. Roger looked to the ceiling. *Days away from crisis and ministers stuck in their own little world of petty intrigue....*

"Tyson San," Ann Thomas said, "I have two policemen to see you."

Roger got up and greeted the plain-clothes officers.

"Konnichiwa, officers. Would you come in."

The officers slipped in and stood in front of his desk.

"Kudasai, sit down," Roger smiled. "I trust the documents showed our business was in order."

There was a long pause. The officers looked at him without emotion and sat down.

"While we were investigating the takeover," the first said, "a more serious matter came to light. Arms produced by your keiretsu are known to have ended up in the hands of paramilitaries responsible for numerous deaths. Do you recognise any of the following groups?"

He pushed a paper across Roger's desk.

"I recognise the names," Roger said, reading through the list, "but this keiretsu has never conducted business with any of them. The arms in question were almost certainly captured or stolen."

"So, you wouldn't object to our conducting an electronic sweep of your files?"

Roger pushed the paper back.

"Be my guest. There's absolutely no truth in these allegations."

The officer nodded and called in the technical team.

"You are aware this isn't the first investigation into this matter," he said, "Some years ago, Diet Member Valerie Whittaker conducted a similar investigation. Months later, she was found dead of a suspected heart attack. I understand you didn't get on."

"That is neither here nor there," Roger said. "Her investigation found no evidence of wrongdoing and she herself described the allegations as 'completely without foundation'." A note of menace entered his voice. "If you're trying to insinuate something, officer, I suggest you desist."

The officer said nothing and the technical team entered. Roger watched in silence as they linked up to the Greenwood information system and filtered through the records.

"Everything's in order," the lead technician said.

The officers looked through the results then stood up.

"Thank you for your time," the first officer said. "If we need any further information, we shall be in contact."

Roger watched them leave, seething with rage. He looked for something to hurl, then stopped himself. Derek Bridges was onscreen.

"Konnichiwa, Roger," he grinned, now looking more jolly uncle than political bruiser.

"Cut the jocularity," Roger growled. "What do you want?"

"I owe you an apology," Derek said. "You were right about liquidation. Two kaishas – English Financial and Albion Investments – are in big trouble and the state finances won't support a rescue."

A faint smile crossed Roger's face.

"And Bill understands this?"

"Bill has no head for figures," Derek said. "He just spends, spends, spends and laps up the praise. We need to act fast. Right now, he's working on a rescue with Graham; something half-baked, no doubt. Without my support, they'll struggle to put anything credible together. The thing is, I can't attack them publicly."

"The fact it's half-baked is neither here nor there," Roger said. "It has to be opposed on principle."

Derek's expression became emollient again.

"Why do you think Bill's keen to bail out every lame duck that gets into trouble? It's not the election; we'll win whatever happens. No, he's worried he won't be leader much longer. These failures are damaging him, Roger. The public's sick of him; they want honest government, but he won't listen. He's become a liability."

"And you think you'd make a better leader?"

"Is that what he said?" Derek let out a horsey guffaw. "He has an amazing ability to turn everything around. Yen Sterling isn't weak, every other currency is strong; he's not paranoid, everyone else is against him. Listen to me, he's made alliances with every hatoha fanatic going and now they have us by the balls. Unless we stop him, he'll continue to move further down the extreme hatoha route or be deposed for an Action Group puppet. Whatever he says, he sees you as a threat and wants you neutralised."

Roger said nothing and Derek punched his fist into the palm of his hand.

"He's vulnerable, Roger. He was caught out by this crisis and a defeat in the Diet will kill him off. It's time to clean up politics. The Party needs a strong figure to restore discipline and the country needs a strong person to restore the economy. Support me and I promise immediate implementation of your Restructuring Plan. Support me and you'll be next Sori Daijin but one."

Roger smiled and thanked Derek for his call.

There was a thin band of crimson and a few wispy clouds in the light blue evening sky. Roger watched the express-way scenery flash past, savouring the mounting panic as news of English Financial and Albion Investments' finances broke. *Win this election and I can turn Bill and Derek's feud into outright war: if Derek blocks a rescue, the kaishas will fail and the LDP split. And once the true state of the government finances are known, the opposition will have to back my plan. Bill will be exposed. I only have to deal with this damned investigation....*

He arrived outside Suzuki Hall and drove into the bomb bay, feeling his doubt return. Had Bill really lost control? If his inner circle controlled what mattered, then ministers attacking each other meant nothing and, if he were the front man, there might be an inner circle within the inner circle. The tracked bomb detector darted beneath his car. Why did they feel so threatened? Was it because he was a barrier to their ambitions? Or was it because they feared what lay inside the innermost box? He shuddered. Who-ever had ordered the police investigation was determined that an election victory would prove pyrrhic at best – and what then? Quickly, he called General Wheeler, but the line went dead.

Roger sat still, listening to the silence. General Wheeler had been arrested. As he stepped out into the cold night air, he could hear Mark's voice ringing inside his head.

"There are some things people will kill for," it said. "In the end, they come for you."

15

A giant holographic image of Roger towered over his campaign headquarters with the caption *ROGER TYSON, THE MAN WHO CAN* underneath. His team stood outside as his helicopter came in to land, bursting into applause as he stepped out. Grinning broadly, he outstretched his arms, giving a double V-for-Victory sign. A party official ran over and pinned a red and white rosette to his chest then dashed back.

"I would like to thank you for your efforts," Roger said. "Your dedication is the reason we will win."

He buttoned up his jacket in the breeze and walked into the building with a confident smile. His entry into politics was the main talking point among the chattering classes. Whether excited, fearful or simply eager to see a punch-up, everyone agreed it was a historic turning point.

"The factions have withdrawn their candidates," an aide said, rushing over. "They're backing Tim. We've dropped in the polls."

He thanked her and watched his rival address a rally on the Kobiyashi media.

"Be under no illusions about this so-called financial crisis," Tim said. "This is not some natural disaster, like a tsunami or an earthquake; it is the deliberate action of spivs trying to drive the economy into recession. There's only one party committed to economic stability. We stepped in once to save the economy and will do so again."

"You've pushed the problem out of sight," Roger bellowed. "The issues haven't been addressed, never mind resolved."

His irritation grew as Tim was followed by a documentary about Greenwood.

"In this programme," announced the presenter, "we uncover hitherto unknown links between Greenwood and the previous administration; an old-boys' network furthering its own interests at the public's expense."

The film cut to a blacked-out interviewee against a murky backdrop.

"There was a kind of revolving door," the robotised voice said. "Ex-Greenwood men joined the Naikaku like it was an extension of the keiretsu. I often wondered whether I was working for an English Government or a Greenwood one."

"But perhaps more damaging," the presenter continued, "was the traffic flowing in the opposite direction. We can reveal that scores of senior politicians and officials gained lucrative positions in Greenwood after holding responsibility for placing orders with the keiretsu."

"This presents a clear conflict of interest," Paul Fox said. "It's time for the Sori Daijin to honour his pledge and root out this corruption. Tyson must be debarred from standing for election."

Roger paced up and down with a foul expression, his team listening patiently.

"Does Kobiyashi Group behave any differently? Every keiretsu has ex-ministers and officials on their boards, but only we have none from the present administration. They benefit, yet we're attacked. This is Andy Hunt's work. Bill wants his people in charge of the keiretsu and now he's got his chance. He won't call it a takeover; no, it'll be 'a rescue.' Not that that will be enough for him. He wants people to equate business with Nastiness, so he can attack it. His takeover won't just be an economic rescue, oh no, it'll be a moral salvation too. Then, having stuffed their faces during the boom, greedy shachos like Teddy Smith will have no choice but to accept. We didn't fall for the New Era rubbish at Greenwood, so we get this."

He dismissed his aides and sat down. The Eikkei had fallen below the lows of the Country and Suburban crisis and money markets had frozen, but would it help? He watched the polls fluctuate in real time, feeling uncertain. *If Bill knows recession is approaching, he knows he has to move fast. Emergency funding won't be enough; English and*

Albion are insolvent; if they don't receive more capital, they will fail. Surely even Bill wouldn't risk the state finances to save them... but does he know the true picture? And can I rely on Derek? He looked up to see his campaign manager waiting. It was time to meet the voters.

The campaign bus arrived at a suburb of medium-rise towers and scruffy parkland, and Roger ascended onto a small platform to address the small crowd, noticing a group loitering on the fringes with hostile expressions.

"I'm glad so many of you could come," he said, ignoring the group. "As your—"

He stopped as a sound truck drove past, its speakers drowning out everything else.

"Vote for Roger Tyson, patriot and national hero," it boomed. "Vote hardline. Vote kouha."

Roger turned to an aide.

"Find out who organised this and stop them. This could be homegoroshi."

The aide scampered off and Roger turned to the crowd.

"As your prospective Diet Member, I've heard your concerns. I've heard from the mother who can't get her child a place at a local school, because she's not a member of a Lifestyle Group. I...."

He raised his voice as the fringe group began chanting, "Roger Tyson, Nasty Man."

"I've heard how the one school that banned pupils from using furigan slang was closed down by the Government Kindness Executive. It's time to get tough and I'm not talking more police patrols and securi-cams; I'm talking about a change of attitude – a new culture of discipline. No longer will furigan gangs be allowed to prey on the elderly."

"Heard it before, mate," shouted out a man with dreadlocks. "Everyone's going to get tough, but it's forgotten the moment the election's over."

The other residents nodded.

"They're all the same," added a fat man in a sweaty T-shirt. "They're only interested in feathering their own troughs."

The crowd started laughing and the chanting momentarily ceased.

"Sir, I disagree," Roger said. "Which of the stuffed dummies in the Diet opposes the Political Consensus? None."

"That's what they all say," a woman called out.

"No, madam, they say the Political Consensus does not exist. I say that I'll string furigans up by their balls. Do they say that?"

Roger paused as shouts of Nastiness came from the fringes.

"Talking tough is easy," Roger continued. "Acting tough is hard. Why should we be apologising to these louts? What right have the Action Groups got to tell us how to think? How dare local officials rig the system so you have to be a member of a Lifestyle Group to get anywhere? It's an outrage."

"Nasty bastard," shouted a protestor. "Scum like you hate the Helpless."

The crowd swelled as residents flocked to watch the commotion.

"If you don't register with a Lifestyle Group," shouted a man, "you can't get a job or a house. They push you to the back of the queue."

"We're being silenced," Roger bellowed. "Look how they shut down debate. If you don't use Nicewords, your opinion is disallowed. If you speak the truth, you're accused of Nastiness. It's a disgrace."

The shouts of "Nasty Scum" and "Thug" increased in volume as the protestors were joined by reinforcements.

"Go on, then," Roger shouted. "What answers do you have for these people? Cuddle a furigan?"

There was a loud cheer.

"We are the people that make this country," Roger continued. "The law-abiding citizens, the diligent students, the hard-working employees. I'm not a career politician; I'm not part of the system. Whenever I raise your concerns, I have goons like this trying to silence me, just as they try to silence you. Ladies and gentlemen, I came here to speak for you. If you want your voice heard, vote for me."

The residents shouted down the chants and cheered as fist fights broke out between protestors and his supporters. Roger walked off with his team to visit a local school.

"How many kids are you going to kill?" shouted a heckler, running alongside him as he crossed an elevated walkway.

Roger pointed to a hospital in the distance, ignoring him.

"Aren't you going to speak?" shouted another, running on the other side. "You think you're too important, don't you?"

Roger walked on briskly, but a third stopped dead in front of him, blocking his path.

"Would you kindly move aside," Roger said.

The man moved forward, getting right in his face. Roger breathed in and tried to walk around him, but he moved sideways. Roger tried the other side, but he moved again.

"I'm a candidate for the National Diet," Roger said, "and you are obstructing my election campaign. Kindly let me through."

His temper fraying, he tried a third time. As he walked past, the man barged his shoulder into him. Roger snapped. His fist landed on the man's nose.

"Nasty pig!" shouted a girl, running over as the man collapsed in a heap. "Look what you've done, you bastard."

"Let me at him!" Roger shouted, his aides restraining him as the man rolled around, howling and clutching his face. "I'll wring his bloody neck."

Roger returned to campaign headquarters, intoxicated by the rush of adrenaline. *The Morning News* was calling for him to be disqualified for using Nastywords, but everything had been overshadowed by his punch. Roger watched with his campaign manager, Angela Taylor, as a reporter jogged behind him on the walkway.

"Wherever he goes," she said, "Roger Tyson seems to court controversy."

Roger, face red and cheeks puffed out, punched the man, who fell to the floor in slow motion, the cameras closing in on his creased-up face.

"This is his true nature," screamed a protestor. "You see his aggression."

"It was just a slap," Roger muttered to Angela. "Look at the big cry-baby. I should have hit him harder. I'd have given him something proper to cry about."

"I wouldn't let it bother you," she said. "It shows you're real. Besides, people like to be entertained."

He waved her comment away as Brian Penney appeared on the news, refusing to answer questions as he left his house.

"An embattled Government came under further press- ure today," the reporter said, "as LDP Chief Fundraiser, Brian Penney, was accused of selling posts in the House of Councillors. Penney San has denied the allegations, saying the appointments had been made in accordance with the law, but investigations have revealed that all of the twenty-seven officials recently arrested were party donors. Margaret Richards described the affair as 'a dreadful stain on centuries of parliamentary democracy' and called for the individuals concerned to be sacked. The Sori Daijin declined to comment but has announced that Lord Emerson's inquiry will be extended to investigate the matter."

Roger breathed out as his tension subsided. *Persist, Tyson, persist. Bill's trying to use Lord Emerson's inquiry as a general-purpose dustbin to dump his scandals in, but there are no scapegoats this time; it's corruption of the system – his system. The Civil Service and the Self Defence Forces answer to the Imperial Crown, not the Sori Daijin; they serve the nation, not the party – and certainly not Bill. Remove the "Iron Triangle of Party, State and Keiretsu"? Rubbish. His reform of the Upper House was just a cover to kick out independent-minded Councillors. Now, with the Diet and Civil Service packed with placemen, the state is under his control. The kleptocracy was no aberration; looting's the very basis of his power: Brian sells official positions and, as long as the buyers support Bill, they're allowed to take whatever they want – it's down-payment for the right to plunder. We must block any rescue attempt; we can't let him bury the evidence a second time.* Angela tapped him on the shoulder. Roger winced at the sight of James Ashley onscreen.

"Roger Tyson's talk of law and order means nothing of the sort. His own behaviour gives us the clearest indication of how he intends to fight his dirty war. Street thugs, beatings, attacks on the Helpless, hooligans turned into paramilitaries, low-level urban warfare in the name of law enforcement; are we to abandon our cities to Tyson and his thugs? No, never."

"Bill's been hurt," Angela said, "but he's fighting back the only way he knows."

She pointed to rumours on the Live Commentary that Roger was proposing to hire paramilitaries to patrol city centres.

"Have you made it clear these allegations are baseless?" Roger said.

She nodded.

"You can fight a war and your enemy will treat you with chivalry," he muttered. "But with these buggers?"

"It gets worse." She handed him a photograph of the sound truck and a blow-up of the driver, a man with a broken nose and a scar on his left cheek. "We've identified the group responsible: they call themselves *Kouha England* and ostensibly are an ultra-kouha movement. They've made no demands, so it doesn't look like extortion. My guess is it's a fake movement Bill's PR people have set up. We're unable to identify the driver."

He thanked her and sat pensively as his lead narrowed.

He was about to leave campaign headquarters when an angry Helen barged her way in.

"What are you doing, Roger? Fooling around in by-elections won't stop the Muhonin. John's been arrested. The purge has begun. Chainsaw has begun."

He took her to a private room in the far end of the building.

"Helen, what's the meaning of this?"

"Give up this fantasy of winning over the people. You're wasting your time. All this pleading with them; you're making yourself look ridiculous. If you don't push into doing what's good for them, they won't do anything. And what if you lose? Have you thought about that?"

"Listen Helen," Roger snapped. "I won't lose. The polls aren't everything: people won't admit to liking me, but that won't stop them voting. Every time something new comes out of the Hentai Scandal, our position grows stronger."

"By-elections don't win wars, Roger." Her voice grew louder. "Only the Self Defence Forces can protect the people. Only—"

He put the media screen on to the loudest setting and leaned in close.

"What do you know about English and Albion?"

"If you want to know how Bill's connected, I don't know."

"Answer the question, Helen."

She took a step back.

"It comes down to furigans. Every government in the past fifty years has followed the same strategy: buy 'em off and keep 'em quiet. What do you think the Financial Aid budget is there for? Not to help residents in hardship or promote development, like the public in its wisdom thinks. No. It's just a giant slush fund to keep furigans happy. Bill, however, has gone further, secretly funnelling money via conduits like the kaishas you mentioned. The ganglords get the bulk, which they spend on flashy weapons and fast cars. What's left over trickles down to the grunts to indulge in recreational violence. When they want more, they riot. They're part of this bubble, too."

"But nobody's being kept quiet, Helen," he said. "The money is fuelling the violence, not buying it off."

An intense anger crossed her face.

"Don't be stupid, Roger. Bill couldn't care less if they're making life hell for us, only that they're not they're making life hell for him. We pay for the Financial Aid, but *he* decides how it's spent. We're paying for them to attack us."

He pressed his face right up against her ear.

"The ganglords are the government in the barracks," he whispered. "There's a tacit agreement: Bill recognises their rule as long as they acknowledge his overlordship. Right?"

She looked around and her manner turned serious.

"No Roger, it's not that simple. Furigan society is one of 'friend today, forgotten tomorrow.' To compromise or show consideration represents a massive loss of face, so relations are highly fluid and loyalty non-existent. With the threat of backstabbing ever present, genuine cooperation is impossible, resulting in a highly unstable social structure: gangs last only as long as an alpha furigan can enforce a pecking order. Furigan culture has radiated out beyond the barracks, infecting the rest of society. Unless you act now, it's where we're all heading...."

Her voice faded away. Roger pressed right against her, his voice harsh.

"Say it, Helen. This goes right into the Government, doesn't it?"

She breathed out and gathered herself.

"Two ganglords – you know who – have acquired more power than they could by crime alone... it's linked to the case of the three businessmen... Roger, kudasai, don't go there: furigans may be our enemies, but they have their friends."

He thanked her and turned the media screen off. She was shaking.

The sun was low and thin wisps of cloud lined the sky creating a band of red beneath the dark grey. Roger cruised down the expressway, his mind fixated on the barracks. *Hiring barbarians to fight barbarians; Bill's trying to maintain an internal balance of power, playing the gangs off against each other and trying to prevent any one from becoming too powerful. The fool. It doesn't matter which gang is "ours" and which one is "theirs" – they're all foe and collectively uncontainable. Politics is becoming furiganised. Who's playing whom, I wonder?* As the sun disappeared beneath the horizon, his thoughts turned to the case of the three businessmen.

The case had begun when Bill's go-to man Nigel Warner had been accused of receiving illegal donations from a small kaisha called Grey Ninja Ltd. Initially, he had denied the charges, but as rumours of links between Grey Ninja and a yakuza protection racket came to light, he had suddenly left the Diet. The matter had gone quiet for a couple of weeks, only to deepen when it had been revealed that then-Fuku Sori Daijin John Davidson had also been receiving payments from Grey Ninja. He had been forced to step down, yet despite the loud demands for reform and claims that even larger donations were being concealed, the Public Prosecutor had declined to investigate. Instead, three junior managers had been arrested. All three had protested their innocence, claiming they had signed confessions under duress, but after other senior figures were implicated, they were denied access to the media and, soon after, one was found dead. Roger rapped his fingers on the armrest. Who was Grey Ninja? Banker to the barracks? Front for furigan criminal enterprises? Conduit for funding dirty operations? Rumours abounded, but only one fact had been established. It was funded by Albion Investments.

Roger stretched out to relieve the tension in his neck and shoulders. Grey Ninja? John Davidson? Nigel Warner? They had fought Jonathan Green and Brian Penney for control of the Urban Regeneration Programme. English Financial? It had spent heavily to drive Albion out of the scheme, causing Albion to cultivate other ministers to break back in. But where did this leave Jaxxi? And what of Fuzzz? Maybe it was time to visit the barracks himself.

Tiredness catching up with him, Roger turned to the news. He sat up in shock: English and Albion had been bailed out, with the Bank of England instructed to purchase their assets on an unlimited basis, printing money if necessary. As calm descended on the Live Commentary, Roger felt unnerved. Where was Derek? *Bill's committing us to rescues we can't afford. Is it that bad? Perhaps he really is completely unaware of the state of the government finances....* He looked again at the comments, alarm turning to fear. The tone had quickly changed as relief that crisis had been averted had morphed into demands for greater action.

"Ad hoc measures aren't enough," said one commentator. "The Government must put its entire resources at the economy's disposal. We need a comprehensive and fundamental rescue package."

Roger tensed up. *Bill must have strong-armed Derek over English and Albion, but he'll still need his support to draw up such a rescue and, even if he got it, the economy would crash before it could be implemented – or before I could put my Restructuring Plan into action. Events are moving too fast. The economy's turning into a landslide that will sweep us all away.* He reached forward to call Amanda, but she was already onscreen.

"Forget my plan," he said without saying hello. "Let's get this coalition going asap."

"Great," she replied. "They've dropped their opposition to liquidation and I've got the accounts. Everything's in place. We can get an announcement out now and confirm details later."

Jane didn't look up when he arrived home, too absorbed in *The Remains of the Day* to notice him. He flung himself in his favourite armchair and checked the polls, feeling sick. Tim Hooper had moved ahead and was swaggering around, kissing babies and confidently predicting victory. *This is a seat I should be winning comfortably and I'm being beaten by a Niceword-speaking nonentity. Surely, I can't lose, surely.* As he got up to go into the garden, Jane put her book down and turned to him with a look of great upset.

"Thanks to your silly campaign," she said, "my father's honour has been put on hold. We've been accused of bribery, Roger. It's a horrible lie! People will think we're crooked and we've worked so hard."

She gave a little sob. Roger looked at her with incredulity.

"When did you become so gullible, Jane? This is a ruse and you've fallen for it."

"Gullible?" She laughed. "Your opposition friends are looking for a sacrificial lamb and you call me gullible. All these years and I didn't realise you were such a dolt."

"Well it's not like your dalliances with Bill are helping me," he snapped back.

She dried her eyes and gave him an angry look. Roger turned away, not wanting to see her. *You must be stupid. They're blackmailing you, getting at you to get at me. They want you to be their star performer in the Chainsaw Trial and they'll keep twisting your arm till they get what they want. Loyalty, Jane, loyalty. How can you have more faith in him than me?*

She returned to her book and he put on the information service. Had his eyes deceived him? Bill had announced a comprehensive rescue. Trillions of Yen of government money would be put at the economy's disposal, overseen by a new Commission for the Economy, reporting to new Minister for Economic Planning Graham Hough; further details be released. He tried to call Derek, but there was no reply. As the Diet vote on the rescue was announced for three days' time, he fell back in disbelief. *It can't be. It's not possible. Even if he had it planned, how could he have done it so fast? He's outmanoeuvred Derek, he's outmanoeuvred me, he's outmanoeuvred everyone – he's outmanoeuvred*

*himself. Do nothing and English and Albion's bad debts will
bring down the economy; bail them out and the state's will.*
The energy drained from his body. A new headline had
appeared onscreen.

DRAMATIC ARRESTS – CHAINSAW PLOT REVEALED

*247 military officers have been arrested for plotting to
overthrow the Government. All are members of
Chainsaw, an ultra-kouha network of serving and retired
officers backed by hardline elements in the state.*

Roger sat down, unable to comprehend what was
happening. The sound truck. Homegoroshi. He was being
killed with praise. Chainsaw needed a ringleader and it
was determined to have one. So what if it were a
fabrication? He thought of the three businessmen and how
the media had taken their guilt as fact and how they had
torn apart their private lives until their public standing
was nil. They had been presented as three dodgy wheeler-
dealers and that was how they had been seen. No-one had
seen the false testimony, trumped up charges and physical
intimidation. As far as the public was concerned, they had
been tried and convicted according to the law and justice
had been done. As the saying went: if it hadn't been seen,
it hadn't happened.

The memory brought him out in a sweat. Contrary to
what Helen thought, he wouldn't lose and Bill knew that:
the attacks were designed to wound, not kill. Without
public support, his position was weak and, win or lose, he
couldn't afford any more damaging smears. However, the
issue was about more than just him. The outer defences
had not fallen and the enemy not yet struck, but they
would attack and it would be vicious. Could he do nothing?
Could he allow his country to sink into an abyss of

187

Muhonin violence? He thought of his Sword of Honour and breathed in. He knew full well what the last line of defence was. If necessary, he would stand and fall there.

16

Roger sat in his campaign headquarters with a forced smile. The declaration of the election result was hours away and exit polls showed him trailing substantially. Worse, the media had been unanimous in its praise for the rescue and, despite rumours Bill had forced Derek into supporting the rescue, both had appeared together outside the Kantei. As the Eikkei registered its largest-ever one-day gain, the mood in Roger's team had turned bleak, with only the announcement of the Sunrise Coalition to lift the gloom – and then only briefly, as the rescue had led to backsliding among the party leaders. What if you lose? What if you lose? Helen's voice provided a constant refrain. Even if he won, the Chainsaw Plot hung in the air and the Muhonin insurgency was still poised to move to Stage Two. Unable to take any more, Roger called his team in, putting Tim Hooper onscreen.

"We have finally dispensed with the insanity of liquidation," Tim said. "This is a time for healing, not sadism. We can't punch the economy into recovery."

He gave an oily grin and lapped up the applause.

"Are we really afraid of this hatoha know-nothing?" Roger said. "He trumpets this so-called rescue, but we haven't heard how it's supposed to work. And let's ignore the media-generated hoo-ha about the punch; people can see I was provoked. The polls understate our support. We will win."

He looked at the ashen faces with a sinking feeling. *I have to win. If Bill gets his rescue through the Diet tomorrow, he'll take on the keiretsu – and there are no prizes for guessing who will be "rescued" first.* He thought of the three businessmen, smiled nervously and left.

The crowd outside the Civic Centre was watching "Your 100 Favourite Political Gaffes" on the big screen. Roger stepped out of his car with a big smile and waved, ignoring the protestors behind the barricades.

"Oi, Tyson," shouted a journalist. "Ain'cha gonna thump someone?"

Roger ignored the laughter and strode into the hall where the candidates had gathered, studiously avoiding Tim Hooper, who was strutting around glad-handing. He greeted his rivals and turned to the studio debate on the wall screen.

"Roger Tyson is the only one who speaks the truth," shouted one panellist. "That's why they don't like him."

"He's a firebrand who's found an issue he can exploit," shouted another. "He's only stirring people up, so he can seize power."

"Do you want mealy-mouthed robots?" the first interrupted. "The man's got principle. Love him or loathe him, we know what he stands for."

"Do we?" the second shot back. "All we know is that he wants power."

The call came for the candidates and Roger braced himself as, one by one, they stepped out onto the balcony. His name was announced and he stepped out to a cacophony of noise, cameras flashing away as he raised his fist.

"The time has come for the results for Chilterns South," the announcer said as quiet descended. "Peter Godfrey, Clean Government Party, 14,764 votes; Tim Hooper, Liberal Democratic Party, 189,987 votes; Roger Tyson,

England Renewal Faction, 193,101 votes. I declare Roger Tyson the elected Diet Member for Chilterns South."

Roger punched his fist in the air as boos mixed with cheers. With a V-for-Victory sign, he returned inside and, took one last glimpse at Tim, who was conferring with his aides. Still feeling uncertain, he stood down his helicopter.

"So, it's happened," Peter Godfrey said as Tim skulked off. "We're into uncharted territory now. By the way, you wouldn't happen to know where the small room is?"

Roger nodded and pointed him the way.

The election over, Roger raced back to Central London to meet the opposition leaders. Would they play silly buggers and renege on their agreement? Would they support Bill in the Diet? He looked at the information service in shock. The Eikkei had collapsed and the markets were reeling.

"Neither fundamental nor comprehensive," said one analyst.

"Figures plucked straight from the air," said another.

"What confidence can we have in a rescue based on a few back-of-an-envelope calculations?" added a third.

Roger read the details of the rescue package, feeling light-headed. *There's nothing behind the headline figures. Nothing whatsoever. Bill has no idea how it will work....* His good cheer increased as he saw reporter standing outside the LDP headquarters above the headline "arrests."

"Several senior figures in the Liberal Democratic Party including disgraced aide Jonathan Green and Chief Fundraiser Brian Penney have been arrested following police raids, which have revealed trillions of Yen's worth of further undisclosed assets from English Landholdings. We have this report...."

Roger laughed deliriously. Brian raising the money, Jonathan doling it out, English and Albion washing it clean;

it was Bill's slush fund in operation – and it had been exposed.

Demand a public inquiry, he wrote to Amanda. *The web of corruption is unravelling; all that remains is the spider.*

His anxiety, however, would not go away. As further disturbances broke out in the Outer Suburbs, he thought about the opposition parties. The financial crisis was approaching the critical point and he couldn't have them backing out as they had over liquidation. If he could get them to subscribe to Edmund's manifesto, they would not just be committed to his leadership; they would be locked in to his vision. And yet…. Roger hesitated, remembering his meetings with Edmund. No, they had not resolved their differences. Edmund might have been right about invented traditions, but he was quite wrong about the state. They were facing civil war and if the state failed, the Muhonin would take over. Strong leadership and firm government were essential: thinking the opposite was not just wrong; it was dangerous.

Sunrise Headquarters was busy with activity when Roger arrived. Behind the sleek reception area, people darted through the corridors, while screens blazed out from every room. Edmund was in the lobby area, talking at length to a group of staffers, one hand in his pocket, while he waved the other around. Roger strode up to him, stopping him mid-sentence.

"You're right," Roger interrupted. "We need to finalise our political philosophy. The leaders aren't due here yet. Do you have a minute?"

Edmund nodded without a hint of surprise and sent his team away. Roger led him into a nearby meeting room and sat down.

"I'm no political philosopher, but this idea the state is strong… it's ludicrous. Bill's state's not only weak, it's disintegrating."

Edmund smiled, as if he had been expecting the conversation for some time.

"You're so wrong; the state is strong, very strong. Look at the powers it possesses. Look how it tries to regulate our inner emotional lives. Look—"

"Edmund," Roger cut in, "the problem isn't that it has too many powers, but that it's using them wrongly. There's an 'us and them' and the Government is supposed to be on the side of *us*."

Edmund laughed.

"The Government is only ever on the Government's side. The real 'us and them' is between state and society: the only people that benefit from a strong state are those that hold its powers. Think about it: what's a state servant without a state to serve?"

"We need a strong state." Roger was emphatic. "What, you think we need a weak one? How would we defend ourselves without an army?"

Edmund shook his head.

"Winning wars might suppress the violence, but not the culture that produces it. In any case, who'd ensure your strong state will act in the national interest? Who'd guarantee your army won't turn its guns on its own population?"

"So how do you explain the infighting?"

Edmund remained composed.

"Just because the state is strong doesn't mean it works harmoniously. The state isn't a single body, but a network of agencies, each consisting of rival groups and competing agendas. The stronger the powers, the fiercer the conflict. Take Bill's Sori Daijin's Department. It's as much an attempt to control these rivalries as a bid for absolute power."

"And his desire for a presidency?"

Edmund ignored his question.

"State power is a source of instability, Roger. It's a destabilising force, radiating outwards and tearing society asunder."

"The state has been strong before," Roger protested, "but it never led to disorder. This is different: the state is disintegrating like the rest of society: established structures are collapsing, rules and positions becoming irrelevant. Look at what's happening in the ministries: official position amounts to nothing more than a fancy job title. Everything is there to take: those without power see their opportunity to seize it and those with power do whatever they can to hold onto it. There's no choice. Without a state, nothing is secure: either you have power or you're at the mercy of everybody else. Look around you, Edmund. Order is breaking down."

"No," Edmund said. "You talk about order in terms of harmony, but it can also mean hierarchy. Harmony may be breaking down, but hierarchy isn't. There are two axes of power: the vertical and the horizontal: the vertical is the relationship between state and society, while the horizontal is the relationships within the state and within society. Leviathan maintains its hierarchy by dividing society, keeping the masses down and the elite up, but that depends on our compliance. State power is more than force; it is the authority to command: without obedience, the power to command is worthless. That's why propaganda is so important. It's essential we believe Leviathan serves us when the reality is the opposite. Without our consent, its power vanishes. Order isn't breaking down; it's changing form."

"I don't understand how you can be so blasé about state failure," Roger sighed. "Our country is about to collapse."

"On the contrary," Edmund replied. "This is a normal political episode. History goes through phases of chaos and stability. The disorder will prove transitory and a new

Leviathan will emerge. It won't be the corporate behemoth of England Inc, but a network of shifting alliances, front organisations and proxy groups. It takes decades, centuries even, for civilisations to decline. Rome might not have been built in a day, but it didn't fall overnight either."

Roger hesitated, his certainty gone. He had been wrong about the nation; could he be wrong about the state, too? Could Edmund have the answer? He breathed in as Edmund stood up with a flourish.

"The strength of a nation is its people, not its government. What is an army but the people in arms? Mobilise the people and not only will you defeat Bill, you will defeat the Muhonin, too. Show them we have a vision. Show them we're not replacing one set of politicians with another. Show them we're returning power where it belongs – to them."

He finished his peroration with a proud look, but Roger was far away. The people were on the streets with him, ready to fight to the last. *Of course. It's obvious. The state is weakening us and strengthening our enemies; return power to the people and the problem resolves itself. But it's not enough to give the lion its roar; we must give it its claws, too. With the people free, the Muhonin and furigans will be swept aside. A leader plus a vision equals victory.* He beamed at Edmund as reception announced the arrival of the party leaders.

Edmund and Roger bowed as they entered in procession. Next to a haughty-looking Margaret Richards was Alan Barker, the urbane elder statesman from the New Frontier Party, Frederick Field, the flamboyant eccentric from the New England Party and the austere stick-like figure of Brian Collingwood of the Pioneer Party.

"Welcome to the Sunrise Coalition," Margaret said, resplendent in her jewellery. "We're agreed: Roger will be Sori Daijin, Brian will be Deputy, I'll take Finance, Alan the

Interior, Frederick Defence and Edmund Justice. Amanda, I've pencilled you in for Education."

They nodded in agreement.

"Before we proceed," Brian said, "I'd like it noted that, while I might have agreed to liquidation in principle, I have grave reservations about opposing a rescue. If we block this rescue, the effects could be catastrophic. We're months away from taking office; there'd be nothing we could do."

"Collingwood San," Roger said, "if Bill gets his rescue through the Diet, we will never take office."

Brian gave him a cold look.

"While these tactical considerations are important," Edmund said, "we must not lose sight of our goal. We need to agree our manifesto."

"Poppycock," Frederick said. "No-one reads the blasted things. They just want us to give Bill a good kicking."

"I agree," Brian added. "Forget this Boy Scout stuff. Are we serious about winning?"

Roger banged the table.

"This is not the national Sumo Championships where winning is all that counts. We're here to speak for England: I insist on Edmund's programme."

Edmund looked on proudly as Amanda handed round the document for signing.

"Don't think you can push us around, Tyson," Brian said. "This coalition isn't a vehicle for your personal ambitions. Our support is not unconditional."

He signed the document and pushed it back to Amanda, his eyes fixed on Roger.

As the party leaders left, Roger called Margaret back. She turned around, her tall figure silhouetted in the doorway.

"Richards San, what do you know about Chainsaw?"

"It's a disgrace," she said. "There's no hard evidence of any wrongdoing. Everything they've presented has been electronic and could easily have been tampered with or forged."

"We need to free those officers," Roger said.

"We would certainly support any campaign for their release," Margaret replied. "You are well known for your integrity. If you were to champion their cause, it would galvanise the public."

"I need your public support," he said.

"I'm afraid I can't," she said. "We know the charges are false, but our supporters are concerned. We can't afford to be accused of siding with them until their innocence can be demonstrated. Politically, it's too dangerous."

With a businesslike smile, she left.

Roger stood alone, filled with mistrust, doubtful they would even vote with him against Bill's rescue. He looked again at the information service. English and Albion had announced they would need an extension of funding and panic was spreading. Chain reactions, cascading defaults, mass bankruptcies, a collapse of the keiretsu sector; fear fed upon fear as markets seized up. As polls showed public support for a bailout, Roger could hear his own warning to Bill: the economy could collapse before an election could be held. He paused as a message arrived from Ann Thomas. The police technical team had been back. A minor detail, they had said, nothing more. Roger breathed in, wondering if the election victory were nothing more than a reprieve. The Chainsaw arrests, the police investigation and the demands for a public inquiry were all of a piece: his enemies were closing in, slowly weaving them into their plot. Of course, the police had found nothing. They didn't need to. They would manufacture whatever evidence they needed.

He put on his coat with a determined pout and prepared to go. As he turned to leave, he caught the news. General Wheeler had been charged with treason.

17

A strange calm had descended ahead of the vote. The widespread fear that English and Albion would bring down the economy if the rescue were blocked was matched by a deeper fear of what might happen should the state default. English and Albion might be large, but the state was far larger. People were now asking themselves: could it really fail?

Roger strode past the cameras with a resolute frown and entered a packed House of Representatives, his fist held aloft as his opponents booed. Gone was the clubbishness Amanda had spoken of; the scene now resembled a Roman amphitheatre ahead of the games. Members sat around the semi-circle, gesticulating and shouting insults, their faces red with fury. Roger smiled to himself, thinking of Brian Penney and Jonathan Green. Should English and Albion fall, many Diet Members would be falling with them.

The hubbub subsided and Roger sat down to jeers from the Gang of Six. Ignoring them, he looked at the mock traditional oak-panelled walls and the huge English flags either side of the Speaker's box, then eyeballed Bill and Derek opposite, who both studiously looked away.

"Welcome to your first day in the House," Edmund said, coming over with Amanda.

"It'll be tight," she added. "If all our members vote against, we'll win, but Bill will try to threaten the waverers. They're scared they'll cop the blame for any recession."

"We know their dirt," Roger said. "They'll find their backbones."

The speaker ascended to his box and the House went quiet.

"This week has seen unprecedented turmoil," he said, tugging his lapels. "After decades of prosperity, long-established names have disappeared as once-mighty kaishas have come crashing down, leaving ordinary people fearing for their futures. We have gathered today in solemn session to vote on the Government's Comprehensive Rescue Bill. I urge all Honourable Members of the National Diet to put aside petty differences and think of the country as we debate these momentous events. The Sori Daijin will address the House."

He sat down with great pomp as Bill rose from his seat.

"My Right Honourable friends, we have seen unprecedented turmoil with kaishas in trouble and the economy under strain. This Government has successfully prevented these problems from getting out of control and today we set out a plan to stabilise the economy and restore prosperity. We do not believe in letting business flounder and fail. With this Comprehensive Rescue Bill, we will do whatever is necessary to put the economy back on track."

Roger watched as Bill launched into flights of rhetoric as cries of "never standing idly by" and "guaranteeing prosperity" were punctuated by applause from his party. Sunrise members however sat mute.

"This is pathetic," Roger whispered to Amanda. "They should be heckling."

"I therefore ask every member of this House," Bill concluded, "to look in their hearts and do what's right, not just to help families fearing for the livelihoods, but also to give our businesses a fighting chance. Let us not give in to the voices of despair, let us put our names to this bill and take pride in ensuring our future prosperity."

There was loud applause from the Government benches. Derek had leaned over with a grin and whispered something to Bill, who nodded and laughed.

"Typical Bill," Edmund grumbled. "All style and no substance."

The speaker then opened the floor to debate and a Diet Member in a checked jacket stood up.

"In normal times," he puffed, "I would savage such a feeble plan, but these are not normal times and a feeble plan is better than none whatsoever. I therefore suggest we make the best of a bad job, because otherwise that's the only job there'll be."

The House nodded in agreement.

"Rubbish," Roger shouted.

As the debate continued, Bill's supporters stood up one after the other to attack saboteurs for seeking to destroy the economy for political gain, while the opposition benches remained subdued. While a few criticised the plan's vagueness, none was willing to speak against it. Boiling with rage, Roger stood up and flourished his printout.

"Speaker San, as a famous person once said, I have in my hand a piece of paper – only this paper is a damning indictment of the financial management of this country. I'm talking about the government accounts. The official figures may look healthy, but hidden from view are trillions upon trillions of bad investments. Put them back and the reality is a gaping deficit and gargantuan debt. If this sounds familiar, it is. It's exactly the same mess the keiretsu are in. This rescue is an irresponsible chimera, committing us to spend money that does not exist. If you put your name to it, you will be responsible for the ruination of the land."

"Lies," shouted Paul Fox. "This is an artificial crisis you created. You're trying to force us into recession."

"Order, order," shouted the Speaker.

"I urge you all to vote against this dangerous gamble," Roger continued. "We have to extricate ourselves from the mire, not plunge in deeper."

He sat down to loud applause, including a few "hear hears." He didn't look round, but one of the voices sounded like Edmund.

The Speaker declared the debate closed and the electronic pads rose from the floor as the loudspeakers sounded the Division Bell.

Government's Comprehensive Rescue Bill – Accept / Decline

Roger selected "decline" and held his breath.

"The votes have been cast," the speaker said. "The noes have defeated the ayes 261 to 250. The Government has been defeated."

There were gasps as he said the words. Even Bill looked stunned. Graham Hough stood up and pointed his finger at Roger.

"This is sabotage. Look behind the patriotic rhetoric; this is a man who seeks power at any costs. He might pretend to be England's saviour, but his kamikaze politics will bring about this country's destruction."

The Diet bar was full of nervous chatter as the session closed. Roger, Edmund and Amanda stood on the riverside balcony, full of excitement as onscreen commentators talked frantically about the implications of the defeat. Inside, he could see the Ministers of Health, Agriculture, and Environment on the leather sofas with Desmond Grey and Paul Fox beside them, all highly agitated. Desmond stopped and looked around before continuing. Roger ordered a beer and slipped behind a wall.

"Nobody deserves to be Figure of Hate more," a voice said. "He's no outsider, he's at the heart of all that's bad in this country."

"MEPTI involvement in creating Greenwood was always a cover for the deep state," a second added. "Tyson has never even left the military."

"Is it any coincidence there's nothing on him when he's erased all trace of his criminal past?" the first replied.

"Imagine if he succeeded?" a soft female voice said. "He must be prosecuted."

"I wouldn't worry," a mellifluous voice said. "He'll be exposed."

Roger strained to hear what they were saying, but gave up as the conversation was lost in the ambient noise.

It was dark when he left the Diet and the Government's defeat dominated the news. While his coalition colleagues were euphoric, panic was turning into paralysis. The Eikkei had nosedived and money markets closed down altogether, while businesses were warning of grave troubles ahead.

"Plan A has been voted down," a commentator said, "but we have no Plan B. We're hurtling towards a catastrophe."

Roger rested his head on the seat and stared upwards at the night sky. Despite his victory, he felt restless. There would have to be a vote of no confidence before a general election could be called and time was tight, but there was something else. Chainsaw. Why was Bill proceeding so slowly? And why hadn't the Muhonin insurgency moved to Stage Two? Were they waiting for Bill to purge the military? The words "temporary alliances," "proxy forces" and "Leviathan" no longer sounded absurd. Roger closed his eyes, trying to blot out the enveloping darkness. *There's more to appeasement than weakness. If Bill sees me as his enemy, he must see the Muhonin as his allies. Why else would he stop people talking about them?*

As he drifted down the expressway, the Diet vote faded into the background. Police investigations, arms to paramilitaries, the death of Valerie Whittaker; Roger let the words wash over him. *They're afraid. They lost over the rescue and they know they'll lose a vote of no confidence. Attacking me with lies won't prevent their collusion from coming out... Yes, that's why they're waiting. They're preparing for defeat... annul the election... a coup. If Bill succeeds, the insurgency moves to Stage Two.*

He dimmed the lights and dozed off as the limo cruised down the expressway, the illuminated lane markings blurring into long smears of silver. A streak of grey to his right caught his peripheral vision; a large car was in front of him. He sat up alert, looking right, left and rear. He was boxed in. A man in the car behind. He was being watched. Seconds later, the cars were gone and the traffic back to normal. His heart racing and his breathing heavy, he tried to remove a handkerchief from his pocket, but his hands were shaking and his cuffs soaked with sweat. Whatever lay inside the innermost box, someone was determined to ensure it would remain shut.

18

Roger and Amanda watched as the Eikkei plunged before them. English Financial and Albion Investments had filed for bankruptcy and many other kaishas were on the verge of collapse. In the space of a week, the economy had come to a halt: factories had closed, people laid off and shops stripped bare. Drivers rioted outside vehicle recharging points, while criminal gangs gunned down businessmen. Roger looked at Amanda in despair. Though both had predicted the country would become ungovernable, neither had predicted it would happen so fast.

"Does anyone honestly think Bill's rescue would have stopped this?" he said.

She looked back despondently as a group of masked men calling themselves the Metal-zoku Defenders announced the formation a new militia, ransacking a house and driving out the owners. The public unveiling of Roger as leader of the Sunrise Coalition seemed lost amidst the chaos.

"We're at a historic moment," he told a press conference. "We have a choice: more No Action Talk Only or decisive action."

The words now sounded empty. As they left for the Diet, the problems seemed insurmountable.

The House of Representatives was in a fractious mood. Roger entered to boos and whistles from the Government benches, while opposition members shouted their approval. Margaret leant over as he sat down, glancing over to a tense-looking Bill with a subdued Derek sitting nervously beside him.

"Look at them, the cowards," she said. "They know they'll lose."

"Order," called the Speaker.

"Order?" yelled a minister. "This man caused a recession."

There were shouts of "rubbish" and "no, you did" from the Sunrise members, leading to further shouts of "Nastiness" from the Government benches. The Speaker sounded the electronic gong and the brouhaha died down.

"The Right Honourable Member for York North," he said, "has called a motion of no confidence in the

Government. If sustained, the Diet will be dissolved and a general election called. We are living in times of historic turbulence and I call on everybody to treat this with the utmost gravity."

He sat down with a flourish, but the atmosphere soon grew charged. Roger watched as a Diet Member threw a paper dart at a long-standing rival, hitting him on the forehead. His rival lunged at him, while colleagues tried to hold him back.

"Order! Order!"

The Speaker sounded the gong repeatedly, but the members were shouting "Fight! Fight! Fight!" After some merriment, the errant Diet Members were hauled back to their seats and debate resumed.

"The Leader of the Opposition will speak next," he said. Roger stood up.

"Speaker San, if there was ever a prize for shooting the messenger, then surely my Right Honourable colleagues in the Government would win."

This time, the jeers were muted.

"For years, I warned of a crash, but no-one listened. I put forward a plan to deflate the bubble, but it was rejected. I pointed out the perils of a flawed rescue plan, but the Government had no Plan B. So, I ask you, who is responsible for this disaster? There has only been one Government in office for the last ten years. It must go."

Roger sat down to cheers from the opposition benches. There was a strange hush as Bill prepared to speak, looking uncharacteristically flustered.

"Speaker San, nobody has done more to aid the recovery than us. However, rather than play a constructive role in managing this crisis, the opposition has chosen to play politics. Are we to trust a rag-tag coalition that sees national emergencies as a chance for power? Only one party has any experience of governing the country and it would be madness to gamble our future on this bunch of spivs."

Bill sat down to muted cheers, while his opponents blew raspberries.

"Feeble," Roger whispered to Margaret.

"He's lost it," she replied.

The Division Bell sounded and Diet Members placed their hands on the electronic pads in front of them.

Confidence in the Government – Yes / No

Roger selected "no" and waited. The result appeared and Diet Members stared at the screen: the Government had been defeated. Not only would there be an election, for the first time in over fifty years the Liberal Democratic Party could lose office. Margaret looked to Roger, her manner suddenly hesitant.

"We're being blamed for the recession and the disorder," she said. "Do you honestly think we can win?"

"They'll blame us for anything," he said. "Recession was unavoidable and the unrest is containable. As long as the barracks stay quiet, we're fine."

She nodded weakly and took her leave.

Amanda was already at Sunrise Headquarters when he arrived. She grinned and gave him a big hug.

"I've prepared some material from the last election," she said. "It'll give you an idea how Bill operates."

She selected a film of a visit to a residential care home in Yorkshire Prefecture where a smiling Bill met cheerful residents.

"Look at that man."

She paused the film and zoomed in on a jolly grey-haired man relaxing in an armchair.

"Arthur Morris," she said. "A long-time party supporter; his family are friends of Bill. He's never been a resident of this or any other home."

She moved on to a second film: Bill at a public Q&A session. She stopped him, mid-gesture, right arm outstretched, left hand clenched tight. Dressed in a dark suit, he cut an imposing figure.

"The questions were planted in advance," she said. "The guests: all his supporters. Not a single member of the public."

"What happens at public events he cannot rig?"

She rolled through a series of clips, stopping at one marked "public questions" and pressing play.

"Is it true, Sori Daijin," a journalist asked, "that reform of the House of Councillors has made it easier for you to appoint your own supporters?"

Bill smiled as though the question had not been asked and a dance troupe ran on stage, screening him off from the audience as rock music blared out.

"Sori Daijin," the journalist said, trying to make herself heard, "will you answer the question?"

Bill waved and left the stage while stocky sokaiya in grey suits surrounded the audience, clapping in unison and shouting, "Let's move things on."

"That's how he constructs his image," she said. "But it's the way he attacks his opponents we need to be wary of."

She played through several clips of Bill being greeted by flag-waving crowds, as he won elections, made announcements or simply emerged from his car.

"I hardly need say they're all stooges," she said. "Any real person to stray too near would have been pushed out by his sokaiya. Now look how his opponents are always dogged by protestors. Notice how it's the same people every time. See how their placards are identical – all planned in advance."

Roger watched as opposition politicians were heckled as they left home, entered the Diet and attended public events.

"We can expect much, much worse. You're seen as controversial, so he could incite troublemakers to riot and bingo! You're inflaming tensions."

She selected another film.

"This was taken outside the home of a small business-man, who had funded literature critical of Bill."

Through the fuzzy camera work and ambient noise, a crowd of people shouting and waving their fists could be made out. The camera jerked upwards as the house was firebombed.

"Freeze the screen," Roger said, pointing to a tall man with a bright red ear-to-ear Mohican. "I recognise that man. Who is he?"

Amanda called over Head of Political Intelligence, Terry Page.

"Terry, could you find out who this is, kudasai?"

Roger sat back, looking at the screen.

"Yes, I remember you: 'We don't want your nationalism or military dictatorship.' So, you're a professional trouble-maker."

Terry hurried back with a small dossier.

"Charles Bonham," he said. "He has quite a history. Eton and Oxford educated, comes from a wealthy landowning family. He used his family finances to support various Aristo-zoku groups before switching to ultra-hatoha causes. He's a core agitator, totally devoted to the cause and utterly ruthless. Former comrades described him as being as dangerous to friends as the enemy. It's no secret his aim is to overthrow the government."

"And he has been seen with known Muhonin terror-ists," Amanda said, studying a photograph.

"Could Bill declare a state of emergency before the election?" Roger said.

"We can't discount it," Terry said. "Faced with defeat, he could always conjure up a dramatic last-minute revelation and have it suspended."

"Unlikely" Amanda interjected. "Far too risky. He has to be seen to win fairly. There's a much greater danger of getting dragged into Bill and Derek's feud."

"I don't see why that should concern us," Roger said.

"Losing two votes in the Diet has dented Bill's leadership badly," she said, "but the financial crisis has hurt Derek, too. Bill's worried because he knows Derek will try to oust him and Derek's sulking because he knows his job's on the line. If Bill were to lose the election, Derek would be sure to attempt a second shot at the leadership."

"Derek as party leader?" Roger said. "I wouldn't have thought he had much chance."

"He doesn't," Terry replied. "Not that it's ever stopped him trying."

"Derek's never forgiven Bill for winning the leadership," Amanda added, "and Bill doesn't trust Derek after running against him. Hiring you would solve two problems at once: eliminating their main rival and splitting the coalition. That's why Bill wanted you in the Naikaku before and that's why he'll try again now. Derek's clumsy – you can deal with him; but Bill's cunning – he'll try to lure you away from Sunrise with false promises, while attacking you via the Gang of Six. He'll step in as your protector and make you dependent on his support, but the moment his position is safe, you're dead. Nastiness, extremist, Chainsaw, you'll get the lot. He's playing the same game with Jane, dangling gongs in front of her daddy's nose. She thinks you'll lose and is planning to sell you out, but once you're gone, he no longer needs her either. Her family may be ruthless, but they lack political nous."

She gave Roger a smile as Terry put the sound up on the media screen.

"It started as a tawdry political scandal, but today it developed into something more serious with the arrest of Shacho of Mouken Security, Darren Phillips. Phillips San stated that former Bill Harris aide Jonathan Green had approached him to provide security for the Sori Daijin and had made a number of payments to the kaisha. He also confirmed that Mouken, which is affiliated to English Financial, had hired yakuza members to provide sokaiya to 'deal with troublemakers' and run 'special missions' against political opponents. Green San has denied any wrongdoing, stating he hired Mouken in good faith, but it is the naming of Bill Harris that raises the most questions. What did he know? Did he too receive payments from English Landholdings? It promises to be a very tricky few days for the Sori Daijin."

Roger looked up, noticing something else: Jaxxi had been arrested. Quickly, he ran through the database. Amidst lurid stories of furigan violence, fast cars and harems, one fact stood out: rival ganglords had been planning a joint plex war to muscle in on his turf. He looked at the aerial shots of his mansion with its fortress-like perimeter wall and gigantic statues of him dominating his harem in a multitude of sexual positions. Jaxxi's furigan empire was as overextended as those of English and Albion and for precisely the same reason: they were two aspects of the same phenomenon. What money had been sent his way? What services had he rendered in return?

As he mulled over the implications, a call arrived from the Office of the Sori Daijin. Roger disappeared to a quiet room before answering.

"Congratulations on a bravura performance," Bill said. "Now the showbiz is over, let's get down to the real business. This is a national emergency and only a national government can deal with it. Let's put our differences aside and work together for the common good: a joint LDP-Sunrise government with you as Fuku Sori Daijin. You can head up a Commission for the Economy with responsibility for economic planning and full authority to implement your Restructuring Plan. It would be in all our interests."

"Why should I prop up your premiership?" Roger said.

"You know the score," Bill said. "Like the shacho of a keiretsu, the Sori Daijin's power is more symbolic than real. Politics has been hijacked by the Action Groups. They're the ones setting the agenda. The public may not always like what they do, but as long as they support their principles, we have to accept their *faits accomplis* or lose public support. The party's terrified of them – yours too – but, without your support, there's little I can do."

"Stand up to them," Roger said. "Show them you won't be bullied. People respect strength."

"If only it were that easy," Bill said. "I've been Sori Daijin for ten years and there are some who think that's ten years too many. Hough and his friends are fronts for some powerful ultra-hatoha interests – people who want you dead. If I opposed the Political Consensus, they'd find a rival to run against me and before you know it, there'd be a leadership contest. I'd be retired and you'd be attacked. The ultras want to push the party further in a hatoha direction and I'm all that's stopping them. I barred them from making you Figure of Hate, but I can't do that if I'm deposed. Don't expect a fair fight, Roger: to them, you are Nastiness and nothing would be too bad. They wouldn't hesitate to hand you over to the Muhonin."

"You can't scare me, Harris San," Roger laughed. "The Action Groups are a tiny minority. People wholeheartedly detest the Political Consensus and now they can vote against it."

Bill's voice turned serious.

"You won a Diet vote, that's all. Even if you win this election, Sunrise won't last. The rivalry between your parties is greater than the rivalry between our factions. Dennis told you about Chainsaw. Brian and Margaret know they could never beat us in a straight fight, but if the Self Defence Forces did the heavy lifting... maybe they could break up the LDP, maybe they could draft a new constitution. By the time fresh elections could be held, they'd hold the advantage. All they lack is a high-profile figure who could land some punches and take the flak: someone plausible with no backing, someone they could dispense with. It won't be pretty, but then politics never is. As for Amanda, I've heard her sob story and it isn't true. She knows there's a place for her in the Naikaku, but she refuses to accept she's not Minister of Finance material. She's been in contact with Jim the whole time she's been speaking to you. She's got her exit route prepared."

"It's easy to cast aspersions."

"When will you see it?" Bill was emphatic. "I'm not your enemy. We both want a strong state and a harmonious society; a patriotic nation where people feel proud to be English. No more Niceness or Nastiness; a return to England Inc. We can stop the Political Consensus, but we must work together. The time is coming for me to stand down and my successor must be someone the public respects. With my support, you can be the next Sori Daijin."

Roger hesitated. There was no grin and no emoting, just a concerned-looking man making a serious proposal. *A national government? Does he need my support against Derek that badly? Could he be telling the truth?* He looked at him again and bit his lip.

"There will be no deals," he said. "Sayonara."

Roger sped down the North Circular Expressway, his head thudding. He couldn't trust his coalition partners, yet he couldn't mistrust his opponents, either. If someone was behind Bill, they could also be behind his allies – and, if Bill were a front man, then his offer might be sincere. Were his Sunrise allies his enemies? Were they behind Chainsaw? Was there anyone he could trust? He looked at the twelve-lane chasm as it scythed through a once-fashionable inner suburbia. So far, Chainsaw existed only on paper, but reality was being made to follow the script. As Mark had said, fabricated plots didn't exist just to deceive the public; they existed to ensnare people. If a network of plotters didn't exist, one would be created. The trap would be set and the victims lured in. An unguarded comment, a rash action; the instant they took the bait, they were finished – they had incriminated themselves and would forever be guilty. Roger thought of Oliver Wells, John Wheeler, the arrested officers and the police investigation. The plot had been concocted and hatched; all that remained was for it to be discovered and suppressed. Then Chainsaw would be complete: fantasy would become reality and fake become fact.

Roger stared ahead bleakly. No, Bill didn't need his support. He was playing on his suspicions, trying to undermine his resolve and make him doubt himself. Amanda was too optimistic. It might be unpalatable, but a coup could not be discounted. He turned to the news, feeling worried. On one screen, a Sori Daijin's personal bodyguard was announced; on another, a mob of Rugian-zoku marched down a street, kicking in windows and torching vehicles.

"We don't want Gepid-zoku scum in our neighbour-hood," shouted a masked man.

"We're subjected to intimidation," a Gepid Party repre-sentative shouted in response, "but the police don't do nuffink."

Roger looked outside with despair. *It's hopeless. While the politicians scheme, the country is dying. No coup can prevent this financial-criminal bubble from bursting. How long before guns and bombs replace knives and baseball bats? Bill might be master of Nagata-Cho, manufacturing disinformation with impunity, but outside anarchy reigns. We're like a routed army, every person for themselves. No, it's worse: routed armies don't turn their fire on each other – we're regressing to a primitive state. Tribal parties and militias, it's a war of all against all. The more the militias attack, the more people turn to them for defence, and the more people turn to them for defence, the more they attack – if this goes on any longer, this election will be the last.* He closed his eyes, wanting to cry. Yet, amidst the chaos, he felt a renewed strength. He thought of Sakura Military Academy and the Sword of Honour, the Chrysanthemum Bridge and Greenwood's rise to power. The Kantei was before him and the people were cheering. He was Sori Daijin, national hero; the new Churchill. *Never give in! Never give in!* He opened his eyes, his fists clenched tight. *Have faith, Tyson. Fads are transient, but the nation is real. People feel no affinity for the Lifestyle Groups. When they see their country in peril, they will remember their true identity. The militia? A handful of troublemakers who will be crushed. Bill? You've defeated him twice and will defeat him again. You are the nation. You are the saviour. This is your hour, Tyson. Take no prisoners.*

The streetlights blurred into the night sky as he hurtled down the empty expressway, the media screen burbling in the background. His eyes were half shut when flashing images on the media screen brought him to. Cars on fire, bombs exploding, mobs on the rampage; the violence had spread to the barracks.

19

The rioting quickly spread from one complex to another until the entire country was ablaze. Roger watched as riot police marched forward behind shields, batons held ready as a screaming mob hurled stones at them. As they advanced, the mob ran off into the maze of buildings and two concrete slabs were dropped from the upper walkways, followed by a short burst of gunfire. Three policemen were dead and a dozen injured. He changed channel. A bullet-ridden corpse sprawled across the pavement in a pool of blood; another businessman gunned down. He changed channel again. Eikoku Sangyo had filed for bankruptcy. He peered out, where he could hear a pair of election drones jostling for position.

"Don't let them in," shrilled the first. "Vote Niceness not Nastiness." It was quickly hustled aside by the second, which screamed, "Kick them out. Vote Patriotism, not Treachery," before the first fought back with, "Many Lifestyle Groups; one Niceness."

Roger turned away in disgust. *What exactly are we contesting? The economy's crashed, kaishas are failing and business assets are disappearing into the black market. The keiretsu and ministries largely exist in name only and criminals are killing each other. Bill has ceded control on the ground to the gangs and militia and now that power is theirs. The result? We only rule with their consent. Damn! Has it become irrecoverable?* He looked around, aware someone was hovering behind him. Margaret was standing in the doorway, her arms folded.

"What's this about a visit to the barracks? Are you trying to lose us the election?"

"We're being timid," Roger said. "People see us and think more of the same."

He put on Bill's latest election diary.

"Day 23," Bill said to camera in his pyjamas. "You know; however long you've done this job, you never stop learning. I've heard your concerns and I'm struck by how much Niceness there is. We're all worried by the violence, yet there's no appetite for Nastiness. I'm proud of that, I can tell you. Oyasumi Nasai." He smiled and turned the camera off with a wink.

Roger switched to the Subversive Service.

"The downtrodden rise up," shouted a masked commentator as riot police pulled back under a hail of petrol bombs. "The complexes will be liberated! The Great Uprising will prevail!"

"The visit stays," Roger said.

Margaret stormed out, unable to contain her rage. As the intercom lit up, Roger allowed himself a brief smile.

"I have a gentleman in the briefing room," the receptionist said. "He didn't give a name; says it's a private matter. He seemed very nervous."

Roger dashed over to find a slim, bespectacled man in his late thirties sitting deep in thought.

"Make this quick," Roger said.

"Major Eric Phipps, army intelligence," the man said. "It's about Chainsaw."

Roger sat down.

"You're in great danger," Phipps said. "The Sori Daijin regards a Sunrise victory as a greater threat than a Muhonin insurgency. They've struck a deal. In return for their support, he's agreed to restructure the Self Defence Forces."

"A purge?"

Phipps nodded.

"Chainsaw's the start. The Sori Daijin has many supporters inside the Muhonin and privately he's more than sympathetic – there's talk he'll convert once the election's over."

"Major Phipps," Roger said, "this is all very interesting, but what evidence do you have?"

"Look into Mouken Security. It's a front for the same criminal activities as Grey Ninja. Plausible deniability. Some very senior figures are involved." He breathed in. "I need your help, Tyson San. I'm being pressured to testify against my fellow officers. I can't do anything on my own, but with your support Chainsaw can be stopped. The Muhonin are planning a terrorist spectacular so Bill can declare a state of emergency. Check out the Subversive Service: hundreds of furigans have been released from prison in advance. Colonel Alexander was killed because they considered him a threat and you will be too. If you don't act now there will be no election. Will you assist me?"

Professor Rowe was standing by the armoured transport vehicle as Roger arrived, surrounded by security officers.

"This is unbelievably foolish," she said. "What if you're kidnapped?"

"Let's just get on with it," he said as the door shut.

They moved off, flanked by police escorts with motor-cycle outriders.

"Okay, the basics," she breathed out. "Never make sustained eye contact: that would be interpreted as hostile. Adopt a neutral position: when unknown furigans meet, both parties look down at the ground while speaking. Use simple language, never long or complicated words. First, they don't understand. Second, they'll think you're patronising them. But never act or talk like them either. You aren't their friend and pretending to be like them will only invite derision. Be confident and strong; they respect strength. You are the representative of the English State and, however much they hate it, they depend on it, so don't be cowed. Never allow them to feel they're the boss: once you've lost their respect, they become unruly and that's when things become dangerous. Don't push them around, but don't be pushed around either."

She selected some images from her gallery: a woman with metal clad to her face like a robot; a chubby teenage girl in leggings with a rifle slung over her shoulder; an old man with shaved head, warpaint and military-style fatigues; and a man wearing a pair of Y-fronts as a hat.

"Furigan culture is highly ephemeral. There are however some standard terms. Gangs are 'staffs,' the bigger ones 'armies.' The barracks are the 'plexes,' while the middle classes are 'Barries' and 'Brendas.' To attend school or have a job is 'actin' barry' – the lowest of the low – and to call someone Barry is a major insult. Furigans incidentally have no collective term for themselves: the word 'furigan' means nothing to them and, apart from the police, they have little conception of the outside world. Although they hate 'the Mollies,' they retain a residual fear, so avoid any reference to anything beyond the complex."

She sat back and Roger checked the news. Bill had moved marginally ahead, while *The Morning News* covered Roger's visit with a photograph of him talking to Helen.

If proof were needed of Roger Tyson's malign nature, it's his choice of Helen Rowe as his chief advisor. A persistent advocate of authoritarian government, she is the spiritual leader of Chainsaw, her talk of law and order a cloak for punitive measures against those she dis-approves of. Most shockingly, not only does she hate the Helpless, she thinks they are less than human. We should be very afraid. They intend the total dehumanisation of society.

"I never said any of that," she scowled. "Criticise the Political Consensus and they paint you as an extremist."

She looked at him, but he wasn't listening. His eyes were fixed on news that bomb-making equipment had been found in a lock up on an industrial estate.

The police radio crackled in the background as they approached the checkpoint. A police officer waved them onto a side lane with anti-vehicle ditches either side and they entered the inspection hangar in single file. Once in, the steel doors slammed shut and the search bay inspection lights came on, casting the vehicles in a harsh glare. Head of Security, Commander Damien Lucas, emerged from behind the blast wall and tapped on the window.

"Sorry about this, sir," he said, climbing in. "We've had to upgrade the checkpoint. Furigans would drive straight through the older barriers."

The green light came on and the exit shutters rose, the lights staying on long enough to reveal large dents as they drove on to the forward secure zone.

Roger's campaign team was waiting with Complex Manager, John Milward, a tired-looking man in corduroy trousers and a red cardigan, while police guarded the route through the complex, which had been cordoned off with metal barriers. Roger held his nose as a pungent smell of bad eggs hung in the atmosphere, wafted along by gusts of warm air. So this was the barracks. He looked up at the towers, struck by how different they appeared from below. Chipped concrete and rotting window frames scarred the façades, while the balconies were stuffed with bikes, fridges and washing machines. On the lowest levels, the windows and doors were shuttered like the checkpoint and the walls coated with crude images of stick men, swear words and gibberish. *Fukkof, Kunt* and *Dikhed* overlaid *Pfsknk, grrb* and *srkrrbvgl*, while the ground was concealed beneath a sea of beer cans, food packaging and putrefying rubbish.

"We ripped up the pavements," Commander Lucas said, "to stop them from being used as missiles. The yobbos you'll meet today are very junior and shouldn't give you much trouble."

They stopped in the main square beside a desolate play area with an overpowering smell of cannabis. In one corner, a couple ate synthetic chicken in the gutter while a solitary man urinated against the heating duct next to them, his free hand holding up a communicator so he could maintain a loud video conversation.

"Domo arigatou, Commander," Roger bellowed as a helicopter patrolled overhead. "Get your team to find what they can."

Four teenage furigans were waiting on electro-bikes alongside four social workers, while a handful of their peers loitered around.

"They have bikes," Professor Rowe pointed out, "and are showing only a little of their underpants, which indicates low rank."

The crew started filming as John stepped forward and bowed.

"Tyson San," he said. "Skaz, Skud, Mbop and Hostesse."

The furigans grunted. Roger looked at their pudgy faces and brightly coloured clothes, festooned with logos and designer labels. The boys wore jackets several sizes too big with coat hangers sown into the shoulders, while the girl wore a catsuit with a cut away midriff from which a flabby stomach bulged.

"I'd like to ask you about life in Deer Park," Roger said, looking down as instructed. "How do you find it?"

"Wochawonna na fo?" said Skaz, spitting at the floor. "Yo don do nuffin fo us. Yo give us nuffin. How mah gonna fid mahseff if yo don give mi munni?"

A social worker leant over towards Roger.

"His allowance was cut last week," he whispered. "He was caught shoplifting."

He turned to the other three, still looking at the floor.

"What makes people want to join a staff?"

There was a pause.

"Yo don' give us nuffin to do," Skud said, "so peepul join staff like an get stuff an like coz we get give no nuffink."

"No nuffink," added Hostesse.

"We shod get give mo," Mbop said.

"Push them a bit," Angela said. "This is too bland. Our supporters want to see you getting tough."

Roger shooed her away.

"We're proposing a training scheme—"

"Wah shod I av to do Barry an Brenda wok," Skaz said. "Ah don wanna be no loya owa kaantant. Yo shod give us proper job like ganglord o porn-star."

"O celeb diva," Hostesse added.

"So, what would you like to see the Government provide?"

The four started fidgeting. There was a prolonged pause.

"Wocha terrogatin us fo?" Skaz yelled. "You fick o sumfin?"

He squared up to Roger, who stood his ground.

"Yo fick, aincha?"

Two large policemen moved either side of him and swaggered back to his bike with a cocky leer, punching fists with the others who folded their arms and adopted passive-aggressive expressions.

"Barry," Skud said, spitting in Roger's direction.

"Okay, interview over," Angela said.

The cameras stopped filming and the security guards shepherded the furigans out of the way.

"Ignorant little shits," Roger muttered as they continued down the secure route.

"They're good kids really," John said. "They just find it hard to express themselves."

They walked past grey ventilation shafts and vandalised ancillary buildings before entering Fibua House. Roger looked at the debris-strewn hallway and burnt-out concierge, thinking of Stalingrad.

"The lifts are working," John said. "Allow me."

He pressed the up button and the sound of the machinery whirred into life.

"The search team hasn't found anything related," Commander Lucas whispered.

"Keep looking," he murmured.

They reached the twenty-eighth floor and entered a cramped corridor of steel doors and battered walls. The lights were smashed and broken glass littered the floor, poking through mouldering food packaging.

"This won't end up another fiasco, will it?" Roger whispered to Angela.

"It'll be fine," she replied. "She's lovely."

John stood in front of the video identification and after a brief wait the door opened.

Violet Walsh, a retired nurse from Jamaica, greeted the group with a cheery smile, which broadened into a beam when she saw Roger.

"Come in," she said, her eyes sparkling behind her glasses.

"Thank you for inviting us into your home, Walsh San."

"It's my privilege," she laughed. "We don't get many visitors in these parts, never mind a Diet Member. Do take a seat, kudasai."

Roger bowed as she showed him to a seat opposite the ikebana display. Thin and of medium height, she had scarcely a wrinkle on her face, giving her a youthful appearance.

"I was told that you like lapsang souchong," she said, returning with a china tea set. "I bought some especially for you, although if you don't mind my sayin' so, I don't much care for it myself."

Roger took a sip as she sat down, looking at the large armchairs arranged around a wooden coffee table and the spotless carpet.

"I understand you're the oldest resident in this block," he said. "You've lived here forty-two years, if I'm not mistaken."

"You know your facts," she said. "I'd have moved but I never won the lottery."

"So, how do you find life here?"

"It is just fine, so long as you don't go out late." She looked at the picture of her three grown-up children and a tinge of melancholy entered her voice. "I just consider myself fortunate. I have a roof over my head and a wonderful family who visits me every day, which is more than many can say."

"I have a little gift for you," Roger said, handing her a bouquet of flowers and a shiny blue box. "Walsh San, you deserve it."

She opened the box. Inside, was a gold coin with her name and the number 42 on it mounted on a wooden frame.

"Oh domo arigatou gozaimasu, it's beautiful."

She took her glasses off and wiped her eyes then hugged him, catching him unawares.

"Walsh San, the honour is mine," he said with a bow. "It is people like you that make our nation great. Thank you most kindly for your hospitality. I wish you all the best."

He bowed and she laughed again.

The crew filmed Roger as he toured the estate, but the scene was no longer peaceful, with furigans lining the route, shouting and swearing. Roger ignored them and stopped to look at a new community centre. As he spoke to the manager, a furigan in a string vest and tea cosy jumped the barricade and gave a two-fingered salute. The cameras swung around and he stuck his hand down his pants, tugging away, before running off sniggering. Before Roger could react, a middle-aged furigan with a shaved head pushed his way to the front and hurled a bottle.

"Niceness indeed," Roger muttered as it smashed some distance away, leaving a splat of excrement. "Flogging would be too good for these animals."

"We really must go," Commander Lucas shouted.

As he spoke, a couple of figures with electro-placards and loudspeakers appeared in the distance.

The noise grew louder as furigans massed outside the tower blocks. The police fired a warning shot, but it had no effect: the crowd pushed over the barriers and charged police lines.

"Pull the men back into a defensive cordon," Commander Lucas yelled into his radio. "Tyson San, come with me."

The police fired tear gas into the crowd and fell back as missiles clattered against riot shields. Furigans poured from the buildings and surged towards them, held back only by the armoured vehicles and water cannon, which had just arrived.

"You're lucky, sir," Commander Lucas said as they reached the forecourt. "If you'd spent any longer, it would have been fridges and concrete slabs."

Roger ducked as a rock hit him on the shoulder. There was a roar of engines and shouts of "Get down! Get down!" Before he could move, two vans careered in from either side, crashing to a halt in front of the police vehicles as gunfire opened up from the towers. Two groups of furigans jumped out, pushing them over and setting them alight.

"They're closing in for an ambush," Commander Lucas shouted. "Fire at will."

The police fired baton rounds and Roger retreated to the vehicles under a hail of petrol bombs.

"Kudasai, no violence," John pleaded. "We need to show empathy; we need to be more understanding."

"Shut up, man," Roger barked. "Pavlov didn't reason with his dogs. In the barracks, the length of the peace is proportional to size of the defeat inflicted. Commander Lucas, do what you must."

The Deer Park riots were already leading the news as Roger left. Images of riot police dragging away injured colleagues were followed by masked furigans silhouetted against burning vehicles. With no police to fight, they went on the rampage, smashing windows and torching cars. Roger rubbed his shoulder as the Kobiyashi media played in the background.

"Sunrise candidate Roger Tyson's controversial visit to the Deer Park Complex has sparked the largest rioting to date," said one reporter. "In what is being described as the most divisive election ever, he caused further outrage by describing residents as 'animals'."

"Talking of flogging shows his sheer disregard for anyone he sees as different," said James Ashley. "The Helpless turn to violence because they have no alternative. He should be listening not demonising."

"This disgraceful provocation is a foretaste," Charles Bonham said. "Forget his stage-managed chit-chats; if Tyson wins, the Helpless, the Lifestyle Groups, the

Movement for Supreme Love will be slaughtered in their thousands."

Roger checked the latest polls. Despite the criticism, his popularity had surged, but he still felt uneasy. *We can't ignore Chainsaw. People may support a tougher stance, but Bill could always suspend the election if thinks he'll lose....* He studied the media, unaware of time passing. The car slowed down, breaking his train of thought and causing him to sit up. A light was flashing ahead, the traffic had gone and a policeman was flagging him down. He got out and walked towards him, knowing that someone must have known he would be there and that this person must have had the power to block the road off. He looked at the deserted service station with its waste hoppers lined up for collection, aware of a figure in the shadows.

"Konbanwa, Tyson San," a voice said.

Roger looked round as a tall, thin man with a narrow, angular face stepped forward and bowed.

"Konbanwa, Sir Gerald. To what do I owe this pleasure?"

"We're facing a disaster of unimaginable proportions," Sir Gerald replied. "Would you step inside, kudasai?"

He pointed to an unmarked car, parked off the road. Roger followed him in and a grey figure closed the door behind him.

"Why now?" Roger said. "You've been part of Bill's inner circle all the time it's been appeasing our enemies."

"I am not part of any inner circle," Sir Gerald said. "With everything so politicised, it's not possible to be the detached official of old. I had to be near the centre of power if I were to have any influence whatsoever. I can assure you, appeasement has never been our policy. We in the Security Services have been quite clear about the Muhonin threat and have worked hard to contain it. Our problem is that the Action Groups have infiltrated the state. Bill lacked the political support to take them on and tried appointing them to state posts to keep them onside – inside the tent pissing out, rather than outside the tent pissing in, so to speak – but it hasn't worked. They're using their position to foment revolution and, if Chainsaw succeeds, we're finished. Bill Harris is a decent man, but the fact is he's no wartime leader. You, however, are."

He paused, looking at Roger with a stern expression.

"However, there are elements of your campaign that give us grave cause for alarm. Let me warn you, Edmund Hope is a man with a track record of preaching sermons and ducking responsibility. He will end up attacking you from the backbenches just as he did with Bill, but what is most disturbing is the way you indulge his ridiculous fantasies of power to the people. The man is the unwitting dupe of subversive radicals who fund him in an attempt to undermine the state. For years he has opposed every measure we have proposed to tackle the violence and now, thanks to you, they see power within their grasp. We in the Service can support you, but not if you insist on pursuing his fantasies."

"Sir Gerald," Roger said. "What is it you want?"

"Tyson San, I want what's best for our country. I don't live in a mansion or own an expensive car. Like you, I come from the old school, I serve the national interest. You're not like those daydreamers; I know that beneath the idealistic rhetoric lies a tough pragmatist. We both know national emergencies can't be solved by moralising. Fukoku kyohei: revive the economy and restore the state."

His expression softened.

"By the way, my condolences on the death of Dr Alexander – he was a first-rate man. He had penetrated an Action Group hit squad intent on assassinating state officials and was close to identifying the individuals. Sadly, they got to him first."

The door opened and Sir Gerald bade Roger farewell.

"I would take what your friends tell you with the greatest care. They are not what we would term 'reliable.' Sayonara, Tyson San."

Roger raced back in a state of unease. Edmund Hope, man of principle or front for subversive radicals? And what about Sir Gerald, could he be trusted? He pushed the questions out of his mind and tried psyching himself up for his speech, but as he arrived at the convention centre he could see Amanda waiting for him in the entrance.

"You were amazing," she beamed. "You really took control."

"Domo," he said with a tired smile.

"I mean it, Roger." She hugged him, tears forming in her eyes. "You were amazing. When they spread their lies, you were my only friend. Everyone thought the worst of me and I wanted to give in, but your support kept me going. I believe in you, Roger."

He looked at her round eyes, his heart pounding harder than ever. What use was victory if he always felt isolated? She made him laugh and smile. She made him happy. She made him.... He shut the thought out, feeling a deep discomfort. As she hugged him, he could see Jane. She was young again, smiling, laughing, cuddling up to him as they set about creating Greenwood. The burning inside went out as his innards twisted up. *No. Jane and I are a team. Her Bill worship is infuriating, but we could never be enemies.* He let go and stood still.

"Stop holding back," Amanda said. "If you don't listen to your heart, you will always be unhappy." She smiled. "I know what they're hiding. We can bring them down."

She clasped his hands and looked into his eyes as the call for people to return to their seats echoed from the intercom.

"Roger, I don't ever want to be alone again. Promise you'll be there for me."

A screen was on as he entered his dressing room: his supporters were being interviewed. He sat down and watched as an assistant made him up.

"He's our man," said a woman, holding a picture of him. "He may not be on cue, but you know where you are with him."

"He's the only person who speaks for us," said the man next to her. "The one man that can save England."

The assistant finished and Roger strode around the room, running through his speech and practising his gestures. He stopped. His supporters had gone. In their place was Bill Harris, sitting behind the Kantei desk.

"Today," he announced solemnly, "two hundred and forty-seven military officers have been charged with treason. These men, part of the Chainsaw network, planned to suspend the election and declare a state of emergency. However, although they have been dealt a severe blow, their network remains active and could yet strike. To prevent any reoccurrence, I have created a Sori Daijin's Department, whose decisions will be enforceable by Imperial decree. Kudasai, remember not give in to fear when you cast your vote. This election is our chance to show our faith in democracy. I bid you all good evening."

Roger stood frozen. Mark Alexander's sunken eyes stared at him as he was cuffed and thrown into a police van. A deep thud-thud-thud boomed out and the policemen turned into clowns, circling around him, jumping up and down and screaming gibberish. A blade sliced through his flesh and blood poured forth, torrents flowing everywhere.

The alarm rang, bringing Roger to. He composed himself and strode out into the hall, arms aloft. His supporters erupted into riotous applause, waving their banners and shouting his name, while Jane waited by the podium with a big smile, clapping delicately. He embraced her and acknowledged the applause with a sweeping wave.

"This election is a contest between right and wrong. On one side, the thuggery of the barracks, aided by the cowardly appeasers in Nagata-Cho; on the other side us – the people, the nation. It's time to stop apologising. Nations are natural. Nations are good. They bring people from different backgrounds and walks of life together into one harmonious whole. Without nations, there can be no civilisation. Nations mean community. Nations mean freedom."

There was loud applause and some were standing up, but Roger gestured for them to remain seated.

"The peaceful transition of power from one administration to the next is one of our country's finest traditions. However, there are those who only respect the people's verdict when it accords with their own. They called me a warmonger. They threatened to make me Figure of Hate. Now, they threaten us all. We must remain vigilant, for their lies serve a sinister purpose. I call on every person present to stand firm and hold our opponents to the same democratic standards we adhere to."

He raised a fist.

"We are England. We shall not be silenced."

The audience rose to their feet as he and Jane embraced with a kiss, cheering as their image projected onto a giant screen like two colossi.

The ovation ended as the lights came on. Roger left the podium and checked the polls, shaking inside. He had moved further ahead, but as the evening turned warm and sticky, the Action Groups had taken to the street, calling for his arrest and clashing with Sunrise supporters.

"We must vote for Bill Harris," Paul Fox said, addressing the Action Groups through a megaphone. "He's only person who can stop Tyson from becoming shogun. He's the only person who can stop military rule."

Roger turned to the news. He searched desperately for information about the bomb-making equipment, but the item had been removed and all he could find was a small notice on the Subversive Service that hundreds of furigans had indeed been released from prison. He stared into space, his anxiety levels at their maximum. *If Bill doesn't suspend the election, there are any number of pretexts he could use to annul the result. I've got to....* Jane was standing in front of him, arms folded and stone-faced.

"Have you ever thought about the pain this is causing me?" she said. "My family has been blacklisted and all because of your silly hankering for public adulation."

"If you think you'll get better from Bill," he roared, "why don't you go and marry him?"

Her voice went quiet.

"Roger, I'm warning you. I won't have my family's name dragged through the mud. If it comes to Chainsaw, you're on your own."

They got in the limo and stared straight ahead, neither wanting to speak to the other.

Within seconds, the forward display was flashing "Unidentified obstruction ahead." They looked out in terror as the car's automated voice echoed around the interior. Roger's security guards were barricaded inside the guardhouse, surrounded by a chanting mob.

ROGER OROSHI! NASTINESS OROSHI!
ROGER OROSHI! NASTINESS OROSHI!
ROGER OROSHI! NASTINESS OROSHI!

"Reverse! Reverse!" he shouted, but it was too late.

The mob charged towards him, faces and shrieks blurring into one as they bashed in the windows with axes and hammers. A flash of red. Charles Bonham? The car tipped from side to side, rocking ever more violently. As it was about to flip over, he and Jane clung tight.

Roger felt his body go light. Lynched? Executed? Wild thoughts rushed through his mind, yet he remained calm. What would happen would happen; he would meet his fate with dignity. There was a loud bang then silence. He was right side up. The screaming had gone, replaced by the sound of squealing tyres, sirens and boots on tarmac. He opened his eyes to find a policeman standing outside.

"Is everything all right, sir?"

"Yes, officer."

"We've removed the troublemakers. You should have no further problems."

Roger thanked him and looked at Jane, who was badly shaken. *It's moments like this reveal one's true character, Jane. I will win, because I have inner strength, but you let them get to you. Kiss Bill's arse all you like; it won't be him in power next week.*

The limo coasted the remaining distance home. Roger sat up straight and looked resolutely ahead, while Jane sat beside him, her face pale.

"I can't take any more," she said as they came to a halt. "I'm going to stay with my family."

"Bill's world is in its death throes," he said, "I will win and your family get its due, but you have to be with me."

She looked at him with undisguised anger.

"You can't see it, can you? Amanda and your coalition partners aren't your friends. She's using you; they're using you. She wants you to have an affair, so you're beholden to her. This isn't kiss and tell, Roger, it's a fishing exercise and you're being reeled in, only you're too pig-headed to realise. Do you think you will still be leader after the election? Do you think you can turn the opposition parties into some kind of patriotic movement? You must be potty. What do you think will happen to you after Margaret Richards and Brian Collingwood have achieved their ambition? And you worried about Bill making you Figure of Hate. You fool. You've been caught up in Chainsaw and now you're being prepared for sacrifice."

They got out and walked up the steps in silence, standing outside as the doors opened. Immediately, her face went white and his smile vanished. The robot valet was standing in the hallway, bearing a large sheet of paper with cut-out letters pasted on.

YOU ARE DEAD

PART III

20

The mood in Sunrise Headquarters was tense as Roger's team awaited the result. The violence had subsided and the Eikkei stabilised, but the prospect of sovereign default had not gone away and there was no guarantee a workable government could be formed. Roger remained quiet, standing anxiously by the window as the crowd outside cheered his name. What if the election were cancelled? Would his supporters turn out for him? Could he survive anything less than a landslide? He turned around, his face lined with worry. Terry was standing behind him.

"Jaxxi was found hanged in his cell this morning," Terry whispered. "He'd been due to testify that he'd been offered a community sentence in return for paying half of his gang's proceeds into an undisclosed fund. The police had threatened him with a lifetime in solitary if he didn't cooperate, but he wouldn't play. An informant in Deer Park told us he'd been boasting that no Barry ever took his money and the Mollies could kiss his lawyer's a-ho."

"Vicious," Roger said, "but not bright."

"We found more. Bill's not the only person making extravagant promises to keep the gangs onside. Derek's aide Charlie Hodge was seen with Fuzzz – and get this: two former Albion executives. The ganglords can see their funding dry up and the police are calling in their investments. Whoever wins today, we face a swift resumption of violence."

They rejoined the team in front of the main screen as the results were declared. The room went quiet as Sunrise gradually pulled ahead before the LDP clawed its way back, the tension increasing as neither side could establish a clear lead. Roger checked his communicator. His helicopter remained at the ready.

Finally, a lead emerged, an incumbent held their seat and the Sunrise majority was unassailable. With a triumphant smile, Roger stepped onto the balcony with Jane.

"Ladies and Gentlemen," the compere said, "we have a new Sori Daijin. This is a historic moment in our nation's history, so please join me in showing your appreciation for Roger Tyson."

There were loud cheers as the crowd applauded, waving English flags and Sunrise banners.

"Arigatou, arigatou," he said. "I couldn't have done it without you, and most of all I couldn't have done it without my beautiful wife, Jane."

He put his arm around Jane and acknowledged their applause, while she smiled at the crowd, saying a quiet "thank you."

The cheers continued for several minutes before they left the balcony. He bounded inside and thanked his team while his Sunrise colleagues slapped him on the back as the first headlines came in.

HISTORY BECKONS – ROGER TYSON WINS LANDMARK VICTORY

THE FIRST NON-LDP GOVERNMENT IN HALF A CENTURY

A NEW DAWN? SUNRISE WINS ELECTION

With a grin, he switched over to Bill's election rally. Triumphal music pumped out as Bill high-fived his ministers with Lizzie grinning beside him. Then, the results were announced. The mood went flat as party members stared at each other, unable to comprehend what had happened. Roger roared with laughter as Bill and Lizzie's smiles remained fixed to their faces.

"Bravo," he clapped. "Encore."

"You only have a majority of ten seats," Jane whispered loudly. "Don't get carried away."

"She's right," Angela said, coming over with the results. "There's been no popular swing: incumbents have retained their seats in every constituency. We only won because Diet Members switched sides. Such a narrow margin of victory means a second election."

Roger looked around the room, trying to hide his disappointment.

"Sori Daijin," Terry whispered as Roger stood down the helicopter, "the windows have been tampered with. Someone has been snooping."

"What else do you know?"

"Nothing." Terry looked at him impassively. "But I wouldn't put too much faith in your colleagues' loyalty. Any of them."

Roger looked at inner London for the first time as Sori Daijin, tears welling up as the Dam Busters' March rang out inside his limousine. *At last! I am part of our island story: Churchill, Wellington, Marlborough.... Bill Harris? That weakling's not fit to wipe their shoes. His foolishness demeaned this great office and made our country ridiculous. Now I shall correct it.* He looked at Jane beside him as he turned into Nagata-Cho, the emotion overwhelming. *For so long, this was just a dream. Action Groups, the media, the Political Consensus; I beat them. Everything was against me, but I held firm. Cometh the hour....* He rounded the corner and there it was: the glass and steel building that had occupied so much of his thoughts. The door opened and he stepped out with a smile, holding Jane's hand as the cameras flashed. Everything looked perfect: the shiny black government limousine with its silver grille and coat of arms, the famous Kantei front door with policemen either side, the well-wishers with their flags. He greeted the people in the crowd before turning to the cameras.

"This victory is not the end, it is the beginning," he said. "I do not promise miracles, only courage, determination and resolve."

The crowd clapped and fluttered their flags. Roger and Jane waved and walked into the Kantei, not noticing the police holding back the anti-Roger demonstrators behind a solid metal fence.

The door shut as they entered the Kantei lobby. Jane left for the living quarters while a robot escorted Roger to the Sori Daijin's office. He looked at the famous marble fireplace, oak desk and the painting of the old Houses of Parliament, familiar from so many broadcasts, feeling proud yet dismayed. *The polls showed I had a clear lead, yet people were not sufficiently moved to vote. With little holding Sunrise together, Bill must feel pretty confident he can return to power. Did he stay his hand over Chainsaw?* He looked at his diary, noticing a briefing with Sir Gerald. He read the attached intelligence report and called in his first meeting.

His personal team – Keith Bird, Economics Advisor, Jez Rice, National Security Advisor and Angela Taylor, Head of Communications – took their seats as Roger stood up to address them.

"Bird San, how close are we to default?"

"The state is running out of cash," he said. "The economy is contracting, businesses failing, factories closed and offices empty. Unless we can secure additional funds in the next few days, default can't be avoided."

"I need you to secure an emergency loan," Roger said. "Beg, grovel, do whatever you have to. We have to avoid any further dislocation."

He turned to Jez Rice.

"How does this impact on security?"

"Furigan gangs are intercepting supplies to the complexes and besieging residents. The most vulnerable are weeks away from starvation. The Lifestyle Militias have been acquiring arms on the black market, so we can expect the violence to spread to the suburbs. Add in a Muhonin insurgency and you've lost control of the country."

"How far away are the Muhonin from attacking?"

"Unknown. The level of furigan violence suggests it can't be long."

"Release the arrested officers from prison," Roger said. "They are to be reinstated with immediate effect."

"I'd advise against it," Angela said. "Bill sees Chainsaw as your weakness and that's where he'll attack. With him so close in the polls and the media sympathetic to him, you can't afford any unpopularity."

"We're beyond that," Roger said. "If the Muhonin attack, we need every man we've got."

Roger dismissed them, except Terry, whom he motioned to stay behind.

"As Head of Political Intelligence," Roger said, steepling his fingers, "who, in your opinion, can I rely on?"

"The Commissions will oppose you whatever you do," Terry said. "The state is too weak to offer any support and the coalition parties are more concerned by the possibility of a Bill comeback than anything else."

"What about Sir Gerald?"

"Waiting on the sidelines to see who wins."

Roger pursed his lips, deep in thought.

"What's the deal between him and Bill?"

"Unclear, but it's part of a long-standing struggle between the state and the parties. The parties wanted to bring the state under political control, while the state wanted to increase its hold over the parties. Bill won round one, putting political appointees in charge of state agencies, but the lack of any political staff within the LDP meant he was reliant on the state to formulate legislation, like every other Sori Daijin. For Bill, Sir Gerald was too formidable an opponent and too useful an ally, so he was moved into Government, where he could maintain his influence. If this is about your planned offensive, you don't have the support to force it through the Naikaku. If you do, you'll splinter the coalition and lose power – and you know what that means."

Roger nodded as reception informed him that the Sunrise leaders had arrived.

He hurried over to the Naikaku Office, slowing down as he walked through the double doorway and pausing before he took his seat at the head of the board table, Amanda and Edmund either side of him.

"Konnichiwa. Welcome to the Kantei," he said. "I have called this emergency meeting of the Naikaku because of the troubles in the barracks. Let me be brief. The violence must stop. All contact with the Lifestyle Groups must cease, police and military reserves must be mobilised and surgical raids on known enemy centres mounted at once."

The leaders shook their heads.

"No, no, no," Frederick said. "On the contrary. We need to develop our links. Only by working with them can we stop the violence."

"Wrong," Roger cut him short. "We are a national coalition not a sectional one. The Lifestyle Groups are the source of the disorder, so working with them will only exacerbate the problem. We're talking about a small number of agitators with no broad appeal."

"This is politically unacceptable," Frederick blustered. "Many of our Diet Members work with them on a range of issues."

"Then they must stop," Roger replied.

Frederick shook his head and sat back with a look of great displeasure.

"The Self Defence Forces are in no condition to mount an offensive, anyway," Alan said. "Bill pared them down, he reduced their budget and cut numbers – you know that. It would be phenomenally risky."

"And military mobilisation would put our finances under immense strain," Brian added. "How are we going to afford it if we're already trying to avoid default?"

"If your visit to Deer Park was controversial," Alan continued, "this would be of an altogether different magnitude. Not only would it be hugely inflammatory, it would lead us to be portrayed as warmongers. Tough measures, by all means, but a military offensive, no."

His fellow leaders nodded unanimously, but Roger was undeterred.

"I called this meeting because the rioting is merely the start," he said, "For the last decade, the Muhonin have been preparing an insurgency and are days away from striking. They and the gangs are intercepting the financial aid to the barracks and diverting it to fund their violence – ordinary residents are starving. We need to break this blockade and ensure aid goes to those that need it. Therefore, all monies will be declared forfeit until unconditional cessation of rioting."

There were gasps of disbelief.

"This is monstrous," Alan said. "You're proposing to starve the Helpless into submission. I can speak for everyone here when I say we could never countenance such an act. Forget the politics, this is utterly inhumane."

The others tapped the table.

"Residents trapped in the barracks might disagree," Roger said. "If it's a State of Emergency for them, it is for us too."

"Is it?" Brian said. "All this belligerent bluster may sound good during an election campaign, but it's no way to govern. Let's stop talking the troubles up as some existential crisis. The violence will pass and we will survive a default. We've already had one presidentially minded Sori Daijin and I certainly hope we don't have a second. Authority is rested in the Naikaku and we are utterly opposed to everything you have proposed."

No-one spoke. Roger looked at Margaret who was sitting awkwardly.

"Margaret," he said. "You've been unusually quiet."

"Sori Daijin," she said. "While I agree wholeheartedly with you about the injustice of Chainsaw and the Muhonin threat...."

Her voice drifted off, before picking up again without its usual confident tones.

"We have to consider the ramifications. If our first action on taking office was a military offensive... how would that be portrayed by our opponents?"

"I hope you're not going wobbly on me?" Roger said. "What happened to the forthright attitude you showed in opposition?"

She looked at him almost apologetically.

"I'm sorry, we cannot afford to alienate public opinion with such a slender majority. We oppose this bellicosity."

"Hear, hear," the others added.

Roger sat with his head in his hands as the party leaders left the room.

"Default?" Brian said in a stage-whisper. "He's got his pals in the financial sector to mount a bond market strike. Mark my words, once he's forced his plans through, the economy will magically recover and he'll claim all the credit."

Roger banged the table. Edmund and Amanda sat quietly.

"They're worse than the other lot," Roger said. "So much for a strong state."

"A strong state doesn't mean a strong Office of the Sori Daijin," Edmund said. "Authority is vested in the Naikaku; you are merely its first minister."

"So how do I get anything done?"

"Amanda beckoned for him to come outside. A look of elation swept over her as she shut the door.

"Forget about them. Take the initiative. Arrest a furigan gang, suppress a Muhonin cell, clean up a residential complex; win over the public and they'll be forced to follow."

"It won't be enough," he said.

She lowered her voice and came closer.

"We know who killed Mark Alexander. A furigan handed himself in yesterday and is prepared to testify. Even better, we have evidence of Bill's complicity – we have proof of Chainsaw."

"Amanda," he whispered. "If you can get that, we've won. Could you get it?"

She pressed her lips against his mouth and kissed him.

"Just promise you will be there for me."

Roger strode back into the Naikaku Office and threw himself onto his seat.

"Okay, Edmund," he said, putting his feet on the desk. "What do you know about Jaxxi?"

"There's an old proverb," Edmund said. "It's better to be an enemy of the state than a friend: a friend can only be sold, but an enemy can only be bought. By converting Action Groups into state agencies, Bill turned radical opponents into loyal defenders. When the public mood was hatoha, he bought the Muhonin and sold you; now it is turning kouha, he will either have to sell them and buy you or increase the price he is paying. Jaxxi? He might have been permitted the trappings of wealth, but he was just a pawn."

"Who ordered his arrest?"

Edmund took a deep breath and looked at him with the utmost gravity.

"Jaxxi's arrest had nothing to do with law enforcement. Leviathan's not interested in punishing crime. It uses the threat of punishment to extract compliance. They had all the dirt on him they could ever need, so it was a straightforward case of 'give us your cash or we'll prosecute.' Believe me, there will be voices trying to tempt you with promises of a quick victory. You must resist. Our victory has frightened Leviathan; it can see its power slipping away, but it thinks you can be captured. It's luring you in, probing for weakness, searching for hidden fears and dirty secrets; anything it can use against you. Whether sympathetic or hostile, you must never be beyond its control. Whatever it promises, you will enjoy its favour while you're useful, but the moment you become inconvenient, you'll be dropped. You'll wake up one day to find your misdemeanours splashed across the media screen or find yourself arrested for crimes it coerced you into committing. I urge you: do not become entangled with Leviathan. Do not speak to Sir Gerald."

Roger leaned across the table, his voice insistent.

"Go on, say it: Sir Gerald is the power behind the throne."

Edmund stood up to leave.

"Just remember, we must always maintain our moral integrity."

Roger tossed Edmund's manifesto to one side, alone in his office. *So, this is appeasement: everyone fighting everyone else over an imaginary pot of gold; Jaxxi and Fuzzz in their plex wars, English and Albion in their bidding frenzies, Bill and Derek in their pathetic little feud. How are they connected? Who's at the centre? Edmund won't say. I need proof, not hot air!* His bleak mood was lifted partially by news that senior police officers had been invited to Jonathan Green's Hentai parties and that Darren Phillips had admitted to providing a sound truck during the Chilterns South by-election after having been approached by a "well-known Public Relations agency." Roger smiled weakly and got changed for the post-election party.

A string quartet played as the dignitaries gathered beneath the chandeliers in the marble hall to celebrate Sunrise's victory. Roger waited in the background, dressed in a crisply pressed evening jacket and bow tie, eager to make the most of this moment. His name was announced and he walked in to loud applause. He smiled warmly and greeted the guests, speaking to every one in turn. There was, however, no hiding the creeping dissatisfaction beneath the cordiality.

"Field San is not happy with Defence," a staffer whispered. "He says he should be Minister of Finance."

"This was agreed before the election," Roger replied. "We're not changing anything."

The staffer ran off and Roger caught sight of Jane, standing by herself in the private garden.

"Come inside," he said, walking over to her. "It's cold."

"Cut the crap," she snapped. "You can't keep this pantomime going forever. Look at them: they've tasted power for the first time and already they're sharpening their knives: first it will be you, then each other. There's only one serious party and anyone who's anyone is in it. You've won your bargaining chip, now use it."

"I didn't win the general election to put Bill back in office," Roger growled.

She looked him in the eye, her expression implacable.

"I've been more than accommodating, but this is where I stop. No deal and you're on your own."

He left her and checked the headlines. *BILL HARRIS: A SETBACK NOT A DEFEAT* was followed by news that Phil Tucker had been knifed in a random attack. In his inbox, a message had arrived from Keith Bird. He opened it, only to close it again. There would be no emergency funding until after a second election.

"Excuse me, Sori Daijin," a staffer interrupted. "Could you come quickly to the Communications Suite."

Roger rushed over to find Sir Gerald onscreen.

"Sori Daijin," he said. "As my report made clear, we are days away from attack, yet we have no plan in place and your Naikaku has failed to reach any agreement. We need to speak."

There was silence as Roger scrutinised his expressionless face. *Which are you: leading proponent of appeasement or champion of the national interest? You're a state official not a politician: you don't have a political ambition to pursue or a public image to protect – and not even Edmund has accused you of abusing his position for personal gain – yet you were an integral part of Bill's Government. If you're right, following Edmund will weaken the country and leave me defenceless against Bill's fabrications, but if he's right, following you will strengthen my enemies and leave me open to accusations of complicity. It's Chainsaw if I do and Chainsaw if I don't.*

"Sori Daijin," Sir Gerald said, "this is more urgent than you realise. Our enemies are one attack away from bringing down the state and instituting a Muhonin government. We must meet."

Roger said nothing. Outside, all conversation had ceased as guests stared at the media screen, where coverage of the election had been replaced by renewed rioting in the barracks.

"Sori Daijin," Sir Gerald said, "will you meet?

Roger turned to him.

"Yes," he said.

21

News that the state had defaulted sent the Eikkei to an all-time low, sparking a fresh round of business failures. Confidence, investment, borrowing, lending, production, consumption, sales, purchases; every index had plummeted. The police were pulling out of the barracks, driven back by the intensity of the violence, while the Naikaku minutes had been leaked, causing uproar. Opponents were outraged by Roger's bellicosity, while supporters were disappointed by his backdown – and all the time Bill was recovering lost ground. As the public mood turned apocalyptic, Roger could feel his position becoming untenable. He sat in his Kantei office, watching impotently as Bill toured the barracks, embracing tearful youths, nodding as he listened to furigan complaints.

"Rage is a cry from the desperate," he implored. "We can't keep neglecting the residential complexes. The time has come to talk."

Roger cursed as Bill's ratings crept up again and switched over. A lorry crashed into a shopping centre, smashing through a window and sending customers everywhere, before a furigan massive steamed through, ransacking shops and beating up people then vanishing into the streets.

With a sour look, Roger opened the conference screen and summoned the chiefs of police.

"Gentlemen," he said. "Withdraw your remaining forces from the residential complexes and redeploy around the city centres – with immediate effect."

"Sori Daijin," said Commander Ian Robertson, England's senior policeman. "Without military backup, we can't hold these centres long."

"You'll have to," Roger said. "We can't afford any further economic disruption. We're on a war footing now and it is your job to maintain order. Use whatever means at your disposal. I don't want to hear anything about soft policing."

An unmarked car was waiting by the rear entrance where a powerfully-built official in an ill-fitting suit greeted Roger. He ushered him into the car and sat down beside him, not saying a word as they twisted through the back streets of Outer Suburbia. They stopped in front of a shabby semi-detached house, not unlike a smaller version of Edmund's home, where an intelligence officer met them. He led Roger past a series of barely furnished rooms to an upstairs bedroom and motioned for Roger to go through. Sir Gerald was standing in the middle of the room in a pin-striped suit, bare floorboards beneath and two armchairs either side of him. He retucked the silk handkerchief into his top pocket and bowed.

"Konbanwa, Sori Daijin," he said, his face betraying no expression.

The officer closed the door carefully and left down the stairs. Sir Gerald waited until he had reached the bottom before sitting down.

"Kudasai, sit down," he said, handing Roger a printed report. "I have prepared a plan for your consideration. In it, you will find a list of foiled plots. Behind the façade of 'appeasement,' as you call it, we scored significant successes and, contrary to your assertions, if it hadn't been for us, the insurgency would already be under way. However, the fact remains: the state's power to combat the Muhonin has atrophied. We need more weapons in our armoury. We need to restore England's sword and shield. Hit them hard and keep hitting them, I say, and with you we have the strong leader we need. I believe we are of like mind."

Roger read through the report and looked up, his fingers pressed against his lips.

"Sir Gerald, I don't believe we are of like mind. This is little more than a policing operation. The Muhonin aren't a furigan gang; we can't defeat them with more arrests and longer detention. They're a paramilitary force who seek to destroy society. We need to mount a full-scale military offensive: take out their strong points, destroy their operational capacity."

"I'm aware of the pressure you are under from the military," Sir Gerald said, "but we don't have the strength to defeat them outright. We have to be smarter. The Muhonin is not monolithic. Turn their sects against the other, exploit jealousies, play on rivalries, cultivate defectors – penetrate the movement. They may not be our friends, but there are elements prepared to negotiate. Grab them by the balls and they have to accept a settlement on our terms, whether they like it or not."

"No," Roger said. "This is a war of irreconcilable opposites. Once they're strong enough, they'll resume the fight. They are our enemies and they must be destroyed."

The lines on Sir Gerald's face hardened.

"I appreciate your sentiment," he said, "but what you propose might not be in our best interests."

Roger put the report down and folded his arms.

"What is that supposed to mean?"

Sir Gerald sat back in his armchair, pulling a cigar and a lighter from his inside pocket. He lit up and paused before inhaling, his actions slow and deliberate.

"We live in a Hobbesian world, Sori Daijin. There are no rules, no prizes for good behaviour. If you don't lie, cheat and steal, you get crushed by those that do. You can jump up and down and complain that's not fair, but if they are strong and you are weak, they will win."

He blew a smoke ring up into the air then turned to Roger with an expression of weary contempt.

"England has no permanent friends, only permanent interests. Today's ally is tomorrow's enemy and today's enemy tomorrow's ally. It's our job to look beyond the present and protect our long-term interests. Sometimes our survival depends on people we don't like, which means we can't turn around and lecture them. If our food supplies run out, we starve; if our fuel sources dry up, we freeze. When your enemy has you by the throat, you put your enmity on hold. But our survival always, always, always depends on maintaining our freedom of action. Friend or foe, everyone is a rival and a strong friend can be more dangerous than a weak enemy. Not only will they pressure us into pursuing their interests against our own, they will sponsor trouble in our country, so they can offer their support to suppress it. We'd be forced to accept their 'help' and become dependent on them; the worse the trouble, the more dependent we'd be. Once we were totally dependent, they could drop us any time they liked and there would be nothing we could do. Tyson San, if you take away our freedom to act, our fate will be determined by others."

He took a leisurely puff as Roger grew impatient.

"The Muhonin may be our enemy, but they are also our enemies' enemy and, when those enemies are fighting the

Muhonin, they aren't fighting us. If we were to crush them, as you propose, our most powerful enemies would be free to turn on us. Our problem is that the Muhonin have grown bold. The older generation knew their place, but they've been a pushed aside by a new generation, cocksure and rebellious. They need to be made to understand we're no soft touch. Once they understand that fighting our enemies is preferable to fighting us, they cease to be a threat. Indeed, they become an asset."

"Sir Gerald," Roger exploded. "The Muhonin an asset? How dare you lecture me with such drivel. This is worse than appeasement. The Muhonin have become your foot-soldiers."

"That's very cheap," Sir Gerald said. "Our work necess-itates close contact with the enemy; without our agents, we would know nothing about them. We can't act on everything we know or we would expose our sources, putting more lives at risk than we would save. Our officers risk their lives to defend the nation and not everything they do will be morally pretty. When you're swimming with the sharks, you can't afford to be burdened with scruples."

"You're assisting our enemies," Roger said. "A nation's strength is its people and your service is undermining them."

"With all due respect, you listen to Hope San too much." Sir Gerald's mouth twitched. "He can spout his idealistic nonsense because he doesn't have to make tough decisions. The people are fickle; one minute they want one thing, the next they want the other. One minute they complain they're being strangled by government regulation; the next they complain it's not doing enough to protect them – and you want to base national policy on their whims?"

He took a draw on his cigar then put it down for a moment.

"Who are *the people* anyway? They're as much a fiction as the Lifestyle Groups. Society is a multitude of individuals pursuing their own contradictory ends; it can never be harmonious."

He picked up his cigar. For the first time, something approaching a smile appeared.

"And let's face it: they've hardly rallied around you."

Roger ignored his remark and looked him in the eye.

"The nation may be an abstraction, but once you remove it there's nothing to stop the representatives acting against the interests of the represented. Remove the idea of 'us' and you also remove the idea of 'them.' If the Muhonin ceases to be the enemy, what's to stop you colluding with them?"

Sir Gerald's face remained inscrutable.

"People like Hope San are a corrupting influence. They sit in their comfortable armchairs, filling people with false hopes, but however much they moan about our work, they still expect us to ensure their safety. I take the world as it is, Tyson San, not as I'd like it to be. Life is rarely a choice between good and bad, but bad and worse. If you're drowning and a murderer throws you a line, you can't wait for someone more agreeable to come along. Hope San can talk about his precious ideals all he likes, but he'd do well to remember the greatest crimes in history have been caused by those who put abstract ideals above reality."

Roger's face went red.

"Have you ever considered that the Security Services might be no more monolithic than the Muhonin? Have you considered that they might be waging the same war as you, playing one against the other, penetrating the state and turning it to their advantage? Sir Gerald, you have allowed your service to become the Ministry of the Muhonin and turned England into a warzone. By using our enemies as shock troops, you've become their sword and shield. We hardly need worry about rival powers turning on us when we're doing that ourselves."

"Sori Daijin," Sir Gerald's voice grew hoarse and his composure strained. "You're failing to see the bigger picture. The Muhonin are little more than a glorified partisan band, furigans not even that. Without air force, navy or heavy weapons, they lack the power of the tiniest state. The amount of damage they can inflict is negligible. Wars aren't won with fine speeches; we need all the powers we can get. Edmund's 'power to the people' nonsense means handing power to people who wish to take it away again."

"You can't measure strength in military terms alone," Roger said. "This is a culture war and they are winning. Look how we are becoming like them with every day. This is a war for who we are."

"Sori Daijin," Sir Gerald said, raising his voice. "You seem to have forgotten that Greenwood would not have won its overseas contracts without our support."

"And may I remind you," Roger said, standing up, "that your job is to maintain security and you have failed. If you won't do your duty, then I shall find someone who will."

He plucked the cigar from Sir Gerald's mouth and stubbed it out on the arm of his chair. Sir Gerald picked up the remains of the cigar and brushed the dust into an ashtray, his fingers twitching.

"Forgive me," he said, standing up. "Please accept my most humble apologies. You are the Sori Daijin and I accept whatever decision you make."

He bowed deeply, his arms straight by his sides.

"Sori Daijin, kudasai, I implore you: you must accept my plan."

Roger bowed.

"The Muhonin are our enemy. They must be defeated."

"Very good Sori Daijin," Sir Gerald, said bowing again. "I shall revise the plan accordingly, but kudasai consider what I say."

Roger sat sullenly as he was driven to the drop-off point. *The power behind the throne? He's just a short-sighted bureaucrat. Does he seriously think the Muhonin can be stopped by police raids? "I believe we are of like mind." Really!* He stared at his shoes, acutely aware how vulnerable he was, then looked outside. Apart from the occasional furigan joyrider, the road was empty and the lack of light gave the streetscape a desolate air. Boarded-up retail cities and deserted office blocks followed one after the other, as if dumped by the roadside. Even the huge video hoardings of gleaming megastructures now looked forlorn.

They stopped in an abandoned car park and he got into his own car, hoping for some good news, but finding instead that trading on the Eikkei had been suspended and a rejuvenated LDP was attacking him on the media. That was not the worst of it. He watched as furigans ramraided shops, torched houses and opened fire on riot police from 4x4s, desperately hoping for something to turn up. *Furigans confident enough to attack police? The Muhonin are testing out our defences. It can't be far off now.* As his ratings fell, he could feel himself trapped. It was dark and he could feel damp on his skin. A concrete floor, a bunker – his friends had deserted him. The Muhonin were massing outside, their knives gleaming, ready to disembowel him. He stared at his speeches, wondering where it had all gone wrong. An explosion, they burst in and....

He sat up in a sweat and summoned up his origami boxes. *Are proxy forces and temporary alliances the new*

Leviathan or are they the intermediate stage to state failure? If the bonds within society can break down, so can those within the state. Without consent to authority, power is determined by force alone and hierarchy reverts to a pecking order, just as it has in the barracks. Without a sense of belonging, social structure is impossible: organisations fail, communities decay, nations vanish. We become like furigan gangs, all structure gone, the legal and illegal blurred into one. This isn't the future, it's happened already. Bill's created a parallel state: the Commissions and Action Groups the official arms; Grey Ninja and Mouken the unofficial – legality and criminality merged. But a change in form doesn't always mean a change in function. Who am I fighting? If the axes of power have broken down, is Bill still in charge? Or has a new furiganised, Muhoninised elite taken over?

A news alert flashed onscreen, causing him to look up. A middle-aged man was dragged out of a riverside penthouse in handcuffs.

"In a dramatic fall from grace, member of the House of Councillors, non-executive director of Country and Suburban, and former National Police Commissioner, Adam Robshaw, has been arrested after a raid on his home revealed undisclosed shares in English Landholdings worth trillions of Yen. Police have confirmed they will be investigating allegations he shielded senior political figures – and ganglords, such as the recently deceased Jaxxi – from arrest and prosecution."

Roger smiled as he was bundled into the back of a police van. *How poetic: the man who claimed crime was "a thing of the past" and withdrew forces from the barracks; the man who compelled his officers to wear furigan costumes and attend Muhonin celebrations while fining ordinary people for name-calling. Uphold the law? No! You turned the police into a protection racket. Ganglords were afforded police protection, while law-abiding citizens were arrested for using Nastywords. You only rose to the top because you were Jonathan Green's mate and now you've been jettisoned. But is it too late? The state is failing and party bosses and police chiefs are striking their own deals with local ganglords: not one policy of appeasement, but hundreds. And Bill?* He stared at the boxes with disquiet. *Either he holds absolute power or he's a power vacuum. Either there's no constraint on his ability to play factions off against each other or there's no constraint on the factions' ability to fight each other. Anarchy or authoritarianism, it's all the same. He's sacrificed his mates, kept his own involvement hidden and created a government-in-exile ready to take over the moment I lose. Is he a front man? Is there an innermost box within the innermost box? Pah! Another incident and the bastard's back in power.*

Suzuki Hall stood empty as he returned. Roger flopped next to the bust of Churchill and put on his speeches, pouring himself a whisky as the famous voice crackled from the speakers.

Hitler knows that he will have to break us.... If we can stand up to him... the life of the world may move forward into broad, sunlit uplands; but if we fail, then the whole world... will sink into the abyss of a new Dark Age.

Roger held the glass, feeling despair. Mobilise the people? Churchill's speeches had inspired a nation, but hadn't that same nation ignored him for a whole decade previously? Sir Gerald. Appeasement. How wrong he'd been. How wrong! Neville Chamberlain had rebuilt the country's air defences, declared war and supported his successor loyally. Even the most ardent appeaser would never have regarded the enemy as an asset.

Whisky followed whisky as he descended into alcoholic moroseness. The windows blurred: flickering streams of red and yellow spinning around the room as bullet trains rushed across a wobbly Chrysanthemum Bridge. Below him, the silvery-grey monoliths of the London Dormitory Suburb of Kent looked magnificent in the glow from the uplighters, only to grow bigger and bigger until they swamped Central London. *The Naikaku is nowhere near agreement, public opinion is against military action and the Self Defence Forces too weak to mount an offensive. I can see it, I can feel it, but I can't stop it.* He collapsed on the sofa and fell into a torrid sleep. The people were trapped in the barracks, slaughtered in their thousands while Bill cowered in his bunker, his presidency gone and Chainsaw a memory. The Muhonin were triumphant, but there was nothing Roger could do, for he – the hated would-be Shogun – was already dead.

He sat up, hair tousled and eyelids droopy, and looked out at the tranquil night. *If Bill wins, all this will become reality. I can't give in. I won't....* His mind drifted off, trying to summon up his remaining resolve, but all he could think of was the dead policeman, shirt open, entrails spilling out onto the floor. Courage and resolve were fine things, but people thrown to the Muhonin had few friends.

22

Passengers crawled from the subway station clutching their throats, the emergency services helping them to safety. Smoke billowed from a side entrance as rescue workers in breathing apparatus hacked their way in, ambulances, fire engines and police cars parked nearby. Roger sat in the Kantei office watching the news reports in silence, trying to look calm. He could feel himself back in the subway concourse, crushed up in the darkness, unable to breathe. The Muhonin had struck. The insurgency had moved straight to Stage Three. As the emergency com-link lit up, his insides were palpitating.

"Sori Daijin," Commander Robertson bellowed. "We've been hit hard. They've used a mixture of smoke and poison gas."

"Wait for Bomb Disposal," Roger shouted. "It could be booby-trapped."

"We don't have time," Commander Robertson replied. "We've got to get them out now."

A search robot was lowered into a service tunnel, its camera panning from side to side in the dim light as the passengers squeezed together by the escalators, piped saxophone music audible beneath their groans.

"How long will it take?"

Roger watched anxiously as the paramedics entered the concourse and stretchered out the first passengers. There was a loud explosion and the screens went dead. He stood alone. The long-awaited bomb attack had happened and everything inside him screamed defeat. Three Muhonin militants appeared onscreen, bearing firearms and wearing back-to-front combat jackets over pyjamas.

"You have brought this upon yourselves," they rasped. "Those who insult Supreme Love will be disembowelled."

They made an X across their chests, rifle in one hand and *The Divine Prophecies* in the other, before Commander Robertson returned onscreen, accompanied by sirens and shouting.

"Get me an armoured vehicle," Roger shouted to Commander Lucas outside. "I'm going to help with the rescue."

"I can't risk that, Sori Daijin," he replied. "The site hasn't been declared safe."

"That's a risk we're going to have to take," Roger said. "The people must see we won't be cowed."

They arrived at the station within the hour, parking in a temporary shelter while the rescue vehicles rushed to and fro down a cordoned-off channel.

"I appreciate the sentiment," Commander Robertson saluted as Roger climbed out. "But I cannot let you assist with the rescue efforts until we can be confident there are no further explosives. I can only show you what's safe."

He quickly escorted Roger round the site, pointing out the location of the bombs and explaining the effect of a gas attack. Roger listened and stepped onto a mound of rubble to address the cameras.

"This is no mere crime; it is an act of war. Whoever attacks our people will find me standing in their way. Wherever they are, whatever they're doing, these murderers will be hunted down and killed."

There were some flashes. Roger raised his fist and left.

Back at the Kantei, activity had given way to resignation. Staffers stared at screens and slouched in seats, overwhelmed by the events. Roger strode in with an air of studied sang froid, straining hard to hide his growing anxiety.

"There's no place for defeatism here," he said, clapping his hands, but the mood remained glum. Everyone was watching Bill Harris on the news.

"I would like to extend my sincere condolences to the victims of this appalling act. In this incident, we see the folly of Nastiness laid bare. Look how cheap demagoguery has inflamed the situation. Look how the Government has sought to exploit tragedy for political advantage. Talk of war is as provocative as it is repellent. Only wisdom, maturity and Niceness can resolve these tensions. We need to sit down and talk."

"Does that mean you'd be prepared to negotiate?" a journalist asked.

Bill paused.

"If the people ask me to, I will do whatever I can to achieve peace."

Terry reached forward and zoomed in on movement in the background. Electro-placards flashing "Negotiate Now" and "Peace First" loomed on the horizon.

"A spontaneous visit?"

Terry shook his head.

"People will see through it," Roger said. "Weakness only encourages violence."

He walked to his office only to find a disconsolate Amanda waiting outside.

"Bill spoke to you about forming a national government, didn't he?" she said.

He nodded wearily and rested against the wall.

"And you didn't tell me? Roger, what's happening? I told you: It's a trap. I've risked everything to help you become Sori Daijin. I believed in you, Roger."

He struggled to think of something to say, but nothing would come out. She looked at him aghast.

"Roger, I didn't do this for a ministerial post, I didn't do this for England. I did this for you. Show some leadership. If you can't do it for our country, at least do it for me."

His silence seemed only to increase her disappointment. She looked at him as if to say, "Have I got you all wrong?" and trudged out.

Roger returned to his office and looked at the latest sitrep with a hollow feeling. Two bombs had failed to detonate and the blast from the third had been absorbed by a parked lorry. Seven people had died, but it could have been far worse. He watched himself standing on the mound of rubble, trying to rouse the people. It all looked so flat onscreen, his defiance sounding like schoolboy bravado. The headlines were even worse: *PAPER TIGER, EMPTY BOMBAST* and *BLUSTER NO SUBSTITUTE FOR*

STRATEGY, not one was supportive. His head dropped as he read *EMPTY BOMBAST*.

How hollow the Sori Daijin's rhetoric sounds. For all his tough talk, he seems powerless to do anything except make matters worse. He has a choice: negotiate or step aside.

It had come from a normally sympathetic outlet.

Roger closed his eyes. As polls showed popular support for negotiations, pressure was mounting within the Naikaku. Unhappiness with his rhetoric, irritation with his leadership, demands for new ministerial posts, the complaints were increasing. *"Keep buggering on," I thought, "show leadership, mobilise the people." Pah! The insurgency has begun and people still want appeasement. How can I mobilise people who lack stomach for the fight? I'm watching a country commit suicide. Even if people do care about their country, they're paralysed by fear. I need to act fast. Bill softened them up with Chainsaw and the moment the Muhonin strike, he'll accuse me of being the ringleader. I need to know what's inside that box. I need to speak to Edmund.* As he got up, he saw the latest briefing from Sir Gerald, his heart beating faster as he read. Rumours of plots, hints of attacks; nothing was definite, but everything pointed in the same direction. The Muhonin would strike again and this time it would be bigger – much bigger.

Roger arrived at Edmund's house and banged on the door. There was no answer. He looked at his watch and banged again.

"Open up, Edmund, damn you."

Edmund opened the door with a sullen look.

"You have a nerve," he said. "Go away."

"I don't have time for this childish behaviour," Roger bellowed, "Grow up, man."

"You're heading for a dark place, Tyson: a place where nothing has a value and everything is sacrificed to power; a vacuum, a void, a pit...."

"What are you babbling about?"

"I told you not to speak to Sir Gerald."

"Stop being hysterical," Roger raised his voice. "He's the Head of the Security Services. I have to speak to him."

Edmund shrank back and Roger's voice softened.

"We agreed our manifesto and I am committed to it. I spoke to him, that's all."

Edmund invited him in and drew the curtains. He pressed a button and a bombastic military march thumped round the room.

"This place could be bugged," Edmund whispered.

"We're past that," Roger said. "We're one defeat away from disaster. If Bill wins, he'll strike a deal with the Muhonin and declare himself president. This won't be money or privileges; it'll be letting them form their own parties, contest Diet seats, hold Naikaku posts and maintain private armies, while he retains a puppet government in Nagata-Cho. He's hollowed out the ministries and created a parallel state outside the state. Confirm it: Bill still holds the power?"

"Bill?" Edmund said. "He's an actor only interested in his own self advancement. All he cares about is getting the star billing and media adulation. He'd just as soon adopt kouha as hatoha politics, only he could never compete with you, so he's been forced further down the hatoha road. The Action Groups are the driving force behind his government. They supply the agendas, the energy, the muscle on the street; he's little more than a rubber stamp. He couldn't care less about their campaigns, but he needs the support they can mobilise."

"Bill's a weak leader, yes," Roger said. "But he's at the apex of a strong machine: the Commissions, the Action Groups, a complex of power – you said so yourself."

Edmund laughed.

"Yes, but the Commissions are as much the means by which the Action Groups captured Bill as the other way around. Bill only avoided answering to the Diet and Naikaku by making himself answerable to them. As for the Political Consensus, it's a hotchpotch of different campaigns with little in common except a vague hatoha theme. Bill's skill was to present it as a guiding vision, but there never was any grand plan, only hot air."

Roger produced his communicator and replayed his Friday luncheon club speech.

"This violence is no coincidence," Roger said as the origami boxes unfolded. "Someone chose to appease our enemies and it's connected with the vilification campaign against me. I need to counter it. I need clear, unambiguous evidence of their complicity. I need to know what lies inside that innermost box."

"Your presentation has it the wrong way around," Edmund said. "It should be the outermost box representing the top of the hierarchy with more and more smaller boxes inside to represent the lower levels. Apart from the shapes, it's fundamentally no different from any other command structure."

"So what's going on at the centre of power?"

Edmund gave him a serious look.

"There is no centre of power." He gently flattened the boxes with the palm of his hand. "Power arises from the interactions between people acting in coordinated fashion. It is diffused across state, parties, keiretsu, action groups, the whole of society. No individual, including those at the top, can hold more than partial power on their own, for an individual, however powerful, is always one among many, always vulnerable to being isolated. If the many gang up against them, their power vanishes, just like the once-mighty despot in a palace coup. State action is the confluence of people making decisions throughout the system. No one person chose appeasement; it suited many."

Roger sank back as Edmund put on a documentary about an unsolved murder. The presenter stood on a sports field holding a photograph of a freckly teenager.

"Neil Bell was a promising sixteen-year-old, keen on sport. Eight years ago today his body was found in the local woods where he had been strangled. No-one has ever been arrested, but evidence has come to light that his killers have been shielded from justice. In what has been described as a reign of terror, the Movement for Supreme Love's Serene Truth Brigade had been responsible for a wave of murders, beatings and kidnappings in the area."

A blanked-out face appeared against a murky backdrop.

"The Serene Truth Brigade contained several deep state agents," said a computer-generated voice. "It was protected from prosecution in return for doing the Services' legwork."

"Legwork?"

"Anything: providing information, running dirty operations, suppressing dissent. As long as they don't threaten the state's core interests, they were allowed to do whatever they wanted. It goes all the way up. Muhonin interests are protected at the highest level. We were told: if someone who understood that could be elevated to supreme power, there'd be no... trouble."

Edmund turned the screen off and remained silent for several minutes.

"Submit or become a victim; it's how they managed the barracks and they're doing the same in the Outer Suburbs.

Leviathan wants power, it wants control, it wants submission. It feeds off insecurity, constantly generating new threats so it can reassert its authority. When people are afraid, they become obedient: instead of fearing Leviathan, they look to it for protection; instead of resenting its control, they demand more. Leviathan knows a harmonious society doesn't need a strong state to protect it; it knows it would be a threat. The people must be broken: unity replaced with division, strength with pliability, independence with subservience. Whether to negotiate peace or fight war, Leviathan's demands never change: the beast must have more power."

Roger thought back to his army days, feeling a growing scepticism. *Okay, there was always the odd bad character, but not everyone. We were motivated by duty, so why should the Security Services be any different? Some officers might have formed their own arrangements with the enemy, but what choice do they have if the state they serve ceases to exist?*

"Leviathan is the enemy," Edmund continued. "The Muhonin and furigans are only its proxies. It nurtures and protects them. It uses them. It needs them. Strengthen Leviathan and you strengthen them."

"They seek to destroy the state," Roger said. "You don't nurture your enemies."

"The insurgency is blowback," Edmund said. "For now, Leviathan finds the Muhonin useful and ignores the odd terrorist attack, but the moment they become too strong, it will chop them down and cultivate new proxies – maybe kouha hooligans. Eventually they too will become too powerful and the cycle will start again. Don't think this is an aberration. Moral conduct means exercising restraint, but when you have power, why exercise restraint? Why punish crime when you could benefit from it? Why behave ethically when it means you lose out? Leviathan rewards those it finds useful and punishes those who seek to hold it to account; it is by its nature amoral, but it still needs us to submit to its authority. It needs us to believe that it stands for democracy, justice and the rule of law. It needs us to believe that Mouken and Grey Ninja are independent organisations, acting on their own initiative. It needs us to believe it is fighting the Muhonin. It needs us to believe the fiction."

"No, Edmund," Roger interjected. "The state is an abstraction. Without people, it cannot exist. Our leaders don't come from outer space; they're products of society, and if that society is corrupt, then so too will be the state. In the past, leaders had a conscience; they regarded themselves as part of the nation and held each other to account. Today, they don't. The problem's not the state; it's the lack of values."

Edmund's eyes filled with zeal.

"No, the problem is always the state. Leviathan always boils down to the question: *quis custodiet ipsos custodes*? If we ask the state to guarantee our freedoms and ensure that justice is done, who guarantees that it does so? It can't arrest itself or put itself in prison and, if it chooses to abuse its power, it will do so. Yes, it's an abstraction, but that abstraction represents the supreme authority – the right to rule. Officially, the state's powers might be limited and its offices divided, but in reality its power is unconstrained. If those in power collude, there's nothing to check their actions: law and morality become meaningless and criminality another method of rule. It can't be any other way: the power to enforce the law is the power to act outside it."

Edmund sat proudly, but the more Roger listened the more he found himself sounding like Jane. *Miscarriages of justice like the three businessmen are rare; bribery, blackmail and intimidation the exception. The system's not perfect, but it works – mostly. You exaggerate, Edmund. Government's not a tyranny. Is it really necessary for the state to generate fear to keep people in line when people accept its authority anyway? There's a residual honesty and you can't – or won't – see it.* He looked at Edmund as he stood up for his peroration, tired with his endless theorising and unable to hide his impatience.

"Dressing Leviathan up in patriotic clothes is not enough," Edmund said. "Even if you won another election, Leviathan would still remain. Our nation originated with self-governing communities of freemen and that's where it must return. We may suffer some initial reverses, but we have to accept that if we are to achieve a harmonious society. You must destroy Leviathan. Anything less will be a hollow victory."

It was nearly midnight. Roger trudged back to his car, dejected. *Suffer a few initial reverses? Does he have any idea what a Muhonin insurgency would look like? Does he have a single practical suggestion? Damn! I'm a fool for investing so much faith in him – and now I have nothing.* He drove off, staring drowsily outside. The streetlights were out, leaving the moonlight to trace the outlines of the boarded-up service stations and warehouses. Too tired to think, he was soon in a shallow sleep. Anger over the subway attack, calls for negotiations, Sunrise members hinting they were prepared to vote against the Government, plummeting ratings; he awoke with a start.

"We could be days away from a vote of no confidence," a reporter said, standing outside the Kantei. "The Sori Daijin is under severe pressure over his handling of the Subway Incident and cannot afford another disaster: any defection would mean the end of the Sunrise Coalition and another general election. Bill Harris could be back in the Kantei within weeks."

Roger lay his head back and let out a laugh. *Coalition? Those traitors would prefer the Muhonin in office than me. Enjoy your pyrrhic victory, Bill. You're a dead man, too. Only a divine wind like in 1588 can save us now. Maybe I could get Derek to defect. No. What could I offer? Perhaps I should commit seppuku.* He thought of the disembowelled policeman and grunted at the irony.

It was 2am by the time he arrived home. As he entered, a call arrived from Terry.

"I think you should see this," Terry said. He put a photograph of Jane leaving Bill's house onscreen. "This was taken yesterday. We don't know any more, but I'd prepare for the worst. If she's struck a deal over Greenwood, his price is almost certainly putting her name to any Chainsaw allegations against you." He put up a photograph of Amanda leaving the Liberal Democratic Party headquarters in broad daylight. "Amanda too has been in contact with Jim Minto, probably to protect herself in case we lose. I wouldn't be surprised if she'd kept her lines open the whole time. She has a record of jumping ship."

"Anything else?"

"Brian Collingwood is ready to leave the coalition. He's waiting for Bill to play Chainsaw – then he's gone. Sunrise is over, Tyson San."

Roger ended the call and looked at the photographs. *I should have known, Jane. No loyalty, you and your arriviste family. Well, let's see how far you get with Bill and his Muhonin friends. Oh, just watch how they shower you with gongs. A national government indeed? But Amanda....* He held back the tears as pain burned inside him. *I'm so stupid. This was always a futile ambition. I've never achieved anything, I was never capable of achieving anything, I'm just an overblown figurehead. The man to save England? No. A junior officer with delusions of grandeur.*

He held his samurai sword and put the media screen on. An effigy of him was lowered from a crane and dropped to the floor before two masked Muhonin ceremonially disembowelled it.

"Death to those who insult Supreme Love," chanted the voiceover as it was set alight. "Death to Roger Tyson."

He turned it off and opened the latest report from Sir Gerald, his eyes straining over the text.

Major terrorist attack imminent. Target unknown. Maximum casualties predicted.

He put it down and lay on the sofa, too tired to go to bed. *Better to die a hero than live like a coward, but I can't even die a hero. I'll be slaughtered like a pig and reviled for as long as anyone can remember. Defeat, dishonour, death, so be it. I'll keep fighting, whether they like it or not. Damn them. Damn them all.* He closed his eyes, turning over and over, unable to sleep. *Victory for the Muhonin, furigans and Action Groups; everything I've strived so hard to avoid and I only ever wanted to serve my country.* He lay silently with the emptiness of the house all around. After several hours, he fell asleep.

23

The police had withdrawn from the barracks and with them went any pretence of government control. Media coverage of the barracks now consisted of self-made films of furigans grinning into the camera, crashing cars into windows and torching buildings, while government control was confined to the town centres and industrial zones, behind the checkpoints, barriers and armed police patrols that had recently sprung up. Roger hunched over the reports coming in, barely able to watch as Desmond Grey addressed an Action Group rally on the Kobiyashi media.

"First, he releases the Chainsaw officers. Then, he plans a military offensive. What next? We must impeach Tyson before it's too late."

Charles Bonham stepped up, rendered unfamiliar by a calm demeanour and closely cropped hair, his plain open-necked suit a contrast to the combat fatigues around him.

"We will say what the politicians won't," he said without hint of a snarl. "Chainsaw is Government policy."

The news moved on to a makeshift barricade straddling a street, but this wasn't the barracks. Roger sat paralysed as three figures in balaclavas and military fatigues appeared in front of a banner stating "Aristo-zoku Defenders." They stood, firearms held across their chests Muhonin style, and declared a "liberated zone" in North London. Mobs rampaged through once quiet districts, kicking in doors and throwing bricks through windows, masked militiamen in the vanguard. A family was dragged from their home and kicked down the streets.

"Goblin-zoku aren't welcome here," screamed a militia-man. "This is Aristo-zoku territory."

Roger watched as a militiaman chased a tubby boy down a street and punched him to the ground. *Many Lifestyle Groups, One Niceness. No, it could never last. They've finally broken free – not that that'll stop Bill trying to play them off against each other. Fake though they are, the Lifestyle Groups are the new reality. The nation couldn't be more irrelevant.* The feeling of powerlessness was overwhelming. He turned to the news with a hangdog expression.

"The residential complexes have been lost," complained a reporter. "Next stop, the country. Where's the Sori

Daijin? Has the tough-talking businessman gone into hiding?"

Roger tried to savour his last moments in his Kantei office as Sori Daijin, but all he could think of was a bunker. He looked at secret photographs of the defences being built around Bill's home then turned to the information screen. His ratings had collapsed and the Pioneer Party was waiting for the most damaging moment to exit the coalition. As the Action Groups called for his arrest, the prospect of lynch mobs and show trials once more filled his mind. He might have been the most unpopular Sori Daijin in history, but with one last look around, he braced himself, determined never to give in.

Angela was waiting in the ante room. She got up and they walked through the main office where staffers sat in gloomy silence, no-one pressing him for action or offering encouragement.

"You might as well cancel," she said as they entered the parking bay. "People are frightened by bellicosity."

"This is a battle for our soul," he said. "We need to challenge the idea we're responsible for the disorder and shift debate back onto our ground. Attack Bill. Attack the Action Groups. Attack the bloody traitors."

She nodded without conviction and they boarded the waiting armoured transporter. The engines growled into life and he looked at his aides looking on glumly. *How do I convince people negotiations are futile if they prefer false hope to blood, sweat and tears? Winning hearts and minds is not enough. The Action Groups don't debate with superior argument: they bully and intimidate until people are too scared to argue against them.* He sat up with a jolt as the transporter swung round and the intercom crackled to life.

"We're taking a diversion," the driver announced. "Disturbances ahead."

Roger put the internal wraparound screen on, his adrenaline levels rising as an Anti-Nastiness Rally marched on Tokugawa Square.

"ROGER OROSHI!" shouted the marchers. "NASTINESS OROSHI!"

"You should feel ashamed," bellowed a man with a megaphone to passers-by. "Your actions are causing suffering."

"This is the real violence," screamed a woman in combat fatigues, pointing at police. "We're being silenced. We're being oppressed."

A drone dipped down, projecting images of crying furigans and dejected Muhonin being trampled underfoot by flag-waving hordes.

"The violence is your fault," boomed its speakers. "The Helpless are suffering and you are to blame."

The noise filled the streets, bouncing off buildings and drumming into ears as column after column of holographic Self Defence Force soldiers marched down the street. A small boy tried to cover his ears.

"Listen to the truth," screamed the man with a megaphone, pulling the boy's hands away as a giant Roger towered above.

"The Movement for Supreme Love is bravely resisting this evil regime. They're fighting for you. Support them! Support them!"

"You should be ashamed," shouted a man with a backpack, pointing his finger. "They're murderers and you're traitors."

There were shouts of "scum" and "Nastiness" and he was hit with a placard as the march pressed on.

"Those thugs have a lot to answer for," Roger said. "Who do they speak for? Who asked for their opinion?"

His aides remained silent as the screen cut to Bill addressing an impromptu crowd from a soapbox.

"Thanks to Sunrise," he said with a commanding demeanour, "we face the worst disorders in our history. While they blunder, the Forces of Nastiness are preparing to strike. These attacks are a wake-up call. Nastiness has driven people to despair and we have failed to heed their grievances. We must feel their pain before it's too late. Peace cannot wait. We must negotiate now."

There was huge applause. Roger paused the screen and looked at the background. This time, there was not an electro-placard in sight.

"I know what you're thinking," Roger said. "People are put off by my tough talk; I make it easy for Bill to brand me a warmonger; I'm allowing him to play the statesman. But giving people the illusion of safety is wrong."

There was no reply. Roger grew angry.

"Have you considered that he might already be in contact with the Muhonin? They know how weak he is. They know how badly he wants to be president. By offering to reward their violence with talks, he's giving them a nod and a wink to attack. This is his plan. He's looking to blame this terrorism on the Forces of Nastiness so he can claim the Chainsaw Plot is real. Once in office, he'll declare a state of emergency, arrest his opponents and purge the Self Defence Forces. Then the Muhonin will pounce. Don't you see?"

Still, no-one spoke. Roger turned to the screen as Bill was showered with applause, the cameras snapping away.

"Look at him. How can he stand there smirking when he's consigning them to their deaths? These aren't negotiations, this is surrender."

He checked the information service, but the polls showed overwhelming support for Bill.

"The Muhonin must think they've as good as won," he sighed. "The Subway Incident is the prelude. They're gearing up for the big one."

Roger looked at the grim expressions listening to him out of duty with an intense despair. *What do they care? They'll work for whoever pays them. Why can't people see Bill for the phoney he is? No, they love him because he tells them what they want to hear. They hate me because I puncture their little dream world, therefore I'm old-fashioned, a fuddy-duddy, an outmoded construct. Bill could never be an outmoded construct. He's whatever people want him to be. He changes with the fashion – and the Lifestyle Groups, too. Victimised outgroups? Rubbish! They're the nation divided: insiders pretending to be outsiders, while the outsiders are now the insiders.... Oh, how I long for the old days. It's not like it was perfect, but you knew where you were. The Political Consensus has burst and everyone is living in their own unreality, speaking their own language; a million myths, but no truth.*

The internal screen deactivated as the vehicle passed through the checkpoint. The engines stopped and the rear doors opened, but Roger was still absorbed in thought. *If furigans and the Muhonin are the parts of society that has rejected its own culture, does that mean they are part of society or outside it? Is it possible for everyone to opt out of their own society? If we all turn against ourselves, will there be any society left to save?*

He entered the conference hall and looked around in shock. Amidst the brightly coloured banners and pictures of him, a mere handful of people dotted the rows of empty seats. Of all the indignities! Never before at any of his speeches had he counted more journalists than members of the public. As he ascended the podium, he could sense them waiting to pick over his carcass. *Look at those jackals grinning away – writing my obituaries already.*

"I wanted to have a little chat," he said over the coughs. "I learned from my days in the Self Defence Forces that, however bleak things look, there's always hope – if one keeps soldiering on. Defeatism offers a false solace. Capitulation cannot bring peace. The terms one gets from giving in are never better than the terms one gets from fighting on."

There were a few claps amidst the coughing.

"However, there are those who pretend that danger can be avoided. They know rewarding violence encourages it; they know the Muhonin and furigans seek to destroy us, but they don't care. They think they can cut a deal for themselves and ignore what happens to us. Be under no illusion: negotiations are not a call for peace; they are an invitation to attack. I call on our nation to rise up. Let us form a citizens' militia and repel Muhonin aggression. If we pull together, we will win."

The mild patter of applause was swallowed up in the hall.

"Sori Daijin," a journalist asked, lounging in his seat. "Isn't this academic? Sunrise is breaking apart and a general election is unavoidable. You've only days left. How on earth do you plan to keep your coalition together and win over the public?"

Roger returned to the armoured vehicle and put the media screen on as Colin defended him in a debate.

"The attacks on Roger Tyson are a disgusting attempt to smear a good man. Who are the people making these allegations? The same people who sold Diet seats to the highest bidder, permitted officials to embezzle public funds, held Hentai parties, solicited bribes and ran illegal dirty operations via front organisations. They have manufactured lie after lie, accusing him of Nastiness and threatening to make him Figure of Hate. They tried to oust him from Greenwood and now they're trying to force him out of Government. These crooks are trying to silence their critics and bury their crimes with their final calumny:

Chainsaw. My friend is an honourable man who puts others' lives ahead of his own safety. When his friend Mark Alexander was drowning, he risked his own life to save him. Now, when the Muhonin threaten to kill him, he puts himself in harm's way to protect us all, even though it goes unappreciated. Roger Tyson is all that stands between us and catastrophe. He's a hero and he deserves our support."

Roger watched with despondency as the debate ended in overwhelming defeat for him. Charles Bonham stood up as his opponents began whistling.

"Lies," he yelled out. "Tyson had Mark Alexander killed, because he knew the truth behind Chainsaw."

Roger jumped up in fury. *Why don't you drop dead, you worthless shit? You think you can accuse me of anything you like. Just because I'm not a grinning patsy like Bill doesn't make me a monster. That bugger gets away with murder because of that stupid bloody smirk. It's character that counts. Do we want to be governed by simpering namby-pambies or someone with the balls to stand up for us?* He stared glumly at the screen as a call arrived on the secure channel.

"Sori Daijin," Sir Gerald said, "I have revised the plan in accordance with your wishes. If it meets with your approval, it is ready to go."

Roger read the plan and nodded.

Roger returned to the Kantei deflated. However, if nothing else, he would not let his enemies rob him of his dignity. He watched as staffers packed and prepared to leave, before his attention was caught by the media screen. Amidst the usual footage of furigans steaming through buildings and hurling people from roofs was an English flag fluttering from an upper-storey window, a flower amidst the rubble. He strode into his office and summoned his team. Obediently, they put their work down and shuffled into his office.

"I want you to know how much your support means to me," he said as they gathered around. "You have been the one thing I can depend upon and if there is anything I can do you only have to ask."

He raised his voice, his fist aloft.

"I know the last few weeks have proved tough and things look pretty bleak, but remember: we're still in office, we're not beaten. So don't give up. The fightback begins here."

There was no applause and they stared back without emotion, returning to their work as dutifully as they left it.

"Sunrise is finished," one staffer muttered, not bothering to whisper, "and he can't even see it."

Terry sidled over and tapped Roger's shoulder.

"It gets worse," he whispered. "Bill's been conducting secret negotiations. We don't know what concessions he's offered, but we're into the endgame now."

Roger nodded and Terry left with the rest of the Kantei staff. He sat alone, thinking of the ruined civilisations of history. He was prepared for the horrors the future held, even if the people were not.

A loud noise pierced the room, forcing him to cover his ears. Bright lights flashed in every direction and a police officer burst into the room.

"Sori Daijin," he shouted. "Are you all right?"

"Yes, apart from this blasted noise."

"We have to get you out," the officer bellowed as a police team arrived.

"I won't run," Roger said. "We stand and fight."

"You don't understand," the captain replied. "We're under attack."

Everyone in the room listened to the reports coming in. The Chrysanthemum Bridge had been blown up.

24

By early morning, the Kantei was in chaos as bedraggled staffers rushed in. Roger watched the first footage of the attack, his eyes bleary through lack of sleep. A couple held hands with the Chrysanthemum Bridge in the background, a blurry bullet train just visible in the rain, before an explosion sent everything sideways and the bridge disappeared into clouds of dust. Seconds later, a staffer came rushing in with a recording from inside the train. Briefly, the office was filled with the everyday burble of a train carriage. A loud blast was followed by the sound of metal ripped apart as the voices became one piercing scream.

The Kantei staff stared at the stumps jutting out of the water then looked at each other in silence. Who were the people on that train? What had been their hopes and dreams? Roger looked at the faces around him. Some were crying, others stoic, but beneath the sorrow, the fear was unmistakable. All knew the attack went far beyond anything the Muhonin were thought capable of and no-one was in any doubt what defeat would mean. As the prospect of a Muhonin victory sunk in, fear turned to terror.

"Wars aren't won by moping around," Roger shouted. "We have work to do."

He clapped his hands as reports of further attacks came in. In West Midlands Prefecture, a group of schoolteachers had been forced to watch as their pupils were herded into the assembly hall and gunned down, before themselves being clubbed to death. In Manchester, a hospital had been blown up with patients and staff trapped inside. In Surrey, residents of a nursing home had been skinned and gutted. Within seconds, the room was a cacophony of radio updates and yelling.

"We could have thousands dead."

"We've been hit. We're coming under heavy fire."

"Chelsea Barracks is under siege. They're taking casualties."

"Get us a chopper. Now. We can't take any more."

Jez Rice walked over to Roger.

"All our military bases are under siege," he whispered.

"Put the police on highest alert," Roger shouted. "And get me the Chiefs of Staff."

He stood calm in the centre of the room and surveyed the room. *While the pressure of war crushes others, I find my inner strength. This is the moment my life has been building to. I will prevail.* His staff looked back anxiously. Though none dared say so, no-one shared his confidence.

"I have the public reaction, Sori Daijin," Angela said, putting on the news.

They watched as people stood open mouthed around public news screens as the Chrysanthemum Bridge collapsed into the sea. Shock once more gave way to fear, before giving way to outrage as rescue workers pulled bodies from the sea and stretchered semi-conscious figures onto ambulances.

"The Government should have seen this coming," a woman shouted.

"They shoulda dun sumfin to prevent it," the man beside her added.

"Angela," Roger said, "organise a visit to the attack site right away. We will show people we are with them."

"I strongly advise against it," she replied. "The site hasn't been secured – and you remember what happened last time."

She paused as a masked Muhonin appeared on the Subversive Service in front of a banner saying, "Supreme Love".

"Behold our Day of Rage," he shouted. "We have destroyed the symbols of your arrogance and will destroy all who defy us. The Supreme Rebeginning is here. All praise Supreme Love."

"You are their number-one target," Commander Lucas said. "They've held off from assassination so far, but we can't stop them forever."

"I'm the Sori Daijin. If the people are in danger," Roger said, "so am I."

The Kantei staff looked at each other with worried expressions.

"Sori Daijin," the Kantei reception announced. "The Joint Chiefs of Staff are here."

Roger got up as a Muhonin demolitions team rushed towards the outer defences of Chelsea Barracks. They blew themselves up before follow-up teams gunned down the sentries and burst through the first line of defence.

"If the military falls," Jez said, "it's over."

Roger powered down the corridor towards the War Rooms with a purposeful look then came to a stop. Amanda was waiting outside.

"Roger," she said. "How have you been?"

He gave a grumpy harrumph, before his expression mellowed.

"I've been trying to get through," she said. "I've got the latest from inside Bill's camp. The Action Groups are planning to sabotage any military action by inciting civil disobedience. I've told the media this is a national emergency and it's their duty to support the Government."

"They can agitate all they like," he said. "They won't stop anything. I shall visit the Chrysanthemum Bridge site this afternoon. You can tell Edmund I shall speak to the people."

"Are you insane?" She looked horrified. "You could be kidnapped, assassinated, anything. Bill is colluding with the Muhonin and furigans and that's exactly what he wants you to do." She handed him a brown envelope. "Jim gave me this."

Roger pulled out a paper.

MEMO: COUNTERING ROGER TYSON

Fighting Tyson on his own terms will fail. We must turn his strengths against him and draw him into indefensible positions, splitting the coalition and isolating him from his support. We should take the following steps:

1. *Draw him into making unpopular public statements*
2. *Attack him for being "controversial" and "divisive"*
3. *Implicate him in terrorist attacks*
4. *Accuse him of leading Chainsaw*
5. *Impeach him*

N.B. Friendly relations with the ganglords must be maintained at all costs. Nothing must jeopardise this. Even from prison, the threat Tyson would pose Bill Harris is too great. Once the trial is over, he is to be handed over to the Movement and eliminated.

"Domo arigatou gozaimasu, Amanda." He smiled at her and held the paper tight. "I knew it. Now I can prove it."

The Chiefs of Staff gathered around the briefing table while Roger stood in front of a giant map of the country.

"Let's be clear what's happening," he said. "A symbolic target has been destroyed in full public view, civilians are being slaughtered in seemingly random fashion and the Armed Forces are under siege. This is a psychological war. The enemy is trying to drive a wedge between us and the people by making them feel we cannot protect them.

Therefore, not only must the enemy be defeated, they must be seen to be defeated. Public fear can only be conquered by showing the Muhonin are not invincible. However, our forces are pinned down, so we must win the defensive battle before we can go on the offensive. General Wheeler, how confident are you the enemy can be repelled?"

"The attacks have been well planned and the enemy has the element of surprise," General Wheeler said. "But our defences should be adequate."

"Should be is not good enough," Roger said. "How quickly can we put together a task force?"

"We have a Rapid Reaction Force on permanent standby, which could be deployed instantly," he replied. "Spearhead troops could be in the field by the end of the day; follow-up troops will take longer."

"What is the general level of readiness?"

"Combat readiness has deteriorated badly over the last decade." A note of hesitancy entered his voice. "We were expressly prohibited from preparing for this eventuality."

Roger pressed a button and the map lit up showing known Muhonin installations with descriptions of size, strength of defences and troop numbers, while the table opened up with copies of the plan appearing on screens.

"Gentlemen, Operation Guillotine. We lack the troops to destroy the Muhonin completely, but by taking out their bases and eliminating their leadership, we can inflict a defeat sufficient to set them back decades. We need to be bold, for the risks are great: their bases are well defended and losses will be high. However, our intelligence is good. By destroying their warfighting capacity, we can force the remnants to accept a settlement on our terms."

He pointed at the London Dormitory Suburb of Kent and zoomed in on the Deer Park Complex.

"Muhonin High Command is located in Lansdowne Tower. We have the architect's plans and the latest photo-reconnaissance, so we know the layout. The complex is well defended with Muhonin and furigan irregulars, so the main difficulty will be gaining entry."

He waved his hand and the exterior of the Lansdowne Tower disappeared, revealing the building's internal structure and the Muhonin strongpoints.

"This is a huge operation," one general said. "We've been cut to nothing. We can sustain an assault of this intensity for one, two, three days at most. After that, we will have to pull back."

The other Generals nodded.

"I expect victory," Roger said. "There can be no failure."

Roger returned to the command centre where sweat-drenched staffers were rushing around trying to fix the air conditioning and collapsed in his seat. Margaret Richards was onscreen.

"Sori Daijin," she said, "why has no War Naikaku been summoned? This is a Naikaku matter and I demand you call one."

"You will be called for when necessary," he replied.

Her voice turned shrill.

"Whatever headlines you win today, you're storing up huge problems for the future. As Minister of Finance, I can tell you you'll be out of money in days and that's only the start. You're not invulnerable. If you think—"

Roger hung up on her as Commander Robertson entered the room.

"Keisatsu-cho Chōkan," Roger said. "How is the clear up operation going?"

"The Chrysanthemum Bridge site is being cleared as we speak."

"Excellent. Scour the site for evidence of Grey Ninja or Mouken involvement. I want proof of Bill's complicity."

He pressed a button and a furigan gang appeared on the screen, jeering as they drove past the smashed illuminations and boarded-up windows of a deserted high street. The film cut to a group loitering by a burnt-out car. There was a hail of bullets and the group fell to the ground. Roger turned to the commander as the gang celebrated their victory by knifing the wounded.

"You know their latest fashion? They're herding people into cars and setting them alight. They call it the 'human petrol bomb'."

"There's nothing we can do, Sori Daijin," Commander Robertson said. "The barracks are beyond our control."

Roger turned the screen off.

"Furigan violence has peaked. The gangs are turning on each other and, without financial aid, they will soon exhaust themselves. When the offensive is over, move in and restore order. I want you to use all necessary force."

He dismissed him and took the lift deep underground. The doors slid open and Angela Taylor led him to the studio. He sat behind the large oak desk flanked by furled English flags as a holographic replica of the Kantei office was projected onto the space.

"Okay," he said, "let's get this done."

The clock counted down 5-4-3-2-1 and the studio signalled "recording."

Roger returned to his office and sat behind his desk, his fingers pressed against his lips as the Subversive Service broadcast films of the Muhonin slicing out stomachs and burning people alive. He looked up with alarm. The Kobiyashi media had interrupted its programming. Major Phipps was speaking to a press conference, flanked by Desmond Grey and Paul Fox.

"I have worked in military intelligence for many years," he said, cameras flashing repeatedly. "I was aware there was a network of ambitious and ruthless kouha officers. It had been rumoured they possessed plans for a military takeover, but I had always doubted its existence. That changed recently when I was called to a meeting with Sori Daijin, Roger Tyson. He told me the Army was our last line of defence and that he would do whatever it took to save the country. I was left in no doubt he was following a Strategy of Tension with the objective of declaring a state of emergency and launching a military offensive. He then pressed me for information he could use against Bill Harris and, when I refused, I was physically threatened. I have been living in fear ever since, but I can ignore my conscience no longer. I can confirm that these terrorist attacks are part of the Chainsaw Plot and that Roger Tyson is its leader."

Roger looked at the memo on his desk, feeling time stop. Stages One to Four had now happened and only impeachment was left. How long did he have left? He gathered himself as Terry rushed in.

"Have you seen it?" he said. "They're ready to move."

"It's too late." Roger said. "I have proof Chainsaw is a fabrication. It's time to arrest Bill for collusion."

He handed Terry the memo and stood impassively. Terry recovered his breath and read it.

"Where did this come from?"

"Amanda got it from Jim."

"No, I mean what is its provenance?"

"I don't know. Why?"

"It's a forgery," Terry said, handing it back. "Or, to be more precise, a counter-forgery, designed to be exposed. No government would ever put such compromising material into writing. Bill's office almost certainly left it for Jim, knowing he'd give to Amanda, who'd give it to you. Use it and you're trapped. There'd be questions of how you acquired it and doubts over its veracity. Bill would expose it as a fake and everything you said would be discredited. The case against him would collapse and you'd be impeached."

Roger said nothing. As Reception announced his armoured transporter was waiting.

"Sori Daijin," Terry said, "whatever you do, Bill will dismiss any allegation of collusion as part of a Chainsaw disinformation campaign. Once you've been impeached, he will fabricate all the evidence he needs to prosecute. There's nothing you can do."

Roger smiled and left.

The convoy drove off, armoured cars to the front and rear, machine gunners poking out of the turrets. Roger sat quietly as the suburbs went past on the internal wraparound screen. *Forgeries turning disinformation into fact, counter-forgeries turning fact into disinformation; that bastard's got me in a pincer again. My allies will vote against me and my enemies impeach me.... We are indeed down to our last line of defence: everything now depends on the military.* The transporter slowed down as the driver announced they were approaching the checkpoint. Roger looked outside at New Folkestone Business District, feeling a sense of grief. Gone were the holográphic logos and the flickering streams of red and yellow; the only light now came from the emergency floodlights and the police vehicles. Was the military strong enough to defeat the Muhonin? Could they win? As he watched the continuous stream of wagons carrying rubble and corpses from the bombsite, he was no longer sure.

The transporter came to a halt and waited for a minute before receiving the all clear. The light came on, the door opened and Roger stepped out to a ripple of applause.

"Come this way, kudasai." Commander Robertson saluted and escorted him to a sheltered spot. "As you can see, the Muhonin have hit more than the Chrysanthemum Bridge: we have thousands dead here alone."

Roger looked at the rubble mountains with twisted steel girders jagging out. Amidst the chunks of concrete and smashed glass, he could see the occasional office seat or desk poking out, indicating what used to be inside.

"The mounds could collapse any time," the commander continued. "We've sent in the robots."

A helicopter patrol flew past as he led Roger past a large white hangar.

"The Field Hospital's at full capacity," Commander Robertson said, as a blood-spattered robot surgeon exited the field hospital, its multiple arms retracted. He stopped outside a second hangar. "You can meet some of the less serious cases."

Roger looked around at the nervous cameramen and the soldiers in full combat body armour surrounding them, then entered. Inside, triple-deck bunk beds ran the full length of the hanger looming over the robots and medical staff at ground level. The Matron greeted Roger and took him down the aisle, leading him onto a platform between the beds.

"Konnichiwa," Roger said to a woman with an extensively bandaged head. "How are you feeling?"

"Not so bad," she said, attempting a smile. "They've been very good to me here." She winced and lay back.

"I wish you a speedy recovery," he said.

The Matron pressed a button and the platform lifted Roger to the second tier.

"Konnichiwa," Roger smiled to a man in stripy pyjamas. "How are you?"

"Could be better," the man said with a cough.

"Hang in there," Roger said, patting him on the shoulder. "Get well soon."

The Matron pressed the button and showed Roger around the hangar, introducing him to staff and patients as she explained their work, Commander Lucas constantly checking his watch.

"Sori Daijin," he said, "we've got to go. We've spent far too long here."

Roger left via the police hangar where the aftermath was plastered on the walls of the incident room. Mangled bodies, dismembered limbs, children impaled on metal; Roger shut his eyes, but the images remained burned inside his head. *This is the Day of Rage no-one will see. How many more lanterns will be floated down rivers?* He stepped out into the cold air and walked slowly to the viewing platform. A small group watched as he ascended the steps and looked at the concrete stumps, bowing his head as he laid a wreath.

"Keep up the good work," he said to the crowd, his eyes moist. "Our people are heroes."

They applauded loudly, their tense expressions betraying their fear.

"I'd like you to look at this," Angela said as the crowd dispersed. She showed him the news. "Now the violence has died down, the Action Groups are back on the streets."

As a sorrowful Bill Harris spoke at length about reconciliation and the need for forgiveness, Roger looked at the electro-placards.

END WAR NOW

DEFY THE BAN – STOP THE AGGRESSOR

NO STATE OF EMERGENCY – NO SHOGUNATE

"This is our last chance," Bill said to rapturous applause. "Only negotiations can prevent catastrophe."

An applauding James Ashley stepped up alongside him.

"Wise words from our former Sori Daijin," he said, "but fine sentiments won't stop Tyson's war. This is a man who revels in violence and worships death; he won't be stopped by appeals to humanity. He has inflamed tensions with his hate-filled Nastyspeech; he has undermined peace by preventing negotiations and now he is driving us into war so he can make himself Shogun. Nothing will stand in his way. Valerie Whittaker, his friend Dr Alexander and now us all – he is sacrificing human life so he can satisfy his lust. These attacks are only the start. We are being plunged into a morass of hooligan violence, slaughter and social decay. We will never be safe until he is behind bars, along with those plutocratic pigs that fund him, the Robinsons. Tyson is evil! Impeach him now!"

The crowd cheered and banged their placards.

"There's only one group planning slaughter," Roger snarled, "and that's the one you support. Angela, get me General Wheeler."

She tapped in the code and the General appeared onscreen.

"Have the attacks been repelled, Taisho?" Roger said.

"Almost all," he replied.

"Good. Proceed with Operation Guillotine."

With a cheery wave, Roger climbed inside his transporter. The engines started and the internal wraparound screen came on. Within minutes, he was on every channel, staring deeply into the camera from the Kantei office.

"This morning," he said with sombre eyes, "our nation came under attack. In a day unparalleled in its barbarity, the Muhonin declared war on us with pitiless slaughter. I urge you all: remain calm. This cowardly attempt to undermine morale will fail. Our nation will never be cowed."

Roger paused, his voice dropping deep.

"As of today, our nation is in a state of emergency: the police have been put on high alert and the Self Defence Forces mobilised. Our enemies have declared war on us and now they will face the full might of the English nation. Our fight may be hard, but we shall prevail, for there will always be an England. I bid you goodnight."

The camera lingered on a solemn-faced Roger, before switching to a public information broadcast.

"There will be several hours before the military attacks," said the voiceover, as a family went about its emergency shopping, "so use that time to make appropriate preparations: stock up on food, water and essentials; identify a safe place where you can shelter. There will be no power, so...."

Roger listened with boredom as every channel returned to its studio and smiling presenters assured viewers that normal programming would return soon. They waved goodbye before a sombre voice announced that all broadcasting had been suspended. There was a buzzing noise and the screens went blank.

A loud blast hurled Roger against the side of the transporter. Everything went dark. His head throbbing, he tried to pick himself up, but another explosion threw him back. His body was burning with pain and his mouth filled with blood. He was upside down and the sides of the transporter were being peppered with rocket-propelled grenades. *The site was sealed off. How did the enemy get in? How....*

"Sori Daijin," a voice shouted. "Crawl towards me."

Roger slid along his stomach towards the escape hatch, where a pair of hands pulled him out.

"You have to get out," the soldier said. "They're bringing in their heavy weapons."

He dragged Roger along, stopping behind an upturned vehicle. Roger peeked out: soldiers were firing at mounds of rubble, the lead vehicles were blown to pieces and corpses lay strewn in pools of blood. A third loud explosion ripped through the air as an anti-tank missile tore into the transporter, sending wreckage skywards. Roger curled up, trying to protect himself from the lumps of hot metal as smoke billowed from the wrecked vehicle. He opened his eyes, coughing as dust got in his lungs and the smell of burning flesh seared up his nose. A bright muzzle flash. He was on the tarmac, bleeding. He could hear shouting as radios crackled "Sori Daijin down," but he felt no pain. With a smile, he lost consciousness.

25

There was no way of knowing how much time had elapsed. Roger doubled over in pain as he came to. The adrenaline had gone and his body hurt, jagging in his ribs, thumping in his head. He looked around, his eyes watering. He was in the back of an armoured transporter, an intravenous drip in one arm and two soldiers either side of him.

"Where am I?"

He turned to the stern looking medic who was watching him.

"You're being taken to hospital?"

"Which one?"

"I'm afraid I'm not at liberty to divulge that information. The Fuku Sori says you will be given the very best medical treatment."

Roger gritted his teeth, trying to block out the pain. *That backstabber Collingwood has assumed power and there's damn-all I can do about it. Those traitors opposed the offensive and now they'll have the Naikaku cancel it.*

"As Sori Daijin," he said, "I request the Kantei's public monitoring service be put on."

The medic nodded and one of the soldiers put the screen on. Roger watched as businesses suspended work and the streets emptied as people stockpiled food and barricaded themselves indoors. Soon, nothing other than armoured convoys carrying soldiers and weapons was on the streets.

"The Fuku Sori requested I relay to you that Operation Guillotine has been given new rules of engagement," the medic said. "To minimise civilian casualties, heavy weapons have been withdrawn from the offensive and troops are not to fire on any position unless they can demonstrate no civilians are nearby."

"The fool," Roger bellowed. "He's depriving it of the forces it needs to succeed. Doesn't he realise this will end in defeat?"

A tear rolled down his check as a helicopter hovered outside Lansdowne Tower where a dense network of defences had been constructed in the outbuildings. *Of course he realises it will end in defeat. Of course he didn't cancel it. He needs the offensive to fail. He needs me to fail with it.* A jet fighter swooped low with a loud roar as murky figures shuffled into position. There was a loud bang and sections of perimeter wall disappeared. The figures burst into view in a blaze of gunfire and shouting.

"They're being sent to their deaths," Roger cried. "The Muhonin don't take prisoners."

The thought of his soldiers being tortured by the Muhonin was too much and he fell back, reeling with pain. Muhonin victory, mass slaughter, England destroyed, everything he dreaded was becoming reality.

He winced as the transporter thudded over rough terrain, the pain proving too much. *I'll be tried, convicted and sentenced, but punishment won't be enough. I'll be forced to submit to the Political Consensus: celebrate furigans, love the Muhonin, apologise for my sins and beg for forgiveness. Well, they won't have that pleasure. I'll die before I dishonour myself.* He tried to sit upright, but a sharp pain shot up his spine. He lay back in despair. *Why fight against it? One person can't stop the forces of nature... You should have given up... You can't save people who don't want to be saved... Give up, you're only dragging out the inevitable....* He froze, gripped by the cold. He was in the furigan vid, chained up, stomach sliced open, kicked to the floor, throat slit. Over and over again, the sequence replayed, each time more vivid: Muhonin and furigans towering over him, glee on their faces as they tortured him. The fear was too much and he instinctively began to struggle. The soldiers held him down as the medic gave him an injection. Roger crashed into his bed as his surroundings drifted away. Bill would fall, barbarism would triumph and his world would be obliterated. Torture, sacrifice, ritual humiliation; he would be consumed by the subculture he detested.

He woke up, feeling queasy. Everything was blurry. The soldiers were still watching him and the screen was playing in the background. Gradually he became aware they were slowing to a halt.

"Roadblock ahead," shouted the driver.

"Everyone out," shouted the commander. "And don't let him out of your sight. We need him alive."

The soldiers jumped out, leaving Roger with the medics. Feeling faint, he strained to look at the screen, then lapsed into unconsciousness. Soldiers were falling back in disarray. The attack had been repulsed.

26

It was dark, except for a small light beside him. Roger awoke again, confused. Jane smiled and held his hand.

"How are you feeling, itoshii?"

"What time is it?" he mumbled, looking up at her.

"3am."

He lay back and closed his eyes.

"What happened?"

"I called John when I heard what had happened and he sent a detachment of troops loyal to you." She kissed him on the forehead. "I'm sorry I was angry with you."

He looked at her, his face drained of life.

"Get some sleep, you need to rest."

Her voice was soft, but he was already asleep.

27

Roger looked around. It was morning and he was in a bright, clean hospital room. His body ached, but his head felt clear. He could hear voices in the next room. General Wheeler? Amanda?

"Good morning, Sori Daijin," a nurse said with a broad smile. "How are you feeling today?"

"What's going on in there?" he groaned.

"Your colleagues have set up a communications suite." She handed him a mirror. "You've lost a lot of blood. You're lucky nothing vital was hit."

Roger looked at himself. His body was bruised and his face swollen.

"You must rest," she said. "You mustn't over-exert yourself."

He ignored her advice and limped to the communications suite, still in his pyjamas. Amanda was remonstrating with a large communications screen.

"You've no authority to countermand the Sori Daijin's orders," she said, "You—"

"While the Sori Daijin's incapacitated I'm in charge," the screen shot back. "And let me remind you, should anything happen to our beloved leader, I am Acting Sori Daijin."

"Our beloved leader is no longer incapacitated," Roger interrupted, his voice weak. "Consider yourself relieved of your duties. Any more from you, Collingwood, and I'll have you arrested."

He coughed and collapsed into a seat, catching sight of the command screen. His heart sank. Helicopters poured gunfire into buildings, while commanders issued orders and troops launched attacks, but nowhere did the Muhonin defences look like falling. It was Day Three and the offensive had stalled.

"Sori Daijin, I have General Wheeler online," a comms operative called out.

"What's the latest, Taisho?" Roger said.

"The offensive can't be sustained much longer," General Wheeler said. "Supplies are low and we're running out of ammunition. We've got to bring our heavy weapons into play if we're to avoid defeat. Their defences are too strong."

"Sori Daijin," Jez interrupted, "we're fighting to defend the public. We have to avoid civilian casualties. If we lose their support, we lose the campaign."

"Nonsense," General Wheeler said. "This is a question of whether they have more cannon fodder than we have cannon – and we can't afford to deprive ourselves of cannon."

Roger bit his lip as the Army was driven back by Muhonin counterattacks.

"What will be left?" Jez said. "A bankrupt country, thousands – possibly millions – dead, cities in ruins, society gone. Even if you win, you'll lose."

"Sori Daijin," the General replied as the nurse tried to order Roger back to his bed. "If this offensive fails, every day from now on will be a Day of Rage."

Roger watched as a group of Muhonin broke out of their envelopment and attacked the fleeing Self Defence Forces.

"Taisho, I authorise you to prosecute this war by all means necessary. I don't want a single Muhonin or furigan left alive."

The General bowed and went offline.

Within minutes, a jet fighter swooped out of the clouds. Roger watched as two bright flashes were followed by two loud blasts. Two Muhonin bunkers were obliterated. Seconds later, a heli-ship hovered outside a tower block, peppering the façade with missiles, red flames shooting out behind. Glass was blown out, leaving a burnt-out hole where a flat had been.

"A Muhonin sniper," a staffer said pointing to satellite imaging of the block. "He'd been picking off our guys for fun."

Flashes and blasts followed in quick succession as buildings crumpled to the ground and vehicles were flung into the air. A staffer pointed to a screen showing aerial film of a furigan 4x4 with enormous wheels and a rear-mounted cannon speeding down an empty expressway. One vivid flash and the vehicle was nothing more than a darkened patch on the road. The staffers stood up and cheered, but Roger was unmoved.

"Tell General Wheeler I want this wrapped up by sunset," he croaked. "Then the troops go in."

The explosions merged into a continuous roar as the airstrikes intensified. Everyone in the command centre sat rigidly, their eyes fixed to the screen as troops prepared to assault the Deer Park Complex. A flotilla of heli-ships landed on the roof and shadowy figures leapt out, running into position. There was a pause, then they abseiled down the sides, placing shaped charges by the windows. With loud explosions and shattering glass, the special forces burst in, covering the rooms with gunfire and hanging enemy bodies from the windows. Progress was swift and the Kantei display turned green as reinforcements poured in and floors were cleared. The central storeys, however, remained stubbornly red.

"We're meeting heavy resistance," General Wheeler said. "We're down to our last reserves."

Roger looked at the head-up display, feeling faint. The entire army had been committed and casualties were mounting. Lansdowne Tower's core continued to hold out despite being completely surrounded. How much longer could it go on? He gritted his teeth, trying to suppress the oncoming nausea. *Come on, lads. They're nearly defeated, they must be. This is where they'll make their last stand. Come on, lads. One last push.* Minutes then hours passed, the casualties increasing. Roger concentrated all his efforts on remaining conscious, feeling his life hanging with the offensive. Bill's personal bodyguard remained at large and would certainly attempt to capture him if the regular army crumbled. Bill's bodyguard? Could they be assisting Muhonin forces? A lift shaft was cleared and a green column appeared. Roger clutched his shoulder as a nurse rushed in, catching him before he could hit the floor. The inner defences were breached and the last defenders eliminated. Lansdowne Tower had been taken.

With their headquarters destroyed, Muhonin resistance collapsed. Troops poured out of buildings either side columns of furigan and Muhonin prisoners, while others crawled from their hiding places to be dragged into line. Roger looked at the enemy faces as they filed past the camera, dazed Muhonin and weeping furigans, some barely able to stand as they were clubbed towards the awaiting prison transports.

"Well done, everybody," he said, his eyes bloodshot. "The Emergency is over."

His team looked at each other with tired smiles before organising the return to civilian life. Roger looked at the casualty estimates and called General Wheeler.

"What's your status?"

"A few isolated pockets of resistance remain, but mopping up operations should eliminate them within the week."

Roger paused. "Taisho, do we know who ambushed my convoy?"

"We think so."

"Hunt them down and eliminate them."

The General bowed as Sir Gerald appeared on another screen.

"The Muhonin and furigan remnants are suing for peace," he said.

"Very good," Roger said. "Ensure that it's punitive."

Sir Gerald bowed and ended the call. Within minutes, the media had returned to air, a pre-recorded Roger on every channel, sitting in the Kantei office, furled English flags either side, accompanied by a bust of Winston Churchill.

"People of England," he said, "the state of emergency is over. The Muhonin and their allies have been defeated. I salute every one of you for your courage."

Slowly, life returned to the streets as police convoys secured the barracks and the emergency services brought supplies. Drones and public screens played Roger's message interspersed with films of surrendering Muhonin. At first, only a few residents appeared, then gradually more until whole streams poured out of the buildings, cheering, waving and helping to clear rubble, while those inside draped flags from the windows. Roger watched with delight as a group of girls showered soldiers sitting on an armoured fighting vehicle with flowers.

"Sori Daijin," Terry said, "what shall we do with Bill?"

"Shoot the bastard," a staffer shouted out, "him and his fifth-columnist friends

There were shouts of "hang him" and "put him on trial" before Roger called for quiet.

"We'll let the people decide," he said.

"You've won an unpopular war," Terry said, pointing to the landscape of burnt-out buildings and craters onscreen. "If you call an election, there's no guarantee the electorate will thank you for it."

Roger looked at the screens in silence as his team looked on nervously. On one, a dog rooted around an upturned garbage train; on another, debris rattled against graffiti covered garage doors; on a third, litter billowed around a collapsed walkway.

"Make preparations for a return to the Kantei," Roger coughed, as he staggered back to his bed. "We have an election to prepare for."

28

Roger watched himself on the Sunrise Headquarters' screen thundering through his election-night speech with Jane and Violet Walsh sitting either side of him and his shoulder heavily bandaged. The colour had returned to his face, but the sound of the crowd outside cheering his name brought him no joy.

"Fourteen seats," he cursed. "Fourteen bloody seats. I won the popular vote by a landslide and we have a majority of a pathetic fourteen seats. After everything, we've gone nowhere." He sighed and sat down with Jane. "You were right."

She smiled and kissed him.

"Never mind, itoshii. You did your best, but you were shackled to a coalition of traitors."

Amanda entered and looked at them with a grin.

"Why the sad faces? You trounced Bill and your approval ratings are stratospheric. Now it's time to capitalise. I spoke with Jim before the election and two factions agreed to join us if we won, which gives us another hundred seats. You will go from head of a coalition to leader of a party, while the LDP will break up into a collection of small parties. The machinery's in place, all you need to do is press the button."

"Excellent," Roger laughed. "Tell your friends they're welcome to join."

Jane beamed at Amanda.

"I've had you all wrong," she said. "We must go for coffee some time."

"I'd be delighted," Amanda said.

Roger left for the Kantei, feeling light-headed as he looked at the London streets. He had won. He really had won. As his motorcade approached Diet Square, he sat up. Masses thronged the street ahead.

"Turn back, turn back," he shouted, his face pale as he turned to Jane.

His heart pounded as the limo slowed down. A police motorcyclist tracked back, stopping beside it.

"Sori Daijin," the policeman said over the intercom, "you're safe to proceed."

Roger looked again. There were no electro-placards, the crowd was waving flags – they were cheering him. Hesitantly, he ordered the car forward. The crowd parted, cheering as he sailed through. Unable to go any further, he stopped and got out, wandering through the crowd with the aid of a walking stick. They were chanting his name, the noise so loud he couldn't hear Commander Lucas next to him. His team brought out a fold-up platform and helped him up.

"This is your victory," Roger said as an aide handed him a megaphone. His voice cracked. "Your victory."

He put the megaphone down and said nothing, listening to the crowd with tears in his eyes.

Two thousand years of history flashed through his mind as he returned to the limo. *Mine is a great country. We avoided a new Dark Age before and we avoided it now. We shall have a second Reconstruction Era. We will be great, greater than ever before.* He got out, smiled at the cameras and, with a wave, walked re-entered the Kantei with Jane.

The building staff lined the entrance lobby, clapping as he walked in. He paused as they gave him three cheers, then took it in turns to thank them personally before heading to his office. There on the desk were the first headlines: *THE RIGHT MAN, ENGLISH HERO* and *VINDICATED BY VICTORY*; even the Kobiyashi Group had penned a grudging apologia. He sat back and watched as people celebrated in Tokugawa Square, throwing Lifestyle Group costumes on a fire and trampling up and down on anything furigan or Muhonin. In one corner, the Action Groups had set up a sound system and big screen.

"Roger Tyson, War Criminal," they chanted.

"Nastiness has won," James Ashley cried. "The Nation-zoku is resurgent. We're heading for a new Great Incident."

"This is your victory," Charles Bonham shouted at the revellers, playing footage of furigans being lynched by residents.

"Why don't you fuck off and die?" shouted a heavily built man as the crowd turned on the protestors, pelting them with stones. "We've had enough of you."

A massive rock crashed into the screen, sending shards of glass everywhere. To loud jeers, the protestors hastily abandoned it and fled.

Roger turned the news off with a smile and reclined his seat, his hands behind his head.

"The Party leaders are outside," the automated secretary announced.

"Keep them waiting," he growled.

He turned to his inbox and read through the messages, while mulling over thoughts for a new speech: *our glorious victory... a proud nation again... never grovel, never surrender... traitors have no place... enemies will be defeated, savagery will be crushed....* He looked up with irritation. The previous Naikaku was onscreen. Derek Bridges, Graham Hough, Andy Hunt, Antonia Richardson and Fred Abbott took it in turns to offer their congratulations, then Bill spoke.

"Congratulations Sori Daijin," he said, bowing deeply. "May I commend you on your victory. Only you could have fought this battle so courageously. It's perhaps for the best you never knew the true extent of the Muhonin threat against you. Jane came to me before the election, worried – very worried. She knew the risks you were taking. She couldn't believe you could be so blasé. She even wondered if you had a death wish.... We might be opponents, Roger, but you know I have never harboured any animosity towards you. We go back too far. I assigned a police team to your protection, so kudasai, remember that."

Roger remained stone-faced.

"Indeed," Bill smiled, "it's my great regret we never formed a national government. Such a pity, such a pity. It's not strong government we need; it's government backed by the people. Let me assure you, the divisions have not disappeared. From one Sori Daijin to another, I can tell you: you have won no victory."

Roger ended the call and summoned in Frank Carter and Angela Taylor.

"I've decided to implement my Restructuring Plan," he said to Frank. "I want MEPTI to manage the process."

"I'll make an immediate start," Frank grinned. "I take it this means the end of the Commissions?"

"No, they stay for now," Roger said. "Under new leadership. I was thinking of you, Bob and Colin."

"Domo arigatou, Sori Daijin. I am gratified to hear that."

Frank bowed as Roger turned to Angela.

"Let the media know the Political Consensus is dead. The people have spoken; we have a National Consensus: savagery and discord are to be condemned. From today, we celebrate harmony, unity and civility. Compassion Day will be abolished. We are a great nation and proud of it. Let this day remembered as Nation Day."

Frank and Angela left as his first appointment arrived. Roger repositioned himself in his leather seat and called in Amanda.

"I would like to thank you for your help," he said, sitting behind the oak desk like on his broadcasts. "You've been a staunch ally from start to finish. I would like you to be my Minister of Finance."

"Domo arigatou, Sori Daijin."

She got up and hugged him. He held her close then straightened his jacket and summoned the party leaders. They shuffled in, not making eye contact, and formed a semi-circle around him.

"Today," Roger said, looking at each one in turn, "we have a new Government and a new England. The Sunrise Coalition is now the Sunrise Party, a patriotic party to speak for the people. Your treachery nearly brought about a Muhonin victory and from now on there will be no more disloyalty. You will all face criminal charges."

They bowed again and were dismissed.

Evening came and Roger sat alone looking at images of the devastation. The thrill of victory had faded and tiredness set in. He had indeed won an unpopular war and there was no guarantee people would thank him for it. He thought of Churchill's second wilderness period, his feelings of doubt still gnawing away. He had at least avoided electoral defeat, but how would people feel once the initial euphoria had died down? He slumped in his chair as a message arrived from Helen.

> *The Muhonin have survived, furiganism remains and the Political Consensus is quiescent. Have you saved the country or given it a stay of execution? You're leader now. You must decide.*

Had he won? Was the victory an end or a beginning? He closed the message. Edmund was standing in the doorway.

"Konnichiwa," he said, his voice more careworn than ever.

"Edmund," Roger smiled, "I'm pleased to see you. I'd like you to be my Minister for the Interior."

Edmund sat down with a sigh.

"I'm afraid I cannot accept. I'm returning to the back-benches."

"Why?"

"I told you: I will never compromise my principles. This was our chance to destroy Leviathan and you...."

"Look here," Roger shouted, "I got shot addressing the people, so don't give me the armchair moralist. What have your cherished principles done for us?"

Edmund looked nervous, his usual certainty shaken. When he spoke, his voice was apologetic.

"I'm sorry: you inspired many with your courage. You stood up for the people when no-one else would, despite the threats against you."

He looked at Roger as if unable to rid himself of the suspicion his opponents might have been right.

"Wartime brings a temporary unity," he said, his voice regaining its indignation, "but only trust can bring harmony. Trust. It's the element that turns groups into teams, strangers into friends and societies into nations; without it, everything will slip back. I can only hope you haven't made a pact with Leviathan. It might flatter you now, but once captured you can never be free. It feeds off mistrust and will toy with you in its jaws, then devour you the moment it chooses."

"Spare me the lectures," Roger said. "There's no such thing as a perfect world, but if I can make it that little bit better, I've done a good job. Now go."

Edmund looked at him as if unable to make up his mind then shuffled off, looking dejected.

"An illusory victory and a rhetorical change of clothes," he mumbled. "Nothing ever changes."

Roger watched Edmund shuffle through the doorway then stared miserably at the wreckage of the Deer Park complex, unaware of time passing. *Illusory victories... rhetorical changes... Leviathan...* There was a loud knock at the door. He raised his head. Sir Gerald was waiting.

"You should be proud," Sir Gerald said. "You've won."

Roger looked at the casualty figures, in no mood to celebrate.

"Sori Daijin, nobody could have stopped the carnage. If it hadn't been for you, this would have been an awful lot worse. Your willingness to take tough decisions in the face of adversity saved untold lives." His voice turned cold. "However, you were very foolish to listen to Hope San. You almost got yourself killed. And because of his daydreams the problems remain. The Action Groups will continue to use him as a front, while working with the Muhonin and furigans to bring down the state. We could have stopped them, but you neutered us. They still loathe you and they will try to destroy you. You do realise these are the groups funding him?"

"Sir Gerald, you would do well to remember that you serve the people. Power is a means to an end, not an end in its own right. I went into politics to serve my country, not to maintain an illusory balance of power. However stable, an England of furigans, Muhonin and Lifestyle Groups is not England. Now I would be grateful if you would leave."

Sir Gerald bowed and left, stopping as if momentarily unsure whether Roger too might be a naive dupe.

Roger undid his collar and put his feet on the desk, watching the street parties with renewed hope. *England's a tough old bird. We rebuilt before and we can rebuild again. Yes, we are a nation again; the divisions will be overcome....* He closed his eyes and smiled as the crowd in Tokugawa Square laughed and sang, not seeing the hooligans loitering on the fringes. As he drifted off, they broke away and ran after the fleeing Action Groups, shouting and hurling bricks. Arms outstretched, they lined the streets, chanting "KOU-HA, KOU-HA, KOU-HA" and making throat-slitting gestures.

He opened his eyes and set the window to the English Channel, smiling as ships passed through the reopened sea lanes. He was about to nod off when the door slid open. Jane peeped around, her expression uncharacteristically shy.

"Roger. I'm sorry, you were right about everything. I was wrong to doubt you."

"No, I'm the one that should apologise. I should have listened."

She began to cry and wiped her eyes.

"I know it's bad of me, but I thought you were going to lose. I thought you would get yourself killed. I'm so proud of you."

They embraced, holding each other for several minutes.

"Jane," he said, "I appreciate all your family has done for me and for the country. It's time that was recognised officially."

She smiled and looked at the Kantei office, her eyes filled with joy.

"President Tyson?"

"Right now, retirement sounds nice."

"Well, not just yet," she laughed. "I like being First Lady."

She gave him a kiss and they turned to the window, holding hands. A big red sun sat on the horizon, casting the water in a crimson glow as it sank ever lower and bowed out for the night. Roger looked on with pride as the floodlights came on and the construction teams commenced work on the new bridge. His feelings of doubt now gone, he smiled and turned to Jane.

"The sun at last has risen. We shall build a new Japan in England's green and pleasant land."

THE END

WRITING GREEN AND PLEASANT LAND

Blood, sweat and tears, Churchill might have called it. Writing *Green and Pleasant Land* proved as enjoyable as dropping a typewriter on my foot. I began way back in 2001, blissfully unaware the final version would not be finished for another seventeen years. I had left university the previous year, having completed a Business Studies degree and was fascinated by Japan. The Japanese bubble of the 1980s had burst and the BBC had produced an excellent documentary *Bubble Trouble*. All the "facts" I'd learned during from business books or heard on the news in the 1990s were now exploded as a myth: Japan was not an economic superpower ready to take over the world, Japan Inc and the mighty keiretsu business empires were a myth, the Ministry of Trade and Industry had never guided the economy, putting the national good ahead of commercial interests, the Liberal Democratic Party, in office for 38 years continuously was riven by factions and there had never been any Iron Triangle of party, state and industry. Having grown up in the 1980s, these revelations were quite a shock and I found myself imagining a story in which a big businessman journeyed to the centre of power in his search for high office, only to find there was nothing there. However, inexperience intervened and the effort was soon discarded, having got no further than three undistinguished chapters.

Something must have appealed to me, though, as I found myself returning to the idea again in early 2008. I had decided I wanted to write seriously and that meant completing a novel. Nothing of the original survived, apart from the protagonist's name, the Japanese influenced England and the idea of a journey into the centre of power. I loved dystopian fiction, Aldous Huxley's *Brave New World*, Anthony Burgess's *A Clockwork Orange* and George Orwell's *Nineteen Eighty-Four* being particular favourites, but the latter had always left me wanting more. What happened inside the Inner Party? How did the government of his world work? The novel showed us no further than what O'Brien was willing to tell. I could remember as a teenager feeling a burning to know what went on behind the curtain. Alas, even literary dystopias proved secretive.

Fired up by these novels, I imagined my own dystopia. The totalitarian governments and regimented societies of so much dystopian fiction seemed a well-worn trope and felt very 1930s or 40s. While totalitarianism is a timeless theme, I wanted to do something new. With the Cold War long over, the reverse seemed much more contemporary. The threat seemed to be less Big Brother and more the opposite: weak governments and fragmented societies and this seemed more likely to lead to social collapse than totalitarianism. Even so, social apocalypse felt far-fetched. State failure might have been a reality in countries like Afghanistan or Somalia, but the idea of a first world country, such as England, becoming a failed state seemed too improbable to make a convincing dystopia.

Then, in September 2008, the world was hit by a massive financial crisis. In the space of a few weeks, Fannie Mae, Freddie Mac, Lehman Brothers, AIG and Bank of America all found themselves in trouble, followed a week later by US Treasury Secretary, Hank Paulson, failing to get his Troubled Assets Recovery Programme (TARP) through Congress, setting off a panic of epic proportions. The events of Japan in the 1990s were being played out again in the West – overvalued stock market and property prices crashed, sometimes to nothing, leaving banks insolvent and economies stuck with mountains of debt that would never be repaid. Could a divided country bankrupt itself into oblivion? Real-life Britain, America and Japan might have been spared sovereign default, but in literary land everything is possible....

My novel began to take shape: an England of the future was in the midst of a bubble, while a corrupt government ignored the rising violence within society, sealing off vast residential complexes behind perimeter walls and using an omnipresent media to present a rosy picture. Only one person stood in its way. Legendary industrialist and Chief Executive of the gigantic Greenwood keiretsu, Roger Tyson, had proved vociferous in his criticism of the government, warning of imminent disaster. Yet, far from being heeded, he found himself under attack, accused of doom-mongering and increasingly ostracised. Determined to bring down the government, he set off on a journey to the heart of power to uncover the dark secrets he believed it was hiding.

But who was he? Was he a goodie or a baddie? My initial thoughts way back in 2001, when he had been named Roger Greenwood, was an innocent who would become increasingly corrupted by the realities of power. However, as my story developed, this seemed implausible. An innocent would never be a credible candidate for high office and would make an improbable business magnate. However, the opposite proved equally problematic. A malevolent mastermind after the fashion of Francis Urquhart or Frank Underwood from House of Cards would certainly be more believable, but a bad guy continuing to be bad hardly made for a compelling story.

I settled on the idea of a character who could be interpreted as good or evil, which added a nice ambiguity: putting us in the uncomfortable position of seeing events from his point of view, but not knowing whether we should be for or against him. However, constructing a character who could simultaneously be interpreted as good and bad proved immensely difficult. I found myself going round and round in circles, editing and changing, even stripping out his inner life to increase the mystery. The result however was a boring nonentity! My long-suffering friends in my writing group groaned as I brought in lifeless scene after lifeless scene to read out. Ditch the novel, they said, focus on your short stories, they're so much fresher. The worst thing was: they were right. I was well and truly stuck.

So stuck that, for the first three years, I struggled to finish the first chapter. Try as I might, my writing never looked like what I had in my mind. It was hugely frustrating. I kept hoping for a lightbulb moment where everything would become clear and the writing flow. No such revelation ever came. Nevertheless, I persisted and eventually scraped together what would become the first three chapters. It wasn't up to much, but it was a start and in 2011 I took voluntary redundancy to finish my novel. I had budgeted myself a year and then I would send it out. The reality was months of plugging away and no progress. There was no one moment where everything fell into place, but I can remember sitting in Cornwall and feeling a block lift. Slowly, slowly, the novel began to take shape. Roger Greenwood became Roger Tyson – a shorter, pun-chier surname with overtones of heavyweight boxer, Mike Tyson. Two years later, I had a first draft.

I can't say what a moment of triumph this felt like! It had taken five years, but I had written a novel. I had also given to a friend, who had found it so unputdownable that he had finished it in one sitting! I was so excited. Now was the time to send the manuscript away to be assessed. Several weeks and hundreds of pounds later, I received a six-and-a-half-page report explaining in polite terms that my novel was an unpublishable load of garbage. I remember being a tad miffed and both my friend and I felt the report was unduly harsh. However, we were wrong. The report was 100% correct, pinpointing the problems that were holding it back and highlighting what would need to be changed for it to work. It proved a necessary stage. I now realised that first drafts are always bad: their purpose is to turn ideas in the head to words on the page. It doesn't matter if it's bad, there's a second draft to edit out the things that don't work and a third draft to craft what's left into something good. With this in mind, I enthusiastically set about redrafting my work.

I restored Roger's inner life, imagining a dour, aggressive character, neither warm nor likeable, but not necessarily bad, either. To maintain the mystery, I externalised the debate about who he was, along with all the characters. Who they were really would never fully be resolved: we would hear their supporters and opponents, but never any conclusive evidence. We would hear hints and accusations, claims and allegations; the debate always getting deeper, never being settled. Hero to his supporters and villain to his enemies; if we are sympathetic, we can't fully refute his enemies' allegations, but, if unsympathetic, we equally can't refute his supporters either. It felt a much more truthful way to depict political characters.

In real life, we decide whether people are good or bad depending on whether we share their views, even if we don't know all the facts. Reality is objective: something either is or isn't. We might not know whether Joe politician took a bribe, but we do know only one answer can be true: they either did or didn't. If we are a supporter, we might suspect the allegation to be false; if an opponent we might suspect it true. Fiction isn't like that: if it isn't stated somehow, it doesn't exist. If the author does not state whether the politician has taken the bribe, then there are no facts to decide the matter: both answers are simultaneously possible. For us to then decide the character is good or bad reveals our own prejudices, not theirs. If we find ourselves rooting for Roger, we are forced to confront the possibility we are rooting for someone evil. If we find ourselves rooting against him, we are must equally face the possibility we are rooting against someone good. Removing the conclusion from the debate forces us to challenge our own opinions.

Over the next few years, I hammered out a second, third, fourth, fifth – even a sixth – draft, so that, by the tenth anniversary of the global financial crisis, I could call the project finished. After ten years and much frustration, I had written my novel! What an adventure it had been and what a bizarre pleasure to have created a world full of suffering and misery! At least, this suffering and misery is fictional and nobody gets hurt.

So here is *Green and Pleasant Land*. Despite all the frustrations, I've had a lot of fun in creating it and I very much hope you have had just as much fun reading it.

Steve
London, May 2019

Get Your Free Ebook!

Did you enjoy this book? Would you like to find out how authors create entire fictional worlds out of nothing? Find out how I created my own fictional dystopia by getting my ebook *A Century of Dystopia Volume 8 – Green and Pleasant Land by Steve Shahbazian* absolutely free!

So don't delay! Follow the link or QR code below to claim your free ebook:

https://www.subscribepage.com/steveshahbazian

If you'd like to leave a review....

If you liked this book and would like to help others enjoy it, please recommend it to friends, family, enemies, colleagues, acquaintances, neighbours, people you vaguely recognise but can't quite place... although please stop at forcing it upon complete strangers in the street – enthusiasm is great, but that would be going too far.

To leave a review, please follow the link or QR code to your local online store.

Amazon US
https://www.amazon.com/dp/1916146007

Amazon UK
https://www.amazon.co.uk/dp/1916146007

About the Author

Steve Shahbazian has won no awards, no competitions and is not critically acclaimed. Some of his best friends have gone so far as to describe his work as "okay in places" and his books have been in huge demand, mostly due to the large number of wonky tables needing propping up. When not writing, Steve can usually be found staring at a blank screen desperately hoping inspiration will come and, like every writer since the dawn of time, he's an avid reader... although bizarrely he mostly reads non-fiction, particularly history, economics and popular science (as long as it's in simple language he can understand). His favourite authors are George Orwell and Alexander Solzhenitsyn and he decided to become a writer after deciding these were the people he would most like to fail to measure up to. To Steve, genre present no barriers. Political dystopian, literary and science fiction, he writes across them all, being equally bad in each. Outside of writing he likes cricket, rugby, music and Belgian Beer as well as boring people to tears talking about cricket, rugby, music and Belgian Beer.

If you would like to find out more about Steve – and there really is no accounting for taste – you can visit his website via the following link or QR code:

www.steveshahbazian.com

BY THE SAME AUTHOR

Approaching Paradise

Wouldn't it be lovely to live in paradise? Perhaps. But what if paradise went wrong? In these short stories, meet the loser who tries to become a winner by undergoing a body transplant, enter a world without money where altruism is the new greed, visit the theme park from hell where shooting up robots isn't all that it seems, run away from a world of perfect health to join the army and take the drug that brings people together in one big psychedelic post-modern shared hallucination.

A Century of Dystopia

Nineteen Eighty-Four, *Brave New World*, *A Clockwork Orange*, *The Handmaid's Tale*, George Orwell, Aldous Huxley, Anthony Burgess and Margaret Atwood wrote arguably the four most famous political dystopian novels ever written, but what makes a political dystopian novel? Does such a genre exist? Author Steve Shahbazian looks at the common themes running through these novels, including *High Rise* by J.G. Ballard and *We* by Yevgeny Zamyatin and how the authors have responded to each other's work. George Orwell famously based his plot on that of Zamyatin and assumed that Huxley had done likewise, something Huxley denied. In fact, many of the novels reflect similar themes and some surprising threads link these famous novels. So, don't wait for the clock to strike thirteen, find out how writers invent dystopia.

COMING SOON

Futility

Life is difficult, life is a struggle. But there is always hope...
to raise our expectations, cheat us and leave us worse than
ever before. Yes, life is difficult, life is a struggle – with
failed hopes and bitter disappointments added in to kick
us when we're down. So, let's look on the bright side. It
ain't so bad when it happens to fictional characters. In fact,
it can be quite fun....

Printed in Poland
by Amazon Fulfillment
Poland Sp. z o.o., Wrocław

65422532R00193